Danish Gold

About the author

Colin J Reed was born in Southampton, Hampshire, towards the end of 1943 when WWII was finally taking a turn for the better.

His first taste of adventure came when he joined the Junior Civil Defence in 1956, and one activity was to recover life sized dummies from under the remains of the roof of a four story bombed-out building opposite the main railway station. When that closed, he joined the Southampton Sea Scouts, and learnt to sail, and row, a 27ft Montague Whaler, the standard ship's sea boat of the day.

He served in the Royal Navy from 1960-70, and his first ship, *HMS Albion,* was the cornerstone of the Borneo War in 1963. During time onshore, he developed a passion for racing dinghies of various classes. After he left the RN he spent 40 years in the upstream oil and gas industry in various categories, and was one of the first crew members on BP's most successful offshore production platform in 1974.

A keen sailor he gained two sailing championships in dinghy racing in the 1980s, and in 1990 orchestrated the historic visit of the Royal Findhorn Yacht Club to Russia, the only UK yacht club to visit and race in the USSR.

He met his second wife in Rio de Janeiro in 1983, two years after losing his Scottish wife after a long illness, in only her mid-30s. He has two daughters from his first marriage. He is now semi-retired, living in the UK and Rio de Janeiro, and is currently involved with the national authority in supporting the 2016 Olympic Sailing Regatta.

Danish Gold

Colin Reed

Also by Colin Reed

Dangerous Voyage

First published 2016 by Tell Tale Books
Copyright 2016 © Colin Reed
All rights reserved.

ISBN-13: 978-1532726699
ISBN-10: 1532726694

www.telltalebooks.uk

Prologue

This story follows my first novel 'Dangerous Voyage' but it is non-contemporary. In my first book, the crew consisted of the older generation, which led to the idea that a second book would be the opposite.

My first experience of sailing started with the local Sea Scouts, still fondly remembered for the excitement and challenge of new things to learn in an outdoor environment.

During my reserve time in the Royal Navy, I had the opportunity to give something back by teaching sea cadets in northern Scotland and the RN base at South Queensferry.

This second novel contains two story lines.

The opening story is set in the present and sets the scene for the final chapters. The schooner joins in an adventurous yacht race for young adults recovering from a traumatic event.

The second story line borrows loosely from real WWII history. With war approaching, the Danish Government attempts to smuggle its remaining gold reserves from the grasp of the Nazi war machine.

They almost succeed, but the large tranche of gold is hidden in a secret Viking's King's Cave, and its whereabouts become lost.

These two stories combine into an exciting conclusion.

A big thanks to all my friends who have helped with the hard work of producing this book.

With special thanks to my wonderful wife, Sonia, and in fond memory of Dad.

Chapter 1

Came that fateful day in the year for every dedicated British yachtsman; 'The Last Sail of the Season'.

It comes at differing times for many. For Calum, it came in the form of an invitation from his good friend Eric, a week before his birthday in mid-October.

Eric loved wooden boats of every description, and over the years had bought quite few special craft, both sail and power. His current pride and joy was an International Six Metre, of some antiquity, in amazingly good condition.

Where Eric found this craft remained a tightly kept secret, especially from Mrs Eric, better known as Kristen. She had a great interest in its origins, as well as the font of cash that paid for it in the first place. When it came to his yachts, Eric dealt in cash. The only bonus, in her eyes, it had only cost a king's ransom to bring it up to Eric's usual astronomically high standards, and it was a liquid asset, i.e. another chump with bulging cheque book would be ready to 'Take it 'oft 'is 'ands'.

At least, she knew where her husband would be at any given moment during the sailing season, either fast asleep at home or massaging clients into parting with their cash.

Eric's new pride and joy had been simply named *Six*, a classic example of the master craftsman's art. Designed by Charles E. Nicholson, and built in 1936 at Camper & Nicholson's Southampton yard, constructed of varnished mahogany on oak. Kristen knew yachts could be made from other materials, but she wasn't sure her husband did.

Eric, on the other hand, didn't care. He had always wanted a 'Six Metre', and here she was. A semi-cruising model with vestigial cabin, complete with red antifouling and gold boot topping. Every part of *Six* glistened inside and out, period. Calum wondered if it would be obligatory to wear slippers onboard. Eric made it clear the scratching of any painted or varnished surface was a definite 'No No'.

The new hi-tech composite mast, painted to look like a new wooden mast, had a finish *Bugatti* would be proud of. The mast's standing rigging consisted of the latest PBO product, a modern and very strong fibre. The local sail loft supplied a superb suit of pale yellow sails to complete the rigging of *Six*. It was love at first sight. Calum admired the sight of *Six*; totally complete in all departments, looks, function, and of course, desirability.

Calum treasured his many fond memories of a six-metre yacht from his earliest sailing days. As a youngster, he sailed from his club at the top of Southampton Water. Calum spent his off-duty hours from Her Majesty's Senior Service learning how to make his white twelve-foot racing dinghy go as fast as everyone else's, and then faster. This expended a lot of effort, which in turn required a high level of refreshment at the end of each race. Being an under aged member of his sailing club, he was barred from purchasing alcoholic drinks at the bar except when his good friend Derek was on duty at the bar.

By far his favourite refreshment after a hard race would be to tie-up alongside 'old Frank's' six-metre cruiser, named *Ruthless*, for Frank's version of a mug of tea. Frank was an old-timer, whose wife, Ruth, had left him some time ago, hence the modified name of his pride and joy.

Frank spent his days resting on substantial laurels. Frank had been there and done that, several times over. Quite what Frank had been up, several times over, would always be a carefully guarded secret, but there were rumours. Frank was a scruffy old bugger, just like his yacht. For some reason, most people assumed Frank wasn't short of a few bob. Where he kept his bobs would also remain a mystery, as he claimed to be always skint.

Frank had retired and liked nothing more than to sit on his beloved yacht watching the tide come in and go out, the bird life on the waterway, and the coming and going of great ocean liners at Southampton's New Docks.

Frank's tea was legendary, and had been since the outbreak of the war, although which war remained a subject of conversation. For sure it was strong. Spoons were known to dissolve if given enough time. The tea was always served with a generous helping of sugar, usually a week's ration during said war, and condensed milk of the kind that can only be persuaded to leave its tin by brute force.

Calum tried to emulate, if not the recipe, but something approaching the style of Frank's tea. The Navy could supply the ingredients, but it still didn't taste quite so good. Perhaps the difference could be traced to Frank's collection of battered enamel tin mugs, rarely cleaned, and incapable of formal recovery to total hygiene. Everyone knew Frank's view on hygiene, that it should be practiced sparingly, especially when it came to his drinking utensils.

Frank's other famous collection was his drawer of assorted cutlery. Every item bore the mark of a long lost airline. The only items that formed a complete set were priceless, to Frank anyway, BOAC desert spoons, some still in their original plastic cover. The knives in the draw had been 'donated' by Pan Am, Caledonian Airways, TWA, and Imperial Airways. Despite all attempts by visitors to grab a memento of the past, old Frank knew to the nearest millimetre where every item lay.

That morning, Calum found himself sitting in his car at the Lymington Harbour municipal car park waiting for Eric. A nice day had been forecast, with a decent south-westerly blowing up the Solent, while high cloud cover precluded the chance of rain spoiling the day's proceedings. Calum fished around in the mess that was his car's glove box compartment for his designer clip-on sunglasses.

Simon arrived. Simon was Eric's boat helper, a queer cove, allegedly a member of the teaching profession, but he looked more like defrocked catholic priest. It took all sorts in this life, but at least Simon knew his boats.

Calum had met him twice before. At the last major session at the 'Dog and Duck', a week ago, Calum plied Simon with enough drink to begin what he hoped would be a subtle interrogation. Calum just had to find out a few of his secrets. Simon was flattered at the attention, but when he saw Marmaduke arrive, his eyes lit up with a deep passion and he was gone.

Marmaduke was the local toff, limp of wrist like you couldn't imagine and on this occasion, definitely in heat. One could tell from his extravagant highly coloured and outrageous attire; a clear warning to the pub's heterosexuals and the biggest kiss-me-quick come-on to anyone else of mixed gender in the vicinity.

'Mornin' Calum,' Simon called out through Calum's open car window. 'Any sign of Eric?'

'Good morning Simon,' Calum replied smiling. 'Not yet, he shouldn't be long.'

'I'll get the tender ready. Be back in a jiff.'

Simon minced his way over to the boatshed. Calum could only conclude that Simon, a well-known bachelor, had not slept alone last night. Neither had Calum, but at least he was sure in his own bedroom of all the genders.

An ageing metallic grey estate car screeched to a halt next to Calum's other love, his weekend only, 'It won't rain today' car, a deep red 1968 Maserati Sebring, a 2-door coupé, totally original, with low miles and drop dead good looks.

'Brought the toy out to play,' chided Eric, as he slammed the door shut on the Citroen.

'It seemed to fit the moment,' replied Calum smiling. 'Not sure who has the most flash kit around; your extravagant yacht, or my modest means of transport. You know the wife bought it for me. I only drive it to keep the peace in the happy homestead.'

Eric snorted an impolite expletive. Calum's love for the Maserati was close to the love of his life. That she had bought this shining example of Italian engineering was a shrewd move on her part. Quite where his wife Adriana found such a rare and much sought after car would never be revealed. And the price was never mentioned either. If one's wife wanted to give her loving husband a nice present, why Calum should care? He enjoyed it immensely and used it sparingly.

A voice came over the harbour wall, as Simon waited to ferry everyone out to *Six*. Simon had been busy. The sails were rigged and ready to go *Six* was lying to her floating mooring can, normally secured on the foredeck.

Eric and Calum safely negotiated the rusting steel ladder to the waiting dinghy. Simon decided to show off today as he quickly sculled the dinghy alongside *Six* without mishap. Within ten minutes, all was ready; sails hoisted, flapping lazily in the slowly building morning breeze. Simon secured the dinghy painter to the mooring buoy and cast off.

Eric took the helm as *Six* slowly drifted astern. Her nose fell away as Eric called out for the mainsail and jib to be sheeted-in on starboard tack. *Six* steadied and surged forward with an ease and grace that Calum fell in love with immediately. No doubt this would be a great day's sailing. Eric steered *Six* over towards the east bank, and called 'ready about'. *Six* tacked smoothly and quickly onto port tack and headed for the other side of the estuary.

Six short tacked down the estuary to the entrance to the Solent, quickly passing the channel marker known as 'Jack-in-the-Basket', and headed out into the main stream of the Solent, with the tide running strongly towards Cowes. Eric altered course for Cowes. 'We going to Cowes?' asked Calum mischievously.

'Could do,' replied Eric. 'You got a better idea?'

'You buying lunch in your favourite restaurant?' asked Calum, hopefully.

'No, we have a picnic hamper onboard, and the wife will be upset if we don't appreciate her hard work.'

'Fair enough,' replied Calum.

Eric called for the jib to be roller reefed. Simon looked at him until he saw Eric staring at the spinnaker that had not been rigged ready for use.

Simon hastened to clip the spinnaker bag into position, open the top, and connect the halyard to the head of the sail and the two sheets to each waiting red and green coloured tacks. Calum removed the spinnaker pole from its stowage position and quickly rigged it flying from the mast. Calum put on his sailing gloves and took both spinnaker sheets in his hands

With the wind coming over the starboard quarter of the six-metre, the spinnaker would provide a lot of power. When all was ready Eric ordered 'hoist', and the spinnaker rose quickly under the lee of the mainsail. Calum sheeted the spinnaker until he was satisfied with its setting. 'Six' healed strongly to the power of this brightly coloured red and yellow sail, dragging a large curving wake behind her.

'Eric,' asked Calum. 'Can you bear away a bit? We're a bit tight on this leg.'

'I've a lot of tide under me,' replied Eric. 'If I bear away we won't make Cowes like this.'

Six continued to power across the Solent, eating the miles quickly. The oscillating wind forced Eric to bear away in the stronger gusts; in all, it was an exciting sail with her crew sitting well outside the yacht. Eric skillfully brought *Six* across the fast moving tidal stream to the shoreline of the Isle of White, bathed in its truly splendid autumn colours.

In no time, after a smooth spinnaker drop, *Six* rounded the sea wall in front of the Royal Yacht Squadron. Calum had never been inside the hallowed grounds of the RYS. He wondered if he would enjoy the experience. Eric put a stop to his musings as he called for the sheets to be brought in as he hardened up on the wind to enter the mouth of the Medina River.

'We going anywhere special?' asked Calum.

'Just down to the municipal landing pontoons. I have 'friend' waiting for me,' replied Eric.

'Thought we made it across the Solent a bit sharpish, anything important?'

'Business,' came the only reply as Eric concentrated on bringing *Six* gently alongside the nearest outside berth on the pontoons. Calum spotted a 'toff' all dressed-up in yachting gear, including regulation dark blue blazer with large club motif, white slacks, club cravat and a peaked cap with club badge and of course, designer sunglasses by Gucci. He moved towards *Six* with a steely look in his eye.

'Ahoy,' said the newcomer in an expected false plumy accent. Calum groaned under his breath, another 'upper-class hooray' was about to become Eric's latest target. Surely he wasn't going to sell *Six* so soon after commissioning.

Eric leapt onto the pontoon and started a quiet conversation well out of range from his waiting crew members. Simon asked what on earth was going on. Calum replied he wasn't sure, but guessed Eric was receiving or had received, an offer he was not about refuse for his gleaming six-metre yacht. Calum watched his good friend intently; vainly trying to get the gist of the conversation. The conversation looked brief and to the point. It looked like a done deal already. Calum watched as Eric and the 'toff' shook hands.

'Deal concluded,' thought Calum.

Eric leapt back onboard *Six* with a slightly glum face as the toff watched Simon push *Six* away from the pontoons back into the midstream of the river. *Six* backed into the river and fell away on to port tack. With sheets quickly trimmed to perfection she sped down the river towards the open sea. Calum saw the toff waving goodbye, turn and walk to a waiting limousine that looked remarkably like the latest Bentley coupe.

Calum turned round to Eric whose face transformed into a grin, larger than your average Cheshire cat.

'OK,' said Calum. 'Pray tell?'

Simon was more than interested too, and eagerly awaited the information to satisfy his curiosity.

'Well gents,' Eric grinned, 'when I found *Six*, I took an option on a second Six-Metre the owner said he was desperate to get rid of. *Six* was easy to get up to standard, but she has an original hull so she's only as stiff was when built. *Six* is a fast yacht, but not as fast as the new composite hulls.

However, she gets an allowance that makes her competitive in fleet racing. The second Six-Metre I found is also a Nicholson hull, with a double skin. Most of the outer skin needs replacing and a few of the frames too. So here I can be smart. By replacing the outer skin, I can also replace the lining between the skins with composite carbon-based materials. By using the latest modern glues, I can rebuild the hull to be very stiff indeed.'

Simon was impressed with Eric's lateral thinking.

'This legal?' asked Calum.

'Nothing specifically banning it in the rule book I can see,' said Eric with a straight face. Calum could tell Eric would have read the rule book a hundred times.

'So be it,' thought Calum.

Six passed the RYS and headed out into the open waters of the Solent. The wind remained in the south-west which quickly built to a solid Force 4 to 5; an ideal sailing breeze. The crew of *Six* proceeded to enjoy an exceptional day's sailing, but all too soon it time came to head back to Lymington.

Six headed towards the East Bramble channel buoy when Calum spotted a strange sight. Four very fast formula racing yachts were heading for the same mark, coming up at a frightening speed from the west.

'Christ,' shouted Calum. 'What a speed. Who's this little lot?'

'The Formula 59 team; they're in full training mode,' replied Eric. 'We'd better get the hell out the way; you've no idea what speed they're up to.'

Eric steered *Six* away from the East Bramble buoy, in the knowledge the racing team would be using it as a turn mark to head on up to their base somewhere on the Hamble River. All Calum could see were four enormous bow waves each with a very large symmetrical spinnaker above each one of them. How could the helms see where the hell they were going? Then he spotted something, even more, unusual.

Positioned at the end of each spinnaker pole, hanging in safety harnesses attached to a spare halyard, Calum saw a crew member waving at them to get out of the way, and bellowing instructions back to the cockpit.

The four yachts screamed by *Six* at speeds that defied logic. They reached the channel buoy almost at the same time and in no time flat, they'd gybed onto the other tack as they tore away into the distance.

Calum looked round at Eric for the expected explanation. Eric laughed. 'You've never seen them before and their favourite party trick?' Calum shook his head.

'It's the future, apparently,' sniffed Eric. 'The yachts are the latest in hi-tech everything. Hulls that weigh a third of anything else afloat, very deep keel foils with large teardrop bulbs. Sails that generate so much power you can't imagine, carbon mast and boom, and sail controls that keep them at full speed all the time. In fact in any wind speed above 15 knots, they can easily maintain speeds around 1.2-1.5 times the velocity of the wind. Today we have 16 knots of wind, so at this moment, they are up to something like 24 knots. Not bad Eh?'

Calum was impressed and asked about the crew member hanging from the end of the spinnaker pole. Eric told him it was for 'safety', as the helms had only a restricted view when the bow waves were up. Calum thought the word 'safety' had been misused yet again.

'Don't they get additional righting moment and speed from this lunacy,' he asked

'Two minutes a hundred,' Eric told him, 'although they only do it in closed waters, it is too dangerous at sea.'

The Formula 59 racing team disappearing quickly as *Six* set a course for home. The tide turned, sweeping *Six* quickly down towards Hurst Castle away in the distance. Eric gave the helm to Calum.

'About time,' thought Calum.

Calum settled *Six* on starboard tack, heading over towards the Island. He called for a little sail trim to ease the power in the beautifully set sails and quickly found the groove. *Six* was a dream to sail, a very taunt yacht, slipping through the Solent chop with little fuss. This was fast sailing indeed. They sailed for another quarter of an hour and soon reached over to the Island shore. Time to tack, and head for the mouth of the Lymington River, as the sun headed quickly for the horizon, and soon it would be the end of a most interesting day's sailing.

As 'Six' started to reach her destination the wind started its expected reduction at the onset of early dusk. Calum asked for more sail trim to put power back in the rig, mindful of the tide he would have to counter to get upstream to the moorings.

Six came up the river estuary with little fuss, slipped neatly past the Isle Of Wight Ferry Terminal and headed smoothly to her mooring and the gently bobbing dinghy waiting to take them ashore.

As the last wind of the day died, Simon used the boat hook to bring the mooring can and chain onboard over the bow roller. It took but a further ten minutes to make everything 'Ship Shape and Bristol' fashion. With the sails stowed, and the protective awning rigged over the boom and deck, Eric and his crew embarked into the dinghy. Simon did the honours with some strong rowing to get them back to shore, landing on the hard to manhandle the dinghy into the club boat park.

'Park your gear. See you in the 'Dog and Duck?' asked Eric.

'Naturally,' said Calum and Simon in one voice, 'and you're buying.'

And so ended a perfect 'end of season' sail.

Chapter 2

Calum went to bed early. His not quite so lean frame ached from head to toe after struggling all day with the garden. Gardens were nice to look at, preferably of the carefully manicured municipal variety with a comfortable deck chair and a stiff drink to hand.

Still, the more immediate tasks were complete, as he relaxed during the evening with a stiff whisky and a good video. Adriana, his beloved wife, had gone to Brazil to visit her beloved mother.

Calum also knew his wonderful wife would be totally preoccupied with the problems of the family at large. Evenings were reserved for watching the latest 'nouvela' on TV. Brazilian nouvelas were rightly famous for their extravagant production and wonderful looking women of any age, but a soap opera is a soap opera in anybody's language.

Calum checked his emails and downloaded the latest weather forecast. The weather forecast predicted a major low-pressure system to come steaming in out of the Atlantic, not quite the Burt Ford special of 1986, but a very close cousin.

Calum had little to worry about his beloved schooner, *Samba Canção*, currently stored high and dry in Barton's Marina in Lymington. At least he didn't until his good friend Eric phoned mid-afternoon to tell him the Formula 59 racing team had just laid-up their sleek racing craft for the remainder of the winter so that the yachts could undergo maintenance and modifications and the race crews could be given time away on holiday.

The yachts had been laid-up next to *Samba Canção*. Eric was concerned that these four racing yachts, with their deep racing keels, were sitting very high on their cradles, with masts still shipped. No one thought to tie them down to stop being blown over gale force winds.

Calum telephoned the marina manager for reassurance, but the manner of the reassurance did sound not reassuring at all. As he put the phone down, the word 'wanker' slipped out of his lips. He considered the man a complete 'oik' at the best of times, who should have stayed on the farm where he originated and almost certainly belonged.

He decided to make an early start the next morning and see the true situation for himself. Knowing Eric as he did, he expected to find substance to his earlier phone call.

During the early hours, Calum awoke to find his duvet on the floor, that he was cold, and badly needed the loo. He finished his visit to the porcelain, becoming conscious of the weather outside. High winds were blowing through the trees protecting his cottage from the south-west winds. This could not be considered good. Gales were rarely heard inside Calum's environmentally friendly cottage, hidden behind a strong line of thick timber.

The level of mayhem outside told him in the light of the new day, many of his neighbours would be looking for a whole host of missing objects; wheelie bins not brought in from front gates, fences that were less than stout, garden furniture and all the other paraphernalia people were wont to waste their hard earned wages on.

Calum returned to bed but slept fitfully, and as the new day struggled slowly over the hill in front of his cottage, he said 'sod it' and got up to make himself a strong cup of tea. His annoyance increased sharply when he discovered the 'digestive biscuit' tin was seriously empty, vaguely remembering he planned a visit to the village shop but managed, with remarkable ease, to forget all about it.

The early morning radio detailed the immense havoc wreaked by the gale. The news presenter had the mistaken impression the gale had subsided.

Calum switched off the radio and slipped back into bed and, as per normal he slept soundly until ten o'clock. These extra few hours worked wonders. Calum arose and leapt out bed, more than a little hungry.

One substantial cooked breakfast later, Calum was full of beans, literally, and looked out into the garden. A transformation had occurred, and it would take more than a magic wand to put it back together. A quick look at next door's garden, however, showed he had little to worry about by comparison.

He wandered into the living room and switched on the television, reporting the widespread chaos the overnight gale had inflicted on the surrounding countryside.

The phone rang urgently. Calum knew it could only be Eric, and if Eric was up and about at this time of day, it did not bode well. His blood rang cold as he picked up the phone and said, 'Hi Eric,' even before the caller spoke.

'That's clever,' said Eric on the other end of the line. 'How did you know it was me?'

'Never mind that,' replied Calum, 'and the bad news is?'

'The bad news is, my friend, as the gale reached its peak and the wind backed to the south, its force produced a domino effect on the four racing yachts I mentioned yesterday, and .....!'

'They crashed onto *Samba Canção*? finished Calum.

'Exactly,' replied Eric. 'The hull is OK, sort of, nothing substantial, but when the mast of the nearest yacht smashed into your main mast, it came crashing down and pulled the top section off the foremast. It's a bit of a mess, I'm afraid.'

Calum muttered an expletive, something about the Marina manager's mother being a nurse, and his father being 'HMS Ark Royal'. Scrotums would be exacted in revenge, nailed to anything processing great altitude, with the owner still attached.

He thought for a moment then told Eric he would come down to Lymington within the hour. 'Don't think so old chum,' said Eric. 'All the roads through the New Forest are blocked.'

'Really,' exclaimed Calum. 'You sure?'

'Yep,' explained Eric. 'The police are preventing traffic entering the Forest except for residents trying to get home, and even then there are a lot of people stranded.'

'Hum,' pondered Calum. 'I could bum a motor boat from my chum at Hythe, and come round by sea, what you think Eric?'

'Nope,' Eric replied. 'The Solent is not the place to be right now. Anyway Lymington Harbour is in such a dreadful state, you wouldn't be welcome unless you happen to have a salvage crew with you.'

'OK Eric. I'll stay at home and chop wood for the fire. I need some practice with the axe. Tell my good friend the marina manager I shall visit soon, preferably with an axe in hand. Oh Eric, could you do me a favour, and take a few photographs and email them up to me?'

'Sure Calum, no problems, I'll ring tomorrow, and we can chat about the next step.'

'Many thanks, Eric. Hear from you tomorrow.'

With that Calum rang off, and a dark mood came over him. He'd worked hard on the refit of *Samba Canção*, and the schooner had been booked for a documentary film in eight weeks' time. There was not much chance of that happening now.

When the promised emailed pictures arrived, his mood got seriously blacker. Calum set about his house tasks and worked off his bad temper chopping wood. Three hours later he'd finished and so little remained but to put his feet up and relax.

Two days later saw Calum standing in the marina, looking at the tangled mess caused by the gale. It was easy to see what had happened. The unsupported metal cradles for the racing team yachts, had rocked to and fro and buried into the ground in its sodden and saturated state. The upwind racing yacht toppled over, taking the other racing yachts with it, crashing domino-like on to *Samba Canção*.

The situation was a shambles, but the rest of the marina was much the same. Out in the river there were yachts everywhere except where they should be. Some were washed-up in the river, rammed under the bridge. Many were washed-up over the mud flats at the exit to the main channel that led out to open water.

It would take a while before even the slightest resemblance of order could be re-established. Calum found his schooner to be at least water tight from the rain that started to fall, so he upped stumps, jumped back into his car and went round to see Eric.

Eric welcomed his old friend with suitable commiserations, and as it was nearly lunchtime and his wife Kristen had gone out, Eric suggested the most sensible plan of all, the pub.

The 'Dog and Duck' was full, full of morose yachtsmen, recounting the damage suffered at the hands of the 'Almighty'. A few were more than well on, steadily swaying at the bar hanging on for grim death. Calum recognised a few of them, the owners with underinsured yachts.

In the far corner, were a couple of skippers in good humour. He thought this strange until Eric mentioned the skipper on the left had been trying the sell his overpriced yacht for some considerable time.

'Isn't he the retired insurance broker?' asked Calum.

'Indeed,' replied Eric. 'And now you know why he's a happy bunny.'

'Perhaps he'll buy everyone a drink?' suggested Calum.

'Fat chance,' said Eric. 'Tight as a duck's arse, that one.'

The two friends continued their convivial lunchtime and retired to Eric's house for coffee and fruitcake.

Kristen returned home and found the two of them in a mellow mood. She asked Calum if he wanted to return home, or stay over. Calum thanked her for the offer, but he felt fine to drive home. The local constabulary would be more than preoccupied with other matters.

A week later, Eric rang at breakfast time and reported the marina had almost returned to normal, and could he come down at eleven o' clock to meet the marina's managing director and the CEO of the Formula 59 racing team.

Calum finished his breakfast, found some warm clothing, his waterproof jacket and safety boots. He took his hard hat from his offshore bag and flung it on the back seat. This meeting would be more than interesting, especially as a good sailing chum in the legal profession had primed him with what to ask for, and what to steer well away from.

The journey to Lymington wasn't too bad as far as Lyndhurst, but getting through the New Forest became slow going. The road was heavily restricted by work crews, either clearing away fallen trees or replacing damaged power lines.

Nonetheless, he made it to the marina only five minutes late. The Formula 59 racing yachts, already back onto their support cradles, now suitably supported by planking. Wire stays had been rigged down to anchors to prevent a reoccurrence of the previous week. The words 'bolted, gate, closing, horse and after' came to mind, to complete a well-known phrase.

It went without saying that Calum wondered why this had not been carried out in the first place. During a quick stop in Lymington Town for the morning papers, the proprietor had told him that on the afternoon before the gale, the Formula 59 racing team and the marina work crew had been more interested in finishing for the day, with a view to making it to the pub at opening time, rather than completing their work despite the weather forecast, which for a change had been one hundred percent correct.

As he parked his car in the marina car park, he was surprised to be met by Mr. Cook, the managing director of the company. Calum considered this a good start and felt in the mood to extract as much as possible in the way of retribution.

He caught sight of *Samba Canção* for the second time since the gale, and was totally dismayed. The mainmast had been, as Eric said, totally demolished. The damage to the fore mast looked bad, with the top section pulled well back from the vertical.

The managing director apologised profusely for the sad state of affairs. Calum asked if he knew the whole story. He said he did until Calum put him straight by mentioning the news he'd obtained, without naming names. He knew the owner of the pub these 'oiks' drank in any way; it wouldn't take long to get chapter and verse of the whole event.

Mr. Cook's shoulders sank. This particular client knew the sorry truth of the matter and would have to be satisfied or else. Mr. Cook asked what actions he considered necessary to resolve all the whole issues.

The hull of *Samba Canção* had sustained damage on the starboard side, but it could be repaired without too much major surgery.

Calum asked the question about replacing the masts? A costly exercise at best, especially as there was a very good chance the mast sections were no longer available. Mr Cook frowned and thought long and hard. Needless to say, Calum had already researched the answer, which in a word, was not good.

In short, not only would the schooner need new masts, and new rigging too. And God knows if the schooner's existing sails would set properly upon the new equipment. There was every chance they wouldn't.

As the scale of responsibility dawned upon Mr. Cook, he tried to change his position in front of his client, but Calum would having none of it. Mr. Cook tried hard to resolve the issues, but the sheer cost of the exercise would be way above the limits he had in mind or were indeed available to him.

Calum could see the situation heading rapidly towards an impasse. So trying a new tack he reminded the general manager most of the responsibility for the sloppy actions of the racing team could be shared with their illustrious CEO. They must have one surely?

Mr. Cook brightened considerably when he suddenly realised he could, with luck, divide the costs between the two entities involved. Some of the tiredness of the last week left him.

A new figure turned up and made his way over the two of them. Calum thought he looked vaguely familiar. The newcomer introduced himself as Mr. C. Whyte, CEO of the Formula 59 Racing Team. Calum faced towards him and said, 'Chalky Whyte, well I never.'

The CEO of the Formula 59 Racing Team looked intently at Calum, and recognition flickered for a moment and then faded away.

'Southampton Sailing Club,' continued Calum. '1964. The SWSA races, you use to win most of them until I bought Zenith #35.'

Mr. Whyte struggled to remember. Calum had one last chance.

'Remember the town regatta in 1963, which I won, just by a few seconds from your good self?'

'It was my last race before HMS Albion sailed to the Far East, and got locked up in the Borneo Conflict.'

'By the time I'd returned to the UK you'd joined a shipyard on the Hamble, and got taken on by a racing team as dogsbody and general washer upper. Mum used to write and tell me all about it until you disappeared, New Zealand I think?'

Chalky Whyte suddenly remembered; it all came back to him. He had indeed prospered when he went abroad. And here stood one of his best adversaries from his earliest sailing days.

He put out a hand to Calum, and Calum shook it vigorously.

Chalky Whyte looked over at the schooner. Recognition dawned over his face. 'Is that the yacht I think it is?' he asked.

'What do you mean,' asked Calum.

'The one that escaped from Florida after the attack on the USA. I hear you had lots of exciting adventures,' said Chalky.

Calum took his arm and pulled him to one side.

'Who told you the story?' he asked. 'We don't broadcast it around here.'

'Sorry old friend,' replied Chalky. 'It came from your lawyer, old 'Sue, Grabbit and Runne' in Winchester.'

'I'll have a stiff word in his ear,' said Calum, more than a little upset.

'Now now, don't get all pet lipped,' soothed Chalky. 'We're old friends, and he was proud to know what you'd achieved. Amazing really, but 'mums' the word old boy.'

Mr. Cook could tell these old combatants were getting comfortable going down memory lane.

'Could I offer you two gentlemen coffee in my office,' he asked. 'Then perhaps we could commence our business?'

'Sure, good idea,' replied Calum. 'Time to get on.'

They made their way to the marina's office block. The feckless one stood by to make the coffee, and generally, make himself useful. Calum gave him a withering look of contempt, which Mr. Cook was not slow to notice.

They made themselves comfortable, with coffees to hand, and began their detailed discussions on how to reach an acceptable result for all parties.

Mr. Cook stated he could agree to almost anything other than a total cash reimbursement.

Calum asked him to clarify his statement, because if he had to repair *Samba Canção* with insurance money, the insurance company concerned would, in his opinion, attempt to recover their costs based on the marina's negligence.

Mr. Cook winced at the word 'negligence' but knew Calum had enough witnesses to stand a very good chance of making that dreaded word stick.

Chalky Whyte saw how the land lay when being quizzed by Calum. He could offer all sorts of things except large amounts of cash, and wished to stay clear of a wrangle with his insurance companies. This event would only put his campaign insurance premiums up, and insurance costs were one of his biggest headaches.

The general discussion on who was going to do what for whom started to drag out. Calum realised at this rate nothing would be concluded. He looked hard at the two gentlemen. They were in heated discussion about responsibilities when they realised Calum had stopped talking and tapping his foot impatiently on the floor.

They stopped to look at him.

'What are you thinking Calum?' asked Chalky Whyte.

Calum replied that at this rate nothing would be agreed. He suggested they draw up the 'minutes of meeting', agree on the wording, agree the actions, by whom, at whose cost, and when the necessary actions would be completed.

Then all parties would sign the 'minutes of meeting', and if anyone defaulted, the 'minutes of meeting' would record the agreement that would make it a lot simpler for the lawyers to sort out. The word 'lawyers' did not go down well.

Chalky Whyte agreed, but Mr. Cook visibly hesitated. Chalky Whyte saw his concerns and suggested he could make notes and draw up the document, otherwise he would defer all responsibility to the marina.

And so the 'minutes of meeting' were duly drafted and agreed. Despite the careful wording, the document screamed negligence, which is precisely how Calum wanted it.

Calum produced an estimate of the total work scope. It added up to a cool ninety-seven grand. Chalky Whyte looked at it horror, but it had the ring of truth about it. He usually spent this kind of money most days of the week when the racing season was busy.

Mr. Cook called in his chief engineer to give his opinion. He agreed reluctantly it was a good a figure as any, and departed, his mobile phone calling him to another aggrieved customer.

The document recorded the event, the damage sustained, and the consequences, which required two new masts to be built by Carbon Masts of Southampton, the racing team's contracted mast developer and supplier.

The schooner would be re-rigged, and require, at the very least, two new mainsails. Calum reminded them the short-handed capability of the schooner must be maintained, so that meant in-boom furling, instead of the existing in-mast furling.

Finally, Calum brought something new to the conversation. The schooner had been chartered for a documentary film in two months' time. Mr. Cook started to stare at the floor; this was turning into a bad day. God knows how much this would eventually cost, but he was in caught between a rock and a hard spot.

Calum could see his despair, and cheered him up with an idea he'd saved for now. He promised when the work on the film documentary commenced, he would insist on the base location of the shooting to be his marina and thereby bring valuable publicity. Mr. Cook thanked him for the offer, but who would see the documentary film.

'Don't worry Mr. Cook,' reassured Calum. 'It will have worldwide coverage, more than that I cannot say.'

Mr. Cook remained only half convinced but accepted the offer at face value.

Eventually, the completed document was duly signed by all three parties. The marina would repair the schooner, waive outstanding storage fees for the last year, reduce the outstanding bill of *Samba Canção's* refit to cost price, complete the exterior painting and anti-fouling for free and waive storage, launch and recovery charges for the next two years.

The Formula 59 Racing Team would use their mast development company to build two new masts and re-rig the schooner, and provide a new suit of sails from their contracted sail loft.

The meeting finished and at last Calum could escape into the fresh air. It had all been heavy going, but he was well pleased with the result, and remaining upset about the damage to *Samba Canção* had little point. What was done was done, and he had successfully managed his way out of an expensive situation.

He wandered around to Eric's house but found Eric on his way out. He bid farewell, and jumped back into his car and headed for home.

When he arrived he made himself a quick snack of Welsh rarebit with a pot of regular coffee, ready for an early night. Tomorrow he had to collect his wife from the delightful Heathrow Airport.

He checked his computer for emails and checked the actual departure of his wife's flight. It had been delayed on departure, but it had been scheduled for on time arrival.

'Fat chance,' thought Calum, the late Adriana would be late again.

Chapter 3

Spring had been a long time coming, so Calum and Adriana left the bleak English winter to take a cheap holiday in the Algarve. They'd never visited the south of Portugal before, so together they welcomed the chance to get some winter sun. The hotel was first class, and in the summer, it would have cost a fortune, due to its proximity to a famous golf course. Calum didn't play golf, never even tried it.

Now they'd returned. Calum spent a very busy time picking up on the progress of restoring the schooner. To his surprise, progress had been good. Even better, the contract from the documentary film company had arrived. All being well, the schooner would be ready just in time. The company agreed to the change of base venue to Lymington, and Calum passed the news along to Mr. Cook, which agreeably speeded up progress.

Calum checked with Chalky Whyte on the progress of the new masts and sails and received the news around about the first of the month. Calum passed on the good news about the charter by the film company and the promise of extra publicity.

'Ah yes, Calum,' said Chalky Whyte. 'I need to speak to you on the subject dear to your heart, finance.'

'Oh really,' said Calum. 'What's up?

'Let's discuss it over lunch, tomorrow OK?' said Chalky Whyte

'Sure,' replied Calum. 'The usual place in town, say 13.30?'

The next day, Calum arrived at the Italian restaurant opposite Southampton Town Quay. This famous old building looked as lovely as ever, having been recently restored and now it had become a smart casino.

Chalky Whyte arrived early and judging by the discreet corner position, pre-booked. Calum asked himself why he deserved this special attention. The restaurant was nearly full of the usual crowd, mostly businessmen and clients, or as always, a businessman with his more than personal assistant. Nothing changes thought Calum. Ah well, let's see what Mr. Whyte wants?

Chalky stood up, beaming at Calum's arrival. Chalky was in a good mood, but then he usually was. It struck Calum how little he'd changed over the years. His deep-set eyes had a wealth of experience, and Calum had difficulty reading his mind. Best to enjoy the lunch, and go with the flow.

Calum waited until the end of the sweet course before Chalky Whyte broached the subject. Calum could see it coming, if only because time had nearly run out.

Chalky Whyte reviewed the situation regarding the repairs to the schooner. To be fair, Chalky had pulled out all the stops, and he must have used up a lot of his team's resources, or rather, his sponsor's money.

Chalky Whyte's review came to a conclusion, which, at the end of the day, Calum would do very well out of the unfortunate incident. His beloved schooner would have a brand new rig, a bigger rig at that, and a new sail wardrobe. It crossed his mind he might have pressed just little bit too hard. Could be time to pay up?

To cut to the chase, Chalky Whyte had cash flow problems that he didn't want to get out of hand and brought to the attention of his main sponsors. It was the dead season for raising funds, and his carefully husbanded reserves were just about finished.

Before Chalky Whyte could bring himself to mention a figure, one he'd obviously been calculating for quite some time, Calum simply asked, 'How much do you need?'

The straight question caught Chalky Whyte off-guard for a moment, but he caught a quick glimpse of a smile in Calum's eyes.

'I hadn't really thought of a figure,' he replied.

Calum struggled to stop his expression from giving away the game. He was smiling inside and knew he would be kind to his old friend.

'Bollocks,' Calum came back to him. 'Just give me the figure you have been revising for the last fifty minutes.'

'That obvious?' Chalky Whyte mumbled, 'OK, perhaps thirty grand?'

Calum looked at him dead-eyed.

'Can we try for twenty' suggested Chalky Whyte.

'OK,' said Calum. 'We can do that. Can you give me a week?'

'Damn,' thought Chalky Whyte. 'That was too easy. Should have tried for the higher figure, goodness knows I need it.'

Calum read his thoughts, time to draw him ever closer. 'A secret for you Chalky, OK?'

'Go on then,' agreed Chalky Whyte. Calum looked around. They were almost totally alone; the restaurant emptying fast.

'It's not strictly my schooner,' he said. 'It's kind of a permanent loan.'

'Who the hell from?' Chalky asked.

'Uncle Sam,' Calum whispered, 'and, I have what is euphemistically known as a 'slush fund' to keep her in good shape.

'How did you manage that?' Chalky asked.

'It's a long story, I'll tell you one day. It'll take me a week to prize the money out its shell, but it's OK.'

'What the whole twenty?'

Calum felt benevolent, which came from drinking too much of the excellent Australian white wine Chalky Whyte had been so careful to ply him with.

'Thirty it is mate, no worries Blue,' grinned Calum.

Chalky Whyte was strangely calm. His moment of inner panic rapidly subsiding.

'Thanks Calum, but how?' he mumbled into his quickly emptying wine glass. 'You come into money or something?'

'Not quite. I received an advance from the film company, for the documentary, and I'll split some of it with you to make up the thirty grand.'

'That's kind of you,' Chalky Whyte said.

Calum told him he would have to put him down as a new sponsor.

'For why?' said Chalky Whyte

'So I can come to the sponsors freebies, and bask in the glory of your successes.'

'And I thought I was the cute one. I'd better pay the bill before I get swept away by your cuteness.'

Calum was well pleased with his lunch, and for that matter so was Chalky Whyte.

As they said farewell to each other Chalky Whyte asked if Calum could bring the schooner round to Carbon Mast's base on the River Itchen, just up past Northam Bridge. Calum stood and looked at him with a blank stare.

'What's that look for?' queried Chalky Whyte.

'When?' suggested Calum.

'Oh yes, sorry, in a week's time, Monday late morning. Arrive at high tide and the technicians will make all the preparations. Your new 'sticks' will be installed and set up straight away at low tide.

'Low tide?'

'Yes, their crane doesn't have the height and the reach for a high tide lift with the new masts you're going to get.'

'Wilco, over and out, see you then, thanks a lot Chalky. Must find you another sponsor.'

Chalky Whyte smiled. Calum might just do that.

Calum arrived home, very pleased with himself, and smiling like an old tabby cat. Adriana wondered what on earth could change old sourpuss, into Mr. Smiley, over one simple extended lunch.

'Tell you later,' Calum told her. It was time for a much-needed nap.

Chapter 4

The Marina at Lymington

The week passed quickly and Calum spent many hours completing all the little tasks to make the schooner ready for her epic voyage from Lymington to Southampton, all of 20 nautical miles.

Calum did not like setting off on a yacht journey with only a main engine. It generated a feeling of nervousness and just didn't seem right having a yacht without sails. Engines were for emergencies only, not the 'be all and end all' of a safe arrival.

Samba Canção looked truly splendid in her new livery, dark blue hull, gold boot topping, and another gold line around the hull one foot below her gunwales. The top hamper had been removed, and the schooner looked naked without her masts and their complicated rigging.

The schooner rested on a temporary cradle at the water's edge of the deep-water quay. The crane, with extra counter weights, would lift the heavy schooner, suspend her over the edge and carefully lower her back into the water.

The crane driver was an old sailing chum of Calum's, in whom he had great confidence. The lift would be a tricky lifting operation at best, with *Samba Canção* close to the maximum capacity the crane had been certified to handle with safety.

With everything nearly ready, the marina foreman arrived and caused a delay of 20 minutes to check the crane, the lifting slings and other equipment were correctly tested and certified. Paperwork, and more paperwork, an ever-increasing requirement by insurance companies and HSE safety inspectors, plagued what he considered normal operations. The crane driver hadn't dropped a yacht in 25 years, and he wasn't about to start now.

A large black car pulled up and backed into the visitor's car park. Two tall heavily built men, dressed in dark raincoats, assisted a third man from the rear seat of the car. Calum paid them little heed, but he did notice they appeared to be heading, purposely, in one direction – towards him. There was something about them. Their easy walk and their casual confident air brought a strange premonition of trouble. Calum instinctively knew they were more than able to handle themselves. Their piercing eyes sent a strong chill down his neck.

Calum began to pay attention to the third man, short, stocky, somewhat overweight, a typical American with a Homburg hat pulled hard down over his head. Pure trouble; it stood out a mile, an American who knew how to get into trouble, and to extract himself from it at everyone else's disadvantage. Short, ugly and bad news all round.

The tall one on the left with a blonde crew-cut called out his name, 'Calum James?'

The words came not as a question, more a statement of fact. Calum didn't reply. The man with the blond crew-cut looked straight at him and his impatience could be seen to be mounting, Calum waited a little longer.

The other man with short dark hair moved to one side and looked out at the river. He too showed signs of becoming very impatient.

Calum answered, 'Who's asking?'

The blonde man asked Calum to step to one side to ask him a few questions. Calum repeated his question, 'Who is asking?' in a polite but cynical way.

Again the blonde man moved to one side, and Calum stepped in his way. The man explained they were police. Special Branch. The American moved away but stayed close to hear Calum's answers.

Calum looked straight at the blonde policeman. Time to be careful he thought.

'Identification,' he asked stubbornly.

The blonde policeman did not look pleased, but as Calum looked over at his friends who worked for the marina, as they began to pay attention to the three strangers.

The blonde policeman pulled out an ID card, showed it and went to return it to his inside jacket pocket. Calum put out his hand and the card was reluctantly handed over. He stared at it, never having seen one before. It could be a bus pass for all he knew.

'Shouldn't it say PC-49?' he quipped.

The look he received in reply was one of pure aggravation.

The other policeman moved closer. 'We wish to ask a few questions about this 'ere boat', he said.

'This 'ere boat is a schooner, and we are very busy trying to launch her,' replied Calum.

The foreman returned satisfied with his mountain of paperwork. The crane man began to inch the schooner out of the cradle and hung *Samba Canção* over the water.

The blonde policeman shouted out over the noise of the cranes engine to stop, but the crane man ignored him, as he watched his jib man guide this tricky lift into the water.

The foreman intervened, and forcibly told them all to clear the area. The area was not safe and angrily told them to bugger off and get the hell out of his way. The foreman's other workmen came to position themselves close to him. They'd picked up on the unusual situation and were not about to let anything get in the way of their operation. They had a busy schedule that morning and time was pressing.

Calum was just about to get involved when his cell phone rang.

'God's teeth, who the hell is this?' he thought. It was Jenny, his erstwhile crew, the lady he'd rescued from Florida, the US Ambassador's daughter.

'Calum,' she said urgently. 'Have you been visited by three strange men, one of them a short unpleasant character; it's very important?'

Calum turned his back on the three strangers.

'Yes, they're all here. We are just about to have an unpleasant conversation on a subject of which I know not,' Calum replied. 'Two of them say they're from Special Branch, the third one I have no idea.'

Jenny continued, 'They're intelligence officers, and they're minders for the short, ugly one.'

'Who is he?' asked Calum.

'I'm with Daddy in his office, and he's not sure. He thinks CIA, but an obscure division and bad news.'

Calum replied he looked like 'Darth Vader'. Jenny asked how on earth he knew that.

'It's not his real name, surely? asked Calum.

'His name is Garth Vidor, but it's his 'nickname' right enough. Be very careful,' she warned. 'You will need help on this one, but Daddy needs say fifteen minutes?'

'OK,' replied Calum, and rang off.

He turned around to face the three intruders, looked past them and saw *Samba Canção* floating in the river being moved to the visitors berth.

He looked at the blonde policeman. 'OK, what do you want, or rather what does Darth Vader want?'

'Who were talking too?' he demanded sharply.

'None of your damn business,' Calum snapped back at him, keeping his growing anger in check.

'Well, we will see about that,' replied the blond policemen. 'You should know your cell phone is being monitored.'

'Fill your boots,' replied Calum and turned to watch his schooner being carefully moored alongside the visitor's pontoon.

The blonde policeman's cell phone rang; he spoke into it in monosyllables. He told the dark haired policeman the origin of the call. The dark haired policeman looked at Calum and thought for a few seconds.

Calum looked directly at him and said nothing. A change of approach should start anytime soon, he thought.

'Mr. James,' he asked. 'We wish to examine your yacht, do we have your permission?'

'Definitely not,' replied Calum. 'I want to know what the hell you want, who the hell you are and why is the Yank involved?'

'State security,' replied the dark haired policeman.

'Bollocks,' said Calum, his temper finally getting the better of him. 'You want to see me, make an appointment. You want the search my schooner, get a warrant. Better still, you can fuck off, and when you've done that, fuck off again.'

The two policemen were not quite expecting this major outburst and were not amused in the slightest. They were about to move into action when Calum's cell phone rang. He snatched it out of his pocket and flipped the lid open.

'YES,' he shouted into it.

'Calum, dear boy.'

The caller was no less a person than Jenny's father, the Ambassador himself.

'You started a war down there yet?' he asked.

'Ah! Yes. Hello Sir,' replied Calum, trying to regain his composure. 'Yes just about. The Round One Bell has just gone, and I think we were about to get physical.'

'Let me speak to Mr. Vidor,' the Ambassador asked.

Calum shouted sarcastically over at the short man, 'Call for you, Sir.'

He didn't mean the 'Sir' of course. The CIA man turned away.

'He won't take the call, Ambassador,' said Calum into the cell phone.

'OK,' replied the Ambassador. 'I have someone here who will speak to one of the two British police officers.'

Calum handed his cell phone to the blonde policeman, 'It's for you, and remember your manners.'

The blonde policeman, his face like thunder, snatched the cell phone from Calum's hand and spoke curtly into it.

The policeman's conversation quickly stopped as he began to listen intently, his vocabulary rapidly reducing to 'Yes Sir', and 'No Sir'. The conversation did not last long. The policeman rang off and roughly handed the cell phone back to Calum.

He moved away and conferred with his colleague, and after a couple of minutes returned.

'Mr. James, I want to ask you about an illegal load of narcotics discovered on your yacht during your voyage across the Atlantic,' demanded the blonde policeman.

'Why?' asked Calum. 'For your information, it's a dead subject.'

The blonde policeman asked on what basis he could possibly make this assertion. Calum told him the incident had been fully recorded in the schooner's logbook, and the entry had been signed not only by him but by the helm on watch at the time.

Furthermore, Calum added, the schooner had been cleared on arrival by the Portuguese Immigration and Customs Service in Lisbon. The US Ambassador to Portugal himself had met the schooner on arrival at the Portuguese naval base, along with the father of the lady he'd rescued from Florida. The father of the lady was the gentleman on the cell phone a few minutes ago.

The drug scam seemed to be common knowledge among the diplomatic community. Calum continued and told the police officers that the schooner's logbook had been taken away, copies made and the original returned to him personally. Calum advised he'd made a certified copy of the original logbook, and the original safely stored in the offices of his lawyer.

What Calum did not tell the policeman was the original logbook had been copied and made to look like the original. This version of the logbook had been used to make copies; identified by a secret mark on the inside cover. This version of the logbook contained the names of the three passengers picked up from a downed aircraft in mid-Atlantic, altered to keep their identity a secret. The passengers were none other than the President of the United States, his wife, and the Secretary of State for Defence. A big secret indeed.

The policeman removed a copy of the schooner's logbook from his inner raincoat pocket, taking Calum by surprise.

The policeman began to ask questions from the logbook, to which Calum pretended not to know the answers. The policeman began to get impatient, but Calum continued to prevaricate. The policeman began to ask even more questions. Calum continued to feign lack of knowledge and asked to see the logbook. He needed to be certain the copy in the hands of the policeman was a copy of the doctored logbook. The real logbook classified as top secret was stored in the US Embassy in London and to Calum's certain knowledge it had never been copied,.

The policeman reluctantly handed the logbook to Calum, who accidentally on purpose dropped it. He quickly bent down to pick it up, and in reopening the logbook, he could see the secret mark on the inside cover. He relaxed, taking care not to show it.

The CIA man started to pay attention, moved quickly into the conversation, and snatched the copy of the logbook away. He began rapidly firing questions at Calum, who for a change, genuinely did not understand.

The CIA man quizzed him about the quantities of narcotics discharged overboard, who'd done the counting, who were the passengers onboard, and what about the gold?

The penny dropped, and suddenly Calum understood. This horrible little man must have been involved from the beginning. There had been no mention in the schooner's logbook of any gold onboard the schooner. At the time, only he knew about the hoard of Kugerands found in the aft master cabin, hidden from view in a suitcase in the master cabin's main locker.

Whatever the CIA operation had hoped to achieve, it could have seriously jeopardised the safety of the schooner and all onboard. Now the horrible little man found himself in a bad situation and desperately needed to get some answers.

Calum fobbed off the CIA man with a few defensive answers and pretended his cell phone had started ringing. He moved away, flipped it open and pressed the callback number. Jenny answered the call.

'It's me,' whispered Calum. 'I think this CIA chap was involved with whoever planted the narcotics on the schooner. I'm not sure when, but certainly when they knew a Brit had planned to buy the schooner and sail her across the Atlantic. Rum sort of an operation, I thought they moved this stuff around the world inside oil field drill pipe'.

Calum referred to a long-held rumour in the oil industry this sort of thing went on all the time at the behest of the secret and murky part of the US Government. Jenny asked Calum if he could be sure of his suspicions. Calum replied being a hundred percent sure would be difficult, but if she was here at this moment, he doubted she would form any other conclusion.

Jenny said, 'Got it. Stay calm and keep out of trouble for ten minutes, please.'

'Okay,' replied Calum, and put the cell phone back in his pocket.

The two policemen started to move towards the schooner. Calum did not wish to let them onboard, but he needed time. Quite what for, he had no idea. No doubt Jenny would be busy.

He accompanied the officers onboard the schooner, insisting they take their thick heavy shoes off. Everywhere the smell of fresh paint, and new wood varnish invaded the interior of *Samba Canção*. The blonde policeman asked what interior work had been completed onboard.

Calum told him the forward cabins had been altered to give better accommodation and increased workshop space. Old bulkheads had been removed, and the furniture replaced. The boat yard had also installed sealable storage bins under the cabin floors, and extra tankage installed under the cabin seating area on both sides of the schooner. By cross connecting the new tanks with gravity feed pipe work, the contents of the windward tanks could be fed down to the leeward tanks just before the schooner changed onto a new tack. Then the full tanks would end up on the windward side of the hull giving a good measure of righting. This arrangement would give the schooner better performance when sailing on the wind.

The blonde haired policeman seemed to understand the basics and looked carefully at the installation to see if he could find anything suspicious. Calum also told him a fair amount of weight had been removed from the hull, mainly from the bow section of the schooner, with the same intention of increasing her performance.

The other policeman moved into the aft main cabin, and Calum went quickly with him. There did exist just a tiny secret in the main aft cabin he did not wish to be known by anybody.

The aft cabin had been stripped bare, following a transformation similar to the forward cabins, and there the bedding on the double berth and the cushions on the bench seats had all been removed. The lockers and other storage spaces were also empty of any contents.

The panelling of the bench-seat backrests had curious rings embedded into the glass fibre structure, sat in deep rectangular grooves. The policeman asked what the rings were for. Calum told him they were to hold the back cushions in place. The policeman tugged on one of the rings quite hard, but it remained firm. Calum told him the rings were screwed deep into the woodwork behind the groove, and wouldn't come out. The policeman remained suspicious for reasons that Calum could not understand.

The cell phone in the pocket of the blonde policeman's pocket started its irritating jingle. He hauled it out of his pocket. He answered the call, but only listened to the voice of the caller.

'Yes Sir and No Sir,' was all Calum could hear. The blonde policeman looked at his hovering colleague. The two of them quickly went ashore, with Calum trailing behind. To Calum's surprise, they bundled the CIA man into the back of their car. The car rapidly disappeared out of the marina and headed up the road to Southampton.

The crane driver, who had been close by putting away the lifting slings said, 'D'you see that Guv, that short geezer, the ugly little shit, was just arrested, 'and cuffed and everyfing.'

Calum smiled to himself, 'How sad,' he thought. 'What a shame.'

Chapter 5

It came to be an early start on Monday morning. Calum had driven down to Lymington the day before to sleep onboard the schooner. He'd busied himself getting the schooner systems ready, and taking on supplies.

Half way through this mountain of work Mike arrived to lend a hand. Mike now lived comfortably in London in an apartment set aside for him by Jenny's father. He and Jenny were not exactly living together, but they spent nights and days preparing for the wedding later in the year, and the arrival of their baby.

The work list onboard was long and the tasks ate heartily into the time they'd hoped to spend in the yacht club bar. They made last orders by a whisker, and fortunately, the barman had no intention of hurrying home.

Calum took out a crumpled map of the Solent from the navigation station shelf and consulted a battered copy of the tide table predictions. If they left Lymington about 07.00, they would catch the last two hours of the flood tide up the Solent and Southampton Water. There would be plenty of time, and with Southampton's double tides, the ebb stream wouldn't start to run strongly until just past 11.00 in the morning.

If they made it to Carbon Masts, say by mid-day, the spring tide would empty the river in less than three hours and the work of getting the masts installed could begin. Calum remained calm about arriving early at the mast factory, and with a bit of luck, he might be able to snoop around and see how these marvels of modern technology were fabricated. Chalky Whyte had told him Carbon Masts might be a bit difficult to get into unless the manager could be persuaded to show him around.

'Just don't turn up with a camera in your hand,' Chalky advised. 'They'll throw you in the river if you do.'

Calum knew the area intimately. He'd started his sailing career in the local Sea Scouts just up river and spent almost a lifetime sailing in and around the Solent and the Isle of Wight.

As the last of the Sunday drinkers left the yacht club bar, Calum could see Mike looked ready for an early night. With a bottle of whisky on the schooner, he could finish preparing for a good night's sleep with a stiff dram.

They shuffled past the barman, busy tidying up, and putting the empty beer barrels outside the back door – a sure sign he was ready to lock-up and go home to face the music.

The night remained calm, and the wind had died with the day. A peaceful night's sleep onboard beckoned, with the promise of clear weather in the morning.

At six o'clock the next morning, Mike was up and about early. He'd caught the English habit of starting the day with a cooked breakfast, and Calum awoke to the sounds and smell of a cholesterol special being fried in the schooner's new and expensive galley.

Calum dragged himself from the comfortable quarter berth behind the navigation table, dashed briefly into the head to answer nature's call and wash his face.

He returned to the main cabin to find a large plate of bacon, two eggs sunny side up, fried tomato, fried bread, fried mushrooms, fried sausage, and a mug of very strong tea.

'We're not rowing this thing round to Southampton, Mike,' Calum teased him.

'I'll soon eat it for you,' replied Mike. 'The woman has me on a low carb' diet, and I'm wasting away.'

'That's American women for you,' Calum came back at him. 'Always the low carb' diet. What is a low carb diet anyway?'

'Well you've never been on one that's for sure, so make the most of it,' chided Mike.

They tucked in and then went on deck for a breath of fresh air. The morning arrived clear, fresh and chilly, with the smell of a touch of frost.

Calum cleared away the breakfast things whilst Mike wandered up to the newspaper shop. He returned with fresh milk, bread rolls and the morning's newspaper.

'Christ,' thought Calum. 'My tame yank's gone native.'

The town clock chimed out the seventh hour of the day – it was time to be going. Calum went below to the main cabin and threw the electrical isolation switch on the main batteries to the 'ON' position. He returned to the main cockpit and stabbed at the start button of the new MB diesel. It whispered into life at the first kick of the starter motor.

Calum nodded to Mike to let go the forward bow line and push the bow of the schooner away from the pontoon. Calum let go the stern line and eased the throttle forward to slow ahead as Mike quickly jumped onboard.

'Nice engine,' Mike said. 'Nice and quiet'.

'It's not run-in yet. I guess we'll have to take it easy, no need to hurry anyway,' replied Calum, as he eased the schooner into the main channel. The tide had long started to flood, and was getting very strong.

The schooner slipped quietly down the river towards the first bend that would take them into open water, with Calum taking in the peace and quiet of the new day. To his annoyance, a loud blast on a ship's horn came from behind. The Isle of Wight ferry to Newquay and her impatient skipper was in a hurry.

With little space for the ferry to squeeze by in this part of the river, Calum bid his time, as Mike went below to switch on the power supply for the depth sounder. The strident blast of the ferry's horn went again.

'OK! OK! Hang on a minute,' muttered Calum. He fiddled with the controls of the depth sounder and slowly edged the schooner closer to the river bank, but could find precious little depth to spare. The ferry, seeing the schooner move over, rang on full speed ahead and surged forward.

'Bloody SUV drivers,' muttered Calum under his breath, and throttled back to let the ferry pass as quickly as possible.

'I'll water his beer the next time I see that old goat in the pub,' Calum said out aloud.

'Who are you complaining about now? asked Mike. 'It's always someone.'

'Ferry Captains. They never change,' replied Calum, as he throttled up to cruising speed now the ferry had disappeared rapidly into the distance.

The schooner made the turn in the river's bend, passed the 'Jack-in-the-Basket' channel marker and headed for the outer channel buoy. A brisk south-westerly breeze picked up, and Calum longed to have the schooner under full sail. Mike made himself busy around the schooner, bringing in fenders and coiling down the mooring ropes.

He jumped lightly back into the main cockpit and asked Calum if he wanted the GPS navigation system switched on.

'Very funny, Mate. I will let you know if we get lost,' Calum answered back smiling.

With the spring tide running strongly in the main channel, the schooner made excellent progress towards Calshot Castle. In the distance, Calum could see the sailing school based at the old flying boat base getting into the rhythm of the new day.

It would be the start of a new course week for the hopeful beginners. No chance they could learn their sailing skills the old way, by trial and error and having fun. Sailing schools had become big business; with complicated curricula to study and exams to pass. Calum had never passed a sailing exam in his life and had absolutely no bloody intention of taking one anytime soon.

He did have an old RN Coastal Instructors ticket for teaching Sea Cadets, and a sailing master's certificate that originated from his wife's country. Quite how he came by it, he wasn't going to say. If it OK for the insurance company to keep his premiums low, by their standard, it was fine by him.

The schooner turned at the Bramble Banks Buoy and headed up Southampton Water. The land along both sides of the waterway was now littered with new buildings and commercialisation. Compared to the recollections of his early childhood Calum felt the march of progress had not been good for the area.

Between oil refineries, military bases and the ever-increasing encroachment by container terminals, there was little left from the past except for the Woolston Shore. Even here the munitions factory had long since given way to endless 'des res' housing estates that had sprung up along the shoreline. At least, they were not too unsightly.

The schooner reached the end of the Old Docks, as Calum turned the bow of the schooner up the Itchen River. The tide started to turn, and progress slowed noticeably.

Calum took the time to observe. Here, change became more evident, the old naval shipyard on the east bank had long gone, and even now new developments could be seen being busily constructed. Even more, apartment complexes were appearing to match those already built on the other side of the river.

The outer Empire Dock had long been developed into a marina and the old Inner Dock filled-in to make way for large commercial premises. Completing the feast of money-making developments, expensive apartment buildings were scattered everywhere, huddled around the marina. A feast of mortgages, all paid for by the up and coming 'yuppie' classes. Quite why they struggled to live in the centre of town, pay expensive mortgages and purchase expensive German motors cars would remain a mystery to Calum. He wondered what the upside to this frenetic activity could possibly be.

The schooner slipped under the 'new' Northam Bridge, as Mike went forward to look out for the premises of Carbon Masts. Calum thought it could be up past the old Nicholson's boat yard but he wasn't sure. Before he could concentrate on his navigation in this constricted part of the river Calum noticed a large open fibreglass rowing boat, about 18 feet long, in a state of total chaos.

Huddled inside the craft, he saw a crew of eight rebellious Sea Scouts. At the stern, an ineffectual scout master with long hair and thick rimmed glasses frantically tried to regain control with little chance of success.

The net result of this unnecessary chaos resulted in the rowing boat being carried quickly downriver by the spring tide. Calum guessed their base would be upriver, and even if the scoutmaster regained control of his rebellious crew, they had little chance of returning; well not until the tide turned anyway.

Calum joined the Sea Scouts when he turned thirteen. His father thought it would do him some good, though although exactly why he wasn't sure. By fifteen Calum had become an expert in the complicated task of rigging and sailing an old ex RN 27 ft. Montague Whaler. One thing for certain, something needed to be done before this rowing boat containing the Sea Scouts got into any more trouble.

Calum steered the schooner behind the rowing boat, and could see the problem. Three of the crew were typical overlarge teenagers, obviously more interested in more earthly matters, and certainly not interested in the discipline required to form a good boat crew.

The three other youngsters were scared, and two of them were crying, adding that extra touch of total disorder. The scout master had lost it completely and started screaming at the crew to no effect. None of them had any idea as to their impending predicament.

Calum gave the helm to Mike and asked him to slowly come behind the rowing boat. So engrossed were these Sea Scouts in their own stupidity they didn't notice the schooner's approach until they saw a no-nonsense skipper standing on the bow of a large yacht.

'OK,' Calum yelled at the top of his voice. 'Just what on earth do you think you're all doing?'

His harsh voice stunned them into silence.

'You stupid people. Don't you know you are about to be washed out to sea on this spring tide. I should let you get on with it.'

Anger rose within Calum, what a dreadful way for a Sea Scout troop to behave. If they were rescued by the harbour authorities it would only cause a great deal of fuss. If the local newspaper got hold of the story, God knows where it would end.

'OK,' Calum shouted. 'We are going to sort his mess out, right now. Everyone get in their place and get ready to row.'

Calum's no-nonsense voice showed he was not to be argued with. The Sea Scouts did as they were told.

'Out oars,' Calum commanded. 'Give way together. In–out, in–out, that's it keep up the rhythm. The rowing boat got under way, and Calum directed the scout master to steer the boat up river. He looked across at Calum, wondering what would happen next.

'Scout master,' shouted Calum. 'Keep them going. We are going to come in front of you, and you can row to my stern.'

Mike took his cue and manoeuvred the schooner around the struggling rowing boat and slowed down to let them reach the stern of the schooner.

Calum took a mooring line from the stern locker and prepared to heave it to the rowing boat.

'Scout master, get ready to receive this towing line, then ship and stow oars. The scout master managed to accomplish the instruction without getting it horribly wrong.

The rowing boat stopped dead in the water, and Mike put the schooner into slow astern. Calum split the heaving line into two, and with the grace of years of practice, heaved the mooring line to the rowing boat. The small boy in the bow caught the rope but had little idea what to do with it.

Calum looked down at him. 'Put the rope through the fairlead on the bow and take two turns around the thwart, that thing you are sitting on, and then make it fast, with what knot?'

'Round turn and two half hitches Sir?' The boy replied.

'Yes, OK, that will do,' Calum replied.

'The rest of you sit down in the boat, face the stern and keep still.'

Mike opened the throttle and the schooner started to move ahead.

Calum looked around to where they were. They'd been carried down river back into Southampton Water.

Calum spoke to Mike, 'Keep over to the Weston Shore, the tide has a bit of slack over there.'

Mike steered the schooner over to the east bank of the river, and slowly but surely they started to pass the pier of the water treatment plant.

The schooner struggled to overcome the drag caused by towing the Sea Scouts rowing boat. Calum gently brought the engine throttle higher, but with only a marginal effect. Calum didn't wish to overstress his new engine.

The schooner was quickly losing time and becoming late for its appointment at the mast factory, but what to do with the rowing boat behind? Mike made a good job of keeping out of the tidal stream, but as the river narrowed under the main road bridge, there was little he could do.

Calum went to the bow of the schooner and considered his options. He could deposit the Sea Scouts at the old 'chain ferry' hard under the bridge, where they could fend for themselves. He looked up river and saw a large powerful, black motor launch coming down-stream. The launch had a blue light on top of the cabin in among an unusual assortment of radio aerials and a small radar set.

'The police river launch, just the job,' Calum thought. He motioned Mike to steer towards the oncoming motor launch, although Mike became slightly puzzled. The police launch approached and Calum waved for it to turn and come alongside. The police launch came alongside, as the Sergeant handed the helm to his constable.

'Can I help you Sir?' the Sergeant shouted over the noise of his engine.

'We've rescued this rowing boat and its Sea Scout crew from being swept out to sea on the tide, but their boat is too large to tow against the tidal stream', Calum shouted back, 'Can you help us?'

'We've been looking for them. They were supposed to go upstream on this tide, but for some reason they came downstream. We received a call to lookout for them.'

'Be glad to hand them over, we need to get upstream quickly to Carbon Masts, can you give me an idea of how far we need to go,' Calum asked.

'About one mile, on the west bank, just past the scrap yard. You can't miss it,' replied the Sergeant.

'Thanks,' shouted Calum. 'I'll let you take the scout boat in tow and we'll be off.'

The police launch dropped back to the Sea Scout rowing boat and handed a towing line to the scoutmaster. Mike brought the schooner to a stop, during the transfer of towlines.

The Sergeant waved over to Calum. Mike gunned the engine of the schooner and headed up river. They were the best part of an hour late, but that couldn't be helped. The tide had another ninety minutes to run so with luck the schooner would arrive with time to spare for the preparatory work.

The schooner passed the scrap yard and the mast factory came clearly into view. Calum took the helm, releasing Mike to prepare for coming alongside the jetty. With fenders deployed, and mooring ropes ready Calum brought the schooner alongside a floating pontoon that would keep the schooner safe from damaging her new paintwork.

A calm voice came down from above, 'Mr. James?

'Yes,' shouted back Calum.

'Jolly good, we are ready for you. Come up when you're ready,' the voice said.

Mike made fast the bow line while Calum made busy with the stern line.

'Mike,' Calum called out. 'You'd best rig a couple of spring lines as well; I am going up to see what's what.'

Calum shinned up the slippery ladder to the top of the dockside. A short dapper man approached him and introduced himself as the director of the company. Calum shook his hand and introduced himself.

'What's the programme?' he asked.

The director told him the preparations were complete and there was little to do. His foreman would check the mooring lines were tight to prevent undue movement when the masts were being lowered into the schooner.

Calum looked across at the main workshop and saw workmen hard at work bringing the first mast on a multi-wheeled trailer across to the dock-side wall. A large mobile crane carefully negotiated its way around the side of the main office building to make its way onto the concourse. A truck arrived with a load of wooden sleepers for the crane's hydraulic outrigger arms to bare down upon. In all, it was a busy scene.

Calum walked over to the mast as the workmen brought it across to the dockside wall. It looked very big, laid there on the ground. Painted in an off-white colour, its profile looked similar to the old mast, pre-rigged to save time.

'It looks very strong,' Calum remarked to the director. 'Is it heavy?'

'It's less than half the weight of the old mast, and it's three feet taller.'

Calum looked at him in a strange way. The director continued to explain the saving in weight would allow an increase in sail area, and enhance the performance of the schooner.

Calum asked who the dickens had completed the redesign of his rig. The director told him Mr. Chalky Whyte employed the services of a naval architect who lived on the Hamble River, a foreign gentleman with a very good reputation.

'Oh really,' mussed Calum.

As the crane manoeuvred into place, a work crew descended to the schooner. Calum was relieved to see they were wearing soft shoes to protect his precious topsides.

With the new main mast lined up along the dockside wall, the riggers were busy laying out the lift and steady lines. The crane's engine roared into life, its main boom lifting from the rest gantry across the front of the driver's cabin.

The crane cab swung round, and the lifting hook lowered to ground level to be attached the lifting bridle on the mast. The foreman consulted a drawing of where its exact position should be. He took out a large tape measure and checked the distance from the bridle to the second set of spreaders on the mast.

It all looked very technical, thought Calum. The director led Calum to one side. The lift crew were almost ready to begin placing the first mast into the schooner.

The director led Calum into the main workshop, to check on the second mast being readied. He showed Calum the two new booms to be installed just as soon as the masts had been installed, their rigging secured and set-up.

They looked very sturdy, but the director assured him they were very light and demonstrated by lifting the end of one boom above his head, gesturing for Calum to try. When he did, Calum was impressed. How could something this bulky be so light?

Calum asked the director about the mast and booms, expressing the opinion he thought his new masts would be much thinner.

The director told him up until now his company had concentrated on the racing market. Their racing masts were generally had a very thin section to give the performance required. Although strong, racing masts were very light and mast bend could be easily controlled to whatever shape the racing teams wanted by the usual array of complicated rigging systems.

Masts for larger cruising yachts were a new venture, and the director expressed his excitement to introduce their new range of masts on such a large schooner. He hoped Calum would send back the trial data promised with regards to their performance and durability.

Calum asked what trial data? The director asked if a Mr Chalky Whyte had advised the terms and conditions for the supply of the masts?

Calum played for time, and certainly unaware of any contractual conditions regarding the supply of the new masts. At that, the man himself arrived.

'Hello Calum,' he called out. 'How do you like your new masts?'

'Very impressive Chalky,' replied Calum. 'What's this about supplying trial data to the mast company?'

'Oh, did I forget to mention that?' hedged Chalky Whyte.

'I think I would remember being set-up. And by the way, what's this about a redesign, I sure don't remember anything about that either.'

'I thought you'd be pleased. My naval architect chum ran his eye over the schooner when you went away. All you have to do is send back reports once a month as to how everything goes with the new rig. Not much to ask surely?'

'Suppose not,' sniffed Calum. 'I don't suppose you cut a deal with your director friend regarding this new line of masts he's bringing to market?'

'Of course not,' replied Chalky.

'Thought so,' replied Calum. 'I knew it would be too good with all this attention I'm getting.'

'Well,' Chalky continued, 'you have a famous yacht here. There's plenty of interest in what you're up to.'

This was all news to Calum.

'Chalky, I told you before. This yacht is not supposed to be famous. It's supposed to have a very low profile. I have given promises to some very senior people on this subject.'

Calum's vexed tone moderated Chalky's attitude. He became quite apologetic, but Chalky being Chalky, always had the last word.

'Won't be long before it does become famous. The newshounds will pick up the scent one day, and then you'll run for cover and no mistake.'

Calum didn't respond, Chalky could be right, but now was not the time.

The crane burst into life as the driver started to take up the slack in the lift line. Slowly but surely the mast rose into the air, and by a bit of clever handling by the riggers, it moved from the horizontal to an almost vertical position.

The crane swung slowly to bring the mast hanging directly over the schooner. A gust of wind caught the mast, but the riggers kept it under tight control. Slowly the mast began its descent to the deck of the schooner as the rigging crew pulled hard on the lines to keep it in position.

The mast heel approached the deck opening, and with that, it disappeared into the schooner. It took a few minutes to get it finally into position, as the riggers quickly attached the standing rigging to the shroud plates. The crane hook lowered itself to the deck as a rigger unhooked the lifting bridle.

The crane driver quickly brought the crane to its original position ready for the next lift. The first operation had gone very smoothly. The director invited Calum into his office for a coffee. Calum followed him across the jetty, well aware workmen preferred to work without an audience.

Mike stayed on the schooner, deeply immersed with so many interesting things to do, with the rigging foreman keeping him very busy.

Half an hour later Calum watched as the second mast was installed onboard the schooner. He felt peckish and shouted down to Mike to come and get some grub.

The director provided sandwiches and beer in his office, and it was not long before Chalky and his minder joined in. Chalky seemed to have a very good idea about the order of the day's events. It would take a while to get the two masts set-up and their rigging tensioned properly. Calum looked out over the jetty and could see the two booms being lowered one by one onto the schooner.

'Chalky,' Calum asked. 'When do the new sails arrive?'

'Oh, they're here already,' he replied. 'It will be a little while before the riggers are ready to get them onboard.'

Chalky's prediction didn't come true, and by the time the riggers finished setting-up the two masts, time had passed quickly. The director apologised, the rigging of the schooner had taken longer than estimated. Mike arrived in the office and told Calum everything ready and the schooner would soon be ready for the new sails.

Calum pointed at the clock, and Mike looked at it in a funny way. 'The day's gone already,' he drawled. 'Just where did it go?'

Calum suggested coming back tomorrow first thing if that was OK, meanwhile, he wished to move to the Marina for the night and get washed up. His cell phone rang, with Adriana wanting to know how the day had progressed. Calum told her everything had gone well, but it had taken longer than expected so he would stay on the schooner overnight in the Marina.

Adriana suggested she came into town and they could go for dinner. Calum readily agreed and she should stay the night. With the domestic scene organised, Calum climbed down to the schooner. Mike followed and prepared to cast off. The pair of them waved to the director, promising to return at 09.00 sharp the next morning.

The schooner motored the short distance down the river, and tied-up at the marina's visitors berth. They found the police launch attending to a suspected break-in on one of the many yachts moored there. It turned out to be a false alarm.

The Police Sergeant was about to leave when the schooner glided past and tied up a little way down the pontoon. The Police Sergeant replaced his mooring ropes and wandered along the pontoon to the schooner.

'Hello there,' he called out to Calum, busy securing the schooner for the night.

'Oh hello Sergeant,' Calum replied. 'Did those boys get back OK?'

'Yes,' the Sergeant continued. 'Thanks for picking them up.'

Calum replied it was no problem, telling the Sergeant once he had been a member of the same Sea Scout troop many years ago. The Sergeant asked Calum for the name of the scout master. Calum told him the name of a police riverboat sergeant called Stan Fright, a big bloke who stood for no nonsense.

'That would be the old man,' replied the Sergeant, introducing himself as Sidney Fright.

'You're joking,' Calum said. 'What a small world. Is your Dad still with us, he must be getting on by now.'

The Sergeant told Calum his father retired many years ago, but had died of cancer only recently.

'Sorry to hear that,' said Calum. 'He was a fine man. You got time for a quick drink?'

The Sergeant told him he would be going off duty in half an hour.

'We will still be here,' Calum told him. 'Come back and we will have made ourselves respectable by then.'

And so an hour later the Sergeant returned out of uniform. Calum and Mike took to him immediately, and the 'quick drink' soon developed into an old pals meeting. Adriana arrived to see three men doing what three men would normally do on a large yacht after a hard day's work.

'Is this party private, or can anyone join in,' she asked.

Calum looked up at his wife; she had certainly dressed for dinner.

'Oh Dear,' said Mike. 'You're in trouble now.'

'Not at all dear boy,' Calum replied. 'Let's dash along to the Town Quay and have a Chinese.' Sidney suggested he should be making his way home, but Calum would have none of it.

'Come along everyone,' he invited. 'Dinner is on me.'

They left the schooner and made their way to the taxi rank opposite the multi-screen cinema. The Chinese restaurant held the usual Monday crowd, just the four of them. Soon they were tucking into the special dinner for four.

Calum was in an expansive mood. He quizzed Sidney about his father, and how he too had entered the police force doing the same job. What interested Calum and Adriana was his charity work. The charity, called 'Sponsored Sports for Recovery', like many others, remained relatively small and generally unknown to the general public. It specialised in looking after young adults suffering trauma after their parents had been the victims of serious crime, severe illness or an accident.

Sidney Fright and his wife looked after the more serious cases. Their activities centred around giving the young adults in question an interest in a sailing activity which would bring a strong physical challenge coupled with strong mental exercise so they would have the chance to build or restore their self-confidence and become part of an integrated team in a technical sport, of which mountain climbing and offshore yachting were the most effective.

Calum and Adriana were more than interested in Sidney's story. 'What a worthy cause,' thought Adriana. 'Getting young people back into the mainstream of life so they could build a future.'

Sidney looked up for a moment and saw he had their undivided attention. He continued by describing a problem causing him a lot of soul searching. Calum could sense something might be about to be revealed and wondered what it might be.

Sidney described a major forthcoming event, a race for cruising yachts crewed by young adults under the age of twenty years. Mostly the participants were generally eighteen years old.

His own charity and three similar charities had been training crews sufficient to man four chartered forty-foot cruisers. The finance for one of the cruiser charters had fallen through, and the combined management team was stuck in a quandary as who to pick for the event and who to leave behind. The young adults had put in a great deal of effort to achieve a very high standard, and it would be very difficult to make choices. The crews had been training hard together and bonded extremely well.

The net result was Sidney badly needed berths for seven crew members, three girls and four boys without success. He tried to split them up among the other yachts in the twenty plus fleet, but with little success.

Calum asked when the race was due. His guest said the event would start in three weeks' time and he had almost given up finding spaces for his young hopefuls. Adriana looked over the table at her husband. She could see her husband was moved by the story, and quickly evaluating his options. He would want to help, of course, but did he have the time?

Calum caught his wife looking at him, and knew she thought the same. Nothing important existed in his diary, it had little to keep him interested over the next few weeks, and she knew the time had come for her husband to have a little adventure.

The duration of the sailing event would be a little over a week; add ten days for preparation and five days for the return and he would be home soon enough. The break would give her time to visit old friends in Aberdeen, although there were precious few left following the usual comings and goings in the oil industry.

Calum found himself looking at the floor deep in thought. He checked himself and looked up at Sidney. He remembered the good training and adventure his father provided all those many years ago. His father had been a good man, strict but fair and always full of encouragement.

Calum remembered the day the Sea Scout troop went Portsmouth for the Trafalgar Day parade onboard HMS Victory. His father returned the salute by the inspecting RN officer a little bit too enthusiastically and nearly demolished Calum and his school chum standing next to him. It felt time to repay the debt.

"OK Sidney,' Calum spoke softly, looking at Adriana to see if she concurred. Her dark eyes flashed her approval.

'If you can let me have the details, say tomorrow; late morning OK?' Calum asked.

Mike looked over at his skipper. 'What am I being let in for now,' he thought out loud, knowing full well his participation had been taken for granted.

He didn't mind, of course, but one day he might just ask if Calum considered the fact he had another life now he lived in England, this strange and foreign land. Sure he had Jenny to help him, as she slowly brought him willingly into her world. Soon they would be permanently entwined through marriage, but Jenny knew Mike was his own man and would take a bit of reeling in.

'If you're sure, that would be fantastic,' said Sidney with great relief, a great weight lifting from his shoulders.

The three of them finished their meal, and Sidney stepped outside of the restaurant to order a taxi whilst Calum paid the bill.

Soon, Calum, Adriana and Mike were safely onboard. Calum hurried to his cabin. It had been a long day, tiredness had sapped all his strength, and after a quick shower, would soon collapse into deep slumber. It was not quite what Adriana had in mind, but she knew he would snuggle into her back as soon as she joined him in the comfortable double bed of the main aft cabin.

Mike did the rounds, turned off the lights in the main saloon and made his way up forward. Tomorrow he would remind his skipper of the nicety of requesting his presence on the forthcoming venture. Looking after a load of kids onboard *Samba Cunção* would be interesting. Their last voyage had been crewed by the older mature generation, as he liked to call Calum and his former crew Bob.

The next morning Calum rose to get breakfast underway and put the coffee pot on to perform the vital ritual of kick-starting his American companion into life. Tea. Why couldn't the outside world realise a good strong mug of tea is the only correct way to start the day?

The two of them settled down to breakfast. Adriana wouldn't join them except for the toast and marmalade. She would stay in bed until the last moment, and then occupy the bathroom for 40 minutes.

Calum remembered Mike stayed quiet the previous evening during dinner. No doubt he would be having a little difficulty understanding exactly what he was being let in for.

'Ooops!' he thought. 'I haven't asked him to join in the new venture, and Jenny would be waiting for him in London.'

'Err. Mike,' Calum began. 'You OK for this little jaunt we planned last night. I forgot to ask if you're going to be free.'

'I might be. You going to keep dancing with your hand on my ass, or you going to tell me what's the deal?' replied Mike, vaguely pleased his skipper had at least thought to ask.

'Not sure really,' said Calum. 'It will be a kind of organised race for the masses. No doubt we'll find out later in the day, otherwise, I am as wise as you are.'

The light of Calum's life arrived at the breakfast table. Adriana sat down and Mike passed her the coffee pot and a bowl of fruit.

'Anything planned for today Darling?' Calum asked, in the certain knowledge Southampton High Street would soon receive its bi-annual stocktaking visit.

'I thought I might look at the shops,' she replied in the certain knowledge her husband already knew this.

'Jolly good,' replied Calum. 'Don't spend too much; you haven't got the wardrobe space.'

Adriana looked up and saw him smile. 'And don't forget to come home after you've finished playing with your toy boat.'

She always said that, and sometimes she meant it. Not today, her husband had an important mission to prepare for.

Adriana left for the shops, as Calum backed the schooner out of the marina. The day remained still and calm, slightly overcast with a gentle breeze blowing up Southampton Water. The forecast suggested the sky would clear within the hour.

The schooner motored gently upriver to return to the premises of Carbon Masts, so that the new sails could be fitted. Soon they were moored alongside the quay, and Calum went below to make a pot of coffee whilst Mike tidied the decks.

They didn't have long to wait before the happy voice of Chalky Whyte could be heard booming out above them.

'Anybody home?' he shouted down to the schooner. The smell of fresh coffee wafting upwards gave a welcome and suitable reply, as he shinned down the boarding ladder to the deck of the schooner. He dropped down through the main hatch just as Calum plonked a mug of coffee on the table before him.

'Good morning Senhor Chalky, and how we are today?' said Calum. 'I trust we come bearing gifts for the natives?'

'The Sail Master will be here in a minute; you got plenty of coffee?' Mike put the kettle on, knowing these two Limeys were about to commence an elaborate conversation about new sails.

The Sail Master duly arrived, dismissed the offer of coffee, and went on deck to look around. On the dockside, the Sail Master's two apprentices, Fred and Bert, were busy unloading a large trailer loaded with four heavy looking rolls, two thin ones and two quite thick. These were the new sails, and within a few minutes, they were being lowered down to the schooner.

The Sail Master proved a busy bee, fussing away, pouring out a myriad of instructions, most of which appeared to be quite unnecessary. Calum, Mike and Chalky Whyte kept well out of the way by fleeing up the ladder to the dockside. Calum could see this might take a while and settled himself on the quayside overlooking the schooner.

The two apprentices lugged the thinner rolls onto the foredeck and quickly removed their covers to reveal two new foresails. One by one each sail was carefully fed into the revolving headsail foils and hoisted to their fullest extent.

The Sail Master went to the bow to check on their handywork and grunted a small measure of his satisfaction. He pulled both sails out and pointed where the apprentices should bend the sheets on. Next he checked the angle given by the sliding sheet cars and chose a position from which he would work later.

The two apprentices moved aft to the main cockpit, wound the reefing lines on their two dedicated winches and quickly furled the two foresails around themselves.

It took four of the Sail Master's men to unpack the mainsail and lay it out along the main cabin roof. With the main halyard shackled to the head, the two apprentices took turns to hoist the sail up the mast, clipping the cringles on to the travelling luff cars as they went.

The sail looked huge, much bigger than Calum expected, but it fitted the mast perfectly. Next came the tricky task of feeding the foot of the sail into the self-furling boom, and with a lot of effort, and not a little swearing, the job was done.

Next, the mainsail was quickly lowered and furled into the boom, and a start made to repeat the performance to install the fore main.

Chalky sat next to Calum, with Mike leaning on a mooring bollard near-by.

'What do you think, Calum?' asked Chalky

'Well they look the business don't they, all that technology in one place.'

Chalky went on about the construction of the sails, hi-modulus aramid fibres with embedded carbon fibres to take the loads. To Calum, the most important observation was they looked good, and they were a lot lighter than conventional sails.

Chalky droned on about how to treat the sails, don't get them creased, blah, blah. Calum knew most of this but said nothing. Chalky drifted into technical heaven, and as he'd paid for the sails Calum didn't see the point of stopping him in full flow.

'When can we go for a sail then?' Calum asked of his erstwhile friend.

'It will be awhile yet,' he replied. 'Old fuss pot will take a fair while making adjustments.'

'Oh good,' Calum replied. 'I'm off to find a coffee and a donut to go with it.'

'Good man,' joined in Mike. 'I'd thought you'd never get around to the basics in life.'

The two of them left Chalky to it, and wandered out into the main street, only to run into Sidney, who'd been trying to find the entrance to the dockside. Sidney looked a trifle anxious carrying a large folder of papers.

'What do you have there, Sidney,' asked Calum.

'Err. It's the information about the young crew members for the race,' replied a hesitant Sidney. 'I hope you haven't changed your mind?'

'Relax, we're going for coffee and a snack; come along and we can go through the details,' Calum said.

The three of them walked quickly down the street until they came across 'The Northam Café', 'A real 'greasy spoon', thought Calum. They went inside. A standard British workman's café.

Still, it was clean enough, and the large lady behind the counter seemed obviously in a good mood. She had a badge pinned to her florid smock proclaiming her name to be 'Rita – Hostess'. The smock said it all.

'Must have worked in Spain, thought Calum. 'Wonder how many years past that was'.

'Good morning Rita,' Calum greeted her. 'You look cheerful for a soon to be a bright sunny morning.'

'Yes Guv', she beamed backed, 'I'ad a good night on the bingo last night.'

Mike looked at the menu board behind the counter. Whatever was on offer, he didn't understand half of it. Why couldn't the Limey's have regular diners, in a language you could understand?

'What's up Mike,' Calum asked. 'You looked confused.'

'Just tell me what's on the menu board I like,' he replied.

Calum turned around and asked Sidney his pleasure. Sidney asked for a large cup of tea and a shortbread biscuit. Calum asked the large smiling lady for two large teas, a large coffee black, one bacon 'butty', a shortbread biscuit, and bacon and eggs for his hungry American friend.

The large smiling lady looked at Mike and asked him 'ow he wanted his eggs 'sunny side up' or 'easy over'.

'There you go chum', Calum interrupted, 'international cuisine. He'd like his eggs easy over, thanks.'

Mike shrugged his shoulders and thought he really ought to be thinking about getting back to civilization, even if the television in America was truly as bad as Calum told him it was.

They sat down at a corner table and Sidney produced a large envelope. He laid two folders on the table and looked up at Calum and Mike. He described the first as information regarding the race event; the second one, marked confidential, contained details about the seven crew persons who needed berths.

Calum picked up the crew folder and handed it to Mike, and opened the first folder containing the details about the actual race. Where to start, the course itself, the finish line, the pre-start reception, the prize giving reception, and a large sub-file full of safety guff, and a million do's and don'ts.

The bulk of the folder contained the expected safety and insurance questionnaires. Did the competing yacht have this, that, and the next thing? All boring bumf' that could be dealt with later.

Calum opened the envelope regarding the race instructions. The scheduled start would come in two and half weeks' time, on Saturday at 11 am, from a start line set from the famous Royal Yacht Squadron garden on the Isle of White. The course would initially head to the west through the West Solent on an ebb tide, through the Needles passage, leaving the 'Varvassi' wreck to port, out to the 'End of Channel' mark and then south-east down to 'St Catherine's Point' at the southern tip of the Isle of Wight, and eastwards to 'Dungeness Point', staying just inside the main shipping channel.

The course would round an inner channel marker, then head directly south across the English Channel shipping lanes, to a local navigation buoy off Cap Gris Nez, and then east along the continental coastline past the Danish port of Esbjerg and on to the Norwegian port of Mandal.

'Looks easy enough,' said Calum after a few minutes. 'What have you got there Mike?'

Mike didn't speak for a few minutes. He looked up and told Calum the experience of the young adult crew members would do just fine; a mixture of proven experience and advanced training.

Calum looked at Sidney and told him as far as he could see everything would be OK. He asked who, or how, he would be reimbursed for expenses, food, provisions, etc. Sidney told him he had funding from a friendly sponsor, and would provide him with an advance of expenses for now and asked him to keep all receipts and reconcile everything at a later date.

Mike looked at his watch and suggested they return to the schooner and see how far the installation of the new sails had progressed.

Calum finished his mug of tea and handed a fiver to the large lady behind the counter. As the three of them marched out of the café, the large woman bid them 'have a nice day'.

Mike shuddered, it just didn't sound right. Calum also shuddered at the mantra; it had never sounded right to his ears. Since when did anybody ever mean it, certainly not in Texas.

Chapter 6

Sidney bid them farewell and the two of them hurried back to the schooner. The work had progressed well, and they found the Sail Master busy having an argument with the Rigging Foreman, discussing the finer points of rig tension. The Sail Master wanted the rigging set up tight as a drum, while the Rigging Foreman argued forcibly the schooner wouldn't take the sort of loads he was taking about.

Calum thought he ought to take an interest and slipped over to the fray. Mike went to the edge of the dockside and looked down at the schooner. The Rigging Foreman's men were testing the tension on the mainstays and shaking their heads. Mike asked what figure they were thinking off and the number horrified him. He didn't know what the correct figure should be, but the one they had sounded way too high. He made a calming gesture and suggested they reduce the figure by a third, and then he'd let them know later if that would do the trick or not.

Mike went over to a confused Calum as he tried to understand the thread of the argument. The Sail Master had it in his head his sails would only set properly if the rig tension was set to the figure he wanted. The Rigging Foreman would have none of it.

Calum saw Mike coming over to him.

'What do you think Mike?' he asked.

'The figure seems way too high. May I suggest we reduce it by a third, go for a sail and see how the schooner handles,' Mike suggested.

The Rigging Foreman readily agreed and told Calum an excessive rig tension would rack the hull. Older yachts were never designed for very tight rigs unless racing in calm seas over a short distance. Ocean passages were not a race, and older yacht hulls had more than enough to cope with the stress of the ocean, without making things worse.

It made sense to Calum, on the basis it was exactly what he did when he'd brought *Samba Canção* across the Atlantic and survived a monster of a storm with wind speeds well off the scale. The only way to find out for certain would be to consult a specialist naval architect and they cost, so he figured he would take a view on the subject once he'd gained some experience with the new rig.

Time to go. The tide would soon turn and Calum wanted to get his precious schooner back to her berth in Lymington. He went over to the Sail Master and suggested he let them take him home if one of his men would return his car. Then he could see what was what, and then they could come to a more informed conclusion. This calmed the Sail Master down a bit, after all, this new product line had possibilities and it would be an expanding market.

The Sail Master continued to grumble, but with a sea trial planned anyway, he was keen to get a move on.

The Rigging Foreman handed over a sheave of papers, regarding the new masts and rigging, and said he would come too; just to see how things went. The two apprentices made up the party.

'How are these two going to get home?' asked Calum of the Sailing Master.

'These two live close by, upstairs,' grumbled the Sail Master.

'These two youngsters belong to you?' asked Calum.

'For my sins, which are many and various, yes,' sighed the Sail Master. 'I'll 'ave to live to a hundred before they become any use, but yah never knows your luck.'

Calum took this inelegant comment as praise of his two sons. They'd worked long, hard and efficiently. Matching Daddy would be next to impossible. Daddy had been in the business a long time, and could rig, and set-up, any sail craft ever built. Rumour had it his display cabinet once collapsed from the weight of silverware he'd accumulated over a long and varied racing career.

Time to get going. Calum handed the helm to the Sail Master. His two boys went fore and aft ready to let go all lines. The Rigging Foreman made aft to sit at the transom to keep an eye on the proceedings and to make comment where necessary; something he was not unknown for.

Calum and Mike made themselves comfortable forward of the helm console to await developments. *Samba Canção* made her way down river under power until she'd passed under the new Northam Bridge. The wind veered to the west, coming off what used to be the Old Docks. The Sail Master brought the schooner under the lee of a large building and motioned his two boys to raise the two mainsails. Calum watched, there was little need to stir and he felt best to let the experts get on with their work.

With both mainsails set, the Sail Master looked at Calum and Mike to get busy. They spilt themselves between the two mainsails, set the mainsheet travellers to their middle position and started to sheet in both sails.

The Sail Master being unsatisfied with the settings barked new instructions at his two boys. Calum had no idea what could be wrong; the sails looked fine to him, but this was new territory. The two boys made a number of, what seemed to Calum, minute adjustments.

With only a moderate breeze blowing the schooner healed over and picked up speed. Calum looked at Mike.

'Christ,' thought Mike. 'The damn ship is nearly fully powered up with only two mainsails set.'

Samba Canção reached a speed of eight knots. This was fast. The Sail Master barked at his two boys, 'those foresails there for ornament, or what?'

'You only have to ask, you old goat,' replied the eldest, the nearest to a family conversation Calum had heard all morning. With all sails pulling hard the schooner started to bury her lee rail as she reached her maximum hull speed.

Calum looked up at the Sail Master. 'This new rig is very powerful,' he commented. 'Did we need the extra height in the new masts?'

The Sail Master smiled. 'I told that young 'whipper snapper' we didn't need no extra height in the masts, but 'e wouldn't listen.'

'This would be Mr. C. Whyte Esq. I take it?' ask Calum.

'The very same,' replied the Sail Master with a great sarcasm. 'Still, if you ever make it back to the Caribbean you'll be all right.'

The Sail Master could see Calum examining the new rig.

'These mainsails shorter in the foot than the old ones?' ask Calum

'Sure,' replied the Sail Master. 'I took the liberty of making them eighteen inches shorter.' Gives a better sail shape and more power you don't need,' he finished.

Calum looked at Mike. Quite who was master of this rebuild was fast becoming doubtful. Mike said nothing, as he looked at where the schooner was heading at a somewhat fearful rate.

The Sail Master waited until the schooner cleared the end of the docks and headed over to the western shoreline. As the schooner reached Hythe Pier, the Sail Master eased the helm and headed down to the Fawley Refinery loading jetty. Calum, Mike and the two boys kept busy trimming the schooner's sails without comment from the Sail Master.

'Christ,' thought Mike to himself. 'We've done something right for a change.'

The wind started to pick up a little now they were in clear air. They eased sheets, allowing the schooner to regain some composure, but the slightest increase in the wind strength had her burying her lee rail into the water rushing by.

'Master,' cried Calum. 'How's the helm? Nice and balanced?'

A balanced helm was always Calum's main concern. A yacht with this amount of power did not need to have any bad habits, like going its own way unannounced. The Sail Master took his hands off the wheel and held his arms out straight. The schooner kept on straight ahead.

'Thanks,' Calum called out. No more needed to be said.

As the schooner headed for the exit of Southampton Water, the Sail Master commented, 'Nice day for a quick whiz around the Island, then I can be sure everything is set-up OK.'

His two boys groaned under their breath. The old man had got 'is hands on a type of yacht he either hadn't seen before or a long time since the last one. Sitting at home was not where this old goat was at. The fact his wife considered him the ultimate impediment to cleanliness in the family home, did not, and never had, encouraged his early return to the nest.

Calum looked at Mike. Mike shrugged his shoulders. He'd nothing to do for the next twenty-four hours. Calum thought hard. He liked the idea, but Adriana came to mind.

'Better not,' he thought. 'I've been absent without planning permission for long enough.'

'Good idea Master,' Calum replied. 'But I have what is known in Portuguese as 'Uma grandé comprimiso', roughly translated as a 'compromise', which is what I'll be if I don't, at least, get home sometime today.'

The Sail Master looked around. The wind steadied in his favourite quarter. Close hauled the schooner could easily make Hurst Castle in one tack, just ten miles down the Solent.

'Hurst Castle do?' the Sail Master, negotiating the next period of the trial, 'Get a mile out to sea, just to check.'

'If you think it's worth it?' shrugged Calum.

Samba Canção made short work of the passage to Hurst Castle. One look at the other side of the narrow channel between the Island and the mainland showed the sea in an angry mood.

The wind rose as the exit to the open sea got closer, and the Sail Master began spilling wind from the very powerful rig towering above. The two boys started to take up position for reefing the two mainsails. The Rigging Foreman knew the drill and moved to help.

A lull in the wind arrived and the Sail Master merely shouted out, 'Positions please.'

With everyone ready in the correct position, the Sail Master called for three rolls in both mainsails.

'Foresails? asked Calum.

'I'll let you know in good time my son, don't worry about your precious ship.'

'That's a relief,' thought Calum. 'I was beginning to wonder who owned this damn schooner.'

Samba Canção powered into the open sea, the Sail Master keeping her tight to the mainland side of the main channel. The open sea looked angry, with the wind over an outgoing tide. This was always a tricky place for any yacht to be. Calum hid his concerns but looked over at the Sail Master's two boys. They were bored, a boredom born of constant sailing over the same piece of water, in the same conditions, and presumably for the same purpose. If they weren't bothered thought Calum, why should he? He buttoned up his sailing jacket and pulled the hood over his head. This was going to be a wet ride. Mike disappeared below for his sailing jacket and goggles. He hated salt water in his eyes.

The Sail Master drove the schooner full tilt into the violent sea. The schooner shot over the first big wave with a bang, burying her nose hard into the steel grey water. The shudder went through the hull, just as he intended, as he intently watched the new masts.

The schooner crashed into the next wave, sending a large amount of cold sea water over her crew. The two boys ducked behind the cabin combing. Mike dropped down into the main cabin, and Calum turned his back to it. The Sail Master and the Rigging Foreman did not flinch, so intent were they in evaluating who was right and who was wrong, about rig tension.

The schooner continued into the confused sea. The Sail Master and the Rigging Foreman were seen exchanging the views on several matters concerning the rig set-up. The Rigging Foreman made his way to the lee shrouds on the foremast and grabbed a hold, feeling the vibrations and any reduced tension in the thick rod rigging.

Another two miles later, the Sail Master had come to a conclusion.

'All hands to your positions,' he bawled out.

A reluctant crew took up positions, prepared for a good soaking. When he was ready, the Sail Master spun the wheel as the schooner turned hard to port on to the reciprocal course to head for home. The Sail Master handed the wheel back to Calum, suggesting he keep to the south side of the channel through the Hurst Castle passageway, and gybe once he reached calmer water.

The schooner shot back into the Solent and Calum felt grateful to be heading back home. The Rigging Foreman brought a cup of tea from the galley and handed it to Calum.

'You OK? You look a bit peaky,' he asked.

Calum took a large swig of the tea, its warmth doing him the world of good.

'Yah. I'm OK, you two boffins come to any conclusions?'

'We certainly have Oily,' he replied. 'The schooner is fine as it is'. E' wants a touch more tension in the rig, I want a touch less, and so it's a draw. It's a bit early to be totally sure, but this new type of rigging won't stretch much, but the hull may move a little under it. I noticed you went below to listen to the noises the hull was making, right?'

Calum said, 'You don't miss much do you. That's exactly what I did do. Trouble with the new internal arrangements the language has changed on me, but I didn't hear anything untoward.'

Calum looked around to concentrate on his steering; his schooner was making rapid progress. The Sail Master came up from the main cabin, much refreshed after a stiff coffee laced with something as close to 100% proof as Calum had ever smelt. He fished a battered cell phone out of an obscure pocket and pushed a fast dial button.

With two rings someone answered, 'You 'bout ready', he barked into it. With the person on the other end clearly in the right place, the cell phone disappeared as fast as it had arrived.

'Calum,' asked the Sail Master, 'can you 'ead over to 'Newtown Creek'. We're goin' to meet a new client of mine with some damn catamaran which needs my tender loving care'. The elder son smirked into a beer he'd pulled from a haversack. 'Tender loving care? My warts are likely to get more TLC than that catamaran,'

His father glowered at him; a tender loving slap round the ear was more likely. True he didn't like catamarans, but this client was rich, and 'e had lots of friends and contacts. Business was business was business.

Anyway, he liked Calum. He wasn't going to say so of course, but saw little point in dragging the poor man all the way up to the Hamble River, and then have to sail the schooner back to Lymington.

A free ride home; a chance to make some money and good contacts. It made sense to him. He just hoped his boys would keep quiet and not spoil anything.

Chapter 7

Calum spent the evening relaxing at home in front of a warm fire, with a hot toddy and a dead TV. Repetitious news and the usual nonsense had Calum reaching for the off button. There were no decent films to watch and his satellite box had recorded just about everything likely to keep him awake.

Adriana had long since disappeared into her study, to get busy emailing her chums. Calum relaxed with a long G&T, slowly perusing the large folder provided by the CEO of the charity to which he would supply the schooner. The race details were standard stuff, and the usual health and safety document made its way to the bottom of the pile for possible examination later. Calum regarded them as 'Rules for the guidance of the wise, and enslavement of fools and the uninitiated'.

Now, his main task was to go through the personal details and photographs of the crew he would take with him on this voyage of adventure and make sure their differing backgrounds and education level didn't get in the way. Calum insisted not so much on a happy ship, but one where everyone knew where everybody else was coming from and respected their point of view.

It was fortunate this crew had been together for some time but had yet to spend a night at sea, even with all their extensive coastal sailing experience. The race to Norway would take at least three, maybe, four nights, given the tides and the late afternoon start time. His crew would be on constant 'watch-on, stop-on' in one of the most congested waterways on the planet. It would take a lot in-depth training to get them up to speed.

So, who did he have? The watch list made out by Mike read:

Starboard Watch

Tom	Lead Helm, watch team leader
Sarra	Watch tactician and winch person
Patrick	Watch winch man

Port Watch

Steve	Second lead helm and watch team leader

Marie	Watch tactician and winch person
Alexander	Watch winch man
Carol	Weather forecaster, GPS navigator, electronics specialist and standby crew.

Calum pondered and saw Mike had made a good start at organising the crew roster. He couldn't see where any changes would improve things. Then he moved on to the highly confidential personal details.

Tom stood out a mile as the star of the crew. The photograph showed a tall strong lad with freckles, tight curly ginger hair and a ready smile. Tom came from the hard East Side of London. His Dad was the last of the 'Thames Barge' skippers. Tom was not so much on probation, but he'd promised the 'beak', the local magistrate, he would get involved in an organised sporting activity that would broaden his horizons on a community basis. Quite how he'd managed to get chosen for this particular charity and his inclusion into this event wasn't stated.

In fact, his background came, in part, to the complex social problems in what had become the last enclave of an old style East End, London community, down past where the docks used to be, in an area hemmed in by ever encroaching modern development. It would be only time before this enclave would go the way of the rest.

The community of this very traditional area of lower working class London had been targeted by recurring gangs of drug pushers. The men folk, based in their usual haunt, the local pub, had seen them off quite a few times. The more the drug gangs pushed, the more the men in the community resisted.

Tom's dad, Bill, could see where this would end up and 'ad a word with the local Police Superintendent, one of the last of the old school who would let the locals defend their own patch providing he could show his bosses he knew nothing about what went on or things didn't get 'too' violent and reach the ears of the higher-ups.

'Too' violent was a measured word in these parts; these were tough people who didn't shirk from dishing out serious GBH if it suited their purpose.

One drug gang in particular wouldn't take no for an answer, and to make matters worse their leader was a former member of the community and known to be close to a major criminal gang in London. Something subtle would be needed and subtlety was a talent no one in the community possessed in abundance.

Of all people, young Tom, an avid reader of old London crime stories came up with the idea to use his Dad's barge for a 'booze cruise' down the river. The hood in question would be invited to join in, for old time's sake, plied with enough booze to knock out an elephant, and when unconscious, two large blocks of solid salt would be tied between his legs before tipping him gently over the side of the barge down somewhere down river.

The salt blocks would take him to the bottom long enough for him to drown, before dissolving, leaving no trace. Bill passed the idea his mates in the pub, and so that's what happened. The barge set off, complete with jazz band and a party of locals known for their ability to look the other way and keep their mouths shut should the police ask any questions.

The barge made it down river as far as Gravesend, at the top of the tide, which those in the know thought a nice touch of irony. Half-way back to the barge's base, just below the Pool of London, a mobile phone call advised the river police of the 'sad' news. The local police, who were not totally unaware of events, smelt a rat and dispatched their Police Superintendent to see what was what, and what could be kept quiet, a sure indication the local police were not exactly heartbroken by the demise of one of London's major criminals.

The Superintendent duly reported the whole event as an accident, despite the accompanying detective from New Scotland Yard wishing to make further investigations. The dead body was recovered the next day, and not a mark found on him. The blood in his alcohol stream broke all records at an all-time low, so that was that.

It was only when a similar incident, which almost went wrong, that everyone got hauled before the local 'beak', the matter eventually straightened out, but not before Tom was hauled into his chambers for what was described as a cosy chat. So here was Tom, older, wiser, and making remarkably good progress in becoming a model citizen.

Next on the list came Patrick, a short stocky Irishman with jet black hair from out-of-town Dublin. A very quiet person, teetotal, who had amazing strength in his hands and upper body. His family were unintended victims of 'The Troubles' and his parents had been killed by protestant thugs from Belfast whilst on holiday visiting family relations near the border.

Patrick had been caught by his local priest earnestly trying to join the IRA. The priest could tell if Patrick joined the IRA, he possessed the resolve and willpower to become a very dangerous man, and in his opinion Ireland, North or South, had a great sufficiency of Irishmen not engaged in God's work. Patrick had been bundled off to the South of England to stay with a strict aunt who had quickly decided a good outdoor activity would do him the world of good. Patrick took to sailing in a big way, where his natural strength and quiet thoughtful manner had stood him in good stead.

Then there was Steve, a thoughtful working class lad, with long blond hair and good physique. He'd recently been cured of cancer but suffered mentally from the effects of the traumatic treatment and needed the physical challenge to restore his confidence. He worked at one of the large service garages in Portsmouth. His employer, a local sailor of note, put him touch with the charity. The experience did him good, and he'd quickly become a very competent helm.

Alexander was the son of a city type from the financial world of the City of London, and his father had supported the SSFR Charity from inception. Alexander had a history of rebelling against his parents, who'd tried hard to keep him on the straight and narrow. Alexander tended to a more active lifestyle whilst his parents continued to push him strongly towards the academic.

His rebellion against his parents took a turn for the worse. He'd become withdrawn and morose, shunning outside contact with his peers. His worried parents were alerted to the need for drastic action when they discovered him unconscious in his bedroom from a barbiturate overdose. The family doctor managed to save his life, and in return for not reporting the event to the authorities, Alexander received a very stiff talking to, who agreed to change his ways. The chance to go sailing and get some fresh air and strong exercise came with relief and considerable enthusiasm all round. The exercise started to trim his somewhat overweight body back to the lean hard condition he'd achieved some years ago with the grammar school rugby team.

As for the girls, Sarra was really good looking, Calum thought to himself, and a very practical middle-class girl. Something about her eyes showed she had enormous potential. Her depleted family lived in Surry. Her mother had been killed by hit and run driver and she had taken the tragedy very badly. The efforts of the SSFR Charity had worked wonders. Her father worked as a senior in government circles close to the military intelligence services. What he did wasn't recorded.

Next on the list was Carol, a slim, shy, timid girl with big glasses and mousy hairstyle. Truth be known she was a bit of a boffin on the side; with a strong knowledge of electronics and meteorology gained from her father. Her father held the position of a senior member of staff at the Met Office in Bracknell. He was a forecaster's forecaster, who always managed to deliver the message of his work in a manner that annoyed his bosses intensely, especially as he always tended to be very accurate. They tried hard to replace him but without success.

His daughter followed in the same mould. Later, Calum picked up most of this scuttlebutt for himself just talking to the girl. With nothing in her file of any consequence, in reality just speaking sensibly to Carol was all it took to discover the wealth of talent underneath. There seemed to be no direct reason why she'd been included in the group, obviously someone somewhere thought it a good idea if only to improve Carols' knowledge of the outside world and to give her the self-confidence she so badly needed.

Last, but not least, came Marie. A Norwegian beauty and then some. Her file indicated she had Norwegian Royal Family background on her mother's side. There was no mention of diplomatic status, but for some reason Calum assumed it was either there or not far away. No doubt she could pick up the phone to the right person and get real results, real quick.

Marie was highly accomplished in many ways and an absolute ace at sailing. The stories about her from Sarra bordered on worship. For some reason there were no details for her inclusion in the party onboard the schooner.

So that was the crew. Calum could see he would have to pull the stops out to get them fully integrated with each other. Their differing backgrounds were not a problem onshore, but Sidney had mentioned that sometimes it got a bit fraught offshore. Did Calum have any recommendations?

Calum thought about the problem, but bedtime called, and it could all keep to another day.

*****

Chapter 8

On the 7th April 1940, a fleet of German naval ships left their home base in the Baltic for the invasion of Norway. The assault, 'Operation Weserübung', was the German codename for Nazi Germany's assault on neutral Scandinavia. The name translates as 'Weser Exercise,' the Weser being a German river.

Early on the morning of 9th April 1940, the Germany military forces invaded Denmark and Norway, ostensibly as defensive manoeuvres against a planned (and openly discussed) Franco-British occupation of those countries. The German government informed the Danish and Norwegian governments that the Wehrmacht had come to protect the neutrality of both countries against Franco-British aggression.

Strategically speaking, Denmark was relatively unimportant to Germany. Denmark's tiny army could offer little-armed resistance. The Danish government capitulated almost instantly in exchange for retaining a large measure of political independence in domestic matters, which resulted in an occupation that became uniquely lenient until the summer of 1943.

On the 7th April 1940, just a few hours behind the Germans, the British Home Fleet left its main port in Scapa Flow bound for Norway.

On the 9th April 1940, Germany forces invaded Norway, beating the Franco-British invasion by only twelve hours.

During the main attack on Oslo, despite orders to the contrary, the Norwegian shore batteries at the Oslo narrows sank three German cruisers, including the 10,000 ton *Blücher*, ten destroyers and eleven troop transports. A battleship and three more cruisers were so badly damaged they had to be pulled out of service.

In concert with the naval invasion of the Oslo Fjord, a German parachute battalion, the first time a parachute force had been used in a war, was dropped at Fornebu Airport, Oslo, which was then quickly overrun.

Partly thanks to the *Blücher* sinking, the Norwegian Royal Family and Parliament evaded the German invasion force, made its escape to the north ahead of the Germans, and was evacuated from Molde by the British Royal

Navy, taking with them the national gold reserves.

The gold reserves were then shipped to North America encased in floatation pallets as deck cargo on various transport vessels, and although one ship was sunk by a German submarine, this part of the shipment floated free and was recovered safely.

Chapter 9

King Christian X of Denmark paced nervously up and down his study. The King's study in his Copenhagen Royal Palace was large. Generally, all rooms in his royal palace were large, and if nothing else he was, at least, getting some much-needed exercise.

What was actually being exercised was his mental processes, in fact he had extreme concern for his small country. In late February 1940 the Second World War, declared by Great Britain and France upon Germany only four months previously, had been going slowly. This period was known as the phoney war, and so far little had happened. Denmark and Norway declared their joint neutrality but increasingly King Christian X could see absolutely no reason why the encroaching German war machine would respect it.

With many reports from his government agencies, plus a lot of rumours circulating in his court and in government circles, he'd taken steps to secretly consult with King Haakon of Norway and although the Norwegian Government remained relaxed about this very subject, King Haakon was not.

So as not to alarm his government, he had acted alone, forming a small committee outside the remit of government. In short he took to acting in the vital need to maintain total secrecy. King Christian waited for his special envoys to report on the situation.

His committee consisted of the Special Assistant to the Prime Minister - Christian Hesselholdt, the Treasury Minister - Eric Horskjaer, the Head of Police - Harald Villemoes, the Superintendent of Detectives - Niels Hammershoej and the head of the Danish Rangers - Major Per Bruus-Jensen.

The members of his committee had the same special qualities; they were the very best in their field, utterly reliable, and good and trusted friends. The meeting the King had called could not be described as a hundred per cent constitutional but in desperate times the King felt it his duty to act in the vital interest of his country.

The members of the committee arrived using different entrances and in a variety of disguises. Eric Horskjaer arrived first, disguised as a policeman. He greeted his King in his customary manner. 'This is fun Majesty,' he declared, shedding his disguise in the anti-room. 'What is the purpose of your meeting?'

King Christian mildly rebuked him. His close friend was always ready for some amusing diversion, all the more surprising since his first wife had died of cancer three years before, and his two sons were studying a long way from home in Canada. The Treasury Minister was never lonely and kept himself very fit and active. He rode wonderfully, skied like a champion and could shoot straighter than anyone he had ever met.

Within the half hour, the others arrived, shedding some rather inventive disguises, before restoring themselves to their personal comforts. The group made themselves comfortable around the large conference table. The Head of the Royal Household brought refreshments, closed the door behind him, and retired to the anti-room to stand guard ensuring his King and his important guests were not disturbed.

The King welcomed everyone on the cold winter's morning and the inventive way they had obeyed the Royal command for total secrecy. No notes or recordings were to be made, and definitely nothing was to leave the room.

The King bid his Head of Police start proceedings. Harald Villemoes was about as tough a policeman as they came, a calm quiet man, very methodical, with a patience born of Job. However, if his patience ran out, people around him knew to make themselves absent very quickly.

His report became long and highly detailed, which only served to reinforce the King's opinion that calling this meeting had been the right thing to do.

Villemoes presented a comprehensive overview of the security situation within the Kingdom. Everything seemed to be calm on the surface, but what appeared out of the ordinary was the numbers of German 'tourists' slowly building up throughout the country.

They were generally couples, pretending to be secret lovers away from their respective family homes or honeymooners. Some of these 'tourists' came on business, and in fact quite a few of them were regular visitors to Denmark. His surveillance teams observed these 'tourists' were monitoring anything out of the ordinary, and keeping a close watch on the ports, airports and railway stations.

In addition, the German border police had recently received a number of extra staff, none of whom, in his opinion looked like any policeman he'd ever known. 'Thugs' was the collective name that came to mind, dressed to a man in long black leather raincoats with suspicious bulges under their left shoulder. Clearly Gestapo.

Niels Hammershoej, the Superintendent of Detectives, spoke next. One of his senior staff members had the task of monitoring their close neighbours. It was hardly tourist season, and the use of couples made surveillance difficult to be sure exactly who was who.

He recalled how one of his ambitious detectives caused a severe case of 'coitus interruptus' of a middle-aged couple deep in the throes of sexual congress in an unusual position, even for Germans. He'd accepted the large bribe offered by the lady to look, as it were, the other way. Whatever this particular couple were doing, keeping an eye on the everyday life of Denmark could not be considered to be one of them.

The Superintendent of Detectives reported he had become sure he'd discovered which couple were controlling the general surveillance. They were staying at a hunting lodge just outside the capital, making frequent trips in and around the countryside. They would meet other couples and some of the known German businessmen in bars or restaurants. The method of contact usually looked totally normal, a sure sign his police force was dealing with pure professionals.

The Superintendent grinned as he continued, 'I also have to report on a bit of one could say luck, but this event occurred out of pure initiative.' The assembly around the King's table leant forward, detecting that something of interest was about to be revealed.

Hammershoej continued, 'A senior detective of mine happened to be in the snug bar of this particular hunting lodge keeping a very low key eye on the couple just mentioned, who were in conference with a number of other German 'tourists' and a couple of regular German businessmen.'

'My detective drinks there on a regular basis as his uncle is the owner. Anyway, a ship's company from a local shipping line had chosen the hunting lodge for a raucous night out with a group of 'ladies' they'd brought with them, for some kind of special celebration, not sure of the occasion and it's of little importance.'

'Anyway, halfway through the evening some of this naval party were getting seriously drunk, rowdy, disturbing just about everyone, including the Germans. My detective came up with a brilliant idea. His uncle had recently commenced renovation of an adjoining function hall, which had been left in a bit of a mess.'

'Then he called for back-up, requesting a microfiche camera, a strong torch, and an army smoke grenade. When the back-up arrived, he sauntered into the function hall, told his uncle to keep tranquil, calmly took the smoke grenade from under his jacket, placed it in a metal bucket, set it off and closed the door behind him.'

'Anyway, to cut a long story short, mayhem ensued a few minutes later. His uncle started rushing around shouting 'Fire' at the top of his voice, and with the assistance of one of my detectives they cleared the building of all guests and staff. My man then slipped down into the basement, and threw the main power switch, plunging to whole building into darkness.'

The assembly warmed to the story with rapt attention.

'My senior then makes his way upstairs with the torch and camera, found the German couple's bedroom and proceeded to photograph every document he could lay his hands on. Having done that he slips downstairs, by which time the local police have arrived.'

He gets the local police to go through every room in the hunting lodge to ensure all the guests are outside and open all windows to ventilate the place and let the smoke out. In order to lay the blame on the sailors, he slips back into the function room, removes the depleted smoke grenade, and leaves the room by the back window.'

'Just as everything starts to calm down, he gets the local police to arrest two of the drunk sailors, who had little chance of remembering anything. He also gets the local police to record all the names of the guests present, a real help as we didn't know some of them, and then let the guests return into the lodge.'

'The Germans rushed upstairs to find a strong breeze had blown their papers all over their room. Uncle, who by this time had been fully briefed by his favourite relative, goes upstairs makes a big fuss of the Germans, apologising for absolutely everything, and organises two maids to tidy up their room.'

'The Germans refuse, asked the maids to leave and started collecting their papers to see what if anything was missing. An hour later they come down to a re-opened bar busy serving free drinks to everyone. From the faces of the relieved Germans, it was assumed they hadn't lost anything. So the evening ended up with smiles all round. The German businessmen left and the remainder of the sailors continued their party into the small hours.'

Hammershoej completed his story, 'Next day, his detective received a real dressing down for possibly giving the surveillance operation away, but on reflection he'd become so taken by his actions, he called him back into his office to tell him, 'Well done'.'

'What they learnt become the subject of a report I received only this morning. The report highlighted the surveillance activities to date and the people employed. It also stated the Germans were confused about the lack of any real wartime preparation or activities by the Danish Government. Military movements to reinforce the border added protection to public buildings, telephone exchanges and other communication centres were all the sorts of things mentioned.'

'There were also comments about the Danish Government's intentions to a range of issues, including the Danish Jews.'

Villemoes broke in to say the report continued to be evaluated, and it would be best to take this conversation off-line.

The King agreed. He sat back in his armchair and thought deeply for a few moments. It occurred to him it might be best to execute some of the mentioned activities, if only to keep the Germans amused. He could think of no military precautions that would worry the Germans.

The King sat upright and addressed his audience. 'OK, let me think aloud and see what you gentlemen think. The shooting war will start as soon as winter relents. Let us assume Germany will attack France, before the French and British attack Germany. The French will sit behind their Maginot Line supported by the British Army. A stalemate might ensue. The Americans will send, or rather sell, huge amounts of war material to the UK and the German submarine fleet will want access to the Atlantic Ocean. The British could invade Norway, it's been openly discussed, and if so, the Germans would have a large threat on their back door.'

'Therefore,' the King continued, 'whatever the outcome, I do not think Germany will respect our neutrality, or for that matter, the Norwegian's. The Germans have much to gain and little to lose.'

The King drew his audience's attention to a map on the table. 'The Danish coast controls the Skagerrak and the Kattegat, the exit of the Baltic Sea into the Central North Sea.'

'The Norwegian coast controls the access to the northern sector of the North Sea directly opposite the Royal Naval Base at Scapa Flow in the Orkney Islands, and then all the way up into the Arctic. Closer to home, their coastline controls the northern sector of the Skagerrak.'

'For these and other reasons I think that they will invade our country first, and then I would guess they will then invade Norway at the same time. Norway may put up a fight. They have a long and difficult country that will be difficult to capture quickly against determined defenders. It will require a great effort from the Germans to capture Norway, especially if the Royal Navy comes out of its lair at Scapa Flow with their big ships.'

'Our small country will present little difficulty to the German army, and we have nothing to gain and a lot to lose by defending our borders. Lives and property will be destroyed for nothing. However, I do not intend to hand them our national treasures on a plate, and it is these I intend to spirit from under their noses.

'The question of 'when' rather than 'if' comes to mind. Realistically, the Germans will wait for winter to loosen its grip a little, and the start of the break-up of the sea ice, especially in Norway. This could come as early as the beginning of April so we have less than eight weeks to put our plans together.'

The King sat back in his armchair and looked around the table at his committee. He could see from their faces his scenario was not popular, but they did recognise the likely possibility of his evaluation.

Major Per Bruus-Jensen, stood up and walked over to the window. The weather outside had turned ugly. The wind had started to rise and snow began to fall in great horizontal sheets across the palace forecourt.

The major was no giant of a man. In fact, he was slightly less than medium height, and of slim build: an ordinary man unless you looked into his deep blue eyes. There, a burning intensity raged, and one never forgot to treat this man with the greatest of respect.

He turned away from the window to face his King. Bruus-Jensen was a trusted advisor to the King, unofficially of course, but the King respected his opinion. This man examined situations from all angles, and sometimes from angles few thought even existed.

'Majesty, you learnt well from your studies at the British War School. I can find little fault with your appraisal. When all this will happen is, of course, the problem? And that makes the timing of any actions an even bigger problem.'

'The fact the German 'tourists' are here at all confirms your thoughts. Their slowly building activities are a good indication. Therefore, your suggestion regarding the date of April has the ring of truth about it, so let's say the first week of April, and no later. We should complete and execute our plans by April 1st. On behalf of all of us here Majesty, what exactly are you thinking we should do?'

The King removed a draft paper from his pocket and consulted it studiously. He handed it to Horskjaer. The Treasury Minister studied it for some time and looked up at the King.

'Majesty this is very ambitious, especially as we do not know how much time we have to complete the actions you suggest,' he remarked.

The other members of the committee waited patiently to be informed of the King's draft proposal. Horskjaer looked up at the King. The King nodded his approval for the Minister to read the draft out loud.

'Gentlemen, the King is suggesting the remainder of the country's national gold reserves be smuggled out of the country, along with the crown jewels and state treasures, the treasures belonging to the church, art and all other artefacts of great value from the museums.'

Hammershoej asked what he meant by the remainder of the country's gold reserves. Horskjaer explained following the commencement of World War II, the Treasury Minister and the Prime Minister had authorised the transportation of a large part of the national gold reserves via Bergen to the Federal Reserve Bank in New York. In total 19.6 tons of gold had been shipped. From there, forty percent of this gold had been transferred to Canada.

In view of the political and military situation in Europe at that time, the USA had to be considered the safest place to store the Nationalbanken's gold. Moreover, this would make it possible to continue to purchase goods in the USA, provided that imports from the USA were still feasible.

The Nationalbanken recommended shipping the remainder of the national gold reserve to the USA so there would be no gold for the occupying forces to seize should the Germans invade.

Horskjaer concluded, 'The main shipment had gone smoothly, but the operation had not been under surveillance from others. Now I fear that if the remainder of the gold is moved, and the 'tourists' got wind of it, the suggested invasion would be brought forward and all the country's treasures would be seized. In any event, the German Navy could intervene outside territorial waters at will.'

The Treasury Minister looked around the table, and in a low voice said, 'Gentlemen there is another matter, which I insist must be treated with the utmost confidentiality. The Danish Treasury is holding, on behalf of others, a large quantity of industrial and gem-quality diamonds. Both are equally valuable, the industrial gems are the more sought after as they will be vital to the production of war materials.'

The King asked, 'How large Minister?' Horskjaer replied the quantity was very large and begged not to be asked any further details. The King agreed, for now, and quickly moved the meeting to other matters. He asked for recommendations from everyone.

The Special Assistant to the Prime Minister, Christian Hesselholdt, spoke first. 'I think this is a matter for the Prime Minister and the government. I would not wish this meeting to presume any actions at this time.'

'Christian,' replied the King. 'You are here as the Prime Minister's trusted advisor, and he is waiting for our recommendations. He knows he has to keep this subject firmly under wraps. We have to decide today, and you will advise him tomorrow. Then he will issue secret orders to the relevant persons at this table.'

Hesselholdt suddenly felt the weight of responsibility heavy on his shoulders. Horskjaer could see his predicament. Hesselholdt was not a man of action; he was an administrator who took the time to decide on any subject. He would worry about the legal position and examine every detail minutely before making a decision or issuing a recommendation from his office.

Horskjaer suggested a comfort break for everyone, and to have some refreshments. The assembly broke up, and Horskjaer cornered the Head of Police in the anteroom. He knew they both thought alike, and pressed him for an opinion. Villemoes turned around to him and said, 'Excuse me Eric, but I do need the bathroom rather urgently. Fix me a drink of something strong, and have one yourself. We're going to need it.'

Horskjaer wandered back into the King's study and poured large measures of Bols into two glasses. He added the mixer and two ice cubes. He was hungry now and filled a small plate from the large silver tray of sandwiches with the usual meat and fish specialties. The King came up to him.

'Any ideas, Eric?' he asked.

'Not yet Majesty, and you?'

'A few,' the King replied. 'But we need more; a lot more.'

The Superintendent of Detectives and the Major moved out of the way into a corner. The Major spoke first, 'I think I will leave this one for the 'grown-ups' to decide.' The Superintendent agreed but thought it unlikely they would be left out for long.

The Head of Police marched back into the study, closing the door to the anteroom behind him. He grabbed the drink from Eric's outstretched hand and downed the contents in one. He took Eric to one side, and whispered, 'Divide and conquer. It's going to be easy.'

'You have a plan, Harald? asked the Treasury Minister.

'Let's all sit down, and pool our ideas. You two in the corner,' he shouted out, 'can't escape over there; trying to hide in obscurity.'

The assembled company resumed their places at the conference table.

Villemoes spoke first. 'Excuse me, gentlemen, I will propose my ideas first, and please add to them as you see fit.'

'First we have to create some fantasy and confusion. Slowly at first, nothing to tip the hand of the Germans. We should close all the important venues, one by one. Building works, annual cleaning of the interior, restoration of the artefacts, are all excuses that can be used.'

'Treasures can be re-assigned between museums, and moved to new venues. When they are in transit the most valuable items can disappear, and hidden inside the country. There are plenty of secret locations. If there any good copies available, these can be substituted for the originals.'

The Head of Police paused for a moment and then continued. 'Moving the gold without being observed could be a problem. I suggest moving it in small quantities to a holding location close to a secure area inside the harbour. There's an old military arsenal that will prove useful, and in fact, the gold can be stored in old ammunition cases. Where are these diamonds, Eric?'

The Treasury Minister replied he could not say, but if suitable ammunition cases were supplied to his office, he would see they arrived at the arsenal.

'Any idea of volume Eric,' asked the Head of Police. Horskjaer paused and replied that four empty cases of rifle ammunition would be sufficient.

Horskjaer continued, 'When suitable arrangements have been made, we'll need a ship, say one of our faster ferries, one that can ship troops, stores and vehicles. It must be able to land at any jetty unaided. We'll disguise the voyage somehow, perhaps to ship workers up to Århus for some urgent repairs to a dock facility, whatever.'

If the army can rustle up, say, four of their best cross-country five-ton trucks, disguise them as army surplus for disposal. Make sure their mechanicals are a hundred percent, all that sort of thing. Building materials can be thrown on top of the cargo being shipped out. All the tricks of deception will be needed.'

Bruus-Jensen broke into the conversation, 'Good ideas Harald. The workers can be my boys, all togged out in donkey jackets and big boots. Who's going to lead this miniature army?' The group around the table looked at him; now he knew why he'd been invited.

King Christian took the chair. 'Gentleman much as I trust my good friend the Major, and despite all his many qualities, I don't think he wants the responsibility of several hundred million Krone on his hands. Our Treasury Minister will be in political charge of the expedition. Yes gentlemen, that's what it's going to be, an expedition. A hazardous one at that.'

'Per you will be in charge of all military and logistical arrangements, working very closely with Eric and the Head of Police.'

'You three are the 'magic circle', the group who will make this expedition work. I will contact King Haakon of Norway. I will request that when he or his most trusted advisors receive a special code word, or words, some very special assistance, of whatever nature, will be required. I hope not to tell King Haakon exactly our purpose, but if he guesses, as I'm sure he will, he will keep everything very close to his chest.'

The meeting relaxed a little and took time to take stock. The plan sounded logical, but the devil would be in the detail. A large number of staff would be needed to organise the different activities, bringing the risk of discovery or infiltration by the enemies of the state.

It was getting late, and little more would be achieved that evening. Before they broke up the King suggested to the Police chief his force should start keeping the attention of the German 'tourists' looking away from the offices of the three members of the magic circle. The 'magic circle' would need to devise ways to keep their operations secret, move locations frequently, and keep as few records as possible. Whatever it took to throw the 'tourists' of the trail.

A nd so, during the next two weeks the activities for success were hammered out. Bruus-Jensen, recruited a team of his best soldiers, all patriots and sufficiently trustworthy not to have to tell them everything. A special op was a special op; the details would fall into place when the time came.

Horskjaer quickly became adept at inventing the tricks and subterfuges to move the remaining gold reserves into the naval arsenal. Most of the activities took place in armoured cars under the guise of transferring stocks around the country. The armoured cars would leave the Central Bank with full bullion boxes, and ammunition cases full of lead weights. The change-over would occur en route, so it would be almost impossible for anyone to know about the switch.

The armoured cars arrived at their destinations, off-loaded the resealed bullion boxes at the receiving depots, and made their way back to the army depot where they were normally stationed at night. Later on, the ammunition cases would make their way via many separate routes to the naval arsenal.

Within three weeks the work had been completed, and the monitoring of the German 'tourists' revealed they had not been alerted to the activities of the magic circle. In coordination with these activities, the Danish government made a show of increasing military defence and other movements as suggested by the secret report.

Finally, a new 'meals on wheels' service opened up at the naval dockyard and its adjacent arsenal, and over the next two weeks four cases of empty rifle ammunition boxes stored at the back of a little-used building slowly gained weight until they could hold no more. The cases were securely sealed and secret marks added to identify them.

Time was passing quickly, and by the end of the fifth week, a fast twin-screw steam ferry arrived at the naval dockyard. Added to many other tasks, the ferry had to be fitted out with anti-aircraft guns, hidden inside collapsible shelters. Its main aft deck had been cleared to receive four army trucks, her two cranes upgraded to lift the trucks fully loaded on to an adjacent quayside, and the cargo deck prepared to receive a range of crates to carry supplies including plenty of ammunition for the expedition.

The King called a hasty meeting at the end of the fifth week. The assembly had grown to include the Prime Minister himself, along with the heads of the army and navy. The atmosphere in the conference room was tense and nervous, everyone feeling the pressure as history started to move against them.

Prime Minister, Eric Scavenius, kicked-off the meeting. He told the group around the table that intelligence reports received from the British Embassy were advising unusual levels of radio traffic in the German sector of the Baltic Sea. This, in their opinion, could herald a large build-up of operations. The PM could give no details, which did not surprise Bruus-Jensen. His Swedish contacts were monitoring all German ship movements in the Skagerrak and the Kattegat. They were all seen to be heading to the German port of Rostock, the closest shipping port to extensive German Army facilities a few miles inland.

The King made his mind up. The information coming to him only added up to one thing. The time had come to move, and to put their careful plans into action.

The King looked around the table, 'Well gentlemen. Are we ready?'

Bruus-Jensen said his men could push-off in less than 24 hours, but it would be difficult to hide their movements from the German 'tourists'. Villemoes advised there was little to worry from the 'tourists' as their number had quickly reduced over the last two weeks and the German businessmen had all left the country despite having pre-arranged appointments with various Danish state departments and industry leaders. In his estimation the 'tourists' would have departed by the weekend, judging by the reports coming back from the detectives monitoring the lodgings where the 'tourists' were staying.

The King became greatly concerned at this news. He knew events were moving fast, but not this fast. He looked up at Horskjaer. 'Are you ready Eric? Is everything prepared?'

'Just about Majesty,' Horskjaer replied, 'just a few papers to shuffle, clear up some personal matters, and I'm ready for the starting gun.'

'You are coming back, aren't you?' asked the King.

'Majesty, Christian, my dear friend, I don't think you will see many of us again. Had you not considered that?'

'Frankly no,' replied the King. 'It's a two or three day operation at most, surely?'

'I think not Majesty if we get out before the Germans move, we'll be lucky. If they invade Denmark and Norway at the same time, which is my guess, we'll all be on the run until either we reach safety, mission accomplished, or we will end up in Norway. If we get that far, we'll end up dodging the German forces and their bullets.'

The King reached a conclusion. 'OK gentlemen, our converted steam ferry, the *Girard*, should sail as soon as possible for Århus. Go the long way round so the Germans will not think we are heading for the open sea. Any outstanding work can be completed on the journey. At Århus, get rid of the civilian workers, and as many of the civilian crew as possible. A navy crew with additional gunners will be waiting for you there. As soon as you are ready, push off, and god speed.'

Bruus-Jensen stood up to take his leave. 'Eric, see you at the ship at twenty-three hundred, OK?'

Horskjaer replied he'd make it although he might be a few minutes late. 'Don't leave without me,' he called at the back of the departing Major.

Villemoes also stood up to leave.

'You are not sailing too I trust?' asked the King.

'No Majesty, I thought about it, but there's going to be enough for me to do here. It looks like it's going to get busy a lot sooner than I expected. I'm off to take the head of the army back to his HQ to see what exactly needs to be done when the invasion starts.'

The meeting broke up. The King wondered what events were about to overtake his small but ancient Kingdom. His mood matched the weather. Both were bad, he could but hope for better days in the weeks ahead.

*****

Chapter 10

The Solent, off the Isle of Wight

Race day at last. 'Thank the Lord for that,' thought Calum as he threw his stuffed sail bag into Mike's waiting hands. The hire of the schooner to the film company had gone off without a hitch, and the funds were about to come in handy.

Mike had arrived the day before with a pregnant Jenny now increasingly showing the shape of approaching motherhood. She wanted to take the last chance to see the schooner in all its new refinements. She was impressed.

Mike fussed around her like an old cock waiting for his first-born. Jenny liked the attention and hoped Mike was not going to overdo the expectant father routine. Still the big moment for both of them had nearly arrived, and none of them were getting any younger. The two of them spent a quiet evening onboard the schooner reminiscing about the past and how they first met.

'Hi Mike,' called out Calum as he reached the deck. 'Everything ready for our guests?'

'Huh,' snorted Mike. 'They arrived an hour ago, well before time. They're over in the Marina Café getting breakfast.'

Jenny stuck her head out of the companionway.

'Hello sailor,' she cried welcoming Calum onboard. 'Love the 'new' schooner, when do I get invited for a sail.'

'Let's go now?' smiled Calum. 'We can leave hubby at home.'

'He's not a hubby yet,' grinned Jenny. 'You've still time to sneak up on the inside rail.'

Calum was flattered, 'I'll check out when the misses is going away to visit her mother, should be able to sort something out. When's baby due?'

Mike broke into the conversation. There was plenty to do apart from chit chat. Calum muttered something about how he couldn't handle the competition and went below. The crew arrived on the jetty from the café at the same time as the van from the marine suppliers arrived.

'That's handy,' thought Calum. 'Many hands make light work.'

He organised the four boys to load the supplies onto schooner's deck, then to load them below into the main cabin. The three girls would stow

77

everything in the correct place.

Within the hour, the schooner was ready to leave and Calum found himself waiting for the love of his life to come back from the post office where she'd been busy distributing postcards from their latest holiday to her close friends.

Adriana planned to take Jenny back home for a few days girl talk in deepest Hampshire. Soon she reappeared without too much delay. A few kisses and hugs later, the two friends were disappearing fast into the distance to begin the expected lengthy conversation, leaving their better halves to play with their boat. Calum thought about waving goodbye, but Adriana was long gone by the time he thought about it. Back to the matter at hand.

Three hours before the start of the race; it was time to be going. All the supplies were stowed and the crew were ready to go, dressed in their smart new outfits.

Mike took the helm, started the main engine, and called for all lines to be released. Tom and Calum fended *Samba Canção* away from the jetty, as Mike slowly brought the schooner into the river. A stiff wind came unrelentingly from the south-west as Mike motored the schooner down to the end of the Old Docks whilst the crew prepared her sails. With the sails hoisted, flapping in the wind, the schooner reached the head of Southampton Water ready for a fast trip down to Calshot Castle.

Mike kept the schooner to the east side of the waterway to keep clear of a busy morning. The Isle of Wight hydrofoil raced past, closely followed by the Isle of Wight car ferry full of spectators anxious to see the start of the race. Clearly the sponsors had done a good job in getting this event into the public domain.

As the schooner reached the mouth of the River Hamble, an armada of yachts and motor cruisers were pouring into the main channel, all headed to the race start line. Calum muttered about the possibility of the event getting out of hand unless the race organisers had a strong fleet of support boats to marshal the spectators well clear of the start-line.

It would be bad enough mixing it with the small racer and cruisers that made up the bulk of the race fleet without getting involved with the great unwashed, as they strove to get near to the competing yachts carrying their nearest and dearest.

Samba Canção quickly reached full speed on a close fetch on starboard tack as they passed Calshot Castle. The sea in front was a mêlée of every kind of yacht imaginable; all heading for the Royal Yacht Squadron start line. Calum remembered another race would also be starting at a slightly earlier time.

Time to go down to the navigation station and check-in with race control. The allocated start line for the charity event had been laid close to the point in front of the Royal Yacht Squadron. The wind direction from the south-west mandated a start on starboard tack, taking the yachts close into the Island shore before they cleared their wind and changed over to port tack to search for clear air in the middle of the Solent.

Calum gave the helm to Tom, with Sarra taking up her position as race tactician at the rear of the cockpit. Calum took up position at the stern of the schooner leaving Mike to organise the remainder of the crew in the pit area of the main cockpit. Tom looked at ease, as he searched around to see where best to position the schooner for the start.

The schooner reached the start area in good time. Tom began practising his start moves whilst it remained reasonably clear, but the start area filled up fast as the other competitors came pouring out of Cowes Harbour anxious to get to grips with the confusion of the day's racing. Calum's concern the spectator craft would get too close to the start line disappeared when he saw the race marshals shepherding the more anxious back into the allotted area.

Tom managed two practice runs before the start area became too crowded for safety. He called for power to be dumped out of the rig as he carefully manoeuvred *Samba Canção* out of the way well up to windward.

Calum called out to Tom, 'You going for a good late start?'

'Thought about it,' replied Tom. 'We're not as nimble as the smaller yachts, don't want to get carved up too early. If I see a gap appear in the line I might just barge in. My guess is this lot are going to be early. Almost anything could happen.'

Calum saw that Tom's evaluation matched his own one hundred percent. The schooner with its tall rig would be less affected by the dirty wind swirling around the start line. The schooner could just sneak a favourable start if the opportunity presented itself, and Tom seemed just the man to take advantage. It pleased Calum to see the remainder of the crew were alert and paying attention. They were keyed up and anxious to do their best.

The ten minute gun boomed out from the RYS start box. The race fleet became even more animated. The competing yachts were crisscrossing in front of each other with little room for error. With general mayhem, the added confusion started to bring a lot of hazards close to the start line. Tom brought the schooner slowly towards the offshore end of the start line on starboard tack, with her sails flapping to leeward. He called for minute changes of sail trim to keep minimum way on as he lined up on the outer start mark.

Carol took out the hand-held GPS and stood just behind Tom. The instrument had been programmed with the start line coordinates to monitor the time needed to reach the line. She started to call out the time to the outer mark of the start line.

'Three minutes late,' she called. Tom briefly turned around and asked if she factored the strong ebb tide that had started to run under them.

Carol reset the GPS and called out, 'Two minutes and forty seconds late at the outer mark.'

Tom grunted his thanks and asked for more power from the two main-sails, leaving the two foresails to continue flapping to leeward. The breeze began to build to a solid Force Four.

The five minute gun boomed out from the RYS start box. The race fleet began their measured run for the line. Calum could see from his long race experience that many competitors would indeed reach the line early, prob-ably by as much as twenty seconds. With little room for manoeuvre, they would run down the start line, bringing that moment of great concern to the few brave souls who fancied their chances on the inshore end of the line ready for a port hand start.

'This should be fun,' he thought. Meanwhile, Tom slowly brought the schooner up to speed. He searched hard but couldn't see any gaps in the mêlée along the start line.

'Three minutes to the gun, less than one minute late,' called out Carol. The mêlée on the line looked like it would get worse. The race fleet crews were indulging in a great deal of shouting, most of it obscene and non-repeatable.

Two over anxious cruiser racers made a vain attempt at a mid-line start, thought better of it and hurriedly reversed course. They were lucky to get away with it. The bulk of the fleet were now sailing down the start line as the countdown seemingly slowed to a crawl, with little room at the far end of the start line, close to the shore, and a large number of yachts were run-ning out of room very quickly.

Tom saw a gap about to break open close to the offshore end of the start line. He called for full sail and started shouting a continuous stream of instructions to get the sails trimmed correctly.

'Forty-five seconds to the line, twenty seconds late,' called out Carol.

Calum looked ahead. The gap had not materialised as fast as Tom hoped, and there were three M-33 sports cruisers coming up fast from behind. Carol looked around and saw them.

'Shit,' she muttered to herself as she called out to Tom, the 'Brother's

Grim' race team were coming up fast from behind. Calum had vaguely heard of them. These were three brothers called Grimsby who raced three very fast M-33 sport cruisers. The trio were well known for being highly competitive, using illegal team race tactics against race competitors who got in their way. That they sailed close to the wind regarding the racing rules was a given.

Tom held his nerve, as *Samba Canção* continued building her speed just as all the yachts around sailed into dirty air. The gap at the outer mark miraculously appeared, just as *Samba Canção* closed on the outer mark.

As expected the three M-33s were attempting to sail around the schooner and barge in on the line. Tom luffed the schooner, as her crew broke into a shouted chorus of 'windward boat keep clear.'

Samba Canção hit the start line ten seconds late, squeezing the three M-33s outside the outer marker. Calum could see the 'Brothers Grim' were not pleased, in fact, their thunderous faces said it all.

Samba Canção crossed the line at full speed. Tom held his course on starboard until he saw his chance to escape from the mêlée in front of him.

'Ready about,' he called, as he smoothly brought *Samba Canção* onto port tack and a started a long leg to cross the tide to the mainland shore. The crew in the work pit put their backs into trimming the four sails to perfection. *Samba Canção* surged forward.

'Nicely judged Tom,' Calum called out, 'and well-done everybody else.'

The schooner pulled hard, quickly getting out of the way of the other competitors. The race fleet chose to short tack down the island side of the Solent, keeping in the strongest part of the tidal stream. This would work for the more nimble yachts but *Samba Canção* needed long straight legs to get to full speed and make the most use of her substantial waterline length. The wind reduced to a varying 10-15 knots.

Fifteen minutes later *Samba Canção* had made magnificent progress. The wind gradient on the Island shoreline was causing problems to those inshore, and most of the race fleet were making little real progress. As the schooner came close to the mainland side of the Solent, the wind started to slowly veer, bringing more of a head wind, giving a big advantage for when she tacked onto starboard and the long leg down to Hurst Castle and the exit to the sea.

Samba Canção closed to within half a mile of the mainland shore. Tom told Sarra to keep a close on the depth sounder. He wanted to get close, but not too close to the crowded shingle shoreline at Lepe Beach.

'See the ice cream van is open in the car park?' suggested Calum.

'Don't worry Skipper, ice creams are bad for my waistline,' smiled Tom.

Sarra tugged at Tom's arm, 'Look behind, trouble with a big 'T', she called out. Out of nowhere the three M-33s were closing fast on the same tack. It didn't take Calum two seconds to work out what their little game would be. Soon the three M-33s were in position, with one astern and to windward, and two slightly behind to leeward in line ahead, a classic trap to try and either run the schooner up the beach or to lose a lot of distance getting out from under. The four yachts were all on port tack, and the only safe manoeuvre would to duck on to starboard tack as soon as possible and get offshore.

The schooner could not tack in front of the M-33 to leeward without impeding its course and incurring a penalty. The M-33s drew a lot less water than the schooner and there was the catch.

Tom looked around, took stock and smiled to himself. He yelled at his crew in the work pit to be ready for whatever. They kept their attention on their star helm. The depth sounder started to show a rapidly decreasing water depth. Tom looked hard at his crew on the mainsheet tracks for both mainsails. They both nodded in readiness.

'Dump all sails to leeward, now,' he shouted out. The schooner lost speed immediately. The first M-33 shot passed to windward before its crew knew what had happened. There was enough space to allow a tack to starboard, but it was going to be mighty close. The depth sounder started its alarm as the schooner came very close to going aground.

'Lee ho,' shouted Tom as he spun the wheel. Would the schooner get to the safety of the right of way starboard tack before the second M-33 was upon them?

'Water to tack,' Tom screamed at the second M-33. Calum figured this the correct and only rule left in the book to use right now.

The second M-33 hesitated. The schooner had rights, it also had 'weight of way', all thirty tons of it. The move Tom had not counted on was when the first M-33 dumped her mainsail to prevent his tack to starboard, not exactly a legal move, and there was little Tom could do. Fortunately, the pit crew were working hard to bring the schooner quickly on the new tack. It almost worked. Calum could see the bowsprit would hit the first M-33. And fortunately its height over the water meant it would miss the transom but impact the M-33's mainmast backstay.

'Crash.' The sound of the bowsprit hitting the backstay of the M-33 and snapping the top section off its mainmast like a dry twig, echoed around the waterway. The schooner remained undamaged, as Tom drove his crew hard to get the schooner back up to speed on the new tack. The Brothers Grim were incandescent with rage as the schooner disappeared in front. The other two M-33s stood by their stricken sister craft, mouthing a wide range of revenge.

Tom concentrated hard on getting the schooner into her groove. The wind increased slightly as *Samba Canção* hit full speed. This was exciting sailing. Sarra called out the wind shifts, advising Tom on the best course, keeping *Samba Canção* on the mainland side of the main channel in the Solent, and picking up useful freeing wind shifts from the influence of the land.

With the tide running strongly under the schooner she made fast progress. The race fleet over on the island shore had slowed, as unfavourable wind shifts still played tricks with the planning of their tactician's best expectations.

Samba Canção drew remorselessly to the head of the fleet as a result of some very concentrated sailing by her young crew. Calum was impressed. Mike had a big grin all over his face as all the effort and training of the last few weeks paid off.

Calum spoke out softly at Tom's side, 'You're doing a really good job today. What's the secret?'

'Not sure Skipper,' grinned back Tom. 'She's kind of sailing herself. I guess what I'm doing is keeping her hard on the wind when we get a strong gust; it lets some of the power out at the top of the rig, and then ease her off a bit when there is a small lull. There's a definite groove where you can feel either side of the equation. Anywhere in between and she goes to full hull speed without effort. Outside the groove, it all goes kind of dead.'

The exit into the English Channel approached quickly as Hurst Castle grew ever larger. Calum took his binoculars scanning the waterway past the Needles and into the English Channel.

Calum looked over at the Needles, the unusual row of three distinctive chalk stacks standing tall from the sea at the western extremity of the Isle of Wight. They took their name from a fourth needle-shaped pillar called Lot's Wife that used to stand in its midst until it collapsed in a storm in 1764.

'Looks kind of nice out there today,' Calum thought to himself. Carol came up from below. She'd been busy at the newly equipped navigation station, enjoying herself with the new electronic gadgets Calum had splashed out on during the refit.

'Skipper,' she said. 'What was the Race Committee's version of the weather forecast?'

'Much as you see it now until evening when the weather is supposed to pick up a little,' replied Calum. 'Why?'

'Hum,' said Carol. 'Well, I have to tell you it's going to bounce up hard within the next two hours, and we'd better be prepared for a rough ride up the Channel.'

Calum looked down at this slight figure of a girl.

'Strange,' he thought. 'She seems different, sure of herself. Delivered the news in a no-nonsense believable manner.'

'You sure?' Calum asked. Her look said it all. 'Did you contact Race Control for confirmation?'

'Of course, but they weren't about to listen to a girl were they now,' she snapped back.

'And just where does this information come from,' Calum asked.

'Daddy. He's just taken over the new shift at the Bracknell weather centre. He can smell things before they happen. His supervisor won't release the information until they're certain. Typical arse covering civil servant,' Carol spat in disgust.

'OK,' said Calum. 'Get on the race net and advise, cautiously mind, any of the other yachts who want to listen and take note. Can't do more than that. Steve, take Marie below and make sure we are rigged for heavy weather.'

'OK,' said Steve, as he collected Marie on the way down below.

Samba Canção made short work of reaching the turning mark into the English Channel, and with a furious unwinding of all four sheet winches, she bore away heading for St Catherine's Point at the southern tip of the Isle of Wight. She was lying in fourth place, a fine effort for a large displacement yacht. The three competitors in front were already up on the plane, flying large asymmetrical spinnakers and would soon disappear from view.

The seas were clear astern for the moment, but no doubt the other sport cruisers would soon come hammering by with their modern sail plans and planing hulls.

The schooner ploughed along at near maximum speed, dragging a beautiful counter wave behind her. This was grand sailing, as Calum got used to the power in the new rig. The new sails certainly looked grand, and they set beautifully. He looked to the west, into the centre of the English Channel hoping to see the new weather that Carol had confidently forecast. He couldn't see much, but his range was limited. He shouted below to Carol to get the latest status. She shouted back to wait a moment, as the radar halfway up the main mast started to turn. A few minutes later she popped her head out of the cabin hatchway.

'The leading edge is about a hundred minutes away, and Daddy agrees,' she said putting away her mobile phone. 'By the way, you have two contacts astern catching up very fast, have you seen them?'

Calum looked astern with his binoculars. 'Oh, bollocks,' he muttered. Yes, he saw them, and just knew who they were: the Brother's Grim.

The two M-33s were up to full speed and some. It would only take another 20 minutes before they caught up. Calum expected trouble. He asked the cockpit crew to bring the two long boat hooks on deck. He couldn't think what else to do, so Calum sat back and awaited events.

He didn't have long to wait. Both he and Patrick were monitoring the M-33s with binoculars. One M-33 had set a course direct for the schooner. The other was intent on passing to windward at about a hundred metres range.

'What do you think Patrick?' asked Calum.

'Not sure, to be sure,' replied Patrick. 'There's something happening on the M-33 to windward. Can't quite see what it is at the moment.'

The M-33 heading for *Samba Canção* was unwavering in its course, but its asymmetrical spinnaker hid any chance of seeing what was happening onboard. Patrick kept his binoculars trained upon the M-33 to windward. Its course gave an ideal wind angle and it was travelling very fast. The M-33 bore away and started to close slightly as it approached to a close position to windward of the schooner.

'Skipper,' shouted out Patrick, 'the lunatic has some sort of weapon. Can't quite make out what it is. Looks like a large jungle machete.'

Calum did not receive this news at all well.

'Keep watching, I'll track the other one,' he blurted out.

Calum looked round at the other M-33 and saw a very unpleasant brute of a man standing at the bow with a weapon definitely looking like a large jungle machete. This could get serious.

'Carol, get a message to race control and the coastguard. When you've done that get your video camera up here and record what these two morons are up to.'

Calum paused to think, 'Tom, take some evasive action, the rest of you keep your heads down. Mike. Take over here.'

The M-33 astern had been momentarily shaken off, but it quickly closed once more. The lunatic, with the machete raised high, was hurling dog's abuse and insults and looking at Calum.

Calum went to stand beside Tom.

'Tom,' he said, 'let's try this. Head downwind, and get the mainsheet trimmers ready to bring the sails onto the centreline. The M-33 will catch us very fast. At the right moment, slam dunk a gybe towards the island shore, harden up on port tack, get Carol below to dump the storage tanks into the leeward wing tanks, then throw in a fast tack to starboard and drive to windward out into the Channel. If the M-33 follows too quickly, they'll likely break something. They won't catch us going to windward in this building weather.'

Tom nodded his agreement and started calling to the work pit to get his crew briefed and ready. The manoeuvre began and the M-33 followed as expected.

'Silly boy,' thought Calum.

The schooner slammed on to port tack, Carol quickly completed the transfer of the water and diesel tanks into the leeward wing tanks, as *Samba Canção* buried her lee rail alarmingly into the sea.

'Ready about, lee ho,' shouted Tom, as he spun the wheel furiously to bring the schooner on to a new starboard tack. The pit crew worked hard to optimise the sail trim and get *Samba Canção* up to full speed hard on the wind.

The chasing M-33, in her haste, got something wrong. Something snapped in the rigging and the mast came crashing down.

'What a shame,' thought Calum, as his schooner powered away from the two M-33s. The other M-33 did not follow. Calum waited another 90 seconds and shouted at Tom to get back on course for St. Catherine's Point, now only a few kilometres away.

Carol poked her head out of the main cabin and shouted out a warning about the weather, which had started to close very fast. As the wind started to rise, the overfalls at St. Catherine's Point were starting to look ugly, and the option of going between them and the headland would become a very bad option. Calum shouted at Tom to get all hands to shorten sail, and get the schooner offshore and fast.

The crew struggled to quickly reef the mainsail to fifty percent, before starting to reef the two foresails. Calum asked Carol for the course to steer to get outside of the overfalls. Carol shouted up the information to Tom who quickly altered course. Mike and his crew were busy in the work pit trimming the sails. He looked up at the fore main and then at Calum questioningly. The large fore main was delivering a lot of power in the rising wind. With the schooner almost on a beam reach, she heeled well on to her side smashing the waves aside.

'Tom,' shouted Calum. 'You need this other mainsail reefed?' Tom looked up at the fore main, and at his instruments. The wind strength was rising quickly. He called to Mike to start spilling wind in both mainsails to bring a better composure to the schooner. A heavy gust of wind battered the schooner as she buried her lee rail well under water.

'Get the fore main fifty percent reefed, and fully reef the mainsail,' Tom shouted out. 'Any time in the next thirty seconds would be ideal.'

The crew in the work pit sprang into action, and as the great sails were reefed into the safety of their booms, some measure of order on board the schooner restored. Tom asked for the inner foresail to be un-reefed, as he struggled to get the schooner's sail plan back into balance.

The schooner reached the seaward side of the overfalls. With the last of the ebb tide running hard, being positioned in the boiling seas of the overfalls could hardly be considered the place to be. In fact at this moment, being in the middle of the English Channel was not the place to be either.

They rounded the overfalls and bore away before the wind. The wind started its expected rise. Carol came on deck with a weather update. The storm would run quickly past, but the next hour would give winds bordering on Force Ten. Then, as it passed by, the winds would drop to gale Force Eight, as the centre of the storm started to wreak havoc upon the English south coast.

Down below Carol kept a listening watch on race control broadcasting advice to the fleet that the race would not be cancelled and all skippers should make their own judgement. They did, however, recommend the slower yachts, if they were still inside the Solent, might want to consider their options.

Calum snorted in disgust. The smaller yachts were well on their way to exiting the protected waters of the Solent into an angry English Channel, heading straight into the oncoming storm. With crews keyed up for the race, they would be reluctant to quit without guidance from the race committee. Calum grabbed the microphone of the cockpit VHF and called HM Coastguards. It would be they, if anybody, who would be left to deal with any emergencies.

Time to look after his own affairs, the safety of his schooner and its young crew. By now the schooner had rounded the overfalls at St Catherine's Point and reset her course for the turn mark further up the coast at Dungeness Point. *Samba Canção* was running hard in front of the approaching storm on a broad starboard reach setting only vestigial sail area from her fore mainsail and a heavily reefed inner foresail.

The watch changed over to Steve and his Port Watch. Mike took the Starboard Watch below to get some rest before the first-night watch, and to help Carol doing sterling duty at the navigation station monitoring the radar, the increasing bad weather, and the local communication networks.

Darkness gained over the last of the daylight, and St Catherine's Point lighthouse, with its one white flash every five seconds, quickly faded away in the gloom. Calum called for the fore mainsail to be reefed down to twenty-five percent. The storm had reached its height, with wind speeds now exceeding the expected Force 10. Fortunately, the tide had turned into the flood, and the sea died down a little as the wind aligned itself with the strong spring tide, giving a respite of less than ten hours before the tide started to ebb and bring with it increased dangers. With just over a hundred miles to the turn mark at Dungeness Point, it would be a close call. True the flood tide would give a little leeway in time, but they still had to traverse the English Channel across one of the busiest waterways in the world.

The schooner continued tracking on a steady course giving the helmsman an easy time. Steve smiled over at Calum as the schooner surfed down the larger of the following waves building up behind her. The crew on deck kept their backs to the wind and heavy spray, their protective hoods pulled well down over their faces. Once or twice *Samba Canção* started to roll in the following seas. Steve quickly altered course to bring the wind on to the quarter. This was no time to start the build-up of a deadly 'death roll'.

One hour later, the weather slowly changed direction as the wind decreased and the storm centre moved away to the north across the south coast of England. A lot of re-arranging would be happening onshore, with trees down, electrical power lines laid over and gardens damaged.

The main cabin hatch opened, to reveal Carol checking if the weather had followed its prescribed course. Calum just smiled at her. She knew well the answer, but she wanted to make sure.

Four hours later the schooner drew level with Beachy Head. *Samba Canção* had made extremely good time, despite the battering from the weather. The crew members were rotating their allotted duties, and Calum had gone off-watch to leave Mike on deck to oversee the Starboard Watch in action. Tom had his watch well in control, with everyone taking turns at the helm and look-out positions.

Calum lay resting up in the sea berth just behind the navigation station. He looked overhead at the repeater instruments watching the schooner's course and speed, plus the data from the weather system. From here he could keep an eye on things and relax at the same time.

Alexander and Marie were busy in the galley. The menu would be usual seven-day stew as the large pot on the galley range slowly bubbled away with fresh ingredients thrown in every now and then; allowing everyone to help themselves went it suited.

Calum was honoured as a large bowl of stew arrived at his berth accompanied by some choice slabs of a crusty brown bread. Luxury indeed. A strong cup of tea completed his repast.

He looked at his watch; it was well past midnight, and Calum realised the routine onboard his beloved schooner continued to run as smooth as it ever did. Both watch captains told him they would keep three-hour watches to enable each watch to put a lot more effort into driving the schooner on its path to glory.

Mike came down from the cockpit. 'What's up,' Calum asked.

'Nothing to do,' replied Mike. 'This crew has got things so well in hand there's nothing to do.'

'Sure?' asked Calum

Mike replied, 'The logbook is up to date. The girls are helping Carol with the radar watch. They even made a table plot to track the radar contacts. The schooner is holding close to maximum speed and we'll make the turn mark in three hours. The weather is slowly moderating and the watch on deck just shook a couple of rolls out of the mainsail. The wind is starting to back, and talking of backs, I'm a'goin to turn in on mine until then.'

'That all?' smiled Calum.

'Huh,' grunted Mike. 'Wake me in three hours, and not before.'

Samba Canção reached the turn mark three hours later. Nobody saw it in the darkness, but the race rules allowed yachts to hit the correct GPS coordinates, and then alter course to cross to the French coastline.

Calum and Mike rose to supervise this busy dangerous crossing, but with both watches stood-to and with all hands on deck, except Carol and Marie manning the radar at the navigation station, it seemed there was little to do except keep a sharp eye out across the two shipping channel lanes, first the westward going and then the eastward going shipping lanes, separated by a zone in the middle kept free of commercial traffic.

Calum popped down to the navigation station manned by Carol and Marie. 'Carol,' he asked, 'have we checked in with Dover Coastguards, and is our radar transponder up and running?'

'Yes Skipper,' she replied, 'and I also checked in with race control as required by the race rules.'

'Well done girls, thanks a lot, everything OK?'

Marie stared intently at the radar screen with a worried look upon her face.

'Skipper, there's a faint radar echo which looks like it could be a coastal ship coming down the west channel. There's something that's not quite right.'

'Why?' asked Calum

'As we started crossing the westbound lane it changed course to maintain a collision heading. Normally it would either make to pass clear ahead or astern,' she replied.

'Check with the Coastguard,' ordered Calum.

Marie picked up the VHF handset. 'Dover Coastguard, Dover Coastguard, this is the schooner *Samba Canção*, Over.'

'Go ahead *Samba Canção*,' replied Dover Coastguard.

'Roger, my position is 51'05.27N – 1'19.08E, course 110 deg. True. We have a faint radar contact at bearing red seven-five degrees, range about five nautical miles. We think a small coaster. It keeps changing its course to maintain a collision heading. Over.'

'Wait,' ordered the voice from Dover Coastguard.

Calum stared at the radar screen. 'Marie, slave the radar display to the schooner's PC. I'll look at it there.'

Two minutes past and then the VHF burst into life.

"*Samba Canção* this is Dover Coastguard, we see your transponder very clearly and there is a contact which appears as you say. We are trying to make contact. Over.'

Calum watched the radar picture on the much bigger screen of his PC, and this did not look good. Something looked wrong; the hair stood up on the back of his neck. Calum shouted up to the deck 'Mike, I need you, quick.'

Mike jumped down and came over to Calum. 'Mike, this contact is trying to close us, and I can't think why. Something is wrong.'

Mike looked at the display for a couple of minutes. 'Whatever he's up to, it's not trying to pass our position. Want to try anything?'

Calum made up his mind. 'Mike, get all hands ready. Give me a sharp course alteration to the south, if it follows, give me a one eighty degree break to the north, OK?'

Marie quickly contacted Dover Coastguard on the VHF to advise the intended manoeuvre.

The schooner healed sharply as she quickly altered course to the south and came hard onto the wind. Marie shouted out the contact had changed course to follow suit. Dover Coastguard came on the air to advise they could make no contact with the mystery target and concurred with their observations. Mike shouted down from the helming position, 'Did that do the trick?'

'Hell no', shouted back Calum, 'come left one eighty and fast'

The schooner bore away with all four sheet winches rattling away. Calum stared at his PC screen. Marie confirmed what he saw; the contact was making straight for them, now less than two miles away. Mike shouted down he'd sighted the strange contact which showed no navigation steaming lights.

'Really,' thought Calum, 'now what?'

'Standby to go about. All hands to your winches.' It was Tom at the helm.

Calum looked up, 'What the fuck is he up to?'

The schooner went into a fast course change and headed west, directly away from the menacing contact. It would soon catch them. The schooner's main engine burst into life.

'Marie, send a Mayday to Dover Coastguard, I'm going on deck. Life jackets everybody,' warned Calum.

Calum arrived on deck. A tense crew were at their positions staring at Tom. Before he could say a word, Tom gave the wheel to Sarra. 'Just do exactly as I tell you, OK.'

Sarra just nodded, trying to stay calm and not making a very good job of it. Tom stood on the side deck of the schooner, holding onto the mainmast's mainstay. He stared at where he knew the contact to be, directly behind and closing fast. Now he could see the bow wave from the fast moving target. Tom made a quick sweep of the horizon, looked down at Calum, smiled and said, 'Watch this.'

'Sarra, when I shout 'go', come to course 'zero three zero' magnetic, and you winch hands wind it on real fast.'

Calum could only hold on and pray. Mike hung on to the steering binnacle, waiting for fate to take a hand. The bow wave from the approaching vessel was starting to get mighty close.

'Now!' shouted Tom. The schooner, its engine running at full throttle, went into another violent course change. The four sheet winches started their frantic rattling as the sails were rapidly sheeted home. The bow wave from the approaching target missed the stern of the schooner by less than ten metres as it healed violently to chase after the schooner.

Calum shouted out an alarm. Another high bow wave was coming quickly in their direction with the VHF loudspeaker blasting a message from Dover Coastguard about a westbound fast container ship at full speed and very close by. The container ship main navigation horn sounded a strident warning. The tension on deck past breaking point.

'Pay attention, standby everyone!' shouted Tom.

Sarra could only look at the compass course she was steering, everyone else hung on where they were. The bow wave of the container ship was almost upon them.

'Come right ninety degrees, trim all sails,' shouted Tom.

The schooner changed course violently, as the container ship sounded four long blasts on its siren.

'She's going astern. Christ what's happening,' thought Calum.

There came a tremendous crashing and tearing of tortured steel as the container ship slammed at full speed into the mystery vessel. Calum ran to the stern of the schooner as searchlights from the container ship lit up the sea. The assailant mystery vessel had been hit full amidships, and laid over at a bad angle, the bow of the container ship buried deep inside its hull. The mystery vessel was doomed.

Meanwhile, Tom kept the schooner's crew busy getting out of range of the mayhem. He looked over at Calum with a big question mark on his face; to stay and assist or to continue?

Calum had no doubts. Whoever were about to be rescued from the mystery vessel were not going to be model citizens, and his crew of young adults were all sufficiently scared, except for Tom, to deal with this. What an adventure Tom was having.

Calum shouted over, 'Steer one ten degrees true and get into the safe zone between the two shipping lanes.'

Tom waved an acknowledgment and got the deck crew busy. The wind fell away slightly, the crew set more sail and the main engine shutdown. Calum hastened down below. Carol and Marie were staring at the radar screen unseeingly.

'Marie, are we are clear to continue crossing the westbound shipping lane? Quickly now,' Calum ordered gently.

'Carol, get me the Dover Coastguard on the VHF, we'd better report in.'

Dover Coastguard was in a high state of alert. A string of urgent questions started to flow. Calum told them what he knew, but he was as confused about events as anybody. He gave them his immediate plans and asked for time to compose.

Sarra came down into the main cabin, rummaged around in a sea bag, and pulled a battered cell phone out. She pressed a fast dial number and hid in a corner at the forward end of the cabin. Calum heard the word 'Daddy'. How could he help, and what did he have to with all this?

How come the mystery vessel seemed to track them down so easily? Another word escaped from Sarra's conversation, 'Albanians. Just what was going on?'

Mike came below to report the schooner had settled down on her new course, and the crew were starting to ask questions to which he didn't have answers. Calum looked again at Sarra. Cell phones, could someone be tracking their cell phone positions?

'Mike, go round every crew member, collect their cell phones from where ever, bring them to me and make sure they are switched off,' he ordered urgently. 'Quickly now.'

Sarra looked over at Calum, 'Daddy wants to know your take on these events?'

'No idea,' he told her, the only really strange thing was the low radar profile of the mystery ship. Calum had caught a brief sighting of this vessel in the searchlights from the container ship. Radar wise, she'd been cleaned up considerably, no working deck masts and rigging, vestigial heavily raked main mast, no other topside hamper or other normal structures which would have given the usual strong radar signature.

The Dover Coastguard came on the VHF to report three survivors had been picked up by the container ship, three frocked priests from Macedonia, just north of Greece.

'Bollocks,' shouted out Calum. 'Sarra, you can tell that one to the Marines.'

'Daddy says thank you for keeping the Marines informed,' Sarra told him, 'and by the way, the schooner is emitting a tracking signal. A very old non-synchronous burst transmission signal from equipment used many years ago by the east European communist states. You need to look for a box, like a small hardback book. It will be quite heavy, with old style long life batteries.'

'Well thank you very much,' said Calum. 'I might just have a look, any other pearls of wisdom. By the way, what's your father's involvement in all this'?

'I'll tell you later. Daddy's rang off,' said Sarra. 'He says you were very clever to think of turning off all the cell phones. He is going to get a spectrum check on our position and see what's going on.'

'Spectrum check, huh?' Calum had heard enough nonsense for one day and went on deck to see how things were going. He collared Steve to get his Port Watch below, washed, fed and to take a half-hour break. That done, Calum would stay with them to daybreak whilst he sought to restore normal routine in the schooner.

The schooner made good progress crossing the English Channel, and with little channel shipping coming up the eastbound lane, they would soon reach the turn mark off the French coast.

The schooner made the turn mark at daybreak and set course for the long haul along the continental coastline to Denmark. The Port Watch had the duty, and with everything being taken care of, Calum turned in for a few hours.

The run along the coast proved reasonably easy, although Carol had been busy downloading the latest weather information. The forecast weather system, which had blighted the race, wasn't finished yet. She told Calum the storm would move into the North Sea, to form part of a new system that would bring strong northerly winds to the whole area.

Calum recognised this possibility earlier on. He did not know what the consequences would be, apart from making the journey to their destination a hard and uncomfortable slog. With the continental coast being a lee shore, it would have a potential to cause disruption to the journey, and possibly the need for a lay-up somewhere if things got too rough. Calum turned in for some much needed sleep.

Mike woke Calum in time for lunch. Mike was pooped and heading to his bunk for a few hours. He told Calum the Starboard Watch had the duty, and Tom was driving the schooner hard on the port tack. The wind remained variable, still from the north-west, as it tried to make its mind up if it would settle down in that quarter.

Calum went to the galley to help himself to lunch from the perennial pot of stew. It wasn't bad, and it filled a hole. Carol had just got up and became busy at the navigation station. She asked Calum if he'd searched for the mystery beacon that Sarra had told him about. Calum's look said it all, he'd forgotten all about it, and that assumed he believed any of the events of the last 24 hours.

He'd spoken to Mike at length about the near collision with the mystery ship, but none of it made any sense. Now he was supposed to look for an electronic bug from a former iron curtain country. Surely not?

He looked around, where to start looking? It was book sized apparently, perhaps disguised as a book. A book would be easy to smuggle onboard and hide. There were a few nooks and crannies that had remained undisturbed for some time. If he reorganised his own private area at least some good would come of what could well become a fruitless exercise.

Calum went to his favourite corner of the schooner, the comfortable quarter berth behind the galley. This was his private world, and apart from letting others use its comfortable single bunk, few were welcome to visit.

He pulled open the large sliding drawer under the sleeping berth and found it full of old shoes, spare clothes wrapped in waterproof plastic zipper bags and a fair amount of junk, most of it from the last voyage. Calum reached for a bin bag and started to idly toss items for which even he had long since forgotten why he'd kept them. A pair of old deck shoes, long past being fragrant, added to the growing collection of rubbish. Below the main sliding drawer were two split drawers, the right-hand one was rather stuck. Calum hadn't used it in a long time, he wondered why?

Grabbing the handle with both hands it pulled open with a bang. Most of the contents spilt onto the deck. More of the same; plus spare parts for machinery which had long gone in the refit. At the back of the drawer he found what looked like an instruction manual, a hard backed instruction manual, for a water maker he'd never heard off? He lifted it out, and thought it too heavy to be an instruction manual. He placed it on the galley worktop, as he emptied the remaining contents of the drawer into the rubbish bag.

'Spare empty drawer', he thought. 'Handy.'

Sarra dropped down from the cockpit to make coffee for the troops on deck. She looked at the object on the galley worktop, and pushed it with her finger. Heavy and solid, whatever it was. Calum came from behind the galley.

'Seen the mystery item,' he asked.

'Yes,' she replied, 'and I don't like the look of it either.'

'Por que ?' asked Calum.

'Don't know,' she replied, taking her cell phone from her pocket, switched it on, waited for it to find a network and pressed a fast dial button. She spoke briefly into the cell phone, describing what she saw. She turned the object over and continued describing the marks and details on the back of the object. Calum suggested opening it up. Sarra placed her hand firmly on top of the object, telling him 'No' and continued to listen to the voice on the phone.

Sarra asked Calum for a heavy metal baking tray from the bottom drawer of the galley to place over the object. After a few minutes, the voice on the phone told her to remove it. She listened intently to some further instructions and then hung-up the cell phone and turned it off.

'That's Daddy's signal specialist. He thinks it could be booby trapped. It's too heavy for anything else, despite its long life batteries. He suggests we wrap it up and make it waterproof, find something that floats, plastic container or similar, put it inside and ditch it over the side,' Sarra told him.

'If it's dangerous, should we not just give it the 'deep six' and have done with?' asked Calum.

'He suggests we don't give the game away and in this wind it should drift onto a beach in a couple of days. If it does, he'll send someone to dispose of it. More likely it will sink and then go off the air.'

'It's still transmitting,' asked Calum.

'Oh, yes, loud and clear,' replied Sarra.

'OK, you fix it,' Calum told her. 'And thanks.'

The long slog along the continental coast continued. Calum continued to be pleased to see his young crew settled down after the previous night's excitement, concentrating hard on driving the schooner at her maximum speed. Carol contacted race control, and was surprised to learn the race was still continuing, albeit with a greatly reduced fleet.

Samba Canção was sailing alone; the race becoming almost secondary. More importantly, the young crew were quickly becoming seasoned experienced sailors, able to handle the big schooner with some ease, and without any real problems. The two watches had settled down, everyone taking turns at the many tasks, with self-confidence building fast.

As the day grew longer the long coastline turned to the north, with the schooner hard on the wind, barely holding its course along the coast. The weather started to build, as did the seas. Short, sharp and making life very uncomfortable for everyone onboard.

The long day turned into a long night, with the schooner thrashing to windward in very wet and uncomfortable conditions. Calum had been monitoring the performance of the new rig. The new masts were certainly standing up straight and tall, and performing as expected. The slight slack in the leeward rigging was, in his eyes, normal considering the strength of the weather. Now he had a spare moment and started to write-up the promised report for Chalky Whyte and his mast maker.

Carol came back on watch and downloaded the latest weather forecast. It started to look touch and go. As the schooner passed the Dutch city of Den Helder the coastline started its slow turn to the east. Calum could see that if the weather continued to build the schooner had every chance of being at the wrong place at the wrong time. With a low-lying lee shore below them and little chance of thrashing to windward to gain mileage from the Danish coast he had to consider whether to lay-up somewhere until things improved.

The new weather forecast was far too general and lacked any detailed information for their immediate area. Calum had little experience in this part of the world. A lay-up would incur lost time, and Calum wanted the journey over and done with before the strength of his young crew started to fall away. Young and keen they maybe, but hardy sailors they were not.

Calum consulted the chart very carefully and brought Carol into his deliberations. It seemed to him they could make the turn to the east without the weather being too difficult, but then it was over 200 miles to safety. The two choices were to duck in early to Den Helder, or to keep on going and if the weather did continue to deteriorate, the schooner could blast reach down to the Island of Terschelling and hide up in one of the creeks behind the island.

The latest weather data did not give a conclusive report and the two watch captains were all for keeping going, as were most of their watch members. Carol, for a change, couldn't make up her mind one way or the other. She tried to contact her father, but either he was off-shift or away from his desk at the Bracknell weather centre and nobody knew where he was.

Calum decided on the second option. Quite why he wasn't sure? Perhaps he had become too keyed up with the race, a rare moment of indecision. During the night the schooner started the slow turn to the east and picked up more speed as the wind freed-off. As the morning watch started at eight am, Calum was roused by Steve, the Port Watch leader. Steve had spent the previous hour steadily shortening sail to the point where he had only the inner foresail set and both mainsails reefed down to fifty percent.

Calum felt the motion of the schooner, crashing around, shaking and shuddering in the short violent seas. He shouted to Steve for their latest position. Their progress had indeed been mighty, as they fast approached the eastern end of the Island of Terschelling. Time to run to safety.

He struggled into his foul weather gear and told Steve to call all hands. From the chart table he looked up at the GPS and marked his position on the chart. He could make straight for the Island at the moment, but it would be a straight downwind run, and in these seas he didn't fancy having the schooner roll her guts out.

He drew a line on the chart to the turn point he wanted and calculated time and distance to run. Twenty minutes would do it, and with a strong east-going tide under him it would bring the schooner's course onto a useful broad reach.

The twenty minutes quickly passed, and with everyone at their positions Steve called a bare-away gybe on to the starboard tack. The schooner was a short five miles out to sea, and the run into safety would not take long, allbeit that they would be running blind on a dark dirty night and relying totally on the GPS, and the radar, for accurate positioning.

Calum ducked down to the navigation station. Carol had the Dutch almanac opened to the right page. The entrance waterway behind the islands was wide, but the seas would be piling up high as the waters became shallower. It would be a wild and dangerous passage, and the schooner would just have to punch through as fast as possible.

Inside the entrance a large sandbank in the middle of the channel presented danger, but by keeping to the west side, the schooner would quickly run into sheltered waters. A firm sandy bottom indicated a good anchorage.

Calum called for the mainsail to be fully reefed. With the wind strength still building the schooner had more than sufficient power. Below, Carol monitored the radar as the schooner approached the shoreline. The boiling surf was all too easy to see on the radar screen. Calum ducked down below to show Carol the line he wanted to take into the entrance channel between the two Dutch islands. The schooner crashed through the waves giving everyone a thorough soaking.

At the helm Steve could see little, putting all his faith into Carol's instructions from the navigation desk. Calum stood in the companionway between the upper deck and the main cabin. The schooner was running hot and hard and taking a lot of punishment from the steep foaming seas. It would be a rough ride in, but thankfully it shouldn't take too long.

The schooner burst into the channel entrance with Carol frantically calling out directions. As the schooner reached calm water, Calum motioned for the helmsman to start the main engine. The schooner began a long slow arc to starboard, bringing the wind onto the beam. With the echo sounder showing a decreasing depth under her keel, Steve let the schooner drift to the south to find a little more depth. In the dark wind-blown night he could still see nothing of the land to starboard.

At last, Carol shouted for the schooner to come head to wind, and hold position on the main engine, as the deck crew rush forward to break out the big 25 kg Danforth anchor. Its deep wide blades would bite deeply into the hard sandy bottom. A torch shone on the anchor to make certain the chain was ready to run cleanly out of the spurling pipe.

Carol shouted for Steve to bring the schooner closer to the island shore.

'Good girl,' Calum thought. 'It would allow a longer length of chain to be run out, and get more weight on the seabed.'

Ten minutes later the schooner safety anchored. Calum went forward and grasped the anchor chain to feel for vibrations caused by a dragging anchor. There were none.

The low laying island provided little shelter from the northerly wind as it howled through the rigging above them at the top of the mast. With all sails safely stowed, Calum sent the Port Watch below to get out of their wet clothing and to get some rest.

Calum and Mike slumped down at the table in the main cabin. They were bushed and needed restoring. Mike reached under the table and a bottle of whisky appeared. Calum provided the water and two glasses.

'Never done that before,' commented Calum.

'What, the blind entrance with a full flood tide under you?' asked Mike.

'Oh, did we have a flood tide, I suppose we did. Just assumed without thought. The east-going stream and all that.'

'The crew did well; did they know the danger?' asked Mike.

'They knew the dangers. See how they totally gelled together, their actions co-ordinated and automatic.'

'A fantastic achievement. I'm real proud and that's a fact,' mussed Calum.

'Hungry?' asked Mike.

'Nope, I'll think I'll turn in until breakfast time, you staying up?'

'Only until it gets light, just to be sure the anchor is holding. I'll got the Starboard Watch rested up too,' said Mike.

Daylight slowly broke over the Island of Terschelling, as her crew prepared for a new day. Carol suggested the bad weather would slowly moderate over the next twelve hours, by which time everyone should be refreshed and ready to go.

Calum rose to answer the call of nature, then went to the galley to make himself some porridge with honey. Alexander, the Port Watch winch man, had the anchor watch. Calum asked how things were. The schooner had pulled her anchor a little during the first four hours but there no movement at the moment. Calum wondered how much force it would take to break the anchor out when they wanted to set sail. It would be buried pretty deep by now. No doubt it would take some coaching to break it free.

Calum finished his porridge and went on deck for a quick look around. The schooner lay in a deep pool, probably half way across the channel of the creek extending to the west. He'd no idea if there was any traffic in this waterway, which he doubted, but it wouldn't hurt to shorten the scope of the anchor chain. He pulled on his waterproofs, and Alexander followed him up on deck.

Calum sent Alexander forward to the winch control, then started the main engine and slowly brought the schooner forward. Alexander reeled in the anchor chain until twenty metres became safely stored in the chain locker. Calum checked the depth sounder. The schooner had reached shallower waters, leaving behind the main channel. The wind continued strong in the upper rigging, but on deck, the wind reduced as the schooner lay in the island's wind shadow.

The tide had begun to ebb, and still had three hours run to go. Still, with plenty of water under her keel, the schooner wasn't so hard on her mooring system. Calum shut down the main engine and waved Alexander back into the comfort of the main cabin.

Having satisfied his craving for activity, Calum took a last look around before heading back to his comfortable bunk behind the galley. He was surprised to see a large powerful fishing trawler smashing its way in through foaming seas at the mouth of the estuary. The trawler rolled hideously in the boiling seas; someone was in a hurry to escape from the bad weather outside in the North Sea.

The trawler rounded into the entrance to the creek but stopped short and anchored about four cables away. Calum looked at the wooden hulled trawler, with an open exposed forecastle, old fashioned high-sided wooden wheelhouse which looked like a dog house. The vessel was about thirty metres long. He didn't recognise the type, but it did not originate from the UK or any of the countries that bordered this side of the English Channel. She seemed devoid of the usual mess of fishing tackle and rigging equipment and painted all over in black. Perhaps she was in transit following a refit. Who knows?

Anyway, it had been another long day, and it was time to turn-in.

*****

Chapter 11

Departure from Copenhagen

Major Per Bruus-Jensen arrived at the Copenhagen Royal Dockyard. · The hour was late, the weather had not improved, and neither had his temper. Following the meeting with his King, the Major had spent most of his time on the telephone. Most of his planning had quickly come into focus, but the loose ends were driving him up the wall. Fortunately, the loose ends were not too serious, but the 'nice to haves' were quickly becoming 'not to haves'. He supposed he could blame matters on the war. His war hadn't started yet, but in his opinion, he wouldn't have long to wait.

At least his aging and tiresome car got him to the Royal Dockyard in one piece. It would later be retired to the back of an unused warehouse, where it would remain until after the operation to get the remaining Danish gold bullion to safety.

He arrived at the Royal Dockyard gate, pleased to see the police guard strengthened with the addition of a police sergeant and two extra men. They were wearing their side arms correctly outside their great coats. His temper further improved when he noticed out of the corner of his eye, one of his own men, fully blacked out and nearly invisible, keeping an eye on the police from a concealed position.

The police sergeant stopped the Major's car, shone a strong torch into his face, efficiently asked for his pass, checked his name off against a list and motioned one of his men to let him through the main gate. The dock-yard was typical of all naval dockyards he'd ever known. A confused mess of what appeared to be discarded machinery, blocking roads and alleyways, things to trip over when walking at night, and an almost hundred percent chance of running into something unlit and damaging the car. He looked around to get his bearings, and hundreds of pairs of eyes belonging to the wild dockyard cats stared at him from every dark recess.

Having stored his car, the Major found the steam ferry *Girard* and made for the gangway. This ferry was not a typical Scandinavian ferry, and had a distinctly British look about her. Her strong riveted hull and two funnels gave her away, probably an old railway ferry, from God only knows where, and more than likely retired from a night ferry service on the Northern Ireland route.

The Major had seen this type of vessel before. Long, low and sleek, the ship would have been constructed, judging by her outline, in the mid-twenties at one of the many shipyards in Glasgow. Her twin funnels were belching a fair amount of black smoke, indicating she was a fuel oil fired steamer, and no doubt with twin propellers. Bruus-Jensen guessed her over-all length at about 200 feet, with a displacement of about two thousand tons.

The ship's open stern deck had been loaded with a large amount of cargo by the ship's crane mounted at the back of the overhanging funnel deck. With any luck the steam ferry would possess a fair turn of speed, which had every chance of becoming a major advantage. The Major could see two of his 'All Terrain' five-ton trucks already loaded onboard.

He made to climb the gangway only to be immediately challenged by another dockyard policeman. The Police Chief had been busy. He made his way onboard and found his Sergeant Major, one Anker Kjaergaard, a short barrel-chested man processed of great strength and sometimes short temper. Like any good Sergeant Major, he was not one to trifle with no matter who you were.

'Good evening Sergeant Major. Everything OK? asked Bruus-Jensen.

'Almost Sir,' he replied, without added information.

'Status report,' ordered the Major testily.

'Yes Sir. The support stores are onboard, as are the men except for the two on gate guard, the two out on the jetty here and two drivers.'

The Major might have known there were two soldiers guarding the dockyard gate; one would never see the second one. He felt pleased.

'Vehicles?' he asked.

Yes Sir,' replied the Sergeant Major. 'Two are loaded onboard and secured for the voyage. They contain the ammunition cases that aren't ammunition. They've been covered over and camouflaged as per your instructions.'

'Where are the other two vehicles, they should be here by now', barked the Major rather annoyed.

'They were Sir, but I sent them on a little mission. I foresaw they would be late back so I've arranged they proceed direct to Århus and we'll load them there'. 'What little mission? Sergeant Major,' the Major started to get annoyed.

'Beg your pardon Sir, but they've gone to a military air force base on the road to Århus to pick up a load of extra equipment which happened to come our way.'

'Extra equipment? What extra equipment Sergeant Major?' snapped the Major.

The Sergeant Major took Bruus-Jensen to one side. 'Well Sir, it's all a bit hush hush, but let's just say a large four engine German transport aircraft with Spanish markings, and a Spanish crew, should by now, have landed at one of our airfields over on the Heligoland side of the country. The afore-mentioned cargo should have been dumped at the end of the runway, and a number of Danish personnel bundled into the aircraft complete with their wives and children. Our two trucks should be there in time pick up the cargo direct from the aircraft.

The cargo should consist of the latest German equipment, lightweight sub-machine pistols, sniper's rifles and scopes', coal scuttle helmets, para-trooper waterproof jackets and trousers, German greatcoats, the latest fashion in hand grenades, light weight mortars, German paratrooper pistols, and ammunition to suit all weapons'.

The Major looked at him astonishment. Well aware he'd been unable to get his men re-equipped with the latest military hardware, and they had made it more than clear that after the two 'holidays' the Major had arranged for them, their standard issue of equipment, most of it left over from the last war, could not be considered suitable in the modern age.

The 'holidays' in question consisted of a month in the Algerian Desert with the 13th Demi-Brigade (D.B.L.E.) of the French Foreign Legionnaires, led by the Major's good friend Coronal Charles de Delacroix, followed by a fortnight with the Norwegian Special Forces Ski Patrol who normally guarded their common border with Russia.

The training had been invaluable, and his men enjoyed bringing them-selves up to the top standard of international soldering. Having overcome the harsh climatic conditions of both venues, and seen a hundred different new ways of becoming real special force soldiers with the appropriate high level of strong esprit de corps, they lacked just one thing, modern Special Forces equipment.

'Any details, Sergeant Major, of the departing Danish personnel?' asked a confused Major.

'Well Sir, the PM's secretary asked me to tell you, in the strictest confi-dence, that as the King has no intention of leaving the country if, or when, the Germans invade, his Ministers are also forced to remain. The personnel being shipped out are junior government ministers and civil servants who are to become a kind of a mini-government in exile. They are being flown under great secrecy to the United Kingdom where they will assist the Brit-ish Government anyway they can.'

'And the Spanish aircrew, what will happen to them?' asked the Major.

'Well Sir, I believe they will end up in the USA clutching large brown envelopes stuffed full of cash. I also understand they have relatives in the USA, and they didn't wish to be on the wrong end of General Franco's somewhat nasty habit of torture and killing off Republican pilots in the Spanish Air Force who'd swapped sides to his Nationalists so as to infiltrate his organisation.'

'Intriguing, said the Major. 'Anyway, these supplies, how many of our men are we able to equip?' he asked.

'About forty, I would say, not sure until we get our hands on the shipment,' smiled the Sergeant Major. 'We'll see when we get to Århus.'

A black limousine arrived at the dockside with two policemen standing on the running boards. 'That will be the Minister,' said the Sergeant Major, 'almost on time. Now we can set sail.'

The Major went over to the gangway to greet the Minister onboard the *Girard*.

'Good evening, Sir', said the Major.

'Thanks, time to get going,' replied the Minister. 'It's too damn cold to be standing around outside. Let's go to the ship's bridge.'

The Treasury Minister and the Major made their way to the pilot house on the ship's bridge. There they found an impatient shipmaster, Captain Arne Ditlevsen and his First Mate Axel Munck, who were anxious to be off. The Captain, a short stocky tough old cove, looked like he'd travelled around a few times. His First Mate looked similar; the pair of them close to being matched book ends thought the Major.

Behind them, looking on with great disinterest, was a large, old black dog, which appeared to be a Labrador. Its name apparently was Kirsty. Its head smaller and thinner than normal, with laid back ears that had the look of a sheep collie. Its large and bushy tail looked Alsatian. Clearly its heritage had not been a carefully planned event.

The Captain and his First Mate shook the hands of their guests and looked hard at them, waiting for some idea as to what was going on. The decision to go the long way round to Århus was, for sure, not his preference. Navigating between the Danish Islands on a dark, rough night would be hazardous given the need for haste. Still, they didn't ask any questions. The rumours of war reached them just over a week ago, so anything out of the ordinary would likely to have a good reason, no matter what it would be.

Captain Ditlevsen spoke to his guests with little ceremony.

'Ready to set sail Sir?' he asked of them.

The Major asked the Captain to proceed as ordered with all haste. Captain Ditlevsen left the bridge's pilot house and went out onto the starboard bridge wing. The cold Arctic wind headed straight down the river channel past the naval docks at Nyholm. Catching his breath, he pulled his cap further down over his ears in a vain attempt to keep his balding head from getting cold.

He waved down at the Second Mate to single-up all mooring lines. When he saw the task complete he yelled into the pilot house to ring on main engines. The engine telegraphs clanged acknowledgement, and the *Girard* was ready to set sail.

The Captain signalled to the Second Mate to remove all lines except the forward spring on the starboard side. The Captain turned to look through the open door into the pilot house and barked at the First Mate, 'Dead slow ahead both, wheel hard a-starboard.'

The First Mate repeated the order, setting the telegraphs for both engines. The telegraph repeaters for both engines clanged their acknowledgement from the engine room. The Captain watched the ship's stern slowly started to swing out into the channel.

'All stop, helm amidships,' the Captain shouted through the bridge door at his First Mate.

The stern of the *Girard* cleared the dockside wall as the dockside gang let go the forward spring. The deck crew quickly reeled it in, anxious to retreat from the cold weather.

'Half astern both,' the Captain shouted. The *Girard* pulled clear from the dockside into mid-stream. Satisfied with the ship's position, the Captain went back into the pilot house and slammed the door behind him.

'Slow ahead both,' ordered the Captain. The First Mate rang the telegraphs down to the engine room. The repeaters rang back with their loud clanging. The Captain looked at the ship's compass, took a bearing down river and ordered, 'Steer zero-one-zero degrees.'

The First Mate spun the wheel bringing the *Girard* on to the correct course. The steam ferry started to move forward, slowly at first, but quickly picked up a little more speed. The *Girard* reached the end of the dockyard jetty, which stuck out like a sore thumb into the channel and went on to pass the Island of Refshalvej.

As the *Girard* cleared the island, the Captain ordered a slow turn to starboard to bring the steam ferry onto a new course to take her south to the channel between the Main Island and Saltholm Island.

The Captain ordered half speed ahead. He looked over at his Boatswain's Mate and ordered him to make sure the four lookouts were closed-up and keeping a sharp eye out.

'Captain,' asked the Major, 'are we running with our steaming lights on?'

'Just navigation lights as per regulations,' replied the Captain.

Horskjaer spoke up, 'Captain, I would ask we make ourselves as invisible as possible. Can we do that?'

'Yes Sir, if we must,' replied the Captain. 'Any reason why?'

Horskjaer briefed the Captain about the security situation. The Captain frowned at the news, as he began to realize how serious things might become. The Captain shouted after the vanishing Boatswain's Mate.

'Boatswain, darken ship completely for the night run. No smoking or naked lights on the upper deck, close all cabin portholes, and get the army detailed off too. Best if the Major's men use the passengers lounge.'

'Aye aye Skipper,' replied the Boatswain mate as he disappeared out of sight.

Bruus-Jensen joined in the conversation. He told the Captain he would be reluctant to give full details of the mission, but with events moving fast, he, at least, ought to know some of the dangers. He outlined the mission in its basic terms, the roundabout journey to Århus, picking up two trucks and more of his men, boarding additional navy crew to man the temporary AA guns, and offloading any of his crew not considered vital to the mission.

'Captain,' the Major continued. 'I have to ask if you have any problems in undertaking what has now become an import mission with more danger than we first thought.'

'Explain?' pressed the Captain.

'I can't explain in any more detail than I have already,' said the Major, 'but I am aware this very important mission is now fraught with potential danger, and after all, you are all civilians. I have a naval crew ready to come onboard at Århus, and the Minister has papers to second your vessel. It's a matter on how you feel being placed under military orders rather than just a simple charter?'

The Captain looked up at the Major. 'Major, myself and my First Mate faced danger in the Great War, and we're not too old to do our duty again should the need arise. In any event, we have been together on this ship for many years, and I doubt if a new naval crew would make a success of her.'

'Do you have any crew you wish to put ashore for any reason?' asked the Treasury Minister.

'Who for example?' asked the Captain testily.

'I was thinking of expectant fathers, anybody with heart complaints, that sort of thing,' replied the Minister.

'Oh I understand where you're coming from,' replied the Captain. 'I have a few candidates, but they won't be pleased.'

'Deck crew or engine room,' asked the Major.

The Captain laughed. 'The Black Squad,' he said. 'You've no chance of getting anyone out of their lair, none whatsoever. You could try, but I wouldn't bother if I were you.'

'Thanks Captain, it's good to meet loyal Danes,' said the Minister. 'We'll let you choose who you wish from the ratings we have waiting at Århus. I do insist on bringing our gunners onboard.'

'Agreed,' said the Captain. 'Please excuse me. I have my duties to attend to.'

The *Girard* came to the end of the long passage between the main island and the Island of Saltholm. Time to fix position, alter course for the Busene Peninsula and then to the turning point at Gedder Odde. As the steam ferry turned onto the new course across the Køge Bugt, the Captain turned around to his First Mate and spoke in a low voice, 'Check with the look-outs, and see if we're clear to come up to full power.'

'Aye aye Skipper,' replied the First Mate. 'But it's a filthy night to be charging around at full speed, but we have no choice.'

'I know, but needs must,' said Captain Ditlevsen.

The First Mate shrugged his shoulders and went on deck to check the two forward lookouts. The two of them had seen little since they cleared the harbour, and complained about being stuck up in the bow of the ship with little chance of seeing anything in the freezing weather.

'I know,' replied the First Mate, 'orders from the Skipper. We're going to be making a fast run across the Køge Bugt. It's full speed ahead, so keep your eyes peeled for anything.'

The first lookout looked around at the First Mate and asked what was going on.

'Why's that?' asked the First Mate.

The first lookout told him a fast trawler had followed in their wake as they left harbour. Did the First Mate know if it was still astern? The First Mate frowned at the news and asked if they recognised the trawler or where it had come from.

'Wasn't Danish,' said the first look-out. 'Could have been German, but hard to tell in this weather and in the dark.'

The First Mate went aft and looked astern intently with his binoculars. He could see little, perhaps a little fluorescence from a bow wave, but it was indeed very difficult to see anything. A clearing in the clouds allowed the light from a weak moon to shine briefly on the sea behind. Yes, there was something there, and for sure it was following them.

He rushed back to the pilot house on the bridge.

'Skipper,' he blurted out, 'know anything about an escort behind us?'

Captain Ditlevsen looked across at the Major, dosing at the navigation table.

'Major,' he shouted out. The Major came to with a start.

'What's the matter?' he asked.

'There's a ship following us, looks like a fast trawler,' said the First Mate. 'One of the lookouts spotted it as we turned south from the harbour entrance. He wasn't sure, and in this weather that's fair comment, but it might have been German.'

'Skipper,' asked the Major, 'can we out run a German trawler, if that's what it is?'

'Should be able to, but I'd rather not in this weather,' replied the Captain.

'I know about the damn weather,' snapped the Major. 'Stop going on about it. Let's go, if you don't want a gunfight on your hands.'

The Captain looked startled.

'You sure?' asked the First Mate.

'Stop and find out if you wish, but I don't wish, so let's go; full speed ahead,' cursed the Major.

The Treasury Minister came from the galley below. 'I heard anxious voices, what's going on?' he asked.

'Eric,' the Major spoke, 'there is a chance we are being followed. They think a German trawler, but nobody's sure.'

'Ah,' said the Treasury Minister, 'that might just be.'

'Oh yes,' said the Major suspiciously. 'Anything else?'

'Actually no,' said the Treasury Minister. 'Someone in the office briefly mentioned the possibility, but no one had any news. I did check.'

The Major looked around at everyone, 'Any ideas, anyone?' he asked.

Captain Ditlevsen looked out the window of the pilot house, but there was little to see. He looked across at his First Mate, who shrugged his shoulders as if to say 'What can I suggest you haven't thought off?'

'Tactics?' suggested the Major.

Captain Ditlevsen turned around with a gleam in his eye. 'I've done this before, and I can do it again.'

The Captain picked up the telephone to the engine room, 'You all awake down there?' he asked of the duty stoker on the footplate.

'Always,' came the reply.

The Captain spoke into the telephone, 'OK. Stand-by for some action,' and hung up the handset.

'Port thirty,' the Captain called over to the helmsman. The *Girard* leant into the sharp turn. 'Revolutions one two zero, speed for fifteen knots, steer 090'. The *Girard* started to shudder as she picked up speed. The First Mate went to the navigation table and marked the change of course, time and the new speed.

'Now let's see if the mystery ship is awake,' said the Captain.

The Captain looked over at his First Mate, 'Give me ten minutes on this course, then come back to our original track, I'm going for a slash.' The Captain disappeared towards the heads.

'The Major followed the Captain. As he passed the galley he saw the cook busy preparing coffee and some snacks for the bridge.

'Good,' thought the Major, feeling more than peckish.

Ten minutes later, the *Girard* heeled to port as the First Mate brought the ship back to its original course. He rang the stern lookout and asked if they'd seen anything. The reply was not polite, and definitely negative.

The Captain returned to his bridge, refreshed. He looked at the updated chart, looked out at the weather, and pulled his cap into place. The weather remained spiteful and inclement, with little to see. He climbed back into his chair in time to receive a large mug of coffee from the cook doing his rounds with refreshments for the deck watch.

As the Captain put away an empty coffee mug the mystery ship broke into clear weather and a strong moon hung low in the western sky bringing an eerie illumination to the sea. The self-powered phone from the stern lookout position rang loudly. The Captain reached forward to answer it.

'Ship bearing Green 90, about 2 nautical miles,' came the report.

The Captain rushed out onto the starboard bridge wing grabbing his binoculars on the way, closely followed by the Major. It took a few moments to adjust his eyes to the darkness, but he couldn't find what he was looking for. In the pilot house, the dog stirred his stumps, wandered out on to the bridge wing, and lifted his front paws onto the wooden cap along the railing. The Labrador looked out over the sea, moved his head up and down a few times, barked conclusively in a direction just forward of the beam, and returned to the undeniable comfort of his dog basket.

The Captain looked intently in the direction barked at by his dog and quickly found the mystery ship sailing on a parallel course. The Major took a little longer, but he too managed to get sight of the mystery ship.

'What do you think Captain,' asked the Major.

'Not sure,' murmured the Captain, unable to make his mind up what he was looking at.

'It's not one of ours,' he said. 'I don't know of any Danish trawler which can match my speed at fifteen knots.'

The First Mate came onto the bridge wing. The Captain slapped the binoculars into his outreached hands. 'You have a look; you've better eyes than mine.'

The First Mate stared hard and long into the distance. Eventually, he said, 'It's German, whatever it is. It's no trawler either, just looks like one.' He paused, continuing, 'For me it's a patrol craft of some kind, can't be sure.'

The radio operator came into the pilot house looking for the Captain. The Captain went back into the warmth of the pilot house. 'What have you got?' he asked.

'A ship Sir, close by, transmitting in code of some sorts. Can't read it, but the radio direction finder has the ship bearing Green 90.'

'Does it now,' muttered the Captain. 'Major, come here.'

The Major returned to the pilot house and asked what was up. The Captain told him the radio operator had picked up the German ship out to starboard, transmitting in code back to shore.

The Major muttered something impolite under his breath and went below to talk to Horskjaer and found him dosing in the cabin he shared with the Major. The unwelcome news merely confirmed his suspicions he'd been secretly nursing.

'Did Villemoes give you any further intelligence before we left?'

'Well Sir, he had nothing concrete, but wasn't sure he'd been a hundred percent successful in hiding our activities,' replied the Major.

'Any suggestions? You're the military wonder onboard this vessel,' said the Treasury Minister.

'Nothing practical; we're not at war, yet. Can't ram or board her. Gun crews aren't onboard yet either, and my men haven't been onboard long enough to find their way around them.'

The Major pondered the situation. He considered if the German ship could slowly overhaul them then out-running her would not be a likely option. Given the dark night, and a good chance they'd not been seen on the parallel course, it might just be that simple to slow down a little and let the German disappear.

The Major went back to the pilot house on the bridge of the *Girard*.

'Captain, I'm hoping he hasn't seen us in the dark, try slowing down and see if the German can be made to disappear in front.'

The Captain turned around to the duty helmsman, 'Revolutions nine zero, speed for 10 knots,' he barked. The duty helmsman set the telegraphs; their loud clanging confirming the change of speed. The Major asked the Captain about a change in course?

The Captain replied, 'Major, we need to get on. Let's see if the German ship pulls ahead. He might even speed up thinking he's lost us in front. Why don't you go below and get some sleep, we'll look after things here. Any fuss, you'll soon hear about it.'

'Good idea,' replied the Major. 'By the way, how long have been using the dog as a lookout?'

'Oh, you mean Kirsty. A long time. I'd use her as a lookout in this weather, but it's too cold for her. She only leaves her dog basket during clement weather, dangerous situations or state occasions. She's a very independent beast, no point in trying to make she do something she has no intention of doing.'

'Weird,' thought the Major as he went on to the bridge wing with his binoculars.

The German ship ploughed steadily on her way and started to pull ahead. The Captain's advice had merit, it was getting late and he could use some shuteye.

He went back into the pilot house. 'Call if you need anything Captain,' as he made his way down to his cabin and found Horskjaer fast asleep.

'Good idea,' thought Bruus-Jensen, as took off his boots, hauled himself into the top bunk and soon fell sound asleep.

Chapter 12

The light of the new day arrived reluctantly. The bad weather had returned and the German ship had either got lost or given up. A further improvement of the apparent situation came when the Radio Operator reported he had tracked the German ship with the direction finder as it continued to pull ahead and then after a burst of traffic, the German ship had gone off the air.

On the bridge, the First Mate was enjoying a quiet morning watch and the Captain had turned in for a few hours. The *Girard* had slipped past the Bunsen Peninsular during the early hours and altered course to the turning point at the tip of Gedser Odde. The duty cook delivered a Smørrebrød of smoked herring with egg and a large mug of Kaffe punch.

Below, the Major rose to take a quick shower whilst the Treasury Minister stayed fast asleep until the coast was clear in the on-suite bathroom. He dressed for the new day, and made his way to the galley. His men had beaten him to it, but arrived in time to see one of his corporals grab the bottom of one of the stewards, causing mirth all round. As the ranger in question was well known to have one wife and two girlfriends, the Major thought the behaviour fitted a familiar pattern.

The steward turned around, and with an enormous 'haymaker' sent the corporal crashing to the deck. The amused soldiers were making one hell of a racket until they caught sight of the Major, with his famous dark look face. Total silence fell in the galley. He looked at the steward. It was a she, a large girl by any standards, more use to wrestling sheep on a farm then dealing with rowdy soldiers. Sheep, soldiers, it was all the same to this girl, no problem whatsoever, they all ended up on their back one way or another.

The Major broke into a grin. His corporal still lay dazed on the floor wondering what on earth had hit him. The Major motioned one of his soldiers to assist the stricken corporal into a waiting chair. He looked at the stewardess and ordered a cooked breakfast. She hesitated until she saw his badge of rank and being unsure did his bidding reluctantly.

The Major called his Sergeant Major over to his table to discuss the day's programme between large mouthfuls of breakfast. Given the events during the night's run, he ordered Kjaergaard to organise three man squads, one to each of the AA guns, and to prepare them for action. The Sergeant Major asked if the Major wanted the guns test fired.

'The ammunition is onboard then?' asked the Major.

'A hundred rounds a gun, and more promised when we dock at Århus,' replied Kjaergaard.

'I leave it to your discretion,' finished the Major. 'I have some other duties to perform.'

He went to the pilot house to find that all was well, so he retreated to his cabin just in time to catch Horskjaer, beginning the struggle to make his way back into action. The last few weeks had been long and hectic, and the chance to recuperate was more than welcome.

'Good morning Major, how are things on deck,' he asked.

'Calm, apparently,' replied the Major. 'The German ship disappeared in front, and we are on the last leg to the turning point at Gedser Odde. My men are up and about, bringing the AA guns into readiness and generally getting on with things.'

'Excellent, well done,' praised the Treasury Minister. 'What's for breakfast?'

'The usual cooked ham and eggs, there's no fish at the moment. The fresh bread is very fresh, quite delicious in fact,' replied the Major.

An hour later the *Girard* heeled to port as it made the turning point at Gedser Odde. The ship's movement caused the Captain, for the first time in twenty years, to partially fall out of his bunk. He laughed at the thought of the last time, a prank played by the 'officer of the watch' on an unsuspecting crew. He wandered up to the pilot house to see what was what before going for his breakfast.

All appeared to be well until he noticed his ship had not increased speed now daylight had arrived. He asked the First Mate the reason why, only to be told he had asked, but the Chief Engineer had advised against it.

'You asked,' bellowed the Captain, his good mood vaporising in a heartbeat, 'you give the bloody orders, get on with it'

The First Mate rang on revolutions for 15 knots. The telegraph repeater did not reply.

The Captain grabbed the engine room intercom and vigorously rang the handle. The Chief answered it promptly, 'You looking for more speed Skipper? Sorry can't be done,' he said apologetically.

'Chief, speed I need, and speed I shall have. You've molly coddled those clockwork toys of yours long enough,' bawled the Captain into the mouthpiece, 'now is their time to deliver.'

'Skipper, for the last time, these engines are as old as you and me, and they're not feeling well today,' the Chief pleaded.

'Not feeling well my arse, give me fifteen knots or else,' shouted the Captain and slammed the phone back into its housing.

'What's up Skipper,' asked the First Mate.

'The engines are not feeling well today, got any aspirin?' said the Captain sarcastically.

The engine's telegraph repeaters rang on the acknowledgment of the new speed, and the Captain, seeing the ship's speed increase, made his way down to the galley. Horskjaer was receiving his breakfast from the blushing stewardess. She'd never met a government minister before, especially one this good looking. She'd heard that tragically he was a single man, but that didn't stop her from dreaming.

'Morning Minister,' the Captain said. 'Sleep well?'

'Like a teenager. Did me the world of good, how are things topside?'

'Great,' replied the Captain, just in time to hear the alarm bells ring in the pilot house and the ship slow down.

'Damn it,' said the Captain as he disappeared back to the pilot house. He found the First Mate busy on the intercom to the engine room. The First Mate brushed the Captain's questions aside as he tried to understand what had happened over the voice of his annoyed Captain.

'The port engine 'forced lube' pump is playing up and the Chief has shut down both engines as a precaution,' he reported.

The 'forced lube' pumps, one of the most vital pieces of engine room machinery, pumped lubricating oil at very high pressure and temperature around the vital parts of the engines including the main turbine bearings, and the propeller shaft main bearings to name but a few. They were sometimes known to shake themselves apart. The lube oil, if released into the environment under pressure, was known to flash-off immediately and cause a very nasty fire.

'You stay on watch,' said the Captain more calmly. 'I'll go and see what the old goat is up to.'

The Captain made his way down into the engine room and found the Chief Engineer bending over the forced lube pump in question. He asked for the status.

'Give me five minutes and I'll get the starboard engine back on-line and we can get underway again at ten knots,' he said. The words 'ten knots' were spat out in disgust.

The Captain beat a hasty retreat, knowing it would be best not to disturb a loving father in his hour of grief. If a way could be found to get the port engine back on-line, the Chief would be sure to find it, and in any event it was time for a well overdue breakfast.

On deck, the Major found his troops busy with the ship's armament. The *Girard* had been hurriedly equipped with six single gun mountings. Two 40 mm guns, mounted port and starboard on the sun deck forward of the bridge, and four 20 mm guns divided between port and starboard, one set between the two funnels, and one set mounted behind the aft funnel.

The task of bringing the AA guns into action would not be as simple as he imagined. These guns had been in long-term storage, and although in reasonable condition, a lot of work would be required to make them fully operational.

However, all things considered, the supply of weapons had been generous, although the Major considered the donors had little idea of their true value. It would be up to him to turn this gift into something serviceable.

It was fortunate that his squad included three experienced armourers, frantically rushing between the six-gun mountings, issuing orders and instructions to a confused group of the Major's men. The guns had been hurriedly disguised, but in removing the wooden frames around each gun, it would not be so easy to restore them when they entered the harbour at Århus. Would it be necessary to continue with the pretence of disguise? The Major couldn't be sure.

He made his way up to the bridge and into the pilot house. 'Is Sparks up and about yet?' he asked of the Captain, dosing in his day chair. The Captain waved his hand in the direction of the radio shack at the rear of the pilot house, which the Major took to be a 'yes'.

Bruus-Jensen entered the radio shack and found the ship's wireless operator busy with a number of messages before him, mostly in army code.

The Major left the bridge to look for his Sergeant Major who was busy harassing his troops on the funnel deck. The Major shouted for his radio man on the double in the radio shack. Kjaergaard waved his hand in acknowledgement and detailed a corporal to find the ranger in question.

Five minutes later the Major's radio specialist arrived in the radio shack. At least, he had brought his decoding equipment with him. Bruus-Jensen shoved the code messages across the desk to him and asked how long to decode them.

'About ten minutes Sir,' I'll be right back with them,' replied the specialist.

The Major stood up, 'Take a seat at this desk, no messages to leave the radio shack, OK?' he ordered.

'Yes Sir,' replied the radio specialist, as he got down to his task.

Ten minutes later the messages had been decoded. Bruus-Jensen saw nothing new and little in the way of updates of the situation from the day before. The hijacked Spanish cargo plane with the supply of new weapons and equipment had arrived and safely off-loaded its cargo at Århus.

The reply to the message concerning the mystery German ship had drawn a blank, although HQ Command did buy into the story. The situation on the border with Germany remained quiet, although troop movements were seen to be slowly building. His overall appraisal of the situation came to the conclusion little had changed, but the feeling was this wouldn't last for long.

The Major wondered what 'soon' meant. He needed time. With the *Girard* limping along at ten knots they would not reach Århus until late evening at the earliest. It would take most of the night to bring the remaining vehicles onboard, supplies of stores, food, fuel, and extra ammunition for the AA guns, which he now considered vital to the success of the mission. In his view, the shooting war could start at any time.

The Major went back into the pilot house and committed the cardinal sin of waking up the Captain in his day chair.

'Excuse me Captain,' he asked gently.

The Captain came to with a start and looked around. All was normal, his ship on the correct course, and now heading northwards to Århus through the Langelandsbaelt Channel for Spodsbjerg. They were making good time all things considered.

'Yes, Major?' he asked sleepily.

The Major asked a range of questions including the time needed to make repairs to the engine room machinery and when could full speed be resumed?

The Captain told him the repairs were going well, the Chief had the spares he needed onboard, and his 'black gang' had been hard at it all night.

All being well, the ship should dock in Århus sometime late afternoon, and if his army support team in Århus got their sorry act together, he forecast sailing on the tide at or before midnight. This included refuelling and taking on ship stores too.

'Was there anything else?' asked the Captain, with a raised eyebrow.

Bruus-Jensen thanked the Captain and went out on deck. He decided against further pretence at hiding the mission. He returned to the Radio Room and found his communications specialist jawing with Sparks. The Major sat down and scribbled out a message to the Chief of Police asking for any intelligence on German surveillance activity in Århus.

'Send that as soon as it's coded, and bring the reply as soon as it comes in,' ordered the Major.

The Major went to his cabin to find Horskjaer busy with ministerial papers. The Treasury Minister asked for an update. The Major gave him the latest news and heaved himself up into his bunk. Horskjaer could do little but accept the situation. The whole mission was now in the hands of fate, whatever that would bring.

The Minister reached into the locker next to his bunk and pulled out a long leather bag, which he opened to reveal a Kreighoff Limited Edition .375 hunting rifle. Horskjaer looked in his haversack, found his rifle cleaning kit, and set about bringing his prized possession into a state of readiness.

The Major leaned over his bunk to watch. 'That looks expensive Minister?' he said.

'It was,' replied Horskjaer, 'but well worth it. There's telescopic sight for it somewhere, I'll find it in a minute.'

'I guess it's accurate?' asked the Major.

'It certainly is,' replied Horskjaer. 'I had the gun specially made. The gun factory tested the barrel before incorporating it into the rifle. It's better than standard sniper quality. It's won me lots of competition medals, as well as good success in various hunting trips.'

'Surely you're not looking to use it on this mission,' asked the Major.

Horskjaer rested the rifle on his knees and looked up at Bruus-Jensen. Their eyes met, recognition of the unspoken realisation the mission could well turn dangerous. There was not one single piece of specific information, but both men had the same gut feeling, the mission would not be going as advertised.

'Have you shot at a target that can shoot back?' enquired the Major softly.

Horskjaer rummaged around in his bag and pulled out a towel carefully wrapped around his favourite telescopic sight. He commenced fitting it to his rifle.

Eventually, he replied to the Major's question, 'No I haven't, but my plan is to be well out of their range when I take my shot. This is not a quick action rifle, so at close quarters I expect your men to protect me. I just hope to make some use of my skills, not provide any competition for your highly trained rangers.'

The Major rolled over and pulled his beret over his eyes. The Minister needed time to himself. He was a brave man to enter into his military world, but at least he'd thought the matter through.

After lunch came welcome news when the *Girard* started to shake and vibrate with a return to full speed. The Major made his way up to the pilot house in time to see the Chief Engineer in conversation with the Captain. An emotional chief expressed regret his beloved ship had let them down, but God willing everything should be OK now.

'Well done Chief,' said the Major in a conciliatory manner. The Captain agreed with the Major, well done indeed.

'Aye aye?' said the Chief, unused to praise, 'just keep your fingers crossed. I'll be going below to keep an eye on things. I'll see what we can get out of the old girl.'

'What age is she?' asked the Major.

'Commissioned in Glasgow in 1924, when me and the Captain were younger but not so wise. Now it's the other way about, grey hair, what's left of it, but plenty of cunning. We should get eighteen knots out of her, at least until we reach port. Hope there's plenty of fuel when we arrive; at this speed the old girl has a big thirst,'

The Chief stomped off back to his world of steam and shining brass wheels. The Captain looked around to check his watchkeepers in the pilot house were all wide-awake. He went outside to the port wing of his bridge, took some sightings, returned to his chart table and updated the *Girard's* position. He took out his slide rule, and calculated the time left on the voyage to Århus.

'Major,' he said, 'we should be berthing about 4.30 pm. I would get some rest if I was you and your men too.'

The Major agreed with the sentiment and went on deck to find his Sergeant Major. He was almost ready to the fire one of the 20 mm AA guns on the funnel deck.

'Having fun Sergeant Major?' he asked.

'Stand back Sir,' as the Sergeant Major loaded the gun and bid his newly trained gunner to take up the correct position to fire. Checking the range was clear he ordered five single shots. The 20 mm gun fired for the first time in twenty years, its loud report echoing over the sea. Satisfied, the Sergeant Major stood back, congratulating his gun crew for a job well done, including not hitting anything in his immediate vicinity.

'Good, well done Sergeant Major,' said the Major. 'As soon as the test firing of the guns has been completed, stand the men down until we dock at 4.30 pm. Muster the men in the passengers lounge at 4.00 pm for a briefing. I'm off to rest and get some sleep. Until then disturb only to announce the 'second coming' of the Lord.'

On his way to his bunk, the Major stopped off at the Radio Room to collect the latest messages.

All he received came in the form of a status report from Århus, where apparently all was ready. With no further communications from the Palace, and on the understanding that 'no news was good news', the Major stood his radio specialist down and made of in the general direction of his bunk for some much-needed shut-eye.

The Minister had also called it a day, and soon the cabin was in restful darkness until it the time arrived for the next phase of the mission.

Chapter 13

Departure from Århus

The Captain was as good as his word when late afternoon saw the *Girard* steaming at full speed towards the harbour of Århus. Familiar landmarks came into view and the Captain felt pleased with the day's progress.

The Major's men mustered in the passenger's lounge as ordered. The Major hurried into the lounge. He hated being late, but he'd at last succumbed to the tiredness that had been dogging him for the last week. He called his men to attention and bid the Sergeant Major sound-off roll call. His men thought this a bit formal and shuffled into some sort of order.

The Sergeant Major, seeing the look of thunder on the face of his Major, quickly took charge and soon had his men smartened up. He stood the men at ease and reported to the Major all were present and correct.

The Major stepped in front of his men and looked them over. They were all in relaxed rig, something he didn't remember ordering. Still, it hardly mattered with all that had been going on. Time to get a grip.

'Right', he started, 'most of you have enjoyed a restful morning, remember it well; it could be your last for a while. When loading has completed I want everyone properly dressed in clean battle fatigues, and that includes berets and a shine on your boots'.

The Major continued, 'When the ship docks, the first to be loaded will be our two missing trucks. They are loaded with the most modern up-to-date equipment for you soldiers; courtesy of the Sergeant Major here. This equipment must be unloaded and set to one side. Sergeant Major, detail four men to sort it ready for distribution after we sail.'

'Yes Sir,' replied the Sergeant Major.

The Treasury Minister unsuspectingly wandered into the passenger lounge. The Sergeant Major snapped his men to attention, and reported them to a startled Minister.

'Thank you Sergeant Major, stand the men at ease,' said the Major.

'Gentlemen this is Eric Horskjaer, our country's Treasury Minister. I'll explain why he's here later'.

119

'Next,' continued the Major, 'a squad of six men will partially unload the two trucks with the sealed ammunition cases under the supervision of the Minister. This cargo will be equally distributed between all four trucks. This cargo will then be covered by the heavy tarpaulins and nailed. Don't ask what's in the cases, it's for your own good.'

When that's finished, load our supplies, food, field rations, water, fuel for cooking, fuel for the trucks, et al, equally among the four trucks. Get your kit bags loaded as well. The Sergeant Major has a list of who is assigned to which truck. Finally, after we arrive at our destination, load your field backpacks and your new equipment into the trucks. I want you to take your discarded equipment with you if there's room.'

'So,' continued the Major. 'What's this all about? Well, war is coming whether we like it or not. The assessment of our King, and our Government, is Germany will invade our country and Norway together. Denmark will not fight, there is little point. But the Norwegians? They have a difficult country they can defend for a long time.'

The Major paused, noting the rapt attention of his men. Fortunately, there were only a few worried faces. He would address that in a minute.

'Our mission; our mission is to spirit away before the very eyes of the German's; yes gentlemen our country has been under the surveillance of German intelligence for some time; something they want very badly. It's our mission to see they don't get it.'

'All being well, we will get to Norway before anybody else, in which case you'll wonder what the fuss is all about. I hope so. The fact the Minister is here with us, tells you all you need to know. The Minister will stay with us until the completion of the mission. He's no soldier, but I don't think he'll be a hindrance. He's one of the best shots in the country. However, I want two volunteers to stay with him at all times soon as we land in Norway, Sergeant Major you choose.'

The Major paused again to introduce the Captain who had just joined them.

'Sergeant Major, I need another two volunteers for two army motor-cycles for scouting and outrider duties. Finally, our stay in Århus will be as short as possible. All those not working for the Sergeant Major will report to the Captain to help his crew. Dismiss.'

The Sergeant Major had his men fall out and make their way to the galley, probably the last chance they would get a hot square meal in peace and comfort.

Horskjaer came up behind the Major. 'That was very efficient; your men look ready for action.'

'Thanks,' the Major replied. 'Most are, there are one or two I shall have a quiet word with later on. They just have to turn the skills they have so arduously learnt into action. Let's eat.'

At the appointed time, the *Girard* sailed into the entrance to Århus Harbour at an alarming speed. The Major didn't know a lot about ship handling, but sensed the Captain had remembered an infrequently executed manoeuvre and waited with interest.

Just inside the harbour wall, the Captain already had the helm hard down to port with the port engine building up to full astern. The stern of the *Girard* swung hard to starboard as she passed inside the outer mole wall. As the *Girard* began to shake and spin about her axis through the intended turn, the Captain reduced the starboard engine to half ahead. With the ship nearing a 180-degree change in her heading, the Captain achieved a fair amount of sideways movement in the *Girard*.

To counter the swing the Captain chose his moment carefully, ordering full astern on both engines with the wheel amidships. To complete the evolution the Captain ordered a finely judge burst of full ahead, bringing the steam ferry to a halt, pointing out to sea, but drifting sideways into the fenders protecting the harbour wall.

Two small harbour tugs moved quickly to hold *Girard* in place against the harbour wall. The dockside gang, ignoring the obvious need to moor the ship, concentrated on getting two fuel-oil hoses onboard and connected up to the *Girard* fuel bunkers. As the fuel hoses started to snake vigorously under the pressure of refilling the ship's depleted tanks, the dockside gang completed the docking of *Girard*.

The Major looked over at the outer mole wall and saw the array of vehicles waiting for the *Girard*. In the vanguard, he saw his two 'all terrain' five-ton trucks and behind them a large assortment of heavily laden transports.

The Major's men and the ship's crew began the race against time to complete loading the *Girard* as quickly as possible. Time was now very much against them, with the vital need to get underway as quickly as possible. The ship's crane swung the two all terrain five-ton trucks onboard. The Major's men worked frantically to secure them for the voyage to Norway.

The soldiers soon had the contents of each truck emptied on the cargo deck of the *Girard* to see what supplies the Sergeant Major had organised. The Major's men shouted with relief and joy, as they found the latest up-to-date equipment they so badly needed.

The Sergeant Major had his men move everything to one side, as it became more important to distribute the sealed ammunition cases containing the gold and gems equally among the four trucks, a task completed under the watchful eye of the Treasury Minister. With the ammunition cases covered over with heavy tarpaulins, now came the time to load the remainder of supplies for the ship and army alike.

The Sergeant Major seemed to be everywhere at once ordering, cajoling and urging his men to even greater efforts. By early evening, the loading of supplies on to the *Girard* had almost come to an end. The last items to load were the two army motorcycles, brought down from the local army base. Their riders did not appreciate being parted from them, but the Major point blank refused to take them with him.

The Major raced up to the bridge deck where the Captain watched progress with growing impatience. 'Ready Major,' he asked.

Receiving an affirmative, the Captain went to the starboard side of the bridge wing to look down at the refuelling operation and saw one refuelling hose in the process of being disconnected and returned to shore, whilst the second hose still snaked vigorously. The Captain sent the Second Mate to ask the Chief Engineer how much longer he needed for refuelling. The question was not well received by the Chief busy monitoring the refuelling operation.

The Captain was at a loss to know where all this bunker fuel was being stored. The operation was well past the time it normally took. The First Mate came onto the bridge wing and looked down at the refuelling operation.

'Where's the old goat pumping all that bunkers?' asked the First Mate.

'Only God and the Chief know that. At a guess, he must have resurrected some tankage in the double bottoms. You could go and ask,' suggested the Captain.

'Not likely,' replied the First Mate. 'I don't think our illustrious Chief Engineer is in any mood for interruptions'.

The Captain went into the pilot house and spoke into the intercom to the engine room. 'You ready down there?' he asked.

The footplate man told him the boilers were close to lifting the safety valves; they had made that much steam. The Captain knew his Chief Engineer hated lifting the boiler safety valves, in his eyes a cardinal sin. That the safety valves were close to lifting was a sure sign the Chief would soon terminate the refuelling operation and get the *Girard* under way.

Five minutes later the Chief stood up, made a signal to the refuelling team on the jetty and stomped below to the engine room. The Captain called the Second Mate to single up all lines. He needn't have bothered, the Second Mate, seeing the Chief disappear below had already ordered the task done. The Captain waved away the gangway, motioned the Second Mate to slip all lines and waited a few minutes to let the wind coming over the outer mole wall to push the bow of the *Girard* away from the dockside wall.

'First Mate, ring on both engines,' he commanded. The boiler safety valves over his head on the forward funnel were starting to lift and chatter, with wisps of live steam starting to seep out.

'Time to go,' he thought. 'Mustn't lift the Chief's precious safety valves.'

The ships telegraphs rang back with their loud clanging noise; the engine room was ready.

'Revolutions nine zero, speed for ten knots,' the Captain barked at the helmsman. 'Keep your wheel amidships.'

'Aye aye Sir,' replied the helmsman.

The stern of the *Girard* squatted deep into the sea as the burst of power got her quickly underway. The slight chattering of the boiler safety valves stopped. The Captain watched as the ship cleared the outer mole wall. He ordered a course change to clear the harbour anchorage zone. The *Girard* passed the harbour outer marker buoy with increasing speed and she was on her way.

'Helmsman, steer new course 130 degrees, and ring on full speed ahead,' ordered the Captain as he went back inside the pilot house to update the chart. The telegraph repeaters clanged their confirmation of the new speed.

The Major, leaning over the wooden cap on the bridge wing bulkhead, looked up at the night sky. The weather had started to close in again. It would be another murky night's run, which would cause everyone in the pilot house to keep a nervous eye on their surroundings.

The two ship's funnels behind him were belching vast clouds of black smoke as the black squad below worked hard to meet the demand for steam.

The *Girard* started to vibrate as the main engines worked their way up to full power.

Tonight's journey would not be an economy run on the long voyage to Norway.

Chapter 14

The *Girard* left harbour just after a quarter to ten in the evening. The turn-around had been an excellent result all round. The ship made good progress as she left behind the safety of the Danish shore and started to reach deep into the Kattegat.

The Captain smiled at the thought of his schoolteacher's irreverent teachings about the name, apparently derived from the Dutch words for Kat (cat) and Gat (hole or rectum). Medieval captains compared this region to a hole so narrow even a cat would have difficulty creeping through the many reefs and shallow waters. This Captain was the master of these waters, and they held little difficulty for him.

The Major relaxed in the radio shack at the back of the pilot House, reading through the latest set of decoded messages. Apart from the usual messages concerning the logistic details of the mission, three messages were marked 'Top Secret', which after primary decoding remained in a simple code for him to complete in the comfort of his cabin. He found the Treasury Minister taking a short nap.

The Major cleared the top of the small cabin desk and got to work.

The first 'Top Secret' message gave a rundown of the situation in the Kingdom of Denmark as of midday that day, which did not make good reading. The exit into the North Sea, as expected, was being heavily patrolled by units of the German Navy North Sea fleet. How tempting it would be on this dark and unpleasant evening to attempt a daring dash across the North Sea to the UK. Unsubstantiated and unconfirmed reports of new minefields also ruled out the option the Major would have loved to consider. Still, he had his orders and saw no little reason to disagree with them.

The second top-secret message gave updated details of contacts in the Norwegian government regarding his mission. A number of senior policemen and army commanders had also been added to the list at the last moment.

The third top-secret message was short, incomplete and left the Major with increasing concern. With a time date stamp barely ninety minutes old, it started off with a warning about increasing German military movements and increasing amounts of radio jamming being carried out by the 'Wehrmacht' signal units. The last two sentences were increasingly corrupt until the words just petered out into garbage.

Radio jamming meant only one thing in the Major's mind. The invasion, had it started? When it would start, and for sure impossible to know, and much too late to do anything about it. Perhaps they were already in a desperate race, how to tell?

Horskjaer rolled over on to his side. 'Anything of interest Per?' he asked, pointing to the folder of messages.

The Major briefed him on his concerns. The Minister's face covered in a dark frown. 'If it's of any comfort, I have the authority given to me by Parliament to order the cargo to be jettisoned over the stern of the ship. This Is very top secret, and you must tell no one.'

'Yes Sir,' the Major replied.

'I must also tell you,' continued the Minister, 'it's of the vital importance to at least get the diamonds to safety. Machine tools will be the vital factor in this war. Not only must the Germans not lay their hands on them, it's vital this resource makes its way to our allies.'

The Major excused himself and went to the pilot house and found the Captain sitting in his day chair looking out at the inky blackness of the night. The Major took the Captain to one side and brought him up to date with a condensed version of the latest news. The Captain's stoic look said it all. He understood fate was about to play its dirty tricks upon his vessel, but he didn't have to accept the impending misfortune.

'Major,' suggested the Captain. 'I think you should do the rounds of your men. Make sure they're all prepared, and make sure they have their life jackets with them.'

'Should they wear them?' asked the Major.

'Not just now, but any alarm, they must don them immediately. Have they practised this yet?'

'Not sure,' replied the Major. 'That's a good idea, I'll go and check.'

The Major went down to the passengers lounge. Someone had opened the bar.

'Sergeant Major,' he shouted out. 'Where is the Sergeant Major?'

One of his corporals told him the Sergeant Major had gone below for a shower, and the two sergeants were checking the gun crews.

'Who opened the bar?' demanded the Major.

The corporal told him the ship's steward opened the bar, as always, outside Danish waters. No one had told him not to.

'OK Corporal,' relented the Major, 'two drinks each, and no more. After, we have practised putting on our life jackets.'

The Sergeant Major hurried back into the passengers lounge.

'It's OK, Sergeant Major,' said the Major. 'Get the men used to putting on their life jackets; then they can finish their drinks. No more than two each, then get them rested. Any alarms, no matter what, they muster here in the passenger's lounge wearing life jackets. Where are the two sergeants?'

'On decking checking the gun crews; the Captain wants them stood-to for the majority of the voyage,' said Kjaergaard.

The Major went on deck and found the guns crews trying to hide from the night weather. The two sergeants were having a hard time with the reluctant sailors. He assessed the situation. Having gun crews freezing in this kind of weather benefited nobody. For a start, they had little warm winter clothing. The Major looked around the deck area and saw a couple of padlocked locker doors. He sent one of the sergeants to fetch the Second Mate.

'Yes Sir?' asked the Second Mate when he arrived.

'Ah yes,' replied the Major. 'I need one of these lockers opened up for the gun crews to shelter in.'

'Right away,' agreed the Second Mate.

He returned in two minutes with the keys and opened them up. The first locker contained only what appeared to be junk, old cordage and had little space. The other, a rarely used workspace, suited the Major's requirements exactly. It even possessed a black electric radiator. He organised the gun crews to take turns in sheltering from the cold, and warned against anyone trying to grab a quick nap. He didn't want to tell them the whole story, but made it plain that if the voyage turned nasty, they had better be fully prepared.

The Major asked where the ammunition brought onboard at Århus had been stored. The Sergeant mumbled something inconclusive, which the Major took as a 'don't know'. Five seconds later the two sergeants and the gun crews were busy hunting down the precise location of the ammunition and bringing it up to where it might conceivably be of use. The Major had the smaller of the two locker rooms emptied by the simple method of ditching everything over the side of the ship, an ideal storage area to make a 'ready use' ammunition locker.

With the task finished, and the gun crews dressed in their German greatcoats and coal scuttle helmets, the Major returned to his cabin for a snooze. He found the Minister lying on his back, wide awake, nervous, but determined not to show it.

'Nervous Minister?' asked the Major.

'No, not really,' came the reply.

'You're no more nervous than anyone else,' said the Major 'It's OK, join the club.'

The watch on the Major's wrist moved slowly to 2 am. 'So far so good,' he thought.

The *Girard* should have passed north of Goteborg by now; perhaps they were going to have a tranquil voyage after all. The shrill noise of the ship's alarm followed by a sharp turn to port ruined that speculation. The Major rushed to the pilot house, with the Minister in close pursuit.

The Captain was busy conning the ship. The Major rushed to the bridge wing to check the gun crews were closed up and pleased to see they had.

'What's up Skipper?' asked the Major.

'I let the damn dog out on the port bridge wing to do her business, and she starts yelping like mad. Then she dashes across to the other side, to the starboard side, same thing,' replied the Captain.

'Did she give a direction?' asked the Major.

'Damn it, no,' said the Captain. 'Her nose is pointing all over the place. We must be in the middle of a convoy for Christ sakes.'

'Rubbish,' snorted the Major.

'Major, Kirsty has never been wrong,' replied the Captain. 'Better stand your men too.'

Before the Major had a chance to take any action the *Girard* narrowly missed the stern of a large troop transport as she cut under her stern.

'Helmsman, revolutions nine zero, speed for ten knots', shouted out the Captain. 'Bring your course twelve degrees to port.'

'Christ that was close,' he swore to himself.

The *Girard's* course became parallel to the transport ship and was still overtaking it. The Captain ordered a further reduction to eight knots and positioned the ferry on the starboard bow of the transport ship. He was still too close. The Captain started a string of minor course alterations to open up the gap between the two ships.

The Captain sensed a new danger and rushed out of the pilot house to the starboard bridge wing with his Labrador behind him.

'Seek, Kirsty,' he ordered.

The dog stood on her hind legs, her paws resting on the wooden cap of the guardrail and started to sniff the breeze. She looked out to the starboard beam and started to bark. The Captain knew another column of the convoy existed over to his right. Judging as best he could, he concluded he could be in the middle of two columns of ships. He ordered all stop on both engines.

The First Mate arrived on the bridge and reported all spare hands had been placed around the *Girard* as lookouts.

The radio operator beckoned for the Captain to come to the Radio Shack door.

'Yes Sparks,' asked the Captain.

'Anybody speak or understand German, someone is broadcasting in plain language,' asked the radio operator.

The Treasury Minister moved to the radio shack. 'Sparks' sat him down and put a set of headphones on his head. The Minister listened intently and looked up at the Captain.

'Someone is calling for an escort warship to investigate a ship out of position in the convoy,' he said. 'Now what?'

The Captain thought furiously. What to do? He turned around to Bruus-Jensen.

'Major,' he ordered, 'make sure the gun crews are closed up, with the guns pointing up and outboard. Get your troops dressed for combat, with their new German weapons, and wearing the German uniforms and helmets. Keep them inside the passenger's lounge for now.'

'Anything else we can do?' asked the Major.

'A German Colonel would be useful, high family name type, black leather coat, a Lugar strapped around his waist, someone with the air of a top level executive Nazi officer.'

The Major looked across at the Treasury Minister. The Minister looked up,

'You need me?' he asked.

The Major shouted for his Sergeant Major to come from the funnel deck organising the gun crews.

'Yes Major?' he asked, as he arrived.

'What do you have in the way of German uniforms in that job lot you acquired from the Third Reich?' he asked.

'Anything in particular?' enquired the Sergeant Major.

'I think the Captain is looked for something like an SS Colonel, the type usually with a double barrel name', replied the Major.

The Labrador started barking again.

'Visitors,' cursed the Captain. 'Didn't take long'.

A fast heavily armed escort ship came quickly into view and positioned herself alongside the *Girard*, her forward gun trained directly upon the ship's bridge.

'Whoops,' thought the Captain. 'This is getting serious.'

The Sergeant Major dragged the Treasury Minister into the pilot house, just as a strong searchlight lit up the scene. The pair of them raced below, past the galley and out onto the cargo deck under the funnel deck overhang. The Sergeant Major dived into a large crate and started throwing its contents over the deck. The Major ducked into the pilot house. It would not be a good idea to be seen at this juncture wearing his distinctive dark green Danish Army Rangers uniform.

On the bridge, the Captain stalled for time. Positioned on the port bridge wing conning position, he switched on the intercom to the helming position inside the pilot house.

'Helmsman, ring down to the engine room, tell them Fritz is alongside, and we are going to need a lot of cunning to get out of this one,' he said.

The German escort ship started to close in; its Commandant with a loud-hailer in his hand. The German Commandant started shouting questions across the gap between the two ships.

Captain Ditlevsen spoke quietly into the helmsman intercom. 'Ask the Chief to blow soot on both funnels, and I need a big blast of steam with it too,' he ordered.

The Captain stood up on his toes as if to answer the German Commandant when the big blast of soot and steam roared out of both funnels accompanied by a fair amount of noise. The black soot landed over the aft section of the German escort ship. The German escort ship moved away. The blast of soot seemed to go on forever.

'OK Helmsman,' he called. 'Cease blowing soot.'

The German escort ship returned to its previous position alongside. As the German Commandant prepared to hail over to the *Girard*, the Captain spoke into the intercom, 'Ring down to the Chief, tell him to stop the port engine, and don't use the telegraphs, the damn things can be heard all over the Kattegat.'

As the *Girard* lost speed, the Captain asked for ten degrees of starboard wheel.

The German escort ship prepared for another attempt to come alongside when the Captain ordered the helmsman to call the engine room for 'all stop' on both engines, with a large release steam from the emergency blow-off vent on the outside of the forward funnel.

The German escort ship went into sudden reverse to stay with the Danish ferry, quickly closing the distance between the two ships. The Captain pretended he was rushing around his bridge in a panic. Just as the German Commandant started to hail over, the Treasury Minister arrived on the bridge wing by way of the pilot house.

The Sergeant Major had excelled himself. Here was the epitome of an

SS Colonel, complete with a long leather overcoat, jack boots, regulation Lugar pistol strapped around his waist, and wearing the correct cap of rank complete with the dreaded skull and bones emblem.

The searchlight from the German escort ship caught the full glory of the SS uniform. With a pounding heart, Eric Horskjaer moved into action. He marched to the edge of the bridge wing and pointed at the searchlight and waved it away. It didn't move. He took out his Lugar pistol and aimed it at the searchlight, holding his arm rock steady.

The German Commandant shouted a command. The searchlight moved its beam to a position aft along the deck of the *Girard*. The Minister slowly lowered his arm and holstered his weapon.

The German Commandant used his loudhailer to ask for details of the ship and its mission. The Minister stood rock still, acted with total contempt for the questions, and indicated Captain Ditlevsen should stand by his side. The Captain brought his loudhailer with him. By this time the Major was getting concerned as to how the next few minutes would go.

The Sergeant Major called him into the pilot house. 'I reckon the Minister could use a hand, put these on,' he said, handing the Major a long black trench coat, a black felt Homburg hat and a Lugar pistol and holster. The Sergeant Major had already so dressed, the spitting image of any Gestapo officer he had ever seen. The Major quickly changed.

'Ready Sergeant Major?' he asked nervously. 'Let's go.'

The two of them marched onto the bridge wing and reported to the Minister with Nazi salutes and shouted 'Heil Hitlers'.

Horskjaer was almost taken aback but recovered in time to give a return salute used only by senior members of the German General Staff. Captain Ditlevsen stood back not knowing what to think. It was hard not to smile, but this was no play-acting

The Minister turned to the Captain and asked for the loudhailer. The Minister shouted across the water to the German Commandant, that his name was 'Coronal Count Friedrich von Esebeck Freiherr' of the SS Polizei Grenadiers Division, commanding a special mission comprised of members of the Waffen SS Special Forces Regiment.

The German Commandant demanded to know the name of his ship and basic details of the 'special mission'.

The Major moved to the side of the Minister and told him the Gestapo wished to know the German Commandant's name.

The Minister gave the Major his most withering look, turned towards the German Commandant and shouted across the Gestapo demanded to know his name.

The German Commandant was in a quandary, these people looked like the real thing. His attention was directed by one of his lookouts to twenty tough looking 'storm troopers', obviously carrying the latest in special forces weapons, drawn up along the funnel deck facing the German escort ship.

Junior Commandants of the German 'Kriegsmarine' were not known for their love of the Gestapo, and this one was no exception. Time to go. The German Commandant gave his name and rank, and told them they should follow his ship. He would guide them to the rear of the convoy's outer western column where they should stay at the regulation distance of two cables until the time came for them to break away to commence their mission. The German Commandant finished with a Nazi salute as he ordered half speed ahead.

The German escort ship began a slow turn to port with the *Girard* following two cables astern. Ten minutes later the two ships came up behind a cargo tramp steamer that everyone on the Danish ferry hoped was indeed the last ship on that side of the convoy. The Major and the Sergeant Major disappeared inside the pilot house.

'That was lucky,' breathed the Major in obvious relief.

'Yes Sir,' replied the Sergeant Major getting out of his Gestapo get-up. 'Shall I get the men on the funnel deck to fall out?'

The Major replied in the affirmative as he looked on as Captain Ditlevsen conned the *Girard* into position behind the tramp steamer.

Fifteen minutes later, the German escort ship disappeared to the head of the convoy, and they were left all alone, trailing two cables behind the tramp steamer in front of them. The Captain came into the warmth of the pilot house.

'Sparks,' he yelled out, 'what's going on in the wonderful world of German communications?'

Sparks popped his head around his door, 'Very little Sir, there's no Morse traffic and any voice traffic is very short and sweet. I think the Escort Commandant made a brief report, presumably to a major warship at the head of the convoy, but I didn't understand much of it.'

The Captain turned around to the Minister. 'That escort ship will be back, maybe just to check or maybe to bring up the rear of the convoy. We'll have to decide when to break away and to where? This convoy must be heading to Oslo, so we need to put our thinking caps on.'

The Minister looked out at the weather, it was still on their side, just, but the time between snowstorms started to get longer.

'Captain, where are we?' asked the Minister.

The Captain moved to his chart table, made some perfunctory updates and confirmed they'd reached the Skagerrak. The shallow water of the Kattegat had been left behind, as he could no longer smell the land. They all looked at each other.

The Major opened the discussion with the options, none of which were very good, and the Minister told him so. The Sergeant Major asked the obvious question; which would be the easiest port to get into, given that the Norwegian coastline along the Skagerrak was fractured and difficult.

The Captain consulted his chart and from the chart table brought out a land map of the area.

'Gentlemen,' he started, 'the German Convoy is steaming at six to eight knots. We can put on seventeen. We could break away, move to the west, swing around ahead of the convoy and try and make it to Oslo before the invasion fleet gets there.'

'The alternative is to head for the port of Larvik. We would arrive at first light. There's a good harbour that's easy to get into. We'll unload your men and trucks and you can hightail to the north as fast as you can go. You could make Oslo in, say, six hours or less.'

The Minister spoke, 'I like the idea of Larvik, we can gain time, warn the Norwegians of the invasion, and it gives you the chance to return your ship to Copenhagen in one piece.

The Sergeant Major spoke up, 'Shouldn't we radio on ahead of the German invasion force and warn the Norwegian government?'

'No,' said the Captain. 'We're too damn close to the German invasion fleet. They'd get a fix right away and be on to us in a minute. No, we'll wait our chance, slip away and high tail it for Larvik.'

The German invasion convoy continued at its plodding pace. The officers manning the bridge of the *Girard* became impatient for the arrival of the next batch of bad weather.

Captain Ditlevsen sat at his navigation table. He needed to fix his position before he started rushing around the Skagerrak at full speed. At last one of the lookouts reported clear sky of which he could make good use. Taking his sextant from its case, the Captain went out onto the bridge wing to take a sighting of the North Star. As he took the sighting, he called out 'fixed', and the Second Mate noted the exact time. Back at the navigation table, the good Captain took only a few minutes to calculate his position. He marked it on the chart and marked his current course on the chart in soft pencil, noting the time.

The skies appeared to be clearing, not what was needed. He went over to the engine room intercom, vigorously wound the handle and waited for someone to reply. The Chief Engineer answered, in his normal wide-awake voice.

'Yes Skipper, can I help you?' he asked.

'Chief, we're waiting for the weather to close in again; then we're going cut and run from this convoy, swing around to the west and make for Larvik at full speed. Whilst we're waiting for the weather I think I'll try falling back and see if we can't slip off the end of the column. Try dropping five revolutions for me, and let's see what we can manufacture.'

The Chief hung up without replying, went over to the main steam valves and slowly adjusted them until the Captain had his reduction in speed. The ruse appeared to be working, as the tramp steamer in front slowly pulled away.

The German escort ship appeared out of nowhere, busy shepherding her flock, a thankless task at the best of times. A Morse lamp started to blink out its message. There was no need to read it, as the Captain called for a resumption of speed. The German escort ship, barely satisfied, moved back up the column of the convoy.

The Captain turned around to his First Mate, 'Efficient bastard, just what we didn't need. Any sign of the weather closing in?'

The First Mate went to the bridge wing; it had at least clouded over and he could smell snow. He returned to the warmth of the pilot house.

'Shouldn't be too long,' he remarked. 'Let's have coffee first.'

He pulled out a bottle of schnapps, as one of the lookouts did the rounds with the coffee pot. He poured a large measure into his coffee.

A strong gust of wind hit the *Girard*, heralding the onset of one of the Skagerrak's most endearing features, a Skagerrak Depression. The Major asked what a Skagerrak Depression was. The Captain told him it came after a secondary depression had formed after the arrival of weather fronts from a primary depression in Norway. The fronts usually stalled because of the mountain chains between Norway and Sweden, intensifying rapidly, bringing bad weather and gales to the whole region. The convoy in front became obscured by the arrival of the bad weather.

The Captain saw his chance and ordered 'Port ten, steer two eight zero degrees, ring on full speed ahead.'

The helmsman put the helm down and brought the *Girard* onto her new course. He rang on full speed: the telegraph repeaters clanging out their strident acknowledgement.

The *Girard* picked up speed as she turned onto the new course, amid the cacophony of sounds and vibrations of a ship running at full speed in increasingly bad weather. The Major came into the pilot house. The Captain told him they were on their way. He went to the navigation table and marked the alteration of course and the time. He planned to hold this course, assuming he wasn't interrupted, for twenty minutes, then he would change course and make directly for Larvik. He completed marking his course on the chart, calculated the distances to run and told the Major they should reach Larvik at 5.30 am, God willing.

The Captain told the Major the sea would build quickly in the storm which would hit them soon, and his men best be prepared for a rough ride.

'Make sure they are all on their backs in the passengers lounge,' he advised.

The Captain was as good as his word. The storm struck with the expected ferocity and the *Girard* started to plough through the quickly building seas. The Major ordered four of his men go aft to check the trucks and cargo were securely fastened, and then he took to his cabin. He wasn't the world's greatest sailor, and getting turned-in on his back, as the Captain suggested, would limit the seasickness that would strike him.

The *Girard* continued to make good time. She was built for this type of weather, her long lean hull made little fuss of the building waves. Short sharp waves, close together, vicious and high sided, unlike the longer waves experienced in the oceans of the world.

Every now and then a wave would break high and hard over the bow of the *Girard* with a bang, causing the ship to shudder and shake as she shouldered the sea aside. Throughout the night the *Girard* made good her escape from the German invasion convoy.

The Captain and crew manning the bridge remained on tender hooks. The radio operator, spent a hectic time monitoring the airwaves for any signs the German escort ship was looking for them or had smelt a rat. The Major assigned one of his German-speaking soldiers to help. He knew a few of the frequencies in use by the German invasion fleet, and these remained thankfully quiet. He picked up the occasional voice traffic, short curt messages, assumed to come from the German Commander of the invasion forces.

The messages meant little except to the intended recipients. The only value gained from monitoring this German traffic was the radio direction loop indicated the source of the radio signals. He passed the relative bearings to the skipper who marked them on his chart, giving some idea of the progress of the German invasion fleet as it made its way up the Skagerrak into the Norwegian Fjords. Captain Ditlevsen, pleased to see an increasing distance open up between his ship and the Germans, as his diverging course hurried them away from possible discovery.

He prayed the sea between himself and Larvik remained empty of other ships, his lookouts would see little in this weather. The storm remained with them for some time, offering welcome cover but increasing the risks associated with charging around without being able to see what lay ahead.

The duty watch changed over at 4 am. The deck crew and the stokers/mechanics in the black gang below were grateful to get a few hours rest. Down in the passengers lounge, the Major's men were getting what rest they could. They were dressed ready for disembarkation in Larvik. They were spread out over the well-worn carpet, using their backpacks as head rests. A few smoked a quiet cigarette. Most were fast asleep, the only known remedy to keep seasickness at bay. The Major joined his men in the passengers lounge, leaving Horskjaer the luxury of having the cabin to himself.

Bruus-Jensen put his thoughts about the new day to one side. He was prepared to admit it could be going to get exciting, but the thoughts of danger tempered his enthusiasm. Danger could bring causalities to his men. They were well trained, more than prepared, but the new day would be their big test.

Up on the bridge, the Captain remained in his day chair in the pilot house. Its deeply upholstered padded bolsters and armrests provided good comfort for a long spell on watch. The Captain dozed and his watch keepers around him did little to disturb his chance to get some rest.

They all knew that tomorrow, already here, would be more than an unusually busy day.

Chapter 15

Lights from the Norwegian mainland came into view just after 5.30am. The first light, the Svenner lighthouse at Indre Skagerak, and its occulant cycle, was immediately recognised by the Second Mate. He made his way to the navigation table, marked the bearing on the chart and measured off the remaining distance to run. They would make the harbour entrance in less than forty minutes.

Below in the galley, the cooks rushed to prepare a substantial hot breakfast for the troops. Get them fed, get them onshore and hopefully return to a normal routine. The Second Mate detailed one of the lookouts to go below and rouse the 'passengers' in the passengers lounge.

Most of the Major's men were stiff from a night on a hard carpet, and some still felt a little queasy from the bad weather. No matter, the Major, now wide-awake from an excellent sleep, leapt into the delightful task getting his men into action. Some of the troops sloped off to the washroom, few bothered to shave. Most of them made the toilet their first and last port of call.

The Sergeant Major brought news from the bridge that all remained quiet, and with no further news of the German invasion force, it was assumed the convoy would shortly pass from the Skagerrak and enter the Norwegian fjords.

On the bridge, the steward served a tired Captain Ditlevsen a hot steaming cooked breakfast on a large tray. The Captain looked out, but there was little to see outside the pilot house. Captain Ditlevsen asked one of the crew to let his Labrador out onto the bridge wing to do his business. Kirsty the Labrador had no interest in leaving his warm and comfortable dog basket. The Second Mate put his coffee down, took a hold of his collar and led him outside.

The dog went to his favourite corner of the bridge, but the bad weather had stripped it off his carefully distributed smells. He raised a tired leg and renewed marking his territory, and looked around the deck. The dog looked out to sea with total disinterest, and wandered back into the warmth of the pilot house, only to be shown the door on the other side. He went reluc-

136

tantly to the other bridge wing. He sniffed the air; there was nothing out there to bark at. The Labrador made his way back inside and sat at the Captain's chair. The expected biscuit failed to arrive. Kirsty made his presence known, and a biscuit duly descended from the hand of his master above. He wolfed it down and retreated to his basket for a well-earned rest.

The *Girard* was fast approaching the outer navigation buoy marking the entrance to the Port of Larvik. The Captain considered arriving at Larvik unannounced being one thing, but arriving at full steam ahead would be another. He looked over at the helmsman and ordered a reduction of speed to fourteen knots.

The steam ferry was still blacked out, and Norway still technically at peace, but not for long he mused. He ordered the steaming lights illuminated, commanded the helmsman to ring on half speed ahead, and maintain course and speed at ten knots.

The Major and his men were getting busy on the cargo deck. The Sergeant Major asked after the Treasury Minister. The Major muttered something impolite below his breath, 'Can't leave him behind.'

'Send one of the corporals to get him and bring his gear aft ready for offloading,' he ordered.

The Corporal found Horskjaer struggling to get into action. To prepare for the new day he had taken a hot shower and even managed a shave, but he still felt another four hours in the more than comfortable bunk bed a good idea. The Corporal was living proof that wasn't going to happen.

He dressed quickly and pointed to the bags he wanted taken on deck. These did not include his rifle, carefully protected in its expensive padded leather bag. He left his cabin to find breakfast and gallons of hot, strong coffee.

The Captain looked out over the city of Larvik. He liked the city a great deal and had visited it many times. Established as a municipality as long ago as 1838, there were little signs of change. A few former girlfriends still lived there, welcome company during the long dark evenings during an overnight stay. Today its main advantage was the short distance to Oslo, a little over 65 miles.

The Captain saw the most important task was to disembark his 'passengers and their impedimenta' off his ship and to make tracks homewards as fast as possible for some well-earned peace and quiet.

The *Girard* entered the inner basin of Larvik harbour. The Captain ordered all stop on both engines and ten degrees of port wheel. The *Girard* started to glide to a stop, turning through a full turn to face the way back out to sea. Captain Ditlevsen went out on to the starboard bridge wing followed by Kirsty the labrador. As the steam ferry stern lined-up with the docks behind, the Captain ordered 'slow astern both'. The telegraph repeaters acknowledged.

The *Girard* came to a stop and gently shuddered as she went astern to the nearest dockside berth available. Aft, the crew removed the sea fastenings from the four trucks, and the ships crane swung into position to lift the first one ashore. On the funnel deck, the second mate was busy organising a secondary gangway down to the dockside.

With the manoeuvre to come alongside the dock wall smoothly executed, two able seamen jumped ashore in time to catch heaving lines attached to the main mooring ropes, which were quickly secured over the bollards. Captain Ditlevsen ordered a burst of full ahead to take all way off the ship. He ordered all stop and waited for the winches to bring his ship alongside the dockside wall exactly as planned.

A gangway from the cargo deck landed on the dockside and the first of the Major's men quickly made their way onshore. A squad of eight soldiers and the Sergeant Major were seen heading up the dockside to the Harbour Masters office. All they found was an irate deputy who'd been abruptly awakened to find an unauthorised ship berthed at his dock. Two soldiers gathered him up and frog-marched him back to the *Girard*.

Captain Ditlevsen went on to the dockside, his labrador trailing behind in search of lampposts. The Deputy Harbour Master was relieved to see a familiar face, and even the dog, but what in earth was going on, his anger rising.

'What the bloody hell is going on?' he shouted out.

The Captain took a hold of him by the shoulders and led him to one side.

'My good friend,' he said, 'listen carefully. The Germans are invading Oslo, and should get there in about eight hours, maybe a little more. Go and get the Harbour Master and also rouse the Police Superintendent. Is the Mayor in town, we will need to get him roped in as well.'

The Deputy Harbour Master didn't believe a word of what he heard and said so. Just then, the first army truck landed on the dockside. More soldiers were streaming ashore carrying backpacks and their weapons. Six soldiers collected their weapons and backpacks and made off down the dockside to secure the exit. The Major was taking no chances.

The third truck landed beside the Deputy Harbour Master, as the soldiers started throwing their backpacks inside. One of the sergeants took a roll call of his section. They piled into the first of the two trucks and roared off down the dockside to the Harbour Master's Office.

The Deputy Harbour Master looked confused as he watched a carefully organised army unit moving efficiently into action.

The Captain grabbed his arm. 'Back to your office,' he said. 'I hope the phones are working.'

'They are,' replied the Deputy Harbour Master, 'but the telephone exchange operator will not be on duty for another hour.'

'That's your first job then; let's go. This is an emergency.'

By the time the telephone operator had been roused from her slumbers, complaining loudly and at length, the Harbour Master arrived in his office demanding to know what the hell was going on.

The Major tried to calm him down when Horskjaer arrived, wearing his best hunting tweeds, an Invertere Field overcoat with his rifle bag slung over his back.

He ordered silence and was pleased to receive it. He was about to outline the actions to be taken when the local Police Superintendent, Gunnar Elgaard arrived. Elgaard recently retired from the Norwegian army as a lieutenant in their intelligence services and had been lucky to move into his current posting courtesy of his brother, the Mayor. This had not pleased the local policemen in-line for a promotion. It had to be said Elgaard brought a fair amount of energy to the job of Police Superintendent in this sleepy out of the way town.

Horskjaer shut them all up with a withering look. He began to tell them the situation and the actions to be taken immediately. He brought out his notepad and tore out a page and handed it to the Police Superintendent. 'I need these people contacted immediately. The message is the Germans are bringing an invasion force up the fjords to Oslo and will arrive in the next few hours. Tell them this entire message comes from me, and they have no time to lose.'

The notepad listed the names of the King of Norway's office, the head of the Norwegian army and the Prime Minister's office.

Gunnar Elgaard spoke for the Harbour Master and his Deputy, 'I don't think this our duty. How do we know the truth of the matter,' he said.

The Captain said, 'Well I saw the damn German convoy, and we almost run into one of their troop transports. That's good enough for me, and should be for you.'

The Major interjected, 'Sir, if I could suggest the Police Superintendent makes these calls, introduces you to ever he gets hold off, and you give the message directly.'

Horskjaer was not pleased with being corrected, but any suggestion to speed things up would be good. He picked up the phone and handed it to the Police Superintendent. Taking the telephone from the Treasury Minister, he got the operator to start calling the names on the list. She repeatedly told him the numbers were engaged, or not working. The Major knew events were moving fast. Eventually, she got hold of an army base outside of Oslo, and she put the connection through.

Elgaard asked to be put through to the base commandant. Fortunately, the tone of his voice brooked no argument and he ended up speaking to an irate Major General. He introduced himself, and apologised for the disturbance but would the Major General speak to the Danish Treasury Minister, Eric Horskjaer? A confused Major General took the call and asked why he was speaking to a ranking member of the Danish Government; why was he in Norway; and what was his business?

The Treasury Minister, detecting the Major General's tone of voice, got straight to the point. 'Sir, I have to advise that the German armed forces are bringing an invasion force up the fjord from the Skagerrak, but we are not sure how far they have got.'

The Major General replied curtly, 'Go on.'

'Yes Sir, I have with me a small force of Danish Rangers and a cargo of national valuables which we wish to spirit away from the Germans. We had hoped to land in Oslo before the invasion, but events have overtaken us. Your Prime Minister knows of our mission, but we can't get through to his or any other offices.'

The Major General told him he had little surprise at his lack of success with the telephone. For his information, and as far as anyone could tell, at about 4:30 am the main German force reached the Oskarsborg Narrows and the forts there. The Norwegian 280mm gun battery on South Kalholmen Island had opened fire scoring major hits on a large cruiser which, after it had been heavily damaged, had sunk; believed by torpedoes.

Other warships had been engaged with some success. As far as he knew, he thought that the Germans had been forced to put their main ground force ashore somewhere south of Oskarsborg, some 20 miles from Oslo city, and were attempting to make their approach by land. He had sent forces to resist, but how long they could delay them would be another matter.

The Norwegian government and the Royal Family were reportedly heading north at this moment in time, and the road north remained clear for now, protected by the Royal Guard.

And last, but not least, simultaneous landings had apparently taken part in other areas of Norway, so in total, the position had become one of total confusion. British and French Allied forces had moved in to try and resist the German invasion, reports were mixed, but he doubted if they would overcome the preparedness and the combined might of the German military forces.

In conclusion the Major General advised he did not know of the minister's mission but in the light of what he just said there was little he or his government could do or suggest.

Horskjaer muttered, 'for helvede', and sat down in his chair not knowing what to think. The Major had heard most of the conversation and asked what to do next.

'Major,' said Horskjaer, 'that is a very good question. Let's go outside and walk, perhaps we'll think of something if we walk a little.'

The morning air was still cold, and the weather appeared to be clearing. The Major preferred overcast. Overcast was good, it hid movement and allowed the opportunity to manoeuvre unseen, especially from the air.

The Minister, the Captain and the Major choose to walk back towards the *Girard*. At the end of the dock, they could see the last of the Major's men and supplies being unloaded.

The Captain asked for a brief run down on what had happened. He wished he hadn't. Now he had few options, the seas would be swarming with the German Navy no matter which way he wanted to go. Either way, his ship would be impounded, and it would make little difference where, Norway or Denmark.

'Captain,' the Major said, 'what are your thoughts for your ship?'

The Captain told him his thoughts. The Minister thought hard and quickly about the *Girard*, The Captain could, of course, tell his future German capturers his ship had been commandeered, but if the Germans knew about the complicitness of the ship and its crew in spiriting away the gold and diamonds from their grasp, matters could easily go from bad to worse.

'Captain Ditlevsen,' began Horskjaer. 'I think myself, the Major and his men are going to make a dash for safety if we can find it, or disappear into the mountains, lose the cargo and do what we have to do. I suggest, most strongly, you make things as good for your ship, your crew and the navy ratings as you can.'

My only suggestion is you set sail straight away, make your way into a quiet fjord, take cover under an overhanging cliff, whatever. Cut the gun mountings from the decks of your ship, heave them overboard, ammunition too, wait for night fall and attempt a home run as soon as it gets dark again. If you can disguise the ship in anyway, it may cause some confusion in the minds of the Germans to give you an edge. The weather may help or it may hinder, no matter what, I think that's about all you can consider for the moment.'

The Major was impressed with the Minister's grasp of the situation. The Captain said nothing. The Minister had appraised the situation almost to the last detail. He even knew of exactly the kind of bolthole the Minister had suggested, a narrow waterway between two mountains that led from the channel up to Kragerø. He had to save his ship, and, more importantly, his crew. They'd all been together a long time.

The three of them reached the *Girard*, the Captain bounded up the gangway shouting for the Chief Engineer. His head appeared out of a skylight, 'You looking for me Skipper?'

'Yes, how much fuel have we got left?' asked the Captain.

'Depends where you want to go to,' replied the Chief. 'Århus should be no problem, Copenhagen if we're economical with the speed, anywhere else I need a hundred tonnes of bunkers.'

'Anything else I can help you gentlemen with?' asked the Captain dryly.

The Minister replied in the negative and told the Captain to make tracks before it became too late.

'And thanks for all your help, good luck and God speed.' They shook hands.

Captain Ditlevsen rattled out a string of orders, 'Chief, come on, let's go, we're going round to park-up at the back of Kragerø, return the ship to normal, and then try a run home tonight.'

The Second Mate looked over the bridge at the dockside. The Captain shouted up to him to get the First Mate on the bridge and 'ring-on' main engines. Then he should think about getting his sorry arse on deck, get the gangways brought in and the mooring hawsers stowed.

The Minister and the Major started the long walk back to the Harbour Master's office. His mind was clear, and his thoughts spilled out for the Major to consider. His plan seemed simple, to explore the route up towards Oslo. If the German forces were held up south of Oskarsborgand, and if the Norwegian Army had the capability to slow them down, if only for a short time, then they might just make the north side of Oslo if they got a move on.

If that option failed there was a difficult mountain road he knew of going west from Holmestrand, not too many miles up the road. This route, up through Berg, would eventually get them over to the deep fjords that would take them to the North Sea. There they would look for local fishing trawlers that could make the journey across to the Shetland Islands once all this damn military activity died down a bit.

The Major considered the Minister's ideas and their options. There weren't many options and the Minister had just about covered the only plan likely to be successful. The chances were still slim.

He looked back down the dockside, as the *Girard* pulled away, smoke pouring from both funnels as the black gang in the boiler room worked hard to build-up sufficient steam for all eventualities.

The Major saw Captain Ditlevsen on the starboard bridge wing and waved farewell, but the Captain didn't see him.

The Major wondered who had the best chance, the *Girard* or his mission. Either way, a lot of luck and cunning would be required, and for sure, the Captain and his crew were not underweight in the cunning department.

Bruus-Jensen knew his first action would be to get his troops together, tell them what would be expected of them, and solicit any helpful suggestions. These were, after all, top soldiers and their future was, to say the least, problematic. If they met German forces, they would have to act quickly and decisively. Their first encounter would have the benefit of surprise. The second would be tough, the Germans would be out for blood, theirs, and use their best troops with, more than likely, their highly trained air force in support.

The Major approached his men and asked them to gather round. He could see their faces were loaded with questions and doubt. He spelt out the situation without emotion or embellishment. His no-nonsense approach was greatly appreciated. A corporal asked about the cargo they were trying to prevent from falling into enemy hands. The Major told them all that they could guess, but he wasn't going to confirm or deny anything. The presence of the Treasury Minister showed the importance their King and their government gave to the mission.

He could but reiterate the utmost importance to prevent their cargo falling into the hands of the Germans, even if it meant dumping the lot in the bottom of Norway's deepest fjord. Much more important, in his opinion, would be to get the cargo to an allied country, with Great Britain the obvious destination.

The Major closed the subject, and with little more to be gained in discussion, he moved to the order of battle. The two motorcycles would scout ahead, the four trucks would follow, and deploy in support should the need arise. One of the sergeants suggested they contact the local police stations as they moved up the line.

The Major noticed Elgaard, looking out the window of the harbour master's office, taking a strong interest in the proceedings. The Danish mission looked exciting and if the war had arrived he wasn't about to remain a policeman. He was looking at top troops, well trained and carrying the latest German arms and equipment. 'Just where did they get them from?' The Sergeant Major had joyfully told only half a story. Clearly someone had been cute. Cute intrigued him.

The Major beckoned to the police superintendent. He quickly established the policeman's interest in his mission, his past service history considered potentially very helpful. He looked fit, had combat training, although he had been stuck behind a desk the last year.

The policeman also had a police car; and if he could get him to join the mission, this would come in very useful. The deal was struck and the Major ordered everyone to their positions.

The Danish convoy started its hazardous journey. Bruus-Jensen sent one of the motorcycle outriders and the police car ahead armed with two of his men to act as guards. The Major sat in the cab of the first truck. The Minister sat nervously in the front of the third truck nursing his hunting rifle, not an easy task given it was such a long weapon.

The Sergeant Major brought up the rear of the convoy in the last truck, making sure his men were alert and attentive.

The convoy sped into the dark gloom that was an early spring morning in Norway. The mountains were covered in low-level cloud, which pleased the Major. He'd taken stock of all he'd heard that morning and became increasing concerned about German air reconnaissance. Even a light aircraft could cover a lot of territory quickly, and help would be just but a radio call away. Fortunately, the road remained deserted, and the Major was hopeful of making good progress.

His optimism became quickly punctured when the motorcycle scout made a sudden stop as the rider laid his bike down on the side of the road and ran for cover. The Major's truck came to a halt at the other side of the road as he shouted for his men to deploy. A section of four men and a sergeant surged forward to take up positions near the motorcycle scout.

The other three trucks took up positions behind the first, the Major's men quickly throwing a protective cordon around the convoy. The Major took a section of rangers on the other side of the road using as much cover as possible. It was not a good place to be stopped, not his choice. Instead of rounding the bend in front of him, the Major took his first section of men in a flanking movement up a small hill.

From his vantage point he could see the lead motorcycle and the police car about two hundred metres up the road, stopped by a felled tree. The police superintendent and the Major's men had been surrounded as they tried to clear the road. With his binoculars the Major could see the attackers were not regular forces, but just who they were he had no idea. He waited to see what would happen next. He waved at his second section of men and signalled them to move cautiously forward but to remain hidden in the undergrowth along the side of the road.

Then he took his men on the hill forward with as little noise as possible. They managed to get within thirty metres of the police car when the Major heard Elgaard having a massive argument with a short stocky bearded man with the thickest crop of reddish hair he'd ever seen. The red mass of hair flowed everywhere so it was difficult the see the man's face; it was obvious to the Major the bearded one's last visit to a barber's shop was clearly decades past.

The red haired man had a gang of real ruffians with him; all placed in perfect ambush positions, all armed to the teeth with an obscure range of weapons. That they knew what to do with them was also obvious. Time to be cautious.

The argument between Elgaard and the red haired man, apparently called Red Eric, got loud and vocal, so much so the rest of the bandits were paying more attention to the shouting than guarding the road. The Major could only pick-up the occasional word. His skill in Norwegian was not that good and certainly not up to the standard of profanities being exchanged.

The Major seized his chance, and motioned both sections of his men into position. It took just a few moments before the Major raised his hand and signalled his machine gun section to send a burst of fire just over the heads of Elgaard and his opponent. The remainder of his men followed suit firing their weapons skywards and rushing quickly into position to cover the remainder of the bandits.

'Right,' thought the Major, 'let's get this settled quickly.'

He slithered down the bank, dropping down next to the prone figures on the road. He turned and waved to his furthest soldier to bring the convoy up to him.

'OK, Superintendent Elgaard,' he said forceful. 'You and the bearded wonder can get up now, explain?'

Elgaard was indeed pleased to see the Major. This is Red Eric he told him, 'Viking warrior, and sometimes fisherman.' He explained that he and his men came from a separate coastal community outside his hometown of Tønsberg just up the road. Standing close behind Red Eric was a giant of a man, apparently called Little Eric. To his left stood another Viking of diminutive stature who was pure poison, called, despite the obvious, Eric the Big.

The Major gave the Police Superintendent a look of some surprise. Elgaard could see he would have to explain the anomaly. He took the Major to one side. 'It's like this,' he said. 'It's a virility thing, building the clan and preventing the decline of the community.'

Little Eric, according to gossip, wasn't, although a lady friend of his did have first-hand knowledge. He was actually an average size, but his sheer bulk had brought about the nickname. Little Eric had more interest in body building, and although most thought he'd exceed his quota, 'Little Eric' kept on getting, well, bigger. Little Eric also liked fighting and was very good at it. Give Little Eric a couple of battles a day, and he slept like a lamb all night. The ladies held little interest for him, which was a pity as there were more than a few of the middle-aged ladies in the region who rather fancied him.

Eric the Big, although a touch on the short side, was hung like a baboon. If anybody was keeping the Viking population up to strength, he was the man.

The Major asked about Red Eric, probably the strongest fittest man he'd ever seen. Elgaard agreed, and for someone who had almost reached the age of nearly sixty-five, he was in remarkably good shape. The Major looked up at the sky in astonishment. Elgaard warned the Major that Red Eric had a very violent temper. If he ever got upset near the Major and his men, it would be best to retreat very fast and leave him to work it off on someone else.

The Major felt sorry he'd asked, but at least, he had been informed. Anyway, back to the business in hand. Why had the Vikings decided to block the road?

It seemed they'd picked up news of the German invasion from the radio on their fishing trawlers and had decided to take action. Quite why was another matter, probably looking for a fight on an otherwise slow day?

'You sure these are Viking warriors?' asked the Major. Elgaard explained Red Eric's community was one of the last to maintain what could be considered Viking traditions and customs. The community was somewhat inbred, but in olden days all communities were to some extent, due to the difficulties of communication and jealous rivalries between the established tribes. His men were extremely tough and would fight anybody on almost any pretext. The Police Superintendent told the Major the whole story about the Viking community would take a long time and could keep for later.

Anyway, he had to hand it to the Major; his men had the drop on the Vikings.

'All very interesting,' commented the Major, 'but if it's all the same to you, we have a war to fight or avoid, depending on our luck. What do the Vikings want?'

'Proof of who you are, and what is your purpose? Red Eric can't think of any reason why a detachment of the Danish army is rushing around southern Norway.'

'He's not the only one,' grimaced the Major.

His men had the drop on Vikings, and he didn't have time to explain unless he became confused himself. He ordered his men to move forward and bring the trucks through the barricade. Just as things appeared to be going to plan, the Major noticed a new and larger group of Vikings had the drop on his men.

All movement came to a sudden stop once more. Red Eric, smiling like a Cheshire cat, repeated his question to the Major.

'God, his breath smelt awful, what did he have for breakfast,' thought the Major.

'OK Mr Red Eric,' started the Major. 'It's like this, and your second group of Vikings have the drop on my men here on the road.'

'Agreed,' said Red Eric.

'But,' continued the Major holding up his hand, 'I have detachment up on that ridge behind you. You can't see them, but they block your escape. Yes? Oh, and they have three heavy machine guns and two-inch mortars. Match that.'

Red Eric looked into the face of the Major. His boyish charm look had gone. His gaze rock hard; his eyes burned with a focus that didn't flinch. Red Eric saw a professional soldier, who looked the part, and quickly came to the conclusion he could act the part too.

Red Eric called his men down to him. They did look a fearsome bunch; just what could they achieve with proper training and the right equipment?

'OK Major, get on with your war,' said Red Eric. 'Bring your men down too. Don't make me look bad by not having any of your people up on that ridge.'

The Major moved forward and shouted for the Sergeant Major.

'Sergeant Major, get the last of the barricade removed, clear this mess up on this road. Move the trucks forward, let's get ready to move out, and bring those men down of that ridge before they freeze.'

The Major's men on the ridge came down. There were only six of them, but Red Eric could see they did actually have three very modern machine guns. The Major asked Red Eric what he would do next. Red Eric told him they would return to their village outside the town of Tønsberg, to get their boats ready for the night's fishing. The Major asked if Tønsberg had a police station. Apparently it did, but the constable would be visiting Holmestrand, the next town on the torturous road to Oslo.

The convoy formed up ready to go; the Major signalled to move forward. Red Eric joined him on his truck, hanging on with one hand standing on the running board. It looked like he'd been adopted. He looked in the rearview mirror only to see that Red Eric's men were also hitching a ride in the same manner.

Red Eric started to talk to him through the open window. Were they in a hurry? Were the Germans looking for his convoy? Where had the invasion reached?

The Major answered 'Yes', they were in a hurry, and 'Yes', it was possible the Germans were looking for his convoy, but he wasn't sure. How far had the invasion got? Hopefully slogging it up on the other side of the fjord against the Norwegian Army, who with luck were making things difficult.

Red Eric said nothing, but the Major picked up on the fact he might have heard something. Red Eric asked the Major what his immediate plans were.

The Major told him he was very anxious to reach the road out of Oslo going north and hopefully catch up with the Norwegian Government believed to be escaping to the west coast. Failing that he intended to head west from Holmestrand, up over the mountains to the west coast of Norway.

Red Eric said nothing, which struck a troubling cord with the Major.

The Danish Convoy reached Tønsberg. Red Eric called a stop at the second house past the entrance to the town. He disappeared towards the house and banged on the door. It was opened by a large stout lady, no doubt the constable's wife. Her greeting of her early morning caller was more than a little familiar.

Her face turned to disappointment when she saw the convoy waiting out in the road. Red Eric brushed past her open embrace, disappeared inside the house, and clearly knew where the telephone was. He came out on the run a few minutes later. He jumped on the running board and told the Major to get a move on.

The Major ordered his convoy forward. Red Eric told him to hurry up. The Major's truck moved up behind the police car, the truck driver honked his horn urgently. The convoy picked up speed, with Red Eric still hanging on the outside, as were all his men.

'And?' asked the Major. 'News?'

'Aye, there's news all right,' said Red Eric. 'Germans Paratroopers landed at Fornebu Airfield, on the west side of Oslo at first light. The airfield is being held waiting for the main column of the German Army to reach Oslo.'

That was the good news. The bad news was a motorized detachment of paratroopers had grabbed some heavy transport vehicles from the airport's commercial transport park and were headed south at full speed. Why he didn't know.

'Numbers?' asked the Major.

Red Eric told him he thought about one company of the 1st Fallschirmjaeger Regiment could be heading south, about sixty men, difficult to be precise hiding behind a heavy stone wall.

'When did they leave?' asked the Major anxiously.

Red Eric didn't know, but it could only have been in the last hour. He reckoned if the Germans landed at first light, getting their equipment together, finding and capturing vehicles at the airfield and getting organised to move out would take two hours at most.

In his opinion, it would take less than four hours for the Germans to get as far as Holmestrand. How much less he couldn't say. In other words, the Major and his men would be unlikely to make it there before they would.

'Shit,' thought the Major. 'Red, can we backtrack and get on another road to the west?

'Not this month, the only other road is buried in snow, and won't clear for another two/three weeks at least,' replied Red Eric. 'Just keep on going and let's see what we can do up the road. There are plenty of places to ambush a German convoy.'

This worried the Major; he wasn't looking for a pitched battle with anyone right now. His Viking friends were clearly enjoying the prospect.

'Major, you got any spare weapons and ammunition?' asked Red Eric.

'Actually, yes. We were going to drop them off in Larvik, but the Mayor didn't seem too interested, and, to be frank, we were short of time to offload them,' replied the Major. 'There are thirty plus Mauser rifles, all in good condition and five MG-34 machine guns. With these, you should be able to make yourself quite unpopular with the Wehrmacht's finest.'

The Major ordered the convoy to a quick stop. Red Eric scowled at the Major and went off in search for the Danish armourer. He returned partially satisfied now his men had got hold of some good quality rifles, some fitted with telescopic sights. The Major noted Red Eric had not been slow in purloining a substantial amount of ammunition. Clearly the Vikings were itching for a good long war.

The convoy resumed its journey to Holmestrand. The Major sent the two motor cyclists on ahead, each carrying one of Red Eric's smaller Viking's on the pillion seat. It would not be long before events started to unfold.

Some five kilometres from the town of Holmestrand, Elgaard car suddenly slewed to a stop at the side of the road two hundred metres from a sharp bend in the road, and one of the motorcycles was seen returning as fast as it could. Bruus-Jensen feared the worst. The convoy came to an abrupt halt, his men pouring out onto the sides of the road, moving forward to take positions overlooking the bend.

The motorcyclist, minus his passenger, screeched to a halt close to where the Major had taken cover. His report was short and to the point. Around the bend lay a natural ambush position fully populated with German 'Fallschirmjaeger'. He'd survived, his pillion passenger having taken a number of shots in the back before his grasp failed, falling dead to the ground. The first motorcycle and its rider had been mown down in a murderous crossfire.

The Sergeant Major busied deploying his men, and along with two scouts, clambered up a small hillock to get a view of the road on the other side of the corner. The position looked very clear; the Germans were holding a very secure position. Red Eric clambered up behind them. He sucked in is breath in between his missing front teeth and chuckled to himself.

'Please share your amusement,' spat the Sergeant Major.

'Oh,' replied Red Eric, 'this will be easy. You see, they think their left flank is protected by the bog between the road and the forest. Well, there's a little-known path that comes behind their position about a hundred metres back. The position is also shielded by dense overgrowth. Give me fifteen minutes and wait for my signals. Some diversion in front of the German position would be helpful, and a smoke barrage from your mortars would also improve matters.'

With that, he vanished with ten of his men. The Sergeant Major moved back to the Major and told him Red Eric had it all in hand, and he shouldn't be long.

'Do I have time for a quick nap?' quizzed the Major.

'Very funny', replied the Sergeant Major, 'you may just want to take an interest and get your sorry butt up that hillock. I'll get the men better positioned'.

The Major looked around. His men were well placed as far as he could see. The Minister and the Norwegian policeman were being shepherded out of harm's way, and there seemed little left to do. He climbed the embankment and took his binoculars out. He saw what had been described; a classic ambush position that would need something he didn't have, a couple of armoured vehicles to break through this position.

He saw no sign of the Vikings who'd vanished into the forest. The other Vikings were crawling on their stomachs along the roadside ditch to get closer to the forthcoming violent event. A few of the Vikings were seen sporting traditional double bladed axes of a fearsome nature, hanging on thongs around their necks down behind their backs.

The Major signalled his machine gun section to move onto the hillock and was impolitely moved aside for his troubles. He thought everyone seemed rather anxious to join the fun. He doubted whether mixing it with German 'Fallschirmjaeger' could be classed as fun, but time would tell.

The Major hissed at everyone to shut up and keep very still. Using a pre-arranged signal, he waved a section of his men forward on the far side of the road. This section of rangers started to creep out of sight around the bend; a purely diversionary move to keep the German's occupied. For now, the Germans would hold their fire, not wishing to give away their position.

The mortar section arrived on the hillock. It was starting to get crowded up here. The Major suggested they move back a little so the Germans wouldn't see their firing position. There was keen and there was keen. Time for a little prudence. All appeared to be ready, but where had Red Eric got to?

Bruus-Jensen didn't have long to wait as the Vikings erupted from very close quarters and threw themselves upon the Germans, with a noticeable lack of gunfire. The Major saw axe blades flashing in the low sunlight and a lot of unholy hollering and shouting. The Vikings in front of the German positions opened fire, just as the Major ordered a smoke barrage from his mortar section. He had the satisfaction of seeing the smoke bombs land exactly on target.

A few of the German 'Fallschirmjaeger' broke cover and ran on to the road. The Vikings on this side of the melee had set up a rifle section almost impossible for the Germans to see. The German Paratroopers were cut down without mercy. In two minutes it was all over. The Major turned around to his machine gun and mortar sections, gave them a well done, and sent them down the embankment to pack up and prepare to move out.

The rangers nearest to the fighting emerged from cover and ran up to the German positions. The lead ranger signalled the Major and the Sergeant Major to come quickly. Bruus-Jensen was not a squeamish man but what he saw shocked him. He found Red Eric, his eyes wide open in vengeful lust, covered from head to toe in blood, with a double bladed axe in one hand,

and a boy of ten in his other arm. The boy had the same mass of red hair, his face ashen white, his expression glazed in shock.

It took some minutes for Red Eric to compose himself. He lowered the boy to the ground, who stood shaking, his arms wrapped tightly around Red Eric's legs. The Major looked around. Nearly every German soldier had been hacked to pieces in the most brutal manner. He looked unflinching at Red Eric and demanded an explanation. Red Eric shrugged his shoulders and moved to a small stream and started cleaning the blood from his half naked body. The boy sat on the grass not moving. Another Viking came to his side to clean and comfort him.

After a while Red Eric spoke. He told him they were about to attack the German positions when a small group of Viking villagers moved into the picture. They told Red Eric the dreadful news their small hamlet had been slaughtered by the very Germans manning the ambush. What'd happened had been brutal beyond belief. They'd saved the boy who, it appeared, was one of Red Eric's half sons. The boy's family had perished, along with most of his community.

The Major saw the deep hatred in Red Eric's eyes, a burning intensity that frightened him. This man was capable of any act of revenge. A revenge that had only just started, and would not finish with this first attack. As he looked helplessly around, Little Eric and Eric the Big came upon the scene. Their eyes burning with the same lust as their leader. Behind, two German soldiers were being held prisoner by a group of Vikings waiting for Red Eric's attention. The Major had a bad feeling about what was going to happen next.

The Major went over to the two captives. The first man, an SS Major, whom he assumed to be the leader of the German 'Fallschirmjaeger', was a brute of a man, hard body, and hard eyes with no compassion. In short, a Nazi thug of the worst kind.

The second man, was a clean-shaven Lieutenant, and although dressed in paratrooper's uniform, looked like a liaison officer from headquarters. Red Eric completed his ablutions, dressed himself and took charge of the prisoners. He went behind them and with lightning judo kicks sent them to their knees. He looked over at Little Eric, who moved forward to the Nazi. As big as the Nazi was, Little Eric's hand clamped around his throat with ease. His grip tightened, but the Nazi Major didn't flinch.

Red Eric started to ask questions in fluent German. The Nazi spat at him in disgust, and Little Eric pole-axed him to the ground with a mighty blow. Most men would have died on the spot, but the SS Major just lay there regaining his breath looking murderously at everyone. Red Eric turned to the Lieutenant who cringed in fear, but not at Red Eric, but at the Nazi lying on the ground.

The Major could see the Nazi Major would never talk, and the other German was too scared. What happened next shocked the Major to the core. Little Eric grabbed the SS Major by an outstretched arm twisted behind his back, produced a double head axe and with a mighty blow severed the arm at the elbow. Red Eric grabbed the SS Major by the hair and started to ask more questions. That Red Eric received the same response surprised Bruus-Jensen.

This could get ugly, and it did. Another mighty axe blow severed the other arm. Red Eric let go of the man's hair and let him slump to the ground, the blood pouring from his body. Another Viking thoughtfully placed his severed arms where he could see them, carefully removing his Nazi ring from one hand and adjusted the position of one severed arm so the victim would see the time on his Nazi watch. The Viking decided to keep the Nazi watch as a souvenir, and replaced it with a watch from another corpse. The Nazi thug did not have long to wait before his life ebbed away.

Bruus-Jensen was sick to the stomach. He looked around and saw Red Eric leading the German Lieutenant away from the scene. The two of them went over to the trucks where the Danish armourers were making a brew up for the troops. Red Eric grabbed a cup of coffee and handed it to the death-white Lieutenant, clearly in shock and shaking in his boots. Red Eric sat him down and started to speak to the Lieutenant calmly and without malice. The ultimate good cop, bad cop routine.

Bruus-Jensen walked over and helped himself to a cup of coffee. Red Eric shooed the Major, and everyone else, away. Within a few minutes, the Lieutenant had regained some composure and started to give Red Eric chapter and verse on just about every subject concerning the invasion, and the presence of the German paratroopers in this area.

When the interrogation had finished, Red Eric came over to Bruus-Jensen and gave him the details. The Lieutenant, a member of the German High Command Intelligence Corps, had to date been in charge of the Danish surveillance activities. He acknowledged the Danes had made it very difficult to complete his work, and surprised at the intelligent steps taken to spirit the valuables out of the country. They'd almost succeeded, but for the chance encounter with the invasion fleet.

He told them the German High Command knew about the cargo in the trucks and were desperate to get hold of it. That piece of news intrigued the Major. Why would the Germans be desperate to get hold of the cargo? A couple of tonnes of gold would be a nice prize, the diamonds a big bonus, but desperate? Surely not?

As Red Eric continued relaying his information, the Major got the distinct impression there could be more detail about the cargo he didn't know and Red Eric wasn't about to tell him.

Red Eric told him specialised German forces were being assembled to cut them off and prevent their escape in any direction. His guess was more detachments of German paratroopers, complete with air support, with the likelihood they would be ready first thing tomorrow. The town of Holmestrand, a few kilometres up the main road, had been captured, blocking the route of escape to the west and to the north.

None of this came as good news. The Major felt the gravity of the situation closing in. He needed time to think and time had rapidly become a very scarce commodity. He wandered down to the Minister enjoying a quiet smoke waiting for news which he assumed would not be all good. He didn't have long to wait.

The Major was a bit gloomy on the prospects, but the Minister put that down to tiredness. It was quite unlike the Major to be anything less than positive, even in the face of total adversity.

Red Eric joined the group and asked what they were going to do next. The Major looked up at him. Red Eric had been driving most of the day's events and now he was asking for an opinion?

The problem was he didn't have one; well nothing he could live with. The Major went through all the issues in a logical manner. Going back to their arrival point was out, and the only options were the routes to the north and the west. The route to the north had been blocked by the German Army in full war paint, so the road to the west looked like the only option. Trouble was getting onto the road when by all accounts the Germans had it well covered.

'Red,' he asked, 'how many men have you got available?'

Red Eric told him he could have fifty or more men to come out of hiding from his decimated community, and if the Major had equipment for them, they were baying for revenge.

'Strip the German soldiers of everything,' said the Major. 'In fact it might be a good idea to dump the bodies in the swamp. If the dead Germans disappeared off the face of the earth, it might save what's left of the community.'

'Major,' replied Red Eric quietly, 'there is no community; they were all murdered, wiped out. We are the last of the Vikings. No more ideas of breeding a pure Viking community. There are no women left. The bastards murdered them all. You don't need to know how either.'

'In that case,' replied the Major, his mind starting to work through the problems, 'let's think about smuggling your men behind the Germans at Holmestrand. Use fishing boats, anything. You know the ground; you can hide, manoeuvre unseen. The Germans at Holmestrand do not yet know what's happened here. There are two German trucks. We'll disguise some rangers as Germans, pretend to have prisoners, anything that'll let us get close. How does the land lie where we need to attack?'

Red Eric went down to his men to consult them. They'd little to lose. The Germans seemed to be intent on tracking them down anyway, God knows why? Ten minutes later he came back with the outline of a plan. He had three fishing boats that could take his men, sail outside the Island of Langoya, and get back to the mainland well behind where the Germans had taken up positions.

If the Major could come up the road with the two German trucks, carrying what looked to be prisoners, they should just be able to manage to get in real close before being exposed. They might even get through the outer cordon. He would give the Major two of his best men to act as scouts to get final information. Red Eric told the Major their prisoner, the German Lieutenant, had little idea of the German dispositions, despite his willingness to talk.

Bruus-Jensen called his Sergeant Major and two sergeants roughed out a plan and went over it a few times to fix the detail. Satisfied the plan had, at least, a fair chance of succeeding, all things being equal, he called the men to him and went through what would be required of them.

His men looked confused and not a little concerned. These were experienced men who instinctively knew their journey to Norway was not going as planned, and a lot of potential downside had become more than evident. One of the corporals asked permission to ask a question. The Major knew what was coming, just exactly what was going on. Before the questioner had finished, the Major raised his hand.

'OK men, it's like this,' he began. 'We are in bad situation, not of our making. We can, however, extract ourselves with some really focussed soldiering. The Germans are aware of our mission, God knows how, because everything, and I mean everything, has been done to keep this mission a secret.'

'The German ambush massacred by the Vikings, are not your ordinary paratroopers. The SS Major, which Red Eric and his men carefully dissected, was a full blown card carrying member of the Nazi Party. Not your average paratrooper I would say? This thug and his men have massacred the last remaining Viking community in Norway, for whatever reason, and we could well be next. So any idea about the Geneva Convention is out, and in any event, war has not exactly been formally declared.'

The Major completed his talk and moved the convoy up the road and found a vantage point to look down on the community of Holmestrand, just under a kilometre away. From this vantage point the Major could see the road junction they had to reach to make their escape west to Berg. The landscape looked quiet and still, which meant the German main force had either not arrived, or more likely, they'd dug in and were waiting to spring a trap on the Danish enterprise.

The Major preferred the latter option. No way could the defeated German patrol be that far in front of the main force. Now he would need precise details before he could commit his small force to a full on battle.

He went back to speak to his men. Bruus-Jensen paused and looked around at his comrades. Giving them an unvarnished appraisal of their situation was appreciated if not exactly welcome. And so to the plan.

The scouts would advance and take-up position to observe the German positions. The Vikings with their fishing boats would come behind the Germans, hopefully with a large element of surprise. When the Vikings were ready to attack the German rear, the two captured German trucks and one of the Danish trucks, minus its cargo, would approach the outlying German position as if returning with Danish Prisoners. They would either take this position or drive further towards the main German position wherever that may be.

The remaining trucks would follow behind and deploy the mortar section to set up fire support as required. The trucks with the cargo, each with machine guns mounted on the cab roof would sweep into action. The Major made it very clear about one thing, no German prisoners. As soon as access to the road west had been achieved, the two trucks with the cargo would head up the road to Berg, and over the mountain road with as many men who were available. The Vikings would be allowed to exact their revenge on the German army, and then whoever remained would pile into the two German trucks and follow behind.

'The situation will be very fluid,' the Major said, 'so keep your wits about you and watch for my commands at all times. The Sergeant Major will now put some detail into this overview. I'm off to brief the Minister.'

Bruus-Jensen found Horskjaer relaxing in the cab of the third truck. For the last half hour he'd kept his eyes firmly closed as he tried to shut-out the barbaric events at the ambush. He struggled with the knowledge he'd brought his countrymen into great danger and had no idea what to do about it. His mind slowly cleared just as the Major tapped on the door window.

The Major; the ever dependable officer, now had a difficult task on his hands. He prayed the Major could see through the confusion and come up with a course of action to get them out of their predicament.

'Major, how goes it?' the Minister asked hopefully.

The Major looked drawn and tired, but the Minister knew he'd something positive to say. Bruus-Jensen outlined the basics of his plan, but clearly he worried about the detail. The Minister could do little but be as supportive as possible.

Further conversation was cut short as his Danish soldiers were called to stand-to as civilians were seen approaching their position, a sorry looking group of three elderly men, four women and a band of ragged looking children. Red Eric was busy questioning them, very vigorously. The Sergeant Major came running up to the Major.

'Good news Sir,' he breathlessly shouted out. 'These are survivors from a local village on an island near the main town. They're safe enough as Red Eric knows most of them.'

The news came from one of the oldest of the men who had, it seemed, hidden in a bell tower of the local church, and watched the Germans take up positions in and around the main town. He had noted with great care the positions the Germans had taken to cover the road junction; their escape route to the west.

The Major returned to his vantage point. Now he knew where to look he could make out the German disposition at the road junction, and saw the position was exposed, with no substantial cover.

His binoculars moved to the edge of the town where the old man said he saw the Germans busy taking up a strong defensive perimeter. At last he found it a large traditional stone barn with strong stone walls surrounding it; a tough nut to crack with his small force, head-to-head. He could also see a route where extra men could be moved up to the roadblock with a reasonable amount of cover.

He rested for a few minutes to let what he'd seen sink in. He needed an edge, but did not know what form it would take. He re-examined the landscape and let his binoculars wander from the road junction on the way to Berg. He paused and saw where part of the road disappeared into a large embankment.

The town side of the embankment appeared quite heavily wooded. If he could place some snipers in there, they could make things tough for the Germans below in the big barn. The range from the embankment to the barn, by his guess about six hundred metres, maybe a bit less. Difficult to be accurate at this distance. Of course, he thought, the Minister, he could be the edge he needed. Get him positioned up there with two or three of his men, and the Minister, with his trusty hunting rifle, could either bring down or keep down, most of the German force located in and around the barn.

Now the Major felt more positive, his plan would work. It just had to. Time to find out.

With reliable information as to the precise whereabouts of the German positions, the Major called a council of war with the Sergeant Major, his two sergeants, the Minister, the Police Superintendent and Red Eric. The plan he had outlined earlier was good to go with, and he only had to fix the timing and communications. He quickly filled in the new details to his audience.

Red Eric said he would need about an hour to get into position. When his men were ready he would make a signal. He wasn't sure what it would be, but the Major would know when it happened.

The Major continued. His men would move into action, eliminate the German position at the road junction and split his force into two.

The Minister and a small escort party would move up the road to Berg and take-up position at the top of the embankment, which he proceeded to mark on the map provided by Elgaard. This position had a clear field of fire over all the German positions and the Minister could use his remarkable shooting skills to good effect. He wanted the Minister to concentrate on eliminating German officers and NCOs to create confusion and a loss of tactical leadership. The Minister could see this would help, but he feared these German soldiers would still be very effective, leadership or no leadership.

The remainder of the Danish force would move quickly to take up positions in front of the main German position on the outskirts of the town. Their frontal attack would take place at the same time as the Viking attack from the rear. When the Vikings reached the main German position, the Danes would withdraw and retreat as fast as possible up the road to Berg.

Red Eric smiled to himself at the thought of his Vikings being left to decimate the German invaders in his own way and in his own time. What fun that was going to be.

The Major doubted the fun part, but this is what they had all trained for. Soon he would find out just how good they really were.

Chapter 16

The Battle of Holmestrand went almost to plan. After a long wait for the Vikings to get into position, the Major signalled for the mini-convoy of two captured German army trucks, with one of his own sandwiched in between, to head for the German position at the road junction to Berg. The German soldier's manning the road junction were taken aback to see the three trucks racing towards them with what appeared to be parachute storm troopers hanging outside of the trucks standing on the running boards with their automatic machine pistols pointed skywards. The centre truck seemed to be full of Danish prisoners.

The first two trucks roared by the checkpoint despite signals to stop. The third screeched to a halt, the soldiers hanging on the outside of the truck hit the ground running in all directions. The truck emptied another ten soldiers as they all began firing at once. Surprise was total as the Danes cut down every German soldier to a man.

With the position cleared, the remaining Danish trucks roared up to the road junction, disgorging the remaining Danish Rangers who quickly piled into the remaining German truck. The Major's heavy weapons and mortar section were quickly transferred, and the truck chased after the van of the Major's main attack force.

The Danish trucks with the Minister's precious cargo made their way up the road to Berg, stopping at the bottom of the embankment. In the back of the last truck, the Minister lay on the floor along with the Police Superintendent. The Minister was unnerved by the sound of battle; the Police Superintendent thought he should have been allowed to join in the action.

A sergeant opened up the back of the truck and called the Minister to jump out and come to the top of the embankment. The Police Superintendent followed, carrying ammunition for the Minister's rifle, and two ground covers to lie on. The other soldiers busied themselves unloading rifles and ammunition to take up station either side of the Minister's firing position.

The Minister removed the cover from his favourite hunting rifle, laid on the ground cover, and made himself comfortable in the prone position. He hid himself well in the undergrowth, a tribute to his big game hunting skills.

He bid the Police Superintendent to use his binoculars to spot his targets and to watch for any reaction from the German force hidden in the barn.

The Minister looked at the Sergeant, told him to keep close and feed him his ammunition when he called for it. The Police Superintendent began calling out targets for the Minister, as he prepared himself for his first experience of shooting at his fellow man. He didn't know how he would react but overwhelmed by the importance of his task he set to and steadied his nerves. His first two shots missed, but the range was long even for him. His next two shots hit their targets, more by luck than good judgement. He wiped the sweat from his forehead and forced his pulse to slow down as he tried to take up a steady rhythm. From then on in he hit his targets with increasing regularity.

The Police Superintendent picked out the targets, guiding the Minister to concentrate on eliminating the German officers and then any NCOs seen taking over command before calling out more general targets.

It would not be long before a German reaction set in. The fighting around the German held strong point slowly increased, as the Police Superintendent kept up a steady commentary of the battle.

The Major's men moved forward to their jumping off point, and began exchanging fire with the German troops. The Major waited for the arrival of the Vikings before he launched his main attack, and was relieved to see the sniper fire from the embankment starting to have an effect.

The Germans were getting restless, wondering whether to break out and take the initiative. That they waited so long began to worry the Major. The shape of the encounter looked strange and he began to wonder if he'd miscalled his strategy. It struck him the opposing forces could be stronger than he'd calculated. It was difficult to tell. If their forces were indeed larger, they could break out in two directions and he didn't have the men to resist such a move.

With both sides carefully dug in, little was happening for the moment, with only sporadic rifle fire being exchanged, as both sides conserved their supplies for their heavier weapons. The Major had little choice. His ammunition stocks were not extensive by any means, and a prolonged battle would be very disadvantageous.

One of his men called his attention to smoke rising from a house on the outskirts of the town behind the German position. The smoke changed in colour. The Major watched intently. The colour of the smoke held steady; he sensed Red Eric was about to attack. He signalled the mortars to open fire with H.E. and smoke grenades, before ordering one of the sections on his left flank to move forward under covering machine gun fire. The Germans reacted strongly to this move and countered it with heavy mortar and machine gun fire. Two of the Major's men were hit, one dropped like a stone, the other, wounded in the lower leg, reached cover behind a stone dyke wall. Not a good start.

The Major's mortars were blanketing the target area, with the smoke interfering with the German forces ability to lay down accurate fire on the Major's positions. The move on the left flank continued, fully occupying the German's attention.

All of a sudden, all hell broke loose in the German rear. Firebombs started to rain down on their positions. A squad of German paratroopers hiding behind a strong defensive position suddenly found themselves out-flanked as murderous fire rained down on them from an unexpected direction.

This is what the Major had been waiting for and ordered an all-out attack. His men were making splendid progress with few serious casualties. The Germans were clearly caught off-guard and their reaction to the two-prong attack became ragged and un-coordinated.

The Major felt elated but quickly realised he'd been out foxed. The number of Germans in front of him had halved. These troops were quickly reorganising and sheer attrition would soon swing the battle back in their favour. The Major called a halt to the advance of his rangers. His mortar section continued to fire with effect but the Major sensed their supply of ammunition was running low.

'Shit,' he muttered to himself. 'What next?'

'What next', took the form of Red Eric and his Viking hoard reaching the German positions. There seemed to be more Vikings than he'd expected. The Major did not know that Red Eric was a trifle late for his appointment on the battlefield as he'd been busy rounding up other sections of the local population. With the news of the atrocities carried out by the German Paratroopers rapidly becoming widespread they were thirsting for blood and revenge.

In a short time blood started to flow in increasing volumes. The in-fighting became barbaric. Many of the Vikings were armed wielding only their traditional double bladed axes. German heads were being cleaved open and a few almost severed at the neck. Limbs were hacked from torsos without mercy. The blood lust in the hearts of the Vikings and the local population from the ravaged town took fighting back to medieval times.

The German paratroopers had no experience of this furious and bloody fighting. For every Viking killed or wounded, two more took his place.

For every Viking who fell, so the next Viking became ever more violent, unstoppable violence that knew no bounds.

The Major was shocked to see some of the attacking Norwegians were women. Coarse brawny fishwives with wicked looking fish knives in one hand and a heavy blunt instrument in the other. They were screaming violent profanities without stop or repetition, urging and swearing at their men folk to even greater efforts and further untold violence.

The Major signalled his men to pull back from the fighting. He didn't want them becoming involved in the level of barbarity before them. He suddenly realised the German soldiers being slaughtered before his very eyes were different from the German paratroopers manning the road junction. These were standard Wehrmacht troops. Where in God's name were the German paratroopers he saw earlier?

Elgaard was under no such difficulties. As the attack by the Vikings built-up in the German rear, Horskjaer took a short breather. The Minister felt pleased with his shooting, but killing men was a new and unnerving experience. He felt buoyed up by the running commentary from Elgaard, and the fact the battle seemed to be going, as far as anyone could tell, more or less to plan. The Police Superintendent relayed to the rangers on the embankment the events going on below them. The Major's men were taking casualties, but they seemed to be slight given the intensity of the conflict.

Now Elgaard was alarmed. The flow of battle changed and he sensed something wrong. With his binoculars, he had brief glimpses of the Major who seemed to have pulled his rangers back from the main fighting and was looking around. The Major was searching for something. The Police Superintendent looked down the slope in front of him.

He saw movement, short brief movements by heavily camouflaged shapes that could only be German paratroopers. He watched for a few minutes. Their movements were skilful and coordinated, maximising use of existing cover, but it was becoming very obvious what was their objective, the embankment. Surely they were not after the Minister?

The Sergeant and his two companions opened fire upon the advancing Germans, with little success. Their targets presented themselves only briefly, and the range was still long.

Elgaard was confused. The advancing Germans returned fire at the flanks of the Danish Rangers positions but not in the direction of the Minister. They knew roughly where he hid in the undergrowth on top of the embankment, his hunting rifle made a very distinctive sound.

The German paratroopers were getting too close for comfort, they would be extremely difficult to stop and the threat unnerved the Sergeant and his two rangers.

'Minister,' he shouted at the top of his voice. 'We need your help; the Germans are coming for you. You must resume shooting.'

The Minister came to with a start. He saw the danger and it galvanised him back into action. His rifle was cooler, more accurate and his first shot didn't miss. In the brief few seconds of exposure, running for new cover, a German paratrooper was hit in the head by a .375 bullet. The back of the unfortunate head exploded, the corpse dropped like a stone.

The Police Superintendent resumed his position next to the Minister, calling out the next best target. The Minister was grateful to divide the task, the Police Superintendent called the shots; he concentrated on his shooting. The Minister fought the rising panic within himself. Six shots later, with six bodies on the ground, his fear started to slowly subside. The advancing paratroopers slowed their advance; they were running out of cover. The Minister continued his methodical shooting.

His success brought a rising feeling of elation. The power of his trusty hunting rifle made him intoxicated. He missed a shot, and the fear instantly returned. The Sergeant nailed the missed target from his right flank. The feeling of support gave him renewed hope. His next two shots were on target, but by now the Germans were less than two hundred metres away and moving purposely his way.

His fear started to rise once more; then it became anger. These bastards were after him, and he knew why. He had a great secret and he sensed, they, the enemy, knew what it was.

The Minister stood up and positioned himself against a tree to lean on. It gave better freedom of movement, with partial protection and a firm support. The sergeant filled his pockets with more fresh rounds. The Minister's right hand a blur of smooth action; pull back the rifle bolt, eject the spent round, remove a fresh round from his pocket and smoothly insert it into the breach. Slide the bolt forward; take aim, pause and fire. Another German paratrooper went to his maker.

Suddenly, upwards of fifteen paratroopers broke cover and sprinted towards his position. The Minister became so intent on his shooting his emotions suddenly disappeared. He continued firing in quick succession. The bodies of dead Germans started to form a line in front of him. His very actions appeared to go into slow motion, like a never-ending nightmare. Load, aim, fire, hit; another mortal fell dead to the ground. The German paratroopers were weaving from side to side, but the Minister was a master at shooting elk on the run. Load, aim, fire, hit. Yet another mortal fell dead to the ground.

A large brute of a paratrooper, possibly the section leader, came at him, weaving and running at speed. The Minister tried to bring him down, but each shot seemed to hit another paratrooper running in front of this beast. He could sense his evil, the beast was coming directly for him. The beast was firing, but not at him. The beast wounded the Sergeant and shot dead one of the rangers. Was there no stopping this man?

He was vaguely aware of fresh rounds being fed into his empty pockets. The Minister kept firing but the brute kept coming. He fired twice more; two more Germans fell to the ground but not the brute coming for him. It was like a bad dream, the worse nightmare ever and panic rose strongly within him. He fired again and his shot hit the brute. At last. But the brute didn't stop. His shot was too low, and it had gone clean through the brute's right side. The round hit nothing vital and the brute kept on coming.

The Minister once shot boar on a shooting holiday and nearly been gouged to death. He'd learnt then to pause, miss a shot, and then make the next shot count at close range. Range so close you could feel the mad breath of the animal in your nostrils. Range so close the .375' round would stop any charging animal. On that occasion, the tactic had worked. The relief of surviving that encounter left him totally elated.

The Minister took a huge breath and steadied his nerve. The brute was nearly upon him, just twenty more metres. He lifted his rifle, aimed at the brute's chest and fired. Nothing! A dud round; the first in ten years. He stood petrified, unable to move.

Eric Horskjaer vaguely heard a shot from his right, and the back of the brute's head exploded. Blood and other debris flew in all direction. Most of it hit Horskjaer full in the face. The momentum brought the brute crashing down upon him, as he was crushed to the ground under the collapsing corpse.

The silence was palpable, almost eerie. The Minister lay helpless under the corpse of the brute, unable to move, all strength drained from his body. He felt movement. Others dragged the corpse to one side. He felt himself being helped to his feet. His legs could not support him. He looked at his helpers and was relieved to see Elgaard, on one side and Per Bruus-Jensen, and his good friend the Major, on the other.

The Major brought his battered but victorious band of rangers away from the battle in the town of Holmestrand. He'd left the fighting in the hands of the Vikings, more to keep his own men safe for when the Vikings ran out of Germans to kill and would be unable to stop their blood lust.

The Minister managed a weak smile and for the first time looked down away from his firing position. What he saw shocked him to the core. A long pile of German corpses stretched out in a ragged line down the slope. The line of German corpses pointed at him. He'd shot and killed nearly every one of them before him, lying cold and lifeless on the ground.

The force of his actions shocked his sensibilities. He'd become a monster, a killing machine. He, Eric Horskjaer, minister of state, family man, widower, academic, and professor of social science. It was all too much. The mental agony felled him like a fatal blow, as he collapsed to the ground in welcome unconsciousness.

The Major shouted for his medic. The medic quickly made his way to the top of the embankment. He saw the Minister laid out on the ground unmoving. He moved to examine the Minister but found no injuries and cleaned his face up as best as he could.

The Minister's breathing had become shallow and very irregular. His face death white, the blood almost totally drained from his face. The medic looked questioningly up at the Major uncertain as what to do next. Fortunately, the Major had some idea of what had happened, although he did not have any previous experience to offer. The Minister was in some kind of deep shock, traumatic shock, from the enormity of his actions.

Bruus-Jensen knew to act quickly to prevent the shock from deepening and kill the Minister. From what little he knew, this type of shock would develop, not instantaneously, hence his feeling of great dread. The Major ordered the medic to administer an anaesthetic to keep the Minister unconscious.

The medic rummaged around in his kit bag and found the correct medication. He lifted the Minister's limp right arm, pulled back his sleeve, found the main vein in his arm above the wrist, swabbed the area with alcohol and injected a large dose of general anaesthetic.

The Minister's breathing slowed and became more regular. A little colour slowly returned to his face, but the man looked very ill. Elgaard called two of the rangers to bring a stretcher and after Horskjaer had been carefully transferred he was carried down to the waiting trucks at the bottom of the embankment.

The Major took stock. He still had two trucks in good shape, and at least, the cargo remained intact. The truck used in the initial assault at the road block and into battle at Holmestrand had been hit many times by rifle fire before a rifle grenade landed in the back blowing the rear of the cab away, severely damaging the chassis, before bursting into flames. His other truck used in the assault had its radiator damaged beyond repair.

As to casualties, overall, seven of his rangers had been killed. Two badly wounded rangers had been dropped off at the local cottage hospital. He'd no idea if they would receive the urgent treatment needed to keep them alive, but at least they had been dosed with morphine and left with a fussing matron.

Now his force numbered twenty tired but uninjured rangers, plus nine walking wounded, none of whom were fit for much but refused to be left behind, a total of twenty-nine.

The Sergeant Major came staggering from one of the trucks. He'd sprained an ankle attempting an activity well beyond his years. As hobbled on his extensively strapped foot, his bad temper, never far behind in stressful times, was in full flow as he bullied his men into order.

The Major suddenly remembered the captured German Lieutenant. He was relieved to find him still handcuffed in the back of the Police Superintendent's car. The Major gave the keys to the Sergeant and asked for their German guest to be released and taken to the cab of the first truck. He signalled for everyone to climb aboard the trucks and move out. At last, they were on the way to Berg.

The Major held up his hand to stop the convoy.

'Where are the two Viking guides Red Eric promised?' he asked the Sergeant Major.

The Sergeant Major looked at him and said, 'you must be joking, Sir. At the first sign of the fighting they were off. I haven't seen them since.'

'What do we do now?' asked the Major. Any ideas?'

'Head up the road to Berg, not much else for it,' suggested the Sergeant Major.

The Major was not impressed.

The road to Berg, in his opinion, was not going to be a joy ride.

Chapter 17

The Major looked up at the road to Berg and shrugged his shoulders.

'OK, Sergeant Major lets go,' said the Major, as he slumped wearily into the passenger seat of the lead truck.

The journey to Berg became rough and tiring. Winter had left the road in poor condition, and with darkness heralding the end of a long tiring and murky day, the journey would appear much further than its thirty-five kilometres.

The Danish army trucks were fitted with 'look down' shielded headlights and the drivers were having great difficulty in keeping to the middle of a wandering road despite following the car driven by Elgaard.

The Major thought about the wounded men in the back of the trucks. The preparation in Copenhagen to hang stretchers from racks in the roof now paid-off, and it was the best that could be done, but the rough ride would still be a severe trial for them in their injured condition.

The second truck had the best of it following behind. It carried the most wounded, but the road conditions were hard on both vehicles and their cooped up passengers.

Sitting in the uncomfortable cab the Major had to admit he was pooped. He needed sanctuary for his men, at least for the night, and the knowledge the German army were making a strong effort to find them meant they could not take any assistance from the local population least they be placed in even more danger.

A nagging doubt at the back of his mind was slowly but surely wrecking his concentration. Something was not quite right but he could not put his finger on it. The defeat of the Germans at Holmestrand had been a mixture of good soldering and good luck. His men performed well above expectations. Being able to leave the conclusion of the battle to the marauding Vikings came as a stroke of good fortune. Their brutality sickened him, but then he supposed if his home city had been massacred in a most brutal way he might have been motivated to act similarly.

The Major hoped the Vikings would carry out their promise to clear away the dead bodies and clean-up the battlefield to confuse the German army expected to arrive anytime soon. Certainly a large number of German paratroopers and regular Wehrmacht had disappeared. Red Eric promised he would strip and bury the German corpses and spirit away all their equipment. Red Eric had nothing to lose, his community was gone, and now he had a great revenge raging inside him. It would burn until the day he himself was cut down. Whatever happened, German armed forces would rue the day they ever crossed paths.

The Major thoughts were interrupted as the truck hit a large pothole and bounced hard into the snow bank lining the side of the road. The second truck narrowly missed ramming into the rear of his truck. At least, there were plenty of willing bodies to push, shove and curse to get the truck back onto the road.

Before the convoy started off again, the Major took the opportunity to look in the back of the second truck and found the medic attending to the wounded. One of the ranger's conditions was far worse than he'd been told, but too late now to head back to the cottage hospital at Holmestrand. Perhaps there were medical facilities in Berg. He just wished the damn town would show up in the headlights.

The Major asked the medic about the Minister. He was still out cold, with a trusted ranger keeping a close eye on him, guarding his precious rifle in its protective leather bag. The Minister's face had regained a little more colour, but he was still plainly in deep shock.

The journey resumed, as the Danish trucks lurched and bounced their way up the road to Berg. At long last the convoy reached the outskirts of the town. The Major directed his driver to head for the town centre. The town was typical Norwegian of traditional brightly painted tall roofed wooden houses and red-roofed neo-Baroque municipal and commercial buildings in the centre of town.

There were no streetlights to show the way. Clearly the local town council saw the need to black out their city with the onset of war.

The convoy entered into a large square. The substantial art nouveau building facing them had a large clock face set into the wall below the roofline. It had to be the town hall. A strong torchlight flashed from a side street. The Major saw a police sergeant heading towards them at the run. Two of his rangers jumped out of the rear of his truck and covered him with their weapons. The rangers from the second truck jumped down and took up defensive positions. Elgaard, jumped out of his car and made his way to the approaching police officer. They conversed for a few moments, and then quickly returned to report to the Major.

'Major Per,' he began. 'Good news, we have been asked to bring the trucks around to the back of the town hall. A meal has been prepared for your men and they can also wash up a little too.'

The Major was lost for words but before he could speak Elgaard told him the Mayor of Berg couldn't offer sanctuary for the night, it would be too dangerous. Clearly the Germans had their contacts in the area. The Major called the Sergeant Major to his side and issued a string of orders to enable half the men to be fed whilst the others kept guard. The Major remained cautious. The feeling of unease from the 'back of his head' feeling still bugged him.

It was warm inside the town hall, a welcome change from the cold raw night air. There were flurries of snow, and the wind started to pick up at this higher altitude. It became a dark dank night, and there was still the problem of where to house his men for the night.

The Mayor of Berg pushed through the crowd and introduced himself. The Major immediately forgot his name, but at least, he remembered to thank him for the hot food being served to his men. The Major asked about hospital facilities. The Mayor pointed to three nurses in the far corner of the hall attending to the wounded. The Major asked about leaving the ranger too injured to go on; his condition worsening all the time.

The Mayor of Berg looked very nervous at the idea of one of the Danish rangers being left behind. He went over to examine the ranger in question, and could see the man definitely could not continue the journey. One of the nurses came over to them, obviously the matron, a large determined woman, one that it would not be wise to cross.

The Mayor of Berg updated her on the situation, and could she get the wounded man ready for the next phase of the journey? Matron held the Mayor in her steely gaze, stony-faced, waiting for him to say something slightly more intelligent. The Mayor of Berg began to panic, apparently a well known trait. Matron would wait no longer, excused herself from the Major and led the Mayor of Berg to one side.

'Rather him than me,' thought the Major. Two Norwegian helpers were summoned by Matron. She turned to the Major and asked for the man's kit bag. The Major sent one of the corporals to fetch it.

'What can you do for him?' asked the Major anxiously.

The Matron saw Bruus-Jensen's worried look. She liked the look of the Major; his priority was looking after his men. She liked that in a commander. The Major didn't know Matron herself had served in the Norwegian army and fully capable of looking after wounded men. In the past she'd revelled in their gratefulness, thus proving if nothing else, their physical fitness. It would be a long time before this handsome blonde Danish Ranger would be in any condition to be grateful.

The Major asked where she was taking him. She smiled back at the Major. 'Not quite sure Major. The Mayor is worried about hiding your man from the Germans. I have an idea which should work, and if he lives, I send him back home somehow.'

The Major gave in. He was tired, and could suggest no other options. He knew not to ask any more questions. Matron disappeared with the wounded ranger and two helpers. The Major grabbed hold of the Mayor of Berg as he passed by. The Mayor looked to the disappearing Matron, turned and smiled.

'He'll be OK if he pulls through,' he said. 'She is a very capable person. She fancies him, he will survive, well, survive his wounds anyway.'

Time for the Major to get his meal. His rangers were being well fed, and they had filled their hungry bellies. The food was hot although the Major wasn't quite sure what it was. Meat and vegetables, with great chunks of fresh bread. He was just grateful to eat something hot and get a short break from the many matters plaguing his mind.

The Police Superintendent came in from the street, served himself and sat down next to the Major. They consumed their food in silence as one of the rangers brought two mugs of coffee.

The Major started to thank the Norwegian policeman but Elgaard held his hand up, apologised, but told the Major the time had come to return to his home in Larvik, to his family, his duties, and to try to lead his community through the trauma of the impending German occupation. The Major knew well the real reason, he wanted to return before being tarred with helping the Danish Force and suffer the consequences of German revenge.

Bruus-Jensen thanked Elgaard for all his assistance. But before he left, he wished to know more about the Viking community. What was the big deal with the Germans, or rather the Nazis, who as far as he good tell, were hell bent on eliminating the Vikings even before the first battle on the road to Holmestrand.

Elgaard drained the coffee from his mug and pulled out a hip flask. He offered it to the Major. He took a large swig, and whatever the contents were, it was strong. It left him gasping for breath as the liquid burnt its way to his stomach. Elgaard drank an even larger draft from the flask, without grimacing, clearly accustomed to the fire water.

He started with the history of the Viking community. Red Eric had always been a dreamer for the past glories of the Vikings. He knew their history from first to last. The Vikings were a strong race, a clever and intelligent people. They'd travelled far and wide, discovered the northern extremities of North America, and populated many areas in Europe. They were traders, farmers and feared warriors. Red Eric had access to ancient records, carefully hidden away. Red Eric had also been brought up on the tales from storytellers, who had passed stories handed down from father to son since time began.

As Red Eric grew up he became the natural leader of what, in the mid-1920s, was a small closely knit community. Red Eric had his family around him, brothers, cousins, and many from faraway lands. Slowly but surely he had brought them together. The community prospered, mostly through fishing, but some farmed, others traded, but all were always active. The Viking men did have a higher natural strength, but their lifestyle ensured their enhanced physical and mental toughness. Local sport competitions showed how much stronger they were in terms of physical activity.

Red Eric had hit upon a method of selecting women, who in his opinion, would bare strong Viking children. God knows how he did it, but the children born into the community were indeed a cut above the local population, especially in raw strength and fortitude.

The Major sat fascinated as Elgaard continued. He told a story about a professor of history working at the Faculty of Humanities in the Centre for Viking and Medieval Studies at the famous University of Oslo, founded in 1811 as Universitas Regia Fredericiana (the Royal Frederick University), the oldest, largest and most prestigious university in Norway.

This Norwegian professor chanced upon the story regarding the Viking community based on a small island on the outskirts of Tønsberg. He'd researched Viking history many years ago, and believed the Vikings, as a race, had died out long ago. The Professor didn't find it easy to get new information. The young Viking men in Oslo knew to keep quiet. Red Eric drummed it into them not to broadcast his, and their achievements. Time had yet to prove the long-term viability of the community. A lot could go wrong, and ridicule and adverse comment could harm any progress achieved. The Professor knew he had stumbled on to something, and made haste slowly in his investigations.

Slowly but surely he assembled the facts as he found them. The Professor carefully and discreetly interviewed the local people of Tønsberg and Holmestrand, the two largest towns close to the Viking community, and built up an impressive file. In the mid-1930s, the professor had spent some time in Hitler's resurgent Germany. The claims by the Nazis and their fixation of the Aryan race nonsense rang a bell. Perhaps one race could indeed be stronger than another. The Professor mistakenly ignored the Nazi propaganda regarding the Jews. He hadn't made the connection that the Nazis were not about to suffer any competition in their views on the master race.

The Professor shared his research on the Vikings with a trusted friend from a German university in Hamburg, little knowing his friend had long been sucked into the Nazi philosophy, and secretly commissioned to build a historical case for the superiority of the Aryan race. Deep down, he knew his research had flaws, but his preliminary reports pleased his Nazis masters, keeping the funds flowing in for more research. He was making a good living at it too. Now here came a chance to tap into some real research and impress his Nazi masters.

Elgaard paused to take another swig from his fast emptying hip flask.

The German professor had, over a period of time, sucked his gullible friend dry and presented a very detailed report as his own work to his Nazi masters. His thesis was that the Aryan race descended from the Vikings and providing proof of their superiority. To his shock, the Nazis considered the Aryan race had been descendant since time began and considered the Vikings as competition.

He thought the matter had died down, just as his stipend took a large drop. In reality, the Nazis sent secret agents to check out the report and were horrified to discover that the Viking Community built by Red Eric had indeed achieved what had been reported. Apparently Hitler himself had been briefed and descended into a terrible rage. The German professor was summoned by Himmler himself.

The very scared professor had been quietly, and with great skill and menace, interrogated by Himmler. Himmler left the room, leaving the German professor quaking in his boots. Two hours later, so the story goes, Himmler returned, thanked the professor for his work, confiscated all his notes, gave him a large packet of cash and told to lose himself in the deepest corner of his university, never to speak or reveal to anyone what had happened. He was left in no doubt to his fate if he did not comply.

And that was the story. Clearly the Nazis kept the information on file, no doubt keeping a close eye on the Viking community from a distance, noting everything down and preparing for the day when they could do something about it.

That day had come and now the Nazis had sown the wind, and Red Eric would provide the whirlwind. Elgaard told the Major that every weapon Red Eric could lay his hands on had disappeared to God know where. Red Eric had networks far and wide, and now he was calling his like-minded patriots to arms. The Germans were in for a rough occupation; only time would tell how rough.

He knew the local population would also suffer the consequences for whatever Red Eric cooked up for the Germans. The local population would have to tread carefully in trying to mitigate some of the effects of the underground resistance against the Germans. No doubt the British would introduce secret agents to coordinate actions and install supply lines. It was all there to be seen, and the war not even two days old.

The Major was impressed by the depth of Elgaard's view of the future. Clearly he'd not been an ordinary member of the Norwegian Army. The Major sat back and searched for a cigarette. The package had survived the exertions of the day although its contents were somewhat bent out of shape.

'Just like their owner,' mussed the Major.

Elgaard sat in silence with the Major before turning to ask why the German paratroopers seemed so suicidally intent on capturing the Minister. The Major knew where this question had come from, and it worried him greatly. It would seem there remained a lot he didn't know. He still felt very uneasy, and could not settle his mind on this and other events that had unfolded during the day.

'Gunnar,' he started, 'to be totally honest, I just don't know. The Germans clearly know something I don't. That they tried to take the Minister alive, despite being cut down to a man in the process, makes no sense at all.'

The Major had become aware his Sergeant Major had taken more than a passing interest in his conversation and had tried to move in his direction without being noticed. What to do?

Time to make a move. Time was passing and there was the small problem of where to get his men bedded down safely for the night.

'Anyway Gunner,' he continued, 'I need to move my men out and get them to safety for the night. Any ideas?'

Gunnar Elgaard replied, 'Sure, the local police sergeant has organised something, let's go and find out.'

The pair of them stood up together and went to search for the local police sergeant. Yes. He had an idea what to do. The Major thought something concrete was called for.

'Major,' began the police sergeant, 'as soon as your men are ready we shall take the road to the west, up through a couple of mountain passes. They still have a lot of snow so your trucks will need snow chains. They're being fitted now, your Corporal told me you had them and I have two mechanics getting them fitted.'

Beyond the second pass, about two kilometres is a turn-off to the north and you will find a large lodge, with a big barn. The barn is used for livestock brought down from the mountains before winter sets in. Sometimes we keep snowploughs up there to keep the road to the west open.'

'The area is clear of snow; it's only the east facing side of the mountains that still has a good covering. Take your trucks there and bed down for the night. You should meet a large farm girl who looks after livestock. Don't mess with her; she's a strong wench and then some.'

The Major smiled at the thought of Red Eric finding new breeding stock for his community.

'Does she have red hair,' asked the Major.

'Yes,' replied the police sergeant. 'Why do you ask?'

'Never mind,' smiled the Major, his suspicions confirmed.

The police sergeant continued, 'I will be coming with you to the second pass with my skis. You'll easily find your way after that.'

'How will you get back?' asked the Major.

'On my skis. It's downhill all the way. I'll need a rifle with a grenade launcher and some grenades. On the way down, I'll fire grenades into the snow overhangs and trigger avalanches in the two passes. It should keep out any uninvited guest for some time. Our snow machines will be awaiting parts and repairs should anyone unwelcome ask. The Germans can't dig out that much snow in a hurry.'

Gunnar Elgaard made a quick departure as the Major nodded his thanks, thankful for the small amount of relief to relax his mind just a little. He made to move among his men and bumped into Sergeant Soeren Koppel, a first cousin, and so far during this epic event, there had been precious little time to talk.

The Major's pre-occupations were building fast and he badly need to talk to someone he could trust implicitly. They'd been good friends for many years, enjoying a natural relationship. They enjoyed sailing together and didn't live in each other's pockets. Koppel was honest to himself and straight forward in his dealing with all his family and friends. He'd joined the Danish Rangers many years before Bruus-Jensen had taken over, and was good at what he did as an armourer and logistics specialist. An order given was always an order carried out, no fuss, and no drama.

'Sergeant Koppel,' the Major called out. 'How are you getting on?'

Koppel knew his man; this small talk was the start of a meaningful conversation. He saw his favourite relation more stressed, probably than he'd ever been in his life, his face drawn, the lines on his face deep and ugly.

'Need to talk, Per?' he asked. 'Let's grab the last of the coffee over at the serving hatch.'

They found quiet in the corner of the town hall. The other rangers were busy in the washrooms and toilets. The Norwegian helpers inside the kitchen were frantically clearing away the wreckage of feeding so many hungry soldiers so quickly. The Major looked around. The Sergeant Major and increasingly his shadow, Sergeant Knut Kirkby, were busy with the many preparations needed to move the rangers out to the waiting trucks.

'Yes Soeren, something is wrong and I can't put my finger on it.'

'Per, our situation has been fucked up all day long, ever since we landed,' replied Koppel. 'We've been lucky though. That was a good scrap back at Holmestrand, everyone did very well, except for those poor sods who didn't make it or were wounded. Anyway, what's on your mind?'

'What's on my mind is a mission that's gone pear-shaped. That I can handle. Wandering around with two tonnes of gold and half the German Army after me, that too I can cope with. But this Viking community being slaughtered and the German paratrooper's attack directly on the Minister doesn't add up. You see, this mission has been put together in great secrecy, so why do I get the feeling that too many damn strangers know what the hell is going on.'

The Major continued, 'Look at the prisoner, the German Lieutenant over there. He knows more about something than I do. I swear he has information I need. The Sergeant Major and Sergeant Kirkby, normally very reliable men, there is something about those two as well. They know something I don't. What is it? The Minister is in shock and has to be kept totally sedated. Did you see all those Germans he killed?'

'No I didn't, heard about it though; he shot how many, thirty plus?

'Easily. Damn fine shooting though. Mostly from long range, but at the end when that Nazi brute almost killed him, that must have been a dreadful experience. The Police Superintendent with him described it in great detail. Lucky for everyone he didn't freeze.'

'Just to finish, this meal here tonight, who on earth organised that? And now we have somewhere to go to for a night stopover, and the local police sergeant has it all figured out how to stop the German army chasing after us for at least two/three days. Interesting.'

Koppel started to see things in a new light. Little things, like the local police mechanics arriving to fit snow chains onto the two trucks. How did they know about them? They were only thrown in the back of the trucks at the last moment, more of a whim than a deliberate action. And yes, the Sergeant Major and his favourite sergeant had shown another side of themselves, to him and to the men. He couldn't put his finger on the change, but change there was.

The Major saw it was time to go. He hadn't mentioned that the Sergeant Major was keeping a close eye on him, the feeling of menace existed, and he could just not explain it.

'Soeren, do me a favour, keep an eye on me whenever the Sergeant Major and his tame sergeant gets too close, OK?'

Koppel could see his cousin was genuinely concerned about something unexplainable but why the concern? Personal safety? Surely not?

Out in the town square, the two Danish army trucks were almost ready as the rangers frantically completed preparations to move out. The Sergeant Major wanted to dump unwanted material and weapons, but the local Mayor wouldn't consider it. Every trace of the Dane's short visit was in the process of being erased. They'd received help, welcome help, but it became very clear the town wished their guests to depart and soon.

The Major was the last to leave the town hall. He ordered the Minister moved into the cab of the lead truck. Koppel took over as lead driver. He had the most off-road driving experience, so this change over could be considered normal although the Sergeant Major took note of the late change. He had his own worries, and he had the German Lieutenant who'd been kept quiet throughout to look after.

The Major checked the wounded in their stretchers were safely strapped in the racks in the back of the trucks. The fit and able rangers were tightly packed in. Comfortable they were not. The Major marched to his truck, thanked the waiting Mayor of Berg for all his help and signalled his small convoy to move out. A Norwegian police car pulled in front of the Major's truck and began to lead them out of town.

'No effort has been spared,' thought the Major.

Why were they in such a hurry to see the back of them? The convoy reached the outer limits of the City of Berg. The police car stopped, the police sergeant got out, took his skis and poles from the roof rack, and threw them in the back of the first truck and jumped in. The convoy renewed its journey and began the long climb up the valley, in inky black darkness, with flurries of snow spinning around in the raw wind. Their departure was hardly quiet as the snow chains assaulted the road surface badly damaged by a long winter of snow and ice.

Koppel kept his speed low. He'd been told the journey to the top of the second pass should take about an hour. The road began to twist and turn, with snow poles lining the road on the inside. The convoy passed the snow line as the Sergeant dropped a gear and engaged the truck's all-wheel drive system. The engine laboured hard as the road gradient sharply increased. The Sergeant dropped another gear, selecting the lowest ratio. The trucks were driving on packed snow, the snow chains biting deeply into the surface.

The Sergeant felt grateful for the added grip of the chains but was rudely reminded things were going to get worse as his truck passed over a section a packed ridged ice. His truck lurched badly toward the road edge. He could sense, rather than see, the drop on the offside. The added blackness promised only severe danger.

A snowstorm hit the convoy, but thankfully blown snow rather than a fresh downfall. The snowstorm vanished as the wind dropped. Koppel's hands were sweating with the effort to keep his vehicle safe, despite the obvious cold in the cab. His passengers sat stony-faced as they peered out into the meagre light from the rapidly obscured headlights.

The convoy continued to grind its way up to the first pass through the deteriorating weather. It passed the first set of snow gates that appeared recently opened. Old tyre tracks were faintly visible in the snow. Sergeant Koppel thought this a positive sign the road would eventually improve as forecast. The Major saw the same thing, but his mind drifted into a blank. He drifted between dosing and just plain staring into the distance, trying to get some space for peace in his head. Normally it would come, but the obviousness of their dire situation prevented it.

The convoy began a small descent and Koppel tested his brakes to find them satisfactory. Despite all-wheel drive and the snow chains, his truck slid and lurched all over the road, sometimes getting too close for comfort to the long drop below. The snow poles were a god send, without them he would have lost the road long before now. The snow blew around in a dizzying swirling action that hurt his eyes. He wanted to reduce speed even further, but daren't. Momentum coupled with smooth driving was a must. He enjoyed driving on snow, but the stress of this task pressed very hard on him.

The road started to climb again. A sharp right-hand turn over a small bridge started the assent up to the second pass. In the back of the truck, the Norwegian Police Sergeant wondered why they were going so slow. Had the Major asked he would have volunteered as lead driver. The ranger driving the second truck had little experience of these conditions, desperately trying to follow the lead truck, mimicking its every movement.

The convoy entered the last stage up the steep mountain pass. The engines of both trucks laboured very hard. The trucks were heavily overloaded, but at least, the extra weight caused the snow chains to bite more deeply through the snow to the ice below. Sergeant Koppel looked nervously out of his misted up window and wondered if the noise from the two trucks constituted an avalanche risk.

Twenty long minutes passed and, at last, the snow stopped as they crested the top of the second pass and the road gradient reduced to a gentle level. The moon shone brightly and for a change, Sergeant Koppel could see where he was going. A loud banging noise on the back of his cab was the message to stop and let the Norwegian Police Sergeant disembark and commence his return back to Berg. He braked slowly to a stop, as the other truck came up behind.

The Major jumped out of the truck cab and helped the Police Sergeant disembark. One of the rangers handed out a German rifle fitted with a grenade launcher and six grenades. The Police Sergeant stuffed the grenades into his backpack. From inside the truck came his skis, bindings and poles. Quickly fitting his ski bindings to his boots, he pulled out a set of goggles from his large backpack and fitted them over his thick woollen ski hat. The Major helped with his backpack. Getting the rifle positioned over his backpack took a bit of a fiddling with the straps, but soon he was ready. The Major thanked him for all his help and shook his hand vigorously. The Police Sergeant merely grunted some words of encouragement, and in a flash he disappeared.

The Major jumped back in the truck. Time to find the promised safe haven and get his men bedded down after what had been a truly adventurous day. He worried about the Police Sergeant getting back to Berg in one piece. He needn't have bothered. The Police Sergeant was a good as his word, skiing swiftly down the road in an excellent graceful telemark style he'd perfected over many years in the mountains. His first stop in the second pass went well. A clear sky allowed the waning moon to illuminate the large overhang of snow that always threatened.

He judged his first grenade to perfection, and as the triggered avalanche roared down behind him he skied quickly out of harm's way. His task at the first pass required two grenades, but he soon succeeded in triggering a magnificent avalanche which crashed down sweeping all before it and covering the road in over thirty metres of snow, ice and rocks, forming a perfect barrier for quite a few days, maybe a week with any luck.

The Police Sergeant continued down the road to Berg. He stopped a few times to reposition some ski poles on the outside edge of the road in the knowledge their new position wouldn't fool the locals, but he doubted if any strangers on this difficult road would notice the difference.

High above the second pass, the convoy found the turn-off to the Mountain Lodge. The Major was relieved to find shelter as promised. The two trucks circled around the back of the buildings. The Major found that the high side of the lodge adjacent to a large barn with the intervening space bridged by a sloping roof forming a perfect shelter for his vehicles.

Now it was time to rest, regroup and get organised.

Chapter 18

To the Major's surprise, the Mountain Lodge had welcoming fires burning in the main rooms, the sauna up to temperature, and the house girl had hot drinks and food ready in large bubbling cauldrons. The house girl was a large, strong, fulsome lass, with a mass of red-blonde hair falling down around her face. She took one hard long look at a Danish Ranger who had ideas of a passing romantic nature. He stopped, rooted to the spot. He'd survived enough activity for one day, and his urges soon left him.

The Sergeant Major waded in, organising and getting his men divided into three groups. One to be fed, one to head to the sauna, and the last group were sent outside to ensure the trucks were hidden from road and air, defensive positions prepared and their arms and munitions deployed ready for use. This last group had barely completed their work, when a slow steady heavy snowfall began, blocking out any chance of unwelcome guests making it to the Mountain Lodge that night.

Within the next two hours, the three groups had rotated, and with only a minimal guard, the weary bedded down for the night wherever they could. The Major did his rounds, checked the wounded, saw that the German officer was secured, and ensured the Minister had been transferred to a large comfortable bunk with the medic cat napping close to hand.

The Major found a camp bed prepared for him and a more welcome resting place would be hard to imagine. At least he was warm and fed. The red-hot sauna, with massive amounts of steam pouring from the room, cleansing his aching body. The pool of his sweat and filth flowed on to the wooden floor along with other rivers of contaminated water, as it flowed down the central drain. The house girl made frequent visits to the sauna to keep the tall wood-burning stove fully charged, and wash the floor with disinfected water. The plunge into the large snow bank just outside the back door of the sauna completed the revival of the Major's aching body.

Afterwards in the recovery room, the Major sat back in a large comfortable reclining chair wearing a huge bath robe nursing a hot steaming mug of spiked wine with herbs. He tried to mull over the events of the day. His brain refused to put them in the correct order and could make no sense of them. There was just too much detail, conflicting detail, facts that didn't fit in anywhere, and too many coincidences.

He found himself falling asleep in the chair. He gathered himself, dressed, headed upstairs to his camp bed, fell into a dreamless sleep and didn't stir until morning. He was pleased to wake to a mug of steaming coffee, and a silence around him that could only come from a Mountain Lodge totally cut-off from the outside world by last night's snow storm.

Per Bruus-Jensen roused himself and looked out at the wintry scene. The blanket of snow formed a thick deep carpet overlaying the countryside. He could see the faint gloomy outline of the two mountains guarding the road back down to Berg. The lack of footprints in the snow around the Mountain Lodge indicated his men had not begun to stir either. He could hardly blame them after the traumatic events inflicted upon them since Larvik. The Major stared into the distance hard and long. A faint line in the clouds to the west appeared to herald a break in the wintery conditions.

The wind abated and the scene before him was as calm as it was beautiful; a fine day for cross-country skiing. The Major looked over at the building opposite, to see a lookout in the upstairs window. The duty ranger waved, his hand signal indicated no untoward movement to ruin the start of a peaceful morning.

The Major finished his coffee and pulled on his boots and battle jacket, donned his cap and went downstairs. The house girl was busy serving a hot breakfast to those rangers who'd risen early. The Major went to look for the Sergeant Major and found him in the washroom preparing for the day.

'Good-morning Sergeant Major, anything to report?'

Anker Kjaergaard finished drying his face and buttoned up his shirt.

'Good morning, Major,' he replied evenly. 'No, not really. Sergeant Kirkby is leading the guard, which changed at 6 am. All the rangers are rested and being fed in shifts. Apart from the lookouts, the men are taking time to prepare their personal items for today. All weapons were cleaned last night by the lookouts, and this morning a detail of rangers will muster all available ammunition. I think stocks are reasonable considering, but depends what comes at us in the next few days.'

Pleased with the report that things were well in-hand, Bruus-Jensen asked, 'How are the wounded, and the Minister?'

The Sergeant Major reported the wounded were much better after being properly cleaned and their wounds re-dressed more calmly than the events of yesterday allowed. The medic remained anxious about the Minister, but he'd organised two rangers to get him bathed and changed into clean clothes.

As far as the medic could tell, the Minister had started to come slowly out of the shock he'd suffered but remained dazed and not fully aware of every circumstance around him. A couple of times he had been found at the window staring out into the distance. The still white snowy blanket surrounding the Mountain Lodge appeared to be a calming influence, so that was the bonus of the morning.

The Major remembered the German prisoner, the intelligence officer, how had he been behaving himself? Kjaergaard said he was being looked after by one of the Vikings who'd arrived during the night, God knows where he'd come from. It was believed he'd arrived on skies, not sure from what direction. It wasn't from Berg, though.

The Viking had been seen having a cosy chat with the German Lieutenant while he carefully sharpened his axe to restore its cutting edge. The Lieutenant hadn't taken his eyes from the axe, answering the questions in calm easy conversation whilst the interrogation continued.

The Major made a note to re-interrogate the prisoner, as his mind wandered back to the doubts he suffered last night.

Outside, two drivers were preparing their vehicles. The engines were proving very reluctant to turn over in the cold, and so far they had been unable to get them started. Two small paraffin stoves were pressed into service to heat their engine's sump oil. An hour later the two trucks were finally started, much to the relief of everyone concerned. The Major went over and ordered the drivers to keep the engines warm at all costs. He left the barn into the light of the new day, which was now improving with the clearing weather.

He heard a commotion from the lookouts at the front of the Mountain Lodge. The Major grabbed for his sidearm but he hadn't suited up yet. Two fully armed rangers rushed by as he chased after them to be surprised by the sight of a German army half-track making its way up the roadway to the Mountain Lodge. The day guard and a number of other rangers took-up positions to cover the approaching threat. The Guard corporal was about to order 'open fire' when the Major spotted Red Eric waving hard to attract recognition. The rangers slowly lowered their weapons as the half-track thundered to a stop outside the main entrance to the Mountain Lodge.

Red Eric leapt from the half-track, his eyes burning bright.

'Good morning Major,' he bellowed. 'Got your men ready?'

'No,' snapped the Major. 'It's only just daylight, I've no real idea where the hell I am, and where have you been? And how the hell did you get here anyway? The road from Berg is supposed to be closed.'

'OK, keep your hat on. For information, the road from Berg is still blocked, but only for one day, two at most. There's an army of Germans clearing snow with equipment brought from Oslo. I borrowed this beastie and got my sorry arse up here to get you and your men moved out of the way fast.'

'How did you get the half-track up from Berg,' quizzed the Major.

'There's a frozen stream and pathway round the other side of the mountain, rough going but we made it, just. The beauty of driving a half-track in reverse on the tricky sections.'

A dozen Vikings were busy piling out of the half-track, taking their personal equipment and knapsacks inside. The Major saw that Red Eric's men had helped themselves to a great deal of German equipment with the back of the half-track piled high with arms of every type, with heavy boxes of munitions and equipment, especially great coats and strong winter boots, no doubt taken from the battlefield at Holmestrand. Their previous, now deceased, owners were no longer in need of them. Clearly Red Eric hadn't finished with the Germans just yet.

Back inside the Mountain Lodge, the Major's day was just about to go pear shaped. His nagging doubts as to what was really going on around him finally got the better of him. He badly needed a coffee, which he laced with some obscure and probably lethal home brew. He went to find the German Lieutenant prisoner. This man knew something the Major didn't, and it was high time to find out what it was.

The German Lieutenant had been locked-up at the back of the Mountain Lodge in a small room, with a small barred window high up, and only a rough wooden table and two uncomfortable chairs for furniture. He bid the German Lieutenant join him at the table. The Major started a slow interrogation. The German Lieutenant sat ill at ease, definitely scared of something, but the Major couldn't put his finger on just what.

After five minutes of small talk, the Major snapped out some very direct questions. The German Lieutenant froze, unspeaking, looking around like a rabbit trapped in the middle of a road with headlights from a speeding car blazing in his eyes. The Major went outside and called in the Viking who had been with the Lieutenant earlier that morning. The German Lieutenant clammed up even more. The Major asked the Viking just what had been discussed earlier. The Viking just stood there, looking at the Major without speaking.

The Major's anger took hold, his hand reaching for his army revolver. He motioned the Viking to leave and began asking the German Lieutenant about the surveillance operation he'd been controlling in Denmark. He received few answers and nothing he didn't know already.

The Major dived into questions about the number of agents and other people used in the operation. Again he received only sparse details, none of it new material. Were any Danes involved? The question came out hard and unexpected. The German Lieutenant froze once more, a sure sign the answer was yes.

The Major pressed for details. The Lieutenant looked stony-faced at the floor. What was so important in the cargo spirited away from Denmark? Was it the gold? Was it the diamonds? What was it?

He shouted the last part of the sentence with great venom. The Major's face set hard, his anger rising quickly; his gun now in his hand. The German Lieutenant started to crack under the interrogation. He started to give a few details about the operation in Denmark but nothing of any real substance. Were Danes involved? The German Lieutenant looked down at the floor and nodded.

'Who?' shouted the Major. The German Lieutenant clammed up again.

'Was it the gold?' shouted the Major. The Lieutenant shrugged an inconclusive yes.

'Was it the diamonds?' shouted the Major. Same answer.

'Was it something else?' shouted the Major, his temper at breaking point.

The Lieutenant hesitated. The Major sensed he was on to something. He pressed further. He shoved his gun hard into the ribs of the Lieutenant. The Lieutenant began to speak, slowly at first. Something about an artefact of great value, something of ....' Bang...the sound of a gunshot filled the air.

The Major spun round to see the hand of an unseen person holding a smoking service revolver that withdrew instantly as the door slammed shut. The Major looked at the Lieutenant's body slumped on the floor. The shot had entered his forehead, blowing off the back of his head, the body thrown backwards over his chair.

The Major was furious; who was the shot meant for? He flew out the door to find rangers rushing to investigate the shooting. The Major shouted rapid questions, who had they seen? Nobody had seen a thing. He lined his men up against a wall. He shouted for the Sergeant Major, who stomped in from outside with snow all over his boots.

'Roll call,' shouted the Major, his gun still in his hand, and he was mad enough to use it too.

The Sergeant Major shouted the order for everyone to muster in the main dining room. The rangers lined up against the wall. To a man they all looked very confused, clearly not understanding what had happened.

The Sergeant Major completed the roll call; only the wounded were missing. The Major shouted for the Vikings to muster. Red Eric stomped in and asked what the fuss was about. The Major snarled at him with the basic details, and he would find the unknown assassin no matter what. Red Eric shrugged, all his men were outside reloading up the half-track ready for the next battle he was planning. The Major stared hard at the Viking but saw no sign to doubt him.

Bruus-Jensen turned around to his own men. He ordered the corporal pat down each man. A few rangers had service revolvers as standard issue. None had been fired. The Major asked the Sergeant Major for his revolver. The Sergeant Major eyes said it all, but his revolver had not been fired either.

The Major knew the moment had almost passed. Who had ever committed the murder of the German Lieutenant had disappeared. Where the hell was the Sergeant Major's shadow, Sergeant Knut Kirkby?

The Major turned on the Sergeant Major with such force he was taken aback. He'd never seen the Major in a rage this strong. The man was capable of anything. He told the Major that Sergeant Kirkby was out on a skiing reconnaissance.

'Why,' snarled the Major, he hadn't ordered any damn reconnaissance. The Sergeant Major shrugged. The Sergeant had been gone over an hour and should be back anytime soon. The Major ordered everyone to stand to attention and not to move a muscle.

He stormed outside and saw ski tracks heading down the approach road. In the distance, he saw a lone skier making his way back, the missing Sergeant. The Major remained unconvinced, but the moment had passed. He went upstairs to check the wounded men. Nothing. None were fit to move unaided.

The Major was still furious, but now he began to get his fury under control and started to think more logically. The one thing that worried the Major, above all else, concerned his good friend the Minister, Eric Horskjaer. The man knew a dark secret, and the Major was sure his Sergeant Major had some involvement. Whatever it could be, everyone seemed to be in danger.

The Treasury Minister stared out over the snowy landscape desperately trying to get his mind in order, a battle he was not winning. He knew within himself it was not so much the shock of the battle at Holmestrand which affected him, although bad enough in itself, but the shock of knowing how far the Germans were prepared to go to get him.

The dark secret was no mystery to Horskjaer. He had become inadvertently involved in the mystery just over a year ago when a parcel unexpectedly arrived at his office by means of an unknown hand. This coincided with the arrival of diamonds, mainly from Eastern Europe. War was coming, and vested interests were desperately scrambling to protect their assets. None more so than the community involved in the diamond trade, run mostly by Jewish interests from Amsterdam. This community was already in deep shock from the Nazis persecution of Jews in Germany and panic had become endemic as a result of the Nazi programme of hate.

The diamonds, unfortunately, arrived after the first tranche of the Danish gold reserves had been shipped to safety in North America. He'd agreed to help the diamond community under the well-established procedure of helping one's friends in the financial world, little knowing what commitment he was letting himself in for.

The diamonds were secretly stored in a number of very safe and obscure locations in and around Copenhagen, and there they would have remained apart from the possibility of Denmark being invaded. The realisation came late in the day, along with the corresponding headaches. Now it transpired that the Nazis had been actively tracking the movement of assets throughout Europe, and quite how secret anything was in Denmark had become a big unknown and huge danger. The extensive surveillance of Denmark shortly before the invasion was not a good sign.

The secret package was an even bigger worry. Horskjaer knew the Nazi philosophy was based on a lot of mumbo jumbo about the Aryan Race, and its mystical but non-existent history. The Thule Society had become known to him through some very discrete investigations made over the last year. This society, formed around 1911, by a strange German Occultist who developed strange beliefs regarding the origins of the Aryan Race, the cornerstone of Nazi philosophy. The Nazis had copied the Thule Society emblem, the swastika. The fact that the swastika, as an emblem, existed in many formats over many hundreds if not thousands of years didn't worry the Nazis. In fact, the swastika had two shapes, with its arms facing either right or left.

The Nazis adopted the right-facing swastika, an emblem now bringing fear and dread to the whole of Europe. The left-facing swastika had been a Buddhist or Hindu symbol for many centuries. Many cultures believed the swastika derived from the swirling arms of the jet streams of passing comets. Comets throughout the ages meant, among other things, a lucky or auspicious object.

The Nazis were out to develop as much proof of the history of the Aryan race as possible, and at the same time, crush any perceived threat to their philosophy. The destruction of the Red Eric's Viking community had been a great shock to Horskjaer, and it merely served to heighten the dread within him.

The secret package contained an artefact of considerable antiquity. This large heavy emblem, measured over three hundred millimetres in a roughly rectangular shape. It had a thick base of solid gold, its colour a good clue as to its age. Horskjaer arranged for some discrete assay tests be done on small gold samples carefully removed from under the base. These showed the gold to be very pure.

The assayer became a little bit too interested in the gold's origin for Horskjaer's liking. He prepared a story that the samples had been taken from ancient Greek artefacts being offered to one of the Danish museums in lieu of outstanding Governmental taxes. The assayer accepted the story at face value, but the experience only served to convince Horskjaer to keep the artefact well hidden.

Embedded in the top surface were an incredible number of large and small gemstones, all uncut but polished, remarkably consistent in terms of size, shape and quality. There was no doubt it was a very rare piece.

In the centre of the artefact was a cross, formed with very rare black diamonds mounted edge to edge. From the ends of the cross four arms in progressively smaller stones, becoming progressively lighter in colour, formed four curved arcs. The symbol of the Buddhist swastika

The Buddhist swastika sat in a circle of small white translucent diamonds mounted on a white enamel base. The outer surface of the artefact had been carefully covered in very small, very dark, red rubies forming an outer mosaic.

Set deep in the four corners of the rectangle were four different strange and mystic emblems, depicted with emeralds, sapphires, diamonds and semi-precious stones. The mystic emblem defied understanding. The Minister could only guess they related to the four seasons.

The overall effect of the design of the artefact showed a strong black swastika on an almost white background surround by a red carpet: the colours of the Nazi Swastika.

All the stones showed a depth of colour known to be very rare and guessed to originate from the Far East, probably Ceylon or Burma. The setting of the stones was also very old and could be compared to Egyptian jewellery of the later dynasties. The age of the artefact would be hard to define but clearly it was many hundreds of years old.

The design of the artefact defied evaluation. Which way up should it be examined; laying down or supported upright? From one angle the outline of the comet symbol was clear. From other angles the stones had a mesmerising quality so that other symbols could be imagined, although it took some deep examination to see them. The only other explanation that could be offered was the object might a derivative 'fylfot', one of the holiest of the 'Jain' symbols.

Somehow the Nazis had learned of the artefact's existence, and, even more, surprising, they knew of its presence in Europe. And they wanted it very badly. And here it was secreted in the bottom of his rifle bag, heavily wrapped in old rags. The secret pressed heavily on Horskjaer, it was a huge danger just to be in possession of it and brought great danger to anybody close to it. The pressure of his many concerns bore down like a huge weight upon the hapless Treasury Minister. He returned to staring out into the unseeing distance from the window, trying to gain some relief from the beauty of the snowy landscape.

Outside, the Major was about to ask Red Eric a thousand other questions about the future of his group when the sound of a low flying aircraft started to reach them.

'Lort,' he cursed, as he legged back to the main building of the Mountain Lodge. He charged through the main entrance almost demolishing two of his rangers. The Major started barking orders left right and centre. First thing, it was too late to move the half-track. He needed six 'German' soldiers to man it. Six rangers grabbed German greatcoats dumped on the floor, rammed coalscuttle helmets on their heads and did what they could to prepare for another episode of subterfuge.

A German reconnaissance aircraft flew by at an agonisingly slow pace as the pilot, and his spotter had a good look at the scene below them, from a high wing, single engine aircraft. The Major recognised it immediately as a Fieseler Fi 156 Storch, its ungainly appearance suited its name, but it had remarkable qualities as a reconnaissance aircraft. It could take-off and land almost anywhere, had a reasonable range, but it did not possess any great speed though, and the Major knew it would struggle against the strong winds that prevailed in Norway. The aircraft, fortunately unarmed, had been fitted with skis to allow take-off and landing in the current wintry conditions.

Upstairs the Major heard the sounds of his rangers taking up positions at the available windows. He bellowed at them to remain hidden no matter what. The Storch flew past and made a lazy sweeping turn to have another look. The Major grabbed a German greatcoat, an officer's cap and found a Lugar revolver with its holster and a belt to wrap around his waist.

He went outside, ordering his rangers to line-up and take positions on the half-track with their automatic machine pistols pointing in the air.

The Major had an idea, a wild one, but one that might just work. As the Storch flew past he strutted out in front of the main building and waved at the pilot, indicating he wanted to talk to him. The spotter in the aircraft could be seen holding up a radio microphone. The Major made a signal that the radio in the half-track was U/S, and awaited results.

To his surprise, he saw the spotter in the aircraft make a downwards signal to the pilot, who swung his aircraft around looking for somewhere to land. The approach road would be the best bet. The Major shouted at one of the rangers to bring a smoke flare from the half-track and bring it to the end of the access road.

Sergeant Koppel joined him, suitably dressed for the part in a German paratrooper's uniform, as the pair of them marched to the end of the access roadway. The Storch lined up for a landing with the lit smoke flare planted in the snow on the side of the road. With very little wind, the Storch made an exemplary landing and coasted up to the two Danish officers.

The Storch slid to a halt. The Major ordered two of his men rush over from the half-track and swing the aircraft through a ninety degrees so it faced across the road into the light westerly wind. The Major and Sergeant Koppel strutted across to the aircraft.

Sergeant Koppel went round to the far side. He looked up at the spotter, smiled and opened the cabin door.

'Gutin tag mein Herr,' he shouted out over the noise of the idling engine. The spotter, a large brutish German wearing the overalls of an Oberstabs-Feldwebel, or Senior Sergeant Aircraftsman, swung his legs over the sill of the doorway. As the German prepared to jump out, Koppel, pulled out a concealed handgun and shot him through the heart. The German slumped heavily to the snow covered ground.

On the other side of the aircraft, the Major wrenched the pilot's door open, shoving his Lugar hard into his side. The pilot's face froze in fear. The Major fixed him with a hard stare, counted to ten and then used his free hand to beckon the pilot from his aircraft. The pilot jumped to the ground, his hands held high. The Major used his pistol to wave the pilot away from the Storch. Two rangers came running and took the pilot inside the lodge. The Major reached inside the cockpit and shut down the engine.

The Major walked around the aircraft to examine the dead body on the ground.

'What's up Sergeant Koppel, didn't he tip you for opening his door,' said the Major with murderous grim humour.

His Sergeant had made the correct decision, this was no aircraftsman. He ripped open the overalls to reveal one of the S.S. led German 'Fallschirmjaeger'. Yet another Gestapo tug guising as a German paratrooper. At least, it confirmed to the Major which branch of the German armed forces were still controlling the hunt for the Danes and their Viking allies.

The aircraft's short-range radio called out; the distant operator getting agitated at the delay in an answer. The Major grabbed the radio handset, placed a cloth over the microphone, and started calling as if the radio could not receive a signal. He moved the microphone in and out from his mouth to give the impression of a serious defect. The Major uttered the only curse he knew in German and turned off the set. He prayed the distant German radio operator would buy into the subterfuge.

The Major turned around to face his Koppel.

'Soeren can you still fly a light aircraft?' he asked nervously, the stress of the day's events starting to get to him.

'Suppose so,' Sergeant Koppel replied. 'My license is out of date, not been able to get the hours on my pilot's logbook.'

'Can you fly this damn aircraft, yes or no?' shouted the Major.

'Where to, for Christ's sake?' answered Koppel, surprised at the Major's tone of voice.

'OK, sorry,' said the Major wearily. 'Look I need you to fly this crate to Sweden. Just fly east, stay low, hide in the clouds, anything, can do?'

'OK, I suppose. Who's going with me?' replied Sergeant Koppel.

'The Minister, I've got to get him out of here. Take two of the wounded too?' asked the Major.

'Too much weight; let me check the aircraft's fuel load,'

Koppel climbed into the Storch's pilot's seat, energised the control panel and studied the gauges, finding the fuel gauge, fortunately, showing three-quarters full.

'Got any aviation gasoline?' he asked.

'Very funny,' replied the Major. 'Will regular do?'

'Should work, the engine is not that high tech,'

The Major shouted for Red Eric to help and bring some of his men.

Red Eric looked confused.

'Red, get one of your men to bring some gasoline, Sergeant Koppel will show where to fill up. Then take two of your men to get the Minister dressed and prepared. Don't forget his rifle. Also, bring the ranger who has the worst injuries. He must be capable of giving some assistance to my Sergeant, even if it's only keeping a lookout.'

Within ten minutes the aircraft had been prepared for flight. A confused and drowsy Minister was bundled and strapped into the co-pilot's seat, and one of the wounded rangers crammed into the back of the aircraft's cramped cabin along with the Minister's trusty hunting rifle in its bag.

The Major rummaged around in his haversack and retrieved a worn copy of a Swedish road map between Malmo and Oslo. He opened it up and spread it out on the ground.

'Soeren,' he started, 'follow the road down to Bern but keep behind the mountains so as to keep from view. From Bern go due east to this town called Sande about 40 kilometres. You will cross the main road from Oslo so expect German troop movements in this area. Fly down the fjord and then head south-east until you get sight of the other side of the waterway. Follow the coastline to the south and try and find the town of Stromstad. Then you will be in Sweden.

If you have the fuel, continue south and try to get to Tanum. The Minister has a good friend who has his family estate in this area. I've marked the approximate location on this map. You should see a large castle, which looks like a stately home. It has the usual Swedish style turrets. This aircraft can land almost anywhere, so you will have plenty of options. Remember you're carrying to safety a ranking member of the Danish government, and he has many friends in Sweden. All you have to do is get him there.'

'Sounds simple,' said Sergeant Koppel hopefully.

The Major beckoned two Vikings to the aircraft and ordered them to manhandle the aircraft to point down the access road. The Mountain Lodge house girl rushed over with a haversack full of hastily prepared sandwiches, a large sausage, and two flasks full of hot drinks. She stuffed the haversack behind the pilot's seat, just as the Major slammed the pilot's door shut.

Koppel waved his thanks, mouthed goodbye to the Major, took the controls, set the wing flaps, took a deep breath to steady his nerves, and gunned the engine to full power. The aircraft shook as its engine reached full power. The aircraft started to roll forward, slowly at first but it quickly built-up speed. The light westerly wind came from just forward of the aircraft's starboard beam. The high wing of the Storch lifted the aircraft skis momentarily from the ground and dumped the aircraft back on the access road.

Nervously, Sergeant Koppel steadied the aircraft, corrected its swinging motion, and gently pulled back on the stick. The Storch rose gracefully into the air with the Sergeant quickly trying to get a feel for the aircraft. It took a few seconds, but the aircraft proved very easy to fly.

The end of the access road quickly approached as Sergeant Koppel tentatively commenced a slow left turn to line up on the road to Berg below him. He reset the wing flaps and throttled the engine back to cruising speed, commencing a slow climb, mindful of the need to conserve fuel.

The Storch slowly gained altitude to eight hundred metres, remaining well below the height of the mountains guarding the valley pass to Berg. Ten minutes later Koppel started to feel a lot more comfortable with the handling of the Storch, and managed to relax a little.

As his flying became more natural he started to look around. Perhaps the journey would be as easy as the Major suggested. Koppel didn't believe in easy. Nothing had been easy since Larvik, but he admitted he was prepared to accept a slight rise in the level of his optimism.

The Storch continued down the road to Berg and reached the sharp turn which led to the descent where the two mountain passes had been blocked by the induced snow avalanches. In the early afternoon light of a clear day Sergeant Koppel could see large numbers of black ant-like figures busy cutting a path through the snow. The lower of the two passes was already clear, and rapidly being widened for the long line of armoured half-tracks and military vehicles waiting below. A large snow blower had been attacking the snow at the higher pass, but it had lost the edge of the road and started to tip into the valley below.

Sergeant Koppel edged the Storch as close as he dared into the dark shadows on the west side of the valley. This side of the mountain pass looked almost bare of snow, hopefully making the camouflaged aircraft difficult to see. The Germans looked up at the sound of the aircraft, but by the time the Storch had been spotted the aircraft was in a shallow dive picking-up speed down the valley. Flying close to the valley wall became difficult in the swirling wind and its updraft. Thankfully he disappeared from the view of the Germans on the ground.

The Sergeant looked intently below and seeing he was flying over an empty roadway, brought the aircraft away from the side of the valley and began a slow climb to give a larger margin for safety. His nerves slowly steadied, as the feeling of panic subsided. He shouted to the injured ranger behind to mark the map with their approximate position and make himself useful.

The ground fell away quickly as the approach to Berg began. Sergeant Koppel slowly lost a little altitude as he edged the aircraft away to the east of Berg. He shouted to the wounded ranger to look for the road towards Sande.

Sergeant Koppel slowly turned to the south-east, hopefully steering the Storch in the correct direction. The aircraft's engine kept up its steady droning beat. The road to Sande came into view and Sergeant Koppel felt his spirits lift a little. He looked around the aircraft's cabin. The Minister stared into the distance, sitting unmoving in a silent trance. The colour in his face began to drain back to death white, but there was little he or the other passenger could do. The Minister just had to hang on for his own sake.

After what seemed an age, the town of Sande appeared in the gloomy distance. Koppel wanted to keep well away from inhabited areas and was tempted to cut the corner to the other side of the fjord to find the road to the south and to safety. He could see little activity on the ground, and what he did see appeared to be normal traffic going about its daily business.

He made a course alteration to the south-east, starting to cross a large finger of open waterway. He hesitated to continue on this course. Realising his aircraft's camouflage would be little use over open water, he swung the Storch back to the east, skirting around the edge of the waterway.

As it narrowed he took his chance and headed south-east. As the Storch made landfall on the other side of the fjord he saw the shadow of a fast moving aircraft coming across the water in his direction. He quickly looked up, into the distance, just in time to see the unmistakable profile of a German Messerschmitt ME-109 heading directly towards him. Sweating profusely, Sergeant Koppel wrenched the controls sending the Storch in a steep left-hand dive towards a forest.

The German fighter overshot and headed up the deep fjord, before returning for a second look. The Sergeant's heart was pounding as he weaved the Storch left and right in a steep dive. The altimeter descended agonisingly slowly as the Storch approached the safety of the tree tops below.

He looked in the rearview mirror and could see nothing. The ranger behind him turned around with some difficulty, and not a little pain, to look out the rear cockpit window. The Messerschmitt weaved violently as the fighter pilot looked down on either side of his long engine, trying to pick-out the Storch against the dark green and brown back-ground of the dark forest floor.

The fighter pilot finally saw the outline of the Storch and dived towards them. Sergeant Koppel slammed on the Storch's' airbrakes, slowing the aircraft to stall speed as he carried out an emergency hard right turn towards the fjord. The Messerschmitt fighter shot past, nearly crashing into a forest covered outcrop of rock. The German aircraft recovered in time to pull-up over the open water of the fjord.

Koppel levelled the Storch and headed back inland over the forest. The winter light was now fading fast as early nightfall came to save the day. The sun began to hide behind the nearest mountain throwing the east side of the fjord into dark shadow. Koppel felt grateful for the obscurity, but he still had a long way to go to cross the border into Sweden and safety.

The Messerschmitt seemed to have disappeared. Koppel carefully checked his instruments. Fuel was running low and he had little idea of his position. He set the Storch onto a southerly course and began a gentle climb back into the last vestiges of the winter daylight, anxious to find his approximate position. He could not fly at night and no matter what, he would have to land somewhere before it became completely dark.

He anxiously searched the ground from both sides of the cockpit. He began edging the Storch to the west to try and find the edge of the fjord. Slowly a few islands came into view and he gratefully swung his aircraft back on the southerly course.

He couldn't match what he saw with anywhere on his map. He gritted his teeth, looked at his watch and studied his control panel gauges. Time and fuel were running out in equal proportions. He took a deep breath to compose himself; to make a decision on what to do next. The next ten minutes passed quickly as he stared into the distance. He thought he saw faint lights in the distance and headed the faithful Storch in their direction. He picked out the lights of a vehicle on a road below him. It too was heading south. The lights on the ground started to get closer. Could it be Sweden? Could it be the lights of a country not at war? He couldn't tell, only hope.

Suddenly the Storch was not alone. Two biplanes closed quickly from behind. Their unmistakeable outline told him they were British Gloucester Gladiator Mk IIs. They just had to be Swedish fighter aircraft. He'd seen them at his flying school near Copenhagen. The leader closed in alongside, the observer pointing frantically at the ground, an unmistakable order to land. The second Swedish fighter took up position close behind him. These two aircraft were almost as manoeuvrable as he was. There would be few tricks he could employ to shake them off. Anyway, he needed help, with no idea of his position.

Koppel shouted for the ranger behind to dive deep into his haversack. 'There's a flag in there. Get it out fast, and show it to the other aircraft.' The ranger quickly found the flag, a Danish flag, opened it up and covered the inside of his window with it.

Koppel carefully watched for a reaction from the Swedish pilot. A Morse lamp began to blink, its message urgently asking for confirmation. He found an emergency torch in the pilot's bag at the side of his seat. He let go of the aircraft controls hoping the Storch would fly straight and level long enough to send a reply. All he could manage to send was 'Danish Rangers' and the name of his destination. His aircraft started to drift across the path of the Swedish fighter. He wrenched the controls to bring the Storch back on course. The Swedish fighter's Morse lamp began to blink again, a single word, 'Follow'.

The Swedish fighter began a slow peel away to starboard. Sergeant Koppel brought the Storch behind it and watched his rear view mirror as the second Swedish fighter kept close behind. The aerial convoy began a slow descent. The daylight was fading fast and had almost gone. A small village appeared in front and a landing strip made itself apparent.

The leading Swedish fighter made straight for it and executed a perfect landing. Koppel hesitated; landing in the increasing gloom suddenly frightened him, but he'd little option. He gritted his teeth as he made himself go through the standard checks for landing an aircraft. He throttled back his engine and fumbled around for the lever to operate the landing flaps. He fixed his gaze on the altimeter and the rate of descent indicator.

He was starting to get low; the landing strip came up at him far too quickly. He pulled the nose of the Storch up briefly to check his rate of descent. It was too much and the Storch began to stall, the ground rushing up towards him. The edge of the landing strip had past. There was nothing for it; just put the aircraft on the ground, it had become too late to think his way out of this one. Sergeant Koppel cut the engine revs to nothing and let his reactions take over.

The Storch hit the ground hard, its long undercarriage soaking up the shock. The tail of the aircraft started to tip up. Koppel pulled back on the stick and braked hard. The Storch slewed to an ungainly stop at the side of the landing strip, its port wheel almost dropping into a deep ditch along the edge of the perimeter fence.

Koppel, his face a mass of sweat, turned off the engine and sat back in his seat unable to move. It took fully two minutes to recover his composure as he realised he and his passengers were safe on the ground.

Two armed policemen came running towards the Storch. Koppel noticed two soldiers behind them. Relief flooded his senses as he realised the soldiers were not wearing German uniforms and their coal scuttle helmets. He sat back and searched his thigh pocket for a crumpled pack of cigarettes. The first policeman reached the Storch and wrenched the pilot's door open with a revolver in his hand.

'Good evening,' Sergeant Koppel called out in Swedish and sat back drawing on his cigarette. The flight commander of the first Swedish fighter came up behind the policeman and took charge of the situation. His questions came thick and fast, interrupted only by the noise of the second Gladiator landing behind them.

Horskjaer, suddenly came to himself, sat bolt upright and introduced himself. Koppel looked on in amazement. The Minister had been semi-conscious throughout the whole flight, looking like death warmed-up. The Swedish commander's attention to the Danish Minister was interrupted by groaning from the rear of the Storch. The wounded Danish Ranger had keeled over in his safety harness.

Help arrived, in the form of an ancient Volvo ambulance. The Swedish commander signalled the first aid men to remove the injured ranger as he went to assist the Danish Minister from the aircraft. As the injured ranger was being bundled into the back of the ambulance he motioned Koppel and the Minister to climb aboard.

The three escapees from Berg were taken to the local police station. Their story, although brief and with many details omitted, amazed the Swedish Air Force flight commander.

Koppel, whilst omitting the precise details of the danger to Horekjaer, pressed his request the Minister be transferred soon as possible to the estate of his friend at Tanum, in secret, as instructed by his commanding officer, Major Per Bruus-Jensen.

The Swedish Police Superintendent went away to make some urgent phone calls. He soon returned but decided it had become too late to relocate his Danish guests. There would be much the Swedish government authorities in the capital would want to know. The arrival of a minister from a friendly foreign state certainly confused the issue.

The three Danes were taken to a comfortable house next to the police station. Koppel was more than relieved to see the two soldiers from the airfield had been assigned to guard them until the next morning. No doubt many more questions would be asked. Later on, the Swedish Police Superintendent came to visit the three Danes. He had good news. Early the next morning they would be transferred under cover of darkness to Tanum. All further enquiries would be conducted there, and they would be held in secret until the situation had been cleared up and the Swedish government understood all the issues.

Koppel relaxed for the first time since first landing in Norway, relieved at achieving success in carrying out his orders. Now tomorrow would be another day. He felt safe, it took a little time to realise he treasured the feeling of safety among all other emotions.

He wondered how his cousin, the Major, and the other rangers were getting on.

Chapter 19

If nothing else, it was time to leave the Mountain Lodge. The Germans were closing in, and the Major was anxious to be off. He briefed his men in front of the Sergeant Major, telling them he would head west with Red Eric and a small force of Vikings in a dangerous attempt to get the cargo to safety or dumped somewhere deep in a hidden fjord. He expected German paratroopers to be dropped in the west to cut them off and block any escape.

The remainder of the Danish Rangers, led by the Sergeant Major, would head north in the remaining truck and the German half-track with Little Eric and his Vikings. The road to the north remained partially blocked with snow and difficult to pass. They expected to be pursued and attacked by German forces. Red Eric assured him, with a wry smile, that the road north would become a natural killing ground for anyone trying to catch-up.

Red Eric promised the Vikings would continue to make themselves highly unpopular with the German Army, and the Danish Rangers would be expected to play their part in the escape to Oslo and safety. Each ranger had to make his own mind up what part he wanted to play in the war against the forces of occupation. Those who served the cause would be received by the Norwegians as heroes, and helped to safety. They could be hidden around the country, and act as instructors to the many volunteers to be recruited into the nascent resistance movement. Deserving cases would be smuggled into Sweden, but under any circumstance they had to keep a low profile and not get caught. The Gestapo would be on constant lookout for them.

The Major thanked his men for their valiant efforts, the successes achieved in the face of overwhelming odds and that he felt very proud of them. He wished them the best of luck and hoped to see them in Copenhagen after the war.

Although he meant his words the Major could not help think his optimism was perhaps a little overplayed. God only knows what would happen to him or his men. Their situation remained extremely perilous and great strength and fortitude would be required just to survive.

Red Eric and his men were ready to move out in an overloaded truck with the dangerous cargo. The Major wearily climbed into the cab with Red Eric standing outside on the running board. In the rear, four Vikings harboured an interesting range of weapons, most stolen from the German army at the Battle of Holmestrand. It was a tight fit crammed on top of the cargo, the famous cargo rapidly becoming a one-way ticket to a violent death.

Early afternoon had passed and as the light started to fade wintry weather moved in from the west. The sound of the snow chains were muffled as they bit deeply into the packed snow on the roadway. The truck towed a heavy chain mat behind to obliterate the wheel tracks.

The Major shouted through the open window at Red Eric watching the sky above. How did he know the Germans would drop parachute troops in front of them? Red Eric wouldn't reveal his sources although he had every confidence in his information. He did, however, tell the Major he wasn't sure when they would be dropped. Weren't they in danger of running slap bang into the middle of them?

Red Eric shrugged his shoulders, the weather should be bad in Oslo, so he hoped for a delay until tomorrow morning, by which time they would be long gone. The Major wasn't convinced. It would be just his luck the Germans would attempt a late afternoon parachute drop no matter what. For the moment, the skies were clear below the snow-laden clouds, but his vision was severely restricted by the surrounding mountains.

The truck passed through the open and most vulnerable part of their escape to the west. A welcoming forest slowly came nearer. The Major strained his eyes looking up at the sky. Red Eric suddenly ordered the truck to stop and shut off its engine. He looked intently at the sky in the direction from where aircraft could be expected. The Major heard only the moaning of the wind as it swept across the snow-bound valley floor.

Red Eric shouted at the driver to head for the forest as fast as he dared. The feeling of dread rose quickly inside the Major. The truck lurched and slithered over the road as the driver made for the welcoming safety. As they reached the safety of the forest, Red Eric shouted for the driver to turn up a narrow access road and hide under the protection of the overhanging canopy. It was not a minute too soon. Low flying transport aircraft came lumbering in from the east, flying into the prevailing wind looking for the best location for a parachute drop. The aircraft pulled into a climb almost directly over the Danish truck. It circled one more time, adjusted its height and soon the billowing canopies of the German paratroopers and their supplies filled the skies.

From his vantage point, Red Eric looked back up the road. The swirling wind brought fresh blown snow over the surface of the road. He prayed the chain mat towed behind the truck had done its work sufficiently well. Time would tell.

Another aircraft dropped a second load of German paratroopers into the snow-bound valley. This was a lot of muscle. Someone in the German High Command had serious intent about cornering the Danes and their Viking comrades. Red Eric chuckled. The Major asked what kept him so amused. Red Eric muttered something about the road north from the Mountain Lodge becoming a target rich environment. Did the man have no fear?

The Vikings took up defensive positions; an unusual step thought the Major, as up to now they only taken positions to get easier access to kill Germans. Presumably, two plane loads of German paratroopers were considered a little too much to get involved with. That thought didn't ring quite true either. Either way, the Major felt glad they were not about to commence another pitch battle. No doubt in the fullness of time the intentions of the Vikings would become clear.

The German paratroopers skied off into the distance, heading towards the Mountain Lodge. Surprised to see how quickly they covered the ground, it didn't take long until the coast became clear. With a great deal of caution the Danish truck backed out onto the roadway, as their journey to the west continued.

The Major worried about his men back at the Mountain Lodge. By now they should have moved out, heading north up the escape route. He need not have worried: the escape was well underway. To the surprise of the Sergeant Major and his men, the road north offered the promised abundance of excellent ambush points. The Vikings set to building intriguing impediments to the progress of the chasing Germans. Little Eric was a cunning man. Explosive booby traps and other surprises were liberally employed to deplete and delay the German advance.

Fixed positions with easy escape routes were engineered with great cunning. Little Eric knew the Germans would not give in. This would be their big mistake. Little Eric would extract a heavy revenge before escaping over the mountains to start the expected long-term resistance to the German occupation.

The Danish force made good their escape after some heroic fighting with only a few extra wounded. They disappeared into the major conurbations of Norway, did their duty by their Norwegian hosts and nearly all them returned to Denmark at the end of the war.

*****

Chapter 20

The Island of Terschelling

Calum got up, went up to the cockpit, saw all was well, and crawled back into his comfortable bunk. He badly needed an extra couple of hours of rest to get himself back to full strength. He quickly drifted off into a deep sleep only to be rudely awoken by a lot of banging and shouting. A dark hooded figure poked a gun in his ribs, motioning him to get up. Calum dragged on his trousers and got knocked to the deck for his troubles. Other members of the crew were similarly manhandled and shoved into the main aft cabin.

As the last members of the crew of *Samba Canção* were thrown into the cabin, the door slammed shut, and sounds of it being boarded up were heard. Calum was in shock but managed to force himself back into some rough composure.

He took a quick head count. Marie was missing.

'Anybody seen Marie?' he shouted out.'

Carol said she'd seen Marie, kicking and screaming, being dragged up the steps to the cockpit. From there she'd no idea where they took her.

Sarra stood at the cabin door looking through the glass spy port. She turned around and told everyone to shut-up. She could hear voices on the other side, a jumble of shouted orders and curses in some strange language.

She listened intently, 'Albanians, fuckin Albanians,' she muttered to herself.

Calum asked what was going on. Sarra told him they'd been kidnapped by a gang of Albanians, hired thugs taking orders from whoever ran this operation.

Sarra continued looking through the glass spy port. She saw frantic activity up forward, but exactly what she couldn't say. She saw a thug standing at the bottom of the companionway up to the cockpit shouting and cursing at the other gang members, and another thug on his stomach reaching into the engine bay access hatch trying to do something she couldn't see what. Mike opinioned from that position he could be trying to reach the seacock next to the main engine.

Calum asked if she knew what they were saying. Sarra told him she could only understand bits and pieces between all the swearing that was going on. Everyone held their breath as Sarra continued to listen through the door.

She turned round, 'Christ, they're going to scuttle the schooner with us locked in the main cabin.' she said. 'What the hell?'

'The fuck they are,' cursed Calum, ordering most of his crew into the heads to make some room.

'Patrick,' he ordered, 'remove the back cushions from the bench seat behind you,' as he fished in his trousers for a pair of pliers. Patrick quickly removed the back cushions, revealing the substantial rings used as connection points.

'I'll take one end, you take the other. Your fingers are strong enough. Turn the rings clockwise to unscrew, clockwise.'

Patrick thought it a bit strange but did as he was bid. The first ring took a hard effort to get moving, the second one was easier.

With the rings unwound at both ends, Calum removed the seat back, reached into the space behind and started throwing large heavy sealed packages on top of the double bed.

'Unwrap these and be quick about it,' he ordered. 'Mike you too.'

The unwrapped packages revealed three Colt .45 Automatics, three AK-47s with preloaded ammunition clips to suit all weapons.

'Fuckin' hell Guv, where did you get the cool gear from,' shouted Tom.

'Never you 'effin' mind, get busy,' grunted Calum.

Patrick started to prepare the AK-47s. 'Nice,' he said. 'Where did you get these special forces grade Russian rifles?'

'How come you know that?' muttered Calum. 'Give them to Mike to get them ready.'

'No need,' said Patrick, 'no need at all.'

Mike prepared the Colt automatics and looked up at Calum for instructions

Calum asked Sarra what see saw now. She told him the Albanians had left the forward cabins and gone up on deck. She could see water starting to flood into the main cabin, although she didn't have a very good view.

Calum looked up at his crew. 'Who knows how to handle these weapons apart from Mike and me?' asked Calum.

Patrick, Tom and Sarra put their hands up. The others backed away, more scared than ever.

Calum put a Colt Automatic in his trouser pocket and picked up an

AK-47. Tom and Sarra took a Colt Automatic each, pulling back the slide, loading a round into the chamber. They were ready.

Patrick picked up an AK-47; clearly it was no stranger to him. Mike picked up the last AK-47, rammed in a loaded ammunition clip, and put the safety catch to 'Off'.

Calum looked around. 'Sarra,' he whispered, 'where are the Albanians now?'

She went back to the spy glass in the door and told him the one at the bottom of the steps stood screaming at the one still lying on the floor, she assumed he was still trying to open the seacock.

'OK, listen up,' called Calum. 'Patrick and Mike; get behind and follow me into the cockpit. Bring extra ammunition clips with you, especially the ones with the red paint. I'm going to fire four times, one high, one low, one not so high and one not so low. Tom, Sarra, when I say 'Go', blast away at the door hinges and Mike you smash the door down. Tom, you move forward and check it's all clear. Shoot to kill whoever you see. Alexander and Steve shut both seacocks and look after the schooner. Ready?'

They all nodded their heads. They looked scared but determined. Calum raised his AK-47 to his shoulder and fired four deliberate shots. Two loud screams could be heard on the other side of the cabin door.

'Go, Go, Go,' Calum shouted. The two Colt automatics blasted away at the door hinges. Mike lunged at the door, which broke away and crashed to the deck. Calum jumped over the broken remains of the door and rushed into the main cabin. The thug on the deck at the engine room hatch was badly wounded, screaming in pain. Calum put a shot into him for good measure, the other thug slumped on the deck of the main cabin. Calum rushed up on deck with Patrick and Mike right behind.

He saw an outboard powered tender making its way back from the moored trawler, full of Albanians. He frantically searched for sight of Marie. He thought he saw her being bundled below decks on the trawler, but his glimpse was too short to be sure.

The three of them hid behind the cockpit combing. The tender started to get close. Calum held his hand out to stop his two companions from making any moves. He popped his head above the combing. It was time. He motioned Mike to go down the blind side to the back of the cockpit, and for Patrick to move forward and lean over the cabin roof. In moments, they were all ready.

Calum stood up, 'Single shot, continuous fire. Go,' he shouted. The heavy bullets from the Russian assault rifles started to tear and smash into the Albanian craft. This amount of firepower they had not allowed for.

Calum rested his rifle on the cockpit combing, took careful aim, switched to automatic fire and emptied a whole clip of ammunition into the Albanian tender. He rammed another ammunition clip into the rifle, one with red paint on it. The clip held tracer and armour piercing rounds. Another long burst of fire.

The tender started to quickly take on water through the many bullet holes in its hull. A tracer round started a fire as it hit a fuel tank. Bodies started to float away in the water, the survivors splashing around in total chaos. Patrick started to pick off the survivors one by one. In moments, it was all over. The three of them rested and took stock. Calum sent Mike below deck to find out what had happened. He quickly returned to report.

Carol had rushed forward and shut off the forward seacock. Sarra had been busy closing the seacock under the main engine, which closed with difficulty. The schooner was now dangerously full of sea water. Mike suggested the schooner was probably being kept afloat by the sealed storage containers under the cabin floors and they were still in danger of sinking unless quick action was taken.

In the main cabin, the Albanians had wrecked the navigation station, smashing all the equipment. The electrical panel had been badly damaged with an axe, and it was impossible to switch on any of the electrical circuits, especially the electric bilge pumps fore and aft.

Calum was furious. He ordered Patrick and Tom to watch the Albanian trawler like hawks and report anything that happened. He stomped off down below. The situation looked as bad as reported. He took Steve and Mike into the engine room to where the main battery banks were mounted. In the deck head above the main battery bank was a coiled cable, its end connection bagged for long-term protection. He told Steve to uncoil the cable and remove the plastic cover. Calum took Mike forward to the workshop compartment that had the forward bilge pump located under the workshop floor. Mike entered the workshop with Calum following behind.

'Mike,' he instructed, 'above your head you'll find the other end of the cable. Uncoil it and take the covers off. See this junction box? Open it up, break the fuse links and connect the cable to the pump side of the terminals. When you've done that shout out, make sure the pump discharge valves are open. I'll be in the engine room.'

Calum quickly returned to the engine room to find Steve almost finished. A few minutes later Mike called out all was ready. Calum took the large cable clips and connected the two leads to the main battery bank. As the last clip connected there was quite a flash as the bilge pump sprang into life.

'Shit,' he cursed. 'Forgot to disconnect the Start-Battery's Inter-connection.'

Steve asked what was wrong. Calum told him sometimes he left the main batteries and the engine start batteries connected when the engine was running to give them a full charge. The bilge pump could easily flatten both battery banks and then they wouldn't be able to start the main engine. Calum broke the battery inter-connector with a large electrical flash.

Mike came aft to report the forward pump was working well, and the water level dropping quickly. Calum asked if he could get the main engine started.

'Not for a while,' Mike advised. 'There's too much water around the engine, and the belts will throw water everywhere and drown the alternator. Calum, is there a spare emergency cable for the aft electric bilge pump?'

Calum told him, yes, but it had been axed during the frenzied destruction of his schooner. He took Steve and Alexander on deck to the back of the main cockpit. He rummaged in one of the lockers and found two handles.

'Use these two hand pumps', he told them, pointing at two units mounted in the outside of the port and starboard lockers. 'Get pumping. Fast as you can.'

He stood up and looked around. He called to Patrick and asked for an update. Patrick said he'd seen nothing yet, which seemed strange. Tom called out that an Albanian crew member was making his way to the open forecastle where the anchor winches were.

Calum reached into a seat locker and took out a pair of binoculars. It looked like the Albanians were going to weigh anchor. With the schooner dead in the water danger signals flashed into Calum's brain.

'Patrick,' he shouted. 'Can you hit that man on the forecastle?'

'I'll have a go; the range is a bit long for this assault rifle,' he shouted back.

Patrick lent over the boom of the main mast, rested his weapon and took careful aim. His first shot fell well short, the second one hit the hull of the fishing trawler, and the third shot hit an anchor winch, showering sparks over the Albanian crew member hiding behind the bulwarks along the main deck.

'Good shooting Patrick,' shouted Calum in delight. 'Keep their damn heads down if nothing else.'

Calum went below to check on progress. Sarra pulled the wounded Albanian back into the main cabin in considerable pain, but Calum wasn't sure if he was still dangerous or not. He called Alexander down from the cockpit. Alexander was a bit of a wizz at first aid.

Alexander found the First Aid kit, took out a file of morphine, and jabbed the needle none too gently in the arm of the wounded man who soon quietened down as the medication did its work. A bullet had passed through the upper leg, narrowly missing the thigh bone, and was still bleeding badly. He quickly sprinkled some antibiotic powder on the wound and applied a field dressing. Sarra worried he might become active again.

'No problem,' said Alexander as he bound his legs together at the knees and ankles with broad bandages, completing his work by binding his elbows to his body. He placed a pillow under his head, told Sarra to keep an eye on him and try to get any information if he came to.

The schooner's main engine at last sprung into life, and the engine driven bilge pump started to slowly empty the water from the engine room and under the floor of the main cabin. But then the forward bilge pump started to slow down. The batteries needed recharging, and with the electrical control panel almost totally wrecked Calum couldn't see how they were going to pump out the forward spaces.

Mike looked into the small compartment that housed the auxiliary generator. The Albanian thugs had overlooked the small but powerful generator and Mike reckoned it would be an easy enough job to get things working again.

Samba Canção lay badly down by the head, and with the stern section nearly pumped dry she was riding very high aft. The remaining water in the main cabin had rushed forward and slopped over the dividing sub-bulkhead further increasing the problem of being very bow heavy.

A shout came from the cockpit. Calum rushed to find Patrick looking hard at the Albanian trawler with the binoculars. Something was going on. The tell-tail discharge of cooling water indicated her main engine was running. Patrick looked at her bow. Someone was doing something with the anchor chain, but it was too difficult to see. Patrick fired a couple of rounds, hitting the top works of the anchor winches but with little result.

Calum instinctively knew the enemy's next move. He couldn't be sure but if they slipped their anchor the trawler would quickly motor to their position and ram them. The schooner would not survive.

'All hands on deck,' Calum shouted with great urgency. He rattled out a string of orders. 'Get the three AK-47s reloaded with red clips, the AP with tracer. There's a heavy canvas bag on the bunk in the main aft cabin, one of you girls bring it up. Quick! Everyone get their life jackets on. Steve, follow me to the foredeck.'

They reached the foredeck in double quick time, the anchor chain unhooked and allowed to run overboard to the bitter end. There was no time to attach a marker buoy and cut it loose. The schooner fell away before the strong wind still tearing at her upper rigging.

Calum ordered Steve to the helm and told him to slowly bring the schooner forward over the anchor chain. Steve glanced at him a bit funny but did as he was bid.

Calum looked over at the trawler. A sharp retort heralded an explosion which cut its anchor chain and the trawler became free. The water boiled at her stern as it swung quickly away. He watched a little longer. The trawler came straight at them, her high bow shielding the wheelhouse from immediate rifle fire. Calum took a huge gamble, positioning Mike, Patrick and Tom on the starboard side of the main cabin. He shouted at Steve to quickly bring the schooner forward over the anchor chain. Events were unfolding fast.

Calum took his automatic from his trouser pocket and took another one from Carol who clearly could not use it effectively. Sarra came on deck and passed the heavy canvas bag to Calum who slung it over his shoulder.

He positioned himself in front of Steve at the forward end of the cockpit. The trawler gained maximum speed and bore down on the schooner very quickly. Steve shouted for instructions. Calum waited a few moments longer, then, shouted for him to come hard to starboard on full power. The trawler did not see the manoeuvre as the schooner moved to starboard, and would pass very close down the port side.

'Mike, Tom, take out the wheelhouse,' he shouted. 'Patrick try and hit the cooling water discharge fitting. If it's a casting it might shatter. Mike and Tom opened up a murderous fire on the wheelhouse of the trawler. Shouts and screams of pain from the trawler filled the air. The two girls handed out the ammunition clips to the men on deck. The trawler passed only two metres down the side of the schooner. Her large bow wave caused the schooner to roll violently. Patrick opened fire at his target. The AP rounds penetrated the hull. The bronze fitting, the discharge for the cooling water system, shattered.

Calum saw shadowy figures inside an opening in the trawler's superstructure. Calum reached into his canvas bag, took out two hand grenades, pulled the pins and tossed them onto the main deck of the trawler. As they went off, more screams from injured men rang out.

Then he opened fire with both automatics, as Sarra used the flare pistol and fired two flares into the trawler starting small fires that quickly started to spread. Mike and Tom continued their steady fire at the fast disappearing trawler's wheelhouse. An unseen hand inside the wheelhouse dragged the badly injured helmsman from the wheel and threw him bodily out onto the deck. The body hit the cap rail and fell into the sea. The trawler veered away sharply and made for the open sea.

'Ceasefire,' shouted Calum. 'Anybody see what happened; it got kind of busy for a while?'

Sarra called from the stern of the schooner. She had followed the retreat of the trawler.

'That was impressive stuff,' she said. 'Their wheelhouse is extensively damaged. Two, maybe three crew were killed. Their cooling water exhaust is damaged and should be leaking water into their engine room. A strange shadowy figure-in-black took charge. He dumped an injured crew member overboard with no more thought than tossing an empty beer can into the sea. He took the trawler out to sea.'

'Ammunition. How much have we left?' asked Calum. Tom raked around the mess over the cabin roof. 'Two, three clips a gun. Any loose rounds in the bags Carol?'

Carol threw the ammunition bag on the cabin roof and told them only a few rounds remained; the bag held mainly spent casings.

'OK,' said Calum. 'Let's get cleared up on deck. Patrick, collect all the ammunition clips together. Load the remaining loose rounds in the empty clips, and then clean the weapons. Everyone else muster in the main cabin.'

Calum made his way to his favourite corner in the main cabin and looked up at a shaken Carol.

'Any tea or coffee?' he asked quietly.

Carol hesitated but set to clean up the mess in the galley to restore some order. The gas supply remained intact and she soon had the kettle on. The rest of the crew made themselves busy tidying up the main cabin into something approaching normality. Within a few minutes tea and coffee was being served, with an unopened packet of digestive biscuits found in the back of a storage locker. Patrick came down and grabbed a cup and sat down.

Calum looked around at his crew. Mike looked OK, he'd seen action before, but Calum had to get his crew settled down. His youngsters had come through a terrifying ordeal and any minute their nerves would catch-up with them as the adrenaline wore off. Calum also knew he had been very hyper shouting orders.

'OK guys,' he started, 'back to normal. First of all I must congratulate you all for your steadfast actions. You all did very well; every one of you.'

That sentence did a lot of healing.

'Second, you'll be wondering what this is all about, and I have to tell you I have no idea, none whatsoever. Maria's been kidnapped. The schooner has no communications, and our cell phones have no local networks here. Sarra thinks the Albanians are heading to the southern tip of Norway, so we'll follow as soon as we can.'

'First, we'll take a break and get ourselves fed. The adrenaline will wear off fast and very soon you'll all be very tired and need some rest. Carol, Sarra and Steve can be cooks, so make a start and rustle up a meal for everyone. Whilst you are doing that Mike and Steve can get the forward bilge pump working and pump out the bow section. The rest of us will go on deck and bring *Samba Canção* to short scope on the anchor. The electric winch has no power, so we'll need the rising tide to break out the anchor, which by now, will be buried very deep in the sand.'

'Finally, when we get to safety, the press will be on to us like a pack of wolves. So the story is that only Mike and I handled guns onboard whilst everyone else took cover below, understood?'

The crew nodded their heads in agreement.

Calum took Tom and Patrick on deck. The schooner had fallen back to the end of a very long scope of mooring chain, swinging in the strong wind howling over the barrier island. Calum turned the engine key and the main engine thankfully started first time. Tom and Patrick went to the bow to haul in the chain and stow it in the chain locker.

Calum took the helm and slowly brought the schooner over the chain. As the schooner reached shallower waters the island wind shadow brought welcome relief and a measure of tranquillity. Calum was right, the anchor had buried deep into the sand and it would take a lot of effort to break it out. With the anchor chain almost vertical, Calum asked Tom to make it fast in the 'bits'.

The three of them checked around the main deck to see if the sails and their control lines were undamaged. Apart from a little tidying up, the schooner would be ready to sail as soon as the crew were fed and rested.

Calum asked his two main crew members if they were OK, with no after effects of the stiff action they had taken part in. They said 'yes', and felt the action had done them little harm. But their faces were drawn and tired.

The girls had a quick meal of hot soup and corned beef sandwiches ready in the galley. Calum nodded to Mike to serve everyone a large tot of brandy and water. Only Patrick refused the offer, teetotal to the last. Calum ordered Port Watch to turn-in for an hour. The Starboard Watch would help Mike do what could be done to restore the many electrical systems on the schooner. The last of the water had been pumped out forward, and at last, the schooner rode normally to her anchor.

Calum consulted the area tide table and found high tide would be in one hour. He went on deck and moved to the bow. The anchor chain was truly vertical despite the strong wind still catching the upper rigging. It must be close to breaking or breaking out, hard to tell. His crew needed the rest period he ordained, so he let out a few metres of chain using the hand lever on the winch.

The weather started to calm down, and it would be dusk in a couple of hours' time. Calum would sail on the high tide. He had to chase after the Albanian trawler, quite what would happen next he had no idea.

An hour later Port Watch arose refreshed. They wanted to set sail and chase after the Albanian ship. If only they had radio communications. Carol came on deck and asked Calum to go down to the main aft cabin. There he found Sarra looking at an unopened package.

'Where did that come from,' asked Calum.

'Patrick put in on the bed when he returned the AK-47s back into their hiding place behind the bench-seat,' she said.

Calum took out his sea knife, opened up the package and found it to be some sort of electrical device complete with a separate headset and microphone. He vaguely remembered where it came from, the last voyage. Sarra looked over his shoulder, 'It's an old Type 31 communicator,' she told him. 'It's got US Navy markings on it, where did you get it from?'

'Err, the US Navy, actually,' replied Calum 'It's a long story.'

'Got any short ones? All your stories seem to be long,' she observed.

'What does it do?' asked Calum.

'Communicate,' replied Sarra mischievously, smiling weakly.

Before Calum could ask any more daft questions, she told him it was a secret service device that could connect with one of the many US Intelligence stations around the world.

Calum passed the communicator to Sarra. She seemed to know what to do with it. She quickly switched it on, and to Calum's surprise, a battery indicator showed a healthy charge. Sarra fiddled around with it some more and pronounced it ready to go.

'You have the procedure to use this thing?' she asked.

'No idea,' replied Calum as he unsuccessfully struggled to remember what he did with the instructions that came with it, not a recent event, that's for sure.

Sarra switched the communicator to a default channel, plugged in the headset and microphone and switched to transmit. She found a 'call' button on the front, which she tentatively pressed. To her surprise, an American voice answered almost straight away.

'Call sign and ID code?' the voice demanded. Sarra hesitated and replied 'WAIT'.

She looked at Calum with her 'what do we do now' look.

Calum took the headset, put it over his head and spoke into the small boom microphone.

'This is Commander James, US Navy, on the US Naval Auxiliary *Samba Canção*, this is an emergency call, over.'

The voice hesitated and repeated the requested for a call sign and ID Code. Sarra had an idea and took back the headset.

'I wish to connect with Commander 'H', Intelligence Section 361, Royal Navy, Whitehall, London. This is an emergency call; we have no call sign or ID.'

The voice replied 'Wait'.

A few anxious minutes passed. The voice returned, 'The requested party is asking for the ID of the Caller,' it said.

'The answer is 'Buttons'. Over,' replied Sarra.

The voice returned once more, 'Colour?'

'Purple and yellow. Over,' replied Sarra.

'Wait,' said the voice.

Another anxious wait. The voice returned, 'Go ahead, you're connected.'

'Thank Christ for that,' thought Calum, getting anxious with the delay.

A strong naval voice came on the air, 'Sarra, what's happened?'

Sarra, in a fit of emotion, started to pour out the story. The strong naval voice cut her dead, told her not to use his paternal name, and report in the correct manner. Sarra looked visibly upset by the rebuff, but Calum had an appreciation of the requirements.

Calum took the headset and gave a concise and factual report of the recent events. He then gave a short statement of intent and asked for advice. The Commander replied 'Wait' and the set went dead. An anxious five minutes passed by slowly. The Commander came back on the air and told Calum to report in exactly two hours' time, and he should set sail as soon as possible, and report his exact position when he made the call. Finally, the Commander gave him a temporary password and ID Code and rang off.

'That was darling Daddy?' he asked.

'It's OK Skipper. Daddy is a very strict about communication procedure. He will be very busy making arrangements; very quickly if I know him.'

It was time to set sail, the evening would soon pass, and it would be best to leave the anchorage before dark. Without radar, and only an old US

Navy GPS handset, navigating out of the harbour would be difficult in the increasing darkness.

Calum mustered both watches on deck and looked intently at them. They appeared ready for action and grateful for the return to normal duties.

'Alexander,' ordered Calum, 'take the helm. Patrick, Tom, go forward to the bow ready to raise the anchor.'

The two of them went forward, as Calum took up position at the base of the foremast. He waved at Alexander to start the main engine and bring the schooner over the anchor chain. Patrick started to haul in the chain, and when it became vertical he locked the chain in the anchor bits and raised his hand to Calum.

Calum turned around and shouted to Alexander to gun the engine in a quick burst of power. The schooner rode hard on the anchor chain. The anchor showed little signs of breaking out.

'Again,' he shouted at Alexander. He gunned the engine hard, achieving the same result.

The schooner lay back on the anchor chain. Calum called Patrick and Tom back to his position. 'Get a 'Handy Billy' connected up to the anchor chain,' he told them. 'I'll get Alexander to bring the schooner slowly forward, as you guys crank the chain in as hard as possible. I'll get all the crew forward to sink the bows.'

When Patrick and Tom were ready, Calum motioned the crew to come as far forward as possible. As the schooner inched slowly forward Patrick and Tom applied considerable tension to the 'Handy Billy'.

'When you're ready lock the anchor chain down.'

With the anchor chain locked down, Tom lifted his hand to Calum. Calum ordered his crew to quickly muster at the stern of the schooner, whilst shouting at Alexander to give a large burst of power on the main engine. At last, the anchor broke free. God knows what state it would be when it landed on deck.

Patrick and Tom returned forward to complete the recovery of the anchor as Calum went aft to the main cockpit. Alexander did a fine job of keeping the schooner in the same position as his deck crew completed preparations to make sail. The anchor arrived on deck, its blades badly bent, but nothing a good blacksmith couldn't repair.

Alexander waited for Patrick and Tom to come aft before kicking the engine into neutral, allowing the schooner to fall away before the moderating wind. He called for all sails to be sheeted loosely on port tack as the schooner headed towards the entrance of the estuary which so nearly became their grave. With no echo sounder to guide him, Alexander kept to the centre of the waterway.

The tide had now turned and the stream was running hard out to sea. The exit to the sea came in sight, the lowering sun revealing an angry bar waiting for them. The wind had changed to the west, driving the seas across the remains of the pounding surf from the north. The exit into the sea would be another uncomfortable and wet ride. The deck crew buttoned up their waterproofs, preparing for a good soaking. Carol and Mike went below, closing the main hatch behind them to make a final check all hatches and openings were soundly locked closed.

The schooner rushed towards the sea boiling over the bar. Alexander shouted for the sails to be trimmed for more power. The schooner powered into the maelstrom with the deck crew hanging on tightly, giving a rough ride while it lasted but soon the schooner reached the open sea.

Alexander asked for a course to steer. Calum ordered 300 degrees magnetic, telling the deck crew he wanted to get away from the Danish coastline, which lay to their lee. Calum sent Sarra below to check the charts. Sarra had briefly heard the name of the port on the tip of Norway she thought the Albanian trawler would head to. The name had not registered, so she examined the charts to trigger her recollection.

Calum looked around the deck of the schooner. Everything looked as it should be as he ordered the Starboard Watch below to take a two-hour rest. He told them to remain dressed ready for action on deck once they had cleaned themselves up a little.

The Port Watch, now totally keyed up for action, settled down for a concentrated period of fast and uncomfortable sailing.

'What next?' thought Calum.

He would soon find out.

Chapter 21

The schooner powered ever deeper into the North Sea. As the water depth increased so the seas became more ordered. The deck crew were learning a sharp lesson in old fashioned sailing, with no electronics to help them. No depth sounders, no radar, no direction finder to pick-up the radio beacons to fix position; there was only Calum's strange hand-held GPS of doubtful accuracy, and fast running out of battery power.

With the schooner running at full speed, fully darkened with no navigation lights, her crew on deck had to be very alert, and constantly scanning the dark horizon in front of them.

The time passed quickly. Sarra came on deck to remind Calum the time had come to phone her father, Commander 'H'. Calum went below with Sarra to the communicator at the navigation table. Contact was quickly established.

Commander 'H' came on the air with short crisp questions, inviting only short factual answers. Calum gave the position readings from his handheld GPS, and marking the data on the chart. Commander 'H' curtly gave him a correction factor, which enabled Calum to quickly update the position on the chart.

Commander 'H' issued a range of instructions. The schooner had to head for a reference point and then hold position there. The journey time would be under two hours at their current speed, and it was important not to be late. Calum broke-off to mark the reference position on the map, drew a rhumb line directly to it, shouted up new instructions to the deck crew and told them to make all haste.

Sarra finished taking notes from her father. Commander 'H' rang-off and Sarra looked up at Calum perplexed.

'And?' asked Calum

'Daddy is sending us four of his best 'hooligans', a night time paraglide drop,' she told him.

'And just who are these hooligans,' asked Calum.

'Err. They're Special Forces. Not many people know about. Some are regular service types with a few free loaders thrown in for good measure.'

'Hired guns you mean?' asked Calum

'Very special hooligans, some rejects from the French Foreign Legion, and some SBS boys in need of more excitement,' Sarra told him.

'And Daddy, Commander 'H', can control these people?' Calum asked.

'Oh yes,' replied Sarra. 'Daddy has a very special talent. All his boys are very special.'

'No names, no pack drill I suppose?' suggested Calum.

'Absolutely,' said Sarra. 'Now here are the rest of our instructions. When we reach point 'X', we hold position on the main engine, with the mainsails fully reefed, also the outer foresail. The inner foresail is to be set, winched in tight, back-winded. OK? And don't forget to have the navigation lights on and the deck lights located up the mast.'

'Oh really, anything else?' asked Calum.

'The first man down will be a 'pathfinder'. When he's aboard he'll take charge of the rest of the drop. Should be exciting,' suggested Sarra.

'Huh,' muttered Calum. 'Get your watch on deck, get a good handover from Alexander, and send Port Watch to rest before the grand event. I'm going to turn-in. If you need to, pester Mike, he's very adept at all this excitement stuff.'

Calum went to his favourite quarter berth behind the galley and threw himself wearily into his bunk. 'Oh for a quiet life; not much chance on this trip,' he thought.

He soon fell into a deep and exhausted sleep. It seemed to last no time at all when he was vigorously woken-up by Carol.

'Show time Skipper,' she said. 'Drink this, it will do you good.'

Calum's hand reached out for a large mug of very strong, very sweet coffee, which did not quite meet the 'drink driving' laws in his nation. He slurped it down whilst listening to the latest updates. The schooner reached the target position with fifteen minutes to spare. Tom had the helm, sailed past position, hove to and now the schooner drifted slowly downwind to the appointed location.

The communicator burst into life. A strong male voice came on the air. Sarra recognised it at once. 'Buffty,' she cried out in excitement.

'Who the fuck is 'Buffty?' muttered Calum grumpily. God, he was tired.

'Buffty' is the pathfinder. He's calibrating our position. He'll jump soon and land close by in a few minutes,' she explained.

'Nice to have a calibrated position,' thought Calum. 'What more could a lost soul ask for?'

Sarra continued outlining a rather hair-raising procedure. The first jumper would launch himself from a high flying aircraft, make a free-fall glide until it was time to pull the rip cord of his main parachute, before gliding onto the schooner. With luck, he might even keep his feet dry.

'Christ,' thought Calum. 'Lunatics, absolute bloody lunatics.'

The crew of the schooner looked up into the sky but could see nothing. The communicator burst into life. 'Descent started', is all it said.

A few moment later the communicator rasped out for the helm to keep in position or else. Tom thought to himself, 'Or else what'? His task was not easy in the restless seaway, and, at least, the backed inner jib damped some of the rolling motion of the schooner.

There came a whooshing noise and a dark compact figure landed on the foredeck. He collected his chute from the sea and rolled it up. This was 'Buffty'. Sarra ran to his side and wrapped her arms around him.

'Must be friends?' thought Mike.

The pair of them made it back to the cockpit. Mike saw a short compact man, hard and very fit, and dressed from head to toe in black.

'The latest fashion,' mussed Mike, who made his way to get the schooner's logbook. On his return he shoved it at the recent arrival, 'You have to sign in; rules.'

'Buffty' looked at him kind of queer, was about to say the obvious, broke into a boyish grin and signed in four persons.

'Eenie, Meanie, Miney and Mo. These are the only names you'll know us by,' said Buffty.

'Yes Buffty, thank you,' said Mike without batting an eyelid. 'Your companions on their way down?'

'Three minutes,' said Buffty, as he pulled out a small GPS handset and gave it to Tom. 'Just keep the northing and easting readings at zero for five minutes and you'll win a prize.'

Tom muttered something impolite under his breath but Buffty let it go.

An alarm rang somewhere in one of Buffty's many pockets. 'In-coming, get ready to drag them aft out the way,' he ordered standing behind Tom.

Another whooshing sound, a loud splash was heard, followed my some very course French, which everyone correctly assumed to totally impolite.

'Sans repetition,' muttered Mike, who hadn't a clue about the French language but recognised a good swearing technique when he heard one. A small grappling iron came flying inboard and wrapped itself around the foremast mainstay. Without effort, the man in the sea pulled himself aboard, and then a large container behind him.

'This is 'Meanie', announced Buffty, and before he could say anything another whooshing sound came from the port side of the schooner and a dark figure bounced off the backed inner jib and inelegantly stopped himself from going over the side. He too pulled a large floating container on board behind him.

'This is 'Miney', announced Buffty, as he berated him for his inelegance. The dark shape of Miney said nothing, and moved aft to unhook his parachute harness and pack his 'chute.

Thirty seconds later, a slow whooshing noise was heard. The crew of the schooner strained their eyes forward to catch sight of the next arrival. Nothing? They looked around only to see a dark shape already standing next to the mainmast.

'Bon Jour, mon amis,' said the dark shape. 'C'est Mo à votre service. This Mo, at your service.'

His heavy French accent with Belgian overtones was polite and gentle. He dragged the last of the floating containers on deck.

'Clever sod,' thought Calum as he ordered the deck crew to make the four containers secure just behind the foremast, as the new arrivals sorted themselves out.

Mo spoke, 'You 'ave ready the coffee?' he asked in a voice suggesting a cross between an enquiry and an order.

'In the galley below,' Mike replied. 'It's fresh, hot, and instant.'

Mo winced. He hated instant coffee, but with a double helping of sugar and a shot from his concealed hip flask he could just about manage to drink the stuff.

Calum went below with the four arrivals and looked them up and down. They were all the same build, below average height, hard compact bodies, piercing eyes and very fit. Crew cut hair styles appeared to be in-style at the moment. Their eyes were their most impressive feature. Eyes that missed nothing, that gave away no clues as to what they were thinking or what they would do next. Total professionals.

Calum shouted up to Tom to resume course for Mandal. The four arrivals finished their coffee and went on deck to unpack their containers. From the first container, Buffty handed over a VHF radio and a new desk mounted GPS unit to be installed in the place of the similarly smashed units.

'There,' announced Buffty, 'that restores some of your systems.'

Calum thanked him. Mo handed Calum a bag of familiar boxes. AK-47 ammunition.

'We thinking 'ou must be running low,' said Mo. 'Let us 'ope you won't have to use.'

'How did you know that?' muttered Calum out load.

'Oh we 'ave photographs of le trawler Albanian,' said Mo. 'We counted three rifled weapons used, plus one maybe two handguns fired by a single person. Not forgetting the hand grenades and the two flares fired, I would guess by Sarra. She's good with the flare pistol. Quite a good team you have onboard considering.'

'I'll look forward to the video replay then?' asked Calum, amazed at the level of information.

Mo smiled, and got on with his unpacking. Calum went below to find four large cartons of fresh milk on the galley table along with the current issue of the Daily Telegraph.

'Thoughtful of them,' mussed Calum, as he put his feet up and drank the coffee Carol put in his hand.

Patrick came below into the main cabin, 'Where are the 'three blind mice plus one' going to sleep?' he asked.

'Is this the crew's new piss take?' asked Calum.

'To be sure. Don't know what to make of them. They're unpacking a mountain of stuff up on deck, running around in ever decreasing circles.'

Calum dragged his weary body on deck to see what was going on. Mo had started setting up a 'comms' station at the back of the cockpit. Haversacks of all descriptions were neatly lined up along the windward deck. Strange looking automatic weapons were being checked, readied, and put back into waterproof bags.

Calum found Mo busy talking in a strange Arabic language to someone. Short sentences, completely undecipherable to almost anybody. Mo shut the set down. 'Excellent reception, voice-over-internet, you know very clear. Commander 'H' sends his regards,' he concluded.

'Well thanks,' said Calum lightly, and went forward to find Buffty.

Buffty dropped lightly into the cockpit, asking about sleeping arrangements.

'The floor, anywhere there's space is about the only real option I can offer, most of the beds up forward are soaking wet. It'll be some time before we're back to normal,' said Calum.

As the enhanced crew of the schooner completed their many preparations, *Samba Canção* continued to power into the night.

Tomorrow would be another interesting day.

*****

Chapter 22

Late afternoon came as the Danish Army five-ton all-terrain truck and its precious cargo made good time escaping to the west. The snow petered out, and it was time to stop for quarter-of-an-hour to remove the snow chains. The Major took the chance to relieve himself in the wind shadow of a large rock outcrop. The wind was biting cold.

The road remained thankfully empty, and the lack of aerial observation from the German Air Force considered a huge bonus. Still, it remained vital to keep a sharp eye open for enemy activity.

The truck continued bouncing down tortuous roads, most of them in very bad condition from the long winter. The road passed through amazing rugged landscapes, as it made its way alongside Norway's many fjords and over its even more numerous mountain passes.

Red Eric was dosing inside the cab, the first time the Major had experienced his company, rather than having to shout through an open window as he stood outside on the running board. His body odour did not add positively to the doubtful fragrance of the cab's interior.

As the truck began to crest what would hopefully be the last mountain pass before the long descent to sea level, ten mountain troops jumped out from behind a rock outcrop and blocked the road. Red Eric came to with a start and made to leap out of the cab to confront them. The Major grabbed his arm and told him to remain still. He'd spotted a partially hidden machine gun off to one side aimed right at them.

The Major relaxed a little. These were not German troops, but Norwegian ski troops. Quite what their purpose was they were just about to find out. A tough looking, heavily armed, sergeant came up to the truck cab.

'Who are you, what is your purpose and I want to see identification papers,' he demanded in perfect English.

The Major looked at Red Eric, 'You got any papers,' he asked.

Red Eric snorted in disgust. He didn't need papers to go anywhere, and said so.

The Norwegian Sergeant did not exhibit any signs of patience as he signalled two of his men to go round the back of the truck. They pulled back the canvas back-flap to stare down the barrels of a lot of German sub-machine guns being held by the scruffiest band of ruffians they had ever seen.

'Vikings, four of them in the back, armed to the teeth, and a small boy,' shouted one of the soldiers. The Major didn't remember a small boy, where the hell had he come from?

The Norwegian Sergeant repeated his demand for identification papers. The reply went something along the lines he should ask nicely if he was that bothered. The Norwegian Sergeant shrugged his shoulders. Clearly Vikings didn't carry identification papers, no need; their body odour said it all.

The Norwegian Sergeant came up to the cab window,

'And you are?' he demanded of the Major.

'Major Per Bruus-Jensen, Special Forces, Danish Rangers, acting under secret orders from King Christian of Denmark, and in cooperation with your government,' he replied.

'Really,' said the Norwegian sergeant. 'Any proof?'

The Major rummaged around in his haversack and pulled out a badly crumpled letter, issued by his Prime Minister's office requesting, in the name of the King of Denmark, all reasonable assistance. He handed it over to the Norwegian Sergeant.

'And just how much reasonable assistance would you like?' asked the Norwegian Sergeant in a sarcastic voice.

'An escort to the nearest sea port would be OK, and whistle up a large Royal Navy ship to take me and my truck to England whilst you're at it,' replied the Major evenly. 'Failing that, if you could tell me what the hell is going on, and stop the Germans from giving me and my men any more trouble for a couple of days, that'll do nicely'.

The Norwegian Sergeant re-read the letter and handed it back to the Major.

'Your sense of humour precedes you Major,' said the Norwegian Sergeant. 'The Germans are looking for you over towards the east. They are unaware you've made it this far west. We believe the German Army is somewhat busy chasing a large gang of Vikings and some of your men up the back road to Oslo. Rumour has it the Vikings are more than holding their own, for the moment.'

'Quite,' said the Major. 'Let me introduce to you Red Eric, Viking and fearless slayer of the German Army. He and his men have become extremely unpopular with the German Army recently, whilst making huge friends with the local undertakers.'

The Norwegian Sergeant almost broke into a smile. He told them to continue making progress to the west as fast as possible, going around the far side of the 'Hardangervidda' plateau and drop down into the Fjords. As far as he knew the German Invasion Forces had not yet moved into the general area. There were Norwegian army units still operating on that side of the country, but they were lightly armed and only doing what they could. Meanwhile, his men would blow this mountain pass and carry on with their mission.

The Major thanked him and looked at Red Eric, 'Move out?'

'Huh,' grunted Red Eric. 'I'm going in that direction anyway, German Army or no German Army.'

'You can't fight them all,' said the Major.

'Yes I can, and yes I will, in my own time, and in my own way,' snorted Red Eric as he stared hard into the Major's face.

The Danish Army truck continued on its way, as it commenced the long and perilous descent to the distant Fjords. Night was almost upon them and time to rest and get a hot meal. Red Eric directed the truck driver to a deserted farm. The Vikings hid the truck at the back of the farm building and the Vikings soon made short work of opening the back door of the farmhouse.

The makings for a fire were quickly produced, and soon a roaring blaze had welcome heat relieving the Major's aching back. He kicked some old blankets into a corner near the fire and sat down. It occurred to him just exactly where they were headed had not yet revealed.

The small boy appeared to be the one from the first German ambush, which seemed such a long time ago. His bright red hair looked a mess, which blended in with the rest of him.

The Major sat the child down in front of the fire and rummaged successfully for a small bar of chocolate. The child grabbed it quickly out of his hands without speaking. 'Poor lad must still be in shock,' thought the Major. He didn't remember any of the Vikings giving him any support or comfort.

'Eric,' the Major called over, 'do you have any idea of where we are going and our options when we get there?'

Red Eric moved to his side and squatted down.

'Major, there is a special place I have in mind. It's very secret. When we get to the second of four fjords, I expect to find two fishing boats, which we will 'borrow', with or without the consent of the owners. We will ship your cargo onto one of them but set sail together. If we're not seen the two boats will stay together.'

'When we get to the secret location, the boat with the cargo will be secreted there, and the other will make its way to the open sea to determine if there is a chance to escape, at night, into the North Sea and over to Scotland.'

'If we are spotted by the Germans, this boat will make a diversionary escape, whilst your boat will stay hidden at the secret location. The boat will never be found, trust me.'

Red Eric looked at the Major's questioning face. The Major looked less than trusting. He also saw a tired Major wondering where the hell he was and what the hell was going on. He didn't blame him.

'OK,' said the Major. 'You've done well so far. I've nothing more to offer. I can but thank you for your efforts, and hope we make it after we leave here. Thanks.'

One of the Vikings dumped a tin plate on the Major's lap and started to ladle a large portion of bubbling food in the cast steel pot taken from the fire. Potato and meat stew, with a few old chopped up turnips thrown in for good measure. A flask of Schnapps was handed down.

'That will make it taste better,' said the Viking. 'One big swig should do the trick'.

The Schnapps did the trick all right, making the food vaguely eatable. No matter, the Major had tasted worse and it filled his empty stomach. Another large swig from the flask of Schnapps prepared the Major for the sleep he badly needed. The adventure in Norway had drained him. He bedded down in a corner using what came to hand to make himself more comfortable. His main worry was how to keep warm, and restore his energy. Tomorrow would be another long and tiring day.

Long before dawn broke, Red Eric roused his party from an uncomfortable night in poor surroundings. The Vikings and the Major finished the last of the food cooked the night before and prepared for the day. Outside was dark with a clear sky and cold wind blowing up the valley; a cold cutting wind that befriended nobody.

The Major and Red Eric climbed into the cab of the truck, whilst the remainder of the party piled into the back. The Major noticed the Vikings had stripped the farmhouse of the old blankets. That they were feeling the cold said it all.

The truck driver completed checks of the truck's engine and tyres, climbed aboard, and the journey resumed. The truck bounced terribly on the journey down to the Fjords, the going slow with very little light from a fast waning moon to show the road ahead.

Within two hours the truck reached the first fjord. The driver carefully checked the turning to take the correct road. The rough ride continued. At the first light of day, the second fjord came into view, and on the far side of the water a small jetty could be seen with the two promised fishing trawlers.

Red Eric woke up from a long snooze and stretched himself as far as he could in the close confines of the truck cab. The Major had tried to nod off but without success. Twenty minutes later, the truck reached the jetty and came to a halt. Red Eric jumped out and roused his complaining Vikings from the rear of the truck, and went to examine the two fishing trawlers.

'Not bad,' he thought to himself, each about sixty feet long, heavily constructed from strong timbers and quite seaworthy.

Red Eric jumped onboard the first fishing boat to rouse the owner from a deep sleep. The Major remained huddled inside the truck cab, where it remained reasonably warm for the moment. Red Eric returned to the truck.

'I need a donation from the cargo,' he demanded.

This was news to the Major, who hadn't thought the matter through. The gold belonged to the Danish Government but the diamonds, well what the hell; a few more or less wouldn't make a lot of difference at the moment. He knew the markings on the case containing cut and polished diamonds.

'Diamonds OK? How many packets,' asked the Major.

'What's in a packet?' asked Red Eric.

'No idea, let's have a look,' replied the Major.

He jumped from the cab and went to the back of the truck. The Vikings had already removed the heavy tarpaulin, allowing the Major to see the ammunition case he had in mind, and motioned it to be dumped on the ground. A crowbar appeared in the hands of one of the Vikings, the Major nodded his head and the case soon opened. The Major took out his hunting knife and slit open the wax paper outer covering. Inside he found small individual packets of diamonds.

'Christ,' he thought, 'this case alone must be worth a king's ransom.' He opened a few of the packets. They all appeared to contain ten diamonds of about one to two carats, which sparkled weakly in the early morning light. He'd no idea of their true value, but ten packets would be a lot of money in anybody's terms.

'Ten Packets do?' he asked of Red Eric, 'about two hundred carats in total.'

'Add two more; that will be more than sufficient,' ordered Red Eric 'Time to be going.'

The Major pulled out twelve packets of diamonds, saw they were all 'much of a muchness' and handed them over. The new owner seemed more than pleased with the deal and left them to it. Red Eric ordered the truck to back-up to the inboard fishing boat, whilst he sent two of his men to check out each engine room.

Twenty minutes later, the cargo had been transferred along with the Vikings hoard of weapons. The large quantity of field rations were equally distributed between the two boats. Red Eric hugged the driver of the truck and sent him on his way.

'Where's he off to?' asked the Major.

'Leading a false trail back up the mountain and over a sheep track to the North. The Germans are looking for Danish Army truck, so with luck, they will spot it and follow behind.'

'I suppose the truck's movements will somehow be communicated to the Germans?' asked the Major.

'Very clever,' replied Red Eric 'Now let's get going.'

The two fishing trawlers set off together down the fjord, hugging the dark east side. The wind whipped up sufficient waves to quickly break down the wake from the two craft. The magnificent scenery almost captivated the Major, but in truth, he remained highly nervous about being on a small trawler in the middle of a Norwegian fjord, highly exposed to observation from the air or anybody high up in the mountains. The Major scanned the scene with his binoculars but saw no movement whatsoever. That didn't mean a lot to the Major, it was difficult to see anything on land except for the endless grey mountains and the sparse mottled brown and green vegetation.

By mid-morning, the two fishing trawlers were well on their way. A sharp turn to the west was safely negotiated when the two vessels changed to the other side of the fjord, keeping in the safety of the dark shadows of the towering mountains. This part of the coastline looked totally unforgiving. The mountainsides rose out of the fjord from great depths, with no places to land. The wind funnelled through the narrows with great force, even on this relatively mild day.

Midday past and Red Eric came on deck to see exactly where they were.

'Not long now,' he said, and went to the bow to look and listen. The two fishing trawlers slowed in the pitching waters of the fjord, coming along the sheer cliff face of the mountain. Suddenly, with a burst of full power, the two fishing boats lined up one behind the other and headed for what appeared to solid rock overgrown with long hanging twisted foliage encased in a shroud of mist.

The Major flinched as the impending collision didn't occur and the two vessels entered a strange narrow inlet, impossible to see from outside in the fjord. The route through this deep entrance was littered with jagged underwater pillars of rock. Red Eric called them 'Drager Tennene' or 'dragon's teeth'. Over the centuries they had kept many an unwary intruder from entering this holy place. Only when weather conditions were favourable was it possible to enter in any measure of safety; a very rare event.

Red Eric motioned for the helmsman to slow down as he stared intently into the deep turbulent waters. With frantic hand signals, he guided his vessel through a torturous channel into a strange lagoon.

The daylight inside the lagoon was strange, very flat with little perspective or depth of view, truly a strange phenomenon enhanced by a gentle mist rising from the surface of the water, the result of a deep underground stream rising to the surface. The far end of the lagoon was shrouded in the mist. The Major asked the distance to the far end of the lagoon. Red Eric didn't answer. How deep was the lagoon? Again Red Eric said nothing.

The entrance, and its deep lagoon, was clearly a result of volcanic activity many millions of years ago. The slow swirling mist made the lagoon an eerie mystic place. Its silence was total, with no wildlife and the only foliage, the long creepers hanging into the water's edge.

Red Eric spoke. He told the Major the ancient Vikings knew this as a holy place, where rituals long since forgotten were carried out on the death of a Viking King. Very few ancient Vikings knew its secrets, and only the most senior of their elders had ever heard of this place. It had remained very secret over the centuries. No Norwegians had ever heard of this location. Quite how Red Eric knew of its location was not about to be explained to a Danish Major traipsing around after an aging Viking.

The two vessels came together in the lagoon as Red Eric called a hurried meeting. He ordered the transfer of extra stores to the Major's boat and sent one of his Vikings to the second boat. After a brief conference and with farewells ringing in everyone's ears, the second boat carefully returned to the fjord.

Red Eric went to the bow of his craft and shouted to the helmsman to open his cockpit window. With Red Eric leaning over the bow he used hand signals to bring the boat forward very slowly. The fishing boat headed for an overhanging cliff face with many large boulders perched perilously above. The Major couldn't see an entrance, but entrance there was as the boat passed through another narrow rock fissure and into a dark cave, its entrance protected by two tall rock pillars.

The Major found the experience of entering the cave very strange, as it did not seem possible the place existed. The fishing trawler moored alongside a large flat rock laying at a strange angle into the water. The other end of this large slab of rock lay high above the floor of the cave, with a man-made pile of boulders, in the middle of the flat surface.

With one end made fast to the windlass, Red Eric leapt ashore with a large coil of rope, and proceeded to make fast to the large slab of rock. His Viking helmsman cranked the windlass and tensioned the rope as hard as possible before making it secure. A stern line was similarly deployed and now the fishing boat was safely moored over the edge of the great slab of rock. Red Eric climbed onboard and gathered up his formidable array of weapons.

'Grab your rifle and follow me Major,' he called out. 'Time for a little exercise.' He looked around at the remaining Viking, told him to stand guard and look after the youngster still sound asleep in the cabin.

Red Eric climbed over the side of the fishing boat, lowered himself down onto the tilted rock, jumped down to the floor of the cave and moved carefully towards its darkened rear. The Major followed Red Eric as he started to climb a barely visible narrow path that wound upwards into the upper reaches of the cave's roof. The climb looked dangerous and in places very tight. The rock path underneath his feet was loose; the Major became very uneasy as he climbed higher.

The Major wondered just where the hell the old Viking was taking him. He didn't need hard exercise right now, but he gamely hung on as Red Eric climbed quickly in front. After what seemed an age, the path led to the top of a cliff. Red Eric signalled the Major to crouch down whilst he carefully scanned the horizon around him. All seemed quiet and with no movement on what appeared to be a deep headland.

Red Eric motioned the Major to follow as he moved towards the edge of the headland. Below, the fjord came into view. They could just make out the second Viking fishing trawler as it made its way carefully to the exit to the open sea, hugging the coastline and keeping in the shadow of the towering mountains.

The Major took his binoculars to scan the fjord in all directions. Looking at the direction from which they had come nothing moved on land or on water. He scanned the sky and saw nothing, hoping they had made their way to safety without being seen, but he could not be sure.

He turned around to watch the second fishing trawler, still some way from the open sea, but it was difficult to see any real detail in the late afternoon mist. The Major tried hard to gauge the distances he was looking at. The strange perspectives gave little idea. Red Eric put his hand out for the binoculars. As he scanned the same view his back stiffened.

'What's up,' asked the Major.

'Trouble,' was the only reply. Red Eric continued to look intently at the distant view, but the Major could make out no detail what so ever.

'Bastards,' came the next comment from Red Eric tight lips. The Major could just make out the fishing trawler, which made a sudden alteration towards the side of the fjord. He saw a powerful patrol boat coming up the fjord at full speed. A German motor launch, fast and well-armed with a 20mm cannon on its foredeck, and two twin machine gun nests each side of the short mast rising out of the rear of the superstructure.

The fishing trawler suddenly resumed its original course. Red Eric chuckled. The Major asked what on earth he could be so pleased about. Red Eric started a running commentary. His Vikings would deploy a large net behind the trawler. If the German motor launch came from astern, the net would be slipped, the motor launch would run over it, and snag its propellers.

That ruse didn't work. The German motor launch approached beam on, turned sharply alongside the Viking's fishing craft and slammed into reverse. The two boats closed each other, side by side.

The next ruse would offer the Germans two baskets of fresh fish. The Major looked at Red Eric strangely. Red Eric explained the fish in the baskets hid about three kilos of TNT. A thin wire loop hanging from the bottom of each basket would activate a five-second fuse.

The German sailors fell for the ruse. The Viking fishermen were careful to hand over one basket opposite the 20mm cannon, the other opposite the rear machine gun nest. With the baskets handed over, the Vikings pulled the wires, dropping for cover behind the thick wooden bulwarks of their fishing boat.

Two powerful explosions wreaked havoc on the German patrol launch. The Vikings jumped up with automatic weapons and finished off all signs of life on deck. Hastily deployed grappling lines held the two craft together, as two Vikings boarded the patrol launch, ran along the deck dropping hand grenades down the ventilation cowlings. They vanished below, extinguishing all signs of life from any remaining Germans. In less than ninety seconds, the Vikings were the proud owners of a somewhat second-hand German patrol launch. Their own craft had been damaged by the two explosions, but what did Vikings need with glass in the windows in their wheelhouse.

Red Eric handed the binoculars back to the Major, well pleased with himself.

The Major asked 'Well, what's going to happen next?'

Red Eric replied, 'If the guns on the German patrol launch are still serviceable, my Vikings will rest up, repair damage as necessary, and go find more German patrol launches.'

'That's a suicide mission,' commented the Major.

'Exactly,' said Red Eric. 'I have two groups of Vikings. Those that want to 'do and die' now, in a blaze of Viking glory, and others who want to indulge in the long-term conflict.'

The Major looked bemused. Red Eric continued, 'Anyway, the German's aren't used to suicide attacks. I reckon they will kill a lot more Germans that way.'

In reality, the Vikings were dead men already, and were merely choosing their demise in their own time, in their own way, remembering their proud traditions.

The Major understood, the Viking community in Norway would go out in style. True warriors to the last, the Germans were not going to enjoy the experience.

Red Eric and the Major turned their backs on the scene and carefully retraced their steps down into the secret cave. On the deck of the fishing boat, a scared looking boy looked anxiously for his father. The boy had woken up and found himself alone in a dark strange cave. The Major couldn't begin to think how bad it would feel to be in the same situation. Red Eric and the Major climbed back into the trawler, and for a change, Red Eric gave comfort to his son.

The Major looked on with an expression of enquiry. 'This is Ericsson,' Red Eric explained. 'He is my youngest offspring, the last of six children. The others are grown-up and living in and around Oslo. Two work for the government, three are studying at various universities.

This was the first time that the Major had been given any information about his family life. The Major knew Ericsson was a half son, but Red Eric was not about to divulge further information regarding wives or other relationships.

He set to and prepared food to fill their hungry bellies. A bottle of Snaps appeared; more homebrew that could strip the paint from any vehicle. The Major ate his food in silence and gave up on the thankless task of worrying about the future. He expected they would rest up and lie low. Red Eric would find a way to safety; when and how would be another matter. It certainly became essential to lie low. Within two days the German Army blanketed the entire area with troops searching for the missing fishing trawler. Worse still, two weeks later and the Germans were still continuing their searching.

Red Eric became concerned. It would be impossible to stay hidden in the safety of the secret cave for an extended stay. Their food supplies were insufficient to feed Red Eric, the Major, his half-son Ericsson and the remaining Viking for more than six weeks. It would be very dangerous to venture outside onto the headland. There would be little wildlife to catch, and their movements would be easily seen from the air.

Red Eric was certain the Germans would play a long waiting game, and if any sign of their presence became detected, it would only narrow the search area and bring an even greater risk of detection. It was time to depart before it was too late and just hope the Germans would eventually come to the conclusion the fishing trawler and the cargo they were seeking were at the bottom of a Fjord.

He had a plan. The cave hid an open four-man rowing boat, a Faering, clinker-built in the traditional Scandinavian way, with riveted overlapping planks. Its history stretched back into time, and although built many years ago the Major could see it belonged to the current century. The Faering had been rigged with a mast and sail in addition to its oars. Red Eric did not offer any information about its origins.

He planned to load their remaining supplies and make their way from the lagoon into the Fjord just before sunset. When the coast was clear, they would sail down the Fjord and make their way to the coast before heading north along Norway's fractured coastline. During the day, they would hide, or mingle with local fishing craft going about their daily business.

The Major expressed his concern at sailing in difficult Norwegian waters at night. Red Eric brushed aside his concerns. He'd sailed these waters from boyhood, confident of making his escape. He explained the northern coastal villages would have few Germans, and it would be easy to hide among the local population. He had many friends and contacts, and Red Eric hoped to find a remote village and wait for the Germans to turn their attention to other matters.

It took two days to prepare the Faering, with a spray cover fitted from the bow to the mast, and two crude bunks constructed underneath. Great care was taken distributing the food and water inside the Faering, with space needed for side arms, sub-machine guns and ammunition. Quite how far north Red Eric was expecting to travel wasn't mentioned. The Major resigned himself to going along with his plan.

Late in the afternoon on the third day, the heavily loaded Faering made its way from the cave into the Lagoon. All was quiet; the stillness eerie and all enveloping. The mist hung like a strange fog on top of the water obscuring the top of the cliffs rising vertically out of the deep still water.

The Major and Red Eric slowly rowed the Faering towards the Fjord, with Ericsson steering to Red Eric's many instructions as they made their way along the narrow passageway. They passed through the exit into the fjord hugging the dark shadows. The Faering stopped among the hanging creepers as Red Eric called for total silence. He searched and listened hard for the sound of German activity in the fjord. As the sun started its final descent, Red Eric carefully opened a passage way through the overhanging creepers and motioned the Major to continue his rowing.

It would be a clear night with a full moon, and a good breeze blew down the Fjord, for which the Major felt entirely grateful. Rowing a heavily over-loaded boat was not his idea of gentle evening exercise. Red Eric hoisted the single lugsail, and young Ericsson looked quite at home as he steered the Faering under full sail along the base of the tall cliffs.

By morning, they were well on their way. The Major dozed under the awning after a two-hour spell at the tiller. The Faering left the fjord during the early hours, and began to make its way north along the rocky Norwegian coast. Strange swirling currents caught hold of the small craft, sometimes assisting progress, more frequently bringing danger from rocky outcrops lurking under the water.

The coast remained clear, and by midday, their progress satisfied Red Eric, continually on the lookout for any signs of the German military. The Faering crossed to a long offshore island to hide in its dark shadows as the weak sun slowly sank in the western sky. The crew of the Faering went ashore and prepared hot food before resting until a strong moon rose in the east. Red Eric prepared to make an overnight sea voyage, an event that filled the Major with unease. Red Eric told him they must pass the entrances of several large Fjords that now led to new German bases being established along the coast.

The Major had to accept he was in the hands of an expert navigator, a Viking navigator who came from a long line of Viking navigators, who'd travelled far and wide, even discovering the northern edge of the American continent.

The night voyage proved tranquil. The wind eased and backed to the south-west, an ideal sailing breeze. The crew shared their time at the helm of the Faering and made remarkably good progress. As they passed the entrance of each fjord, distant lights showed the German military hard at work.

As the weak morning sun slowly crept above the mountains the signs of a fierce naval battle were everywhere. The Royal Navy had left its mark before retreating back to its lair in Scapa Flow. Flotsam and floating wreck-age littered the water over a wide area. A beached German destroyer had obviously been hit by the big guns of a British battleship. The remains of German ships were everywhere. An abandoned British destroyer floated listing at a big angle, its topside almost totally consumed by fire.

Red Eric was eager to reach the safe haven he had in mind. The Major asked how much further they had to travel. Red Eric grunted three hours, if the wind held fair. The Faering was being hard pressed, its square sail straining almost to destruction. Two hours later a headland came into view. Red Eric gave the helm to his son and raked around in a pile of boxes in the stern of their overloaded craft. He found what he want, a box of hand gre-nades. Apparently it was time to go fishing. Red Eric reluctantly explained that they were heading for a fish processing factory, and it would be useful to arrive with some fish. A good friend owned the fish factory, but a craft coming from distant waters would look very odd if it didn't have any fish to discharge. It would look very suspicious.

The Faering reached the headland, and Red Eric pointed to where he wanted to go, above an old steamship wreck. After quickly dropping four hand grenades into the clear waters around the shipwreck stunned fish soon started to float to the surface. The fish were quickly collected, filling what little space remaining in the bottom of the Faering. The Major worried their small craft would be swamped, but their journey continued, and as they entered into a small fjord, the waters calmed down. Red Eric steered the Faering alongside a fishing boat on the same course, and after a brief con-versation, Red Eric bid his Viking crew member farewell with instructions to get lost in the fishing community and not get caught.

At last, the fish processing factory came into view at the end of a long quay. Many local fishing boats were headed in the same direction, anxious to unload their fish so their catch could be processed in time for the evening train to Oslo. Adjacent to the fish processing factory the Major could see a small shipyard with external and internal slipways.

As the Faering came closer to the quay, German soldiers watched care-fully the scene before them. The Major looked questioningly at Red Eric. No one would miss seeing his tangled red hair flowing all over his face. Red Eric grunted and raked around in a canvas haversack, pulling out three woollen Balaclava hats. He tossed one to the Major and his son. The Major looked around and saw that the crews in the other fishing boats were simi-larly protected against the cold biting wind. Why wait until now? It had been cold all night and the woollen garments would have been welcome.

Red Eric steered the Faering toward a tall stout man wearing a Russian 'ushanka' hat, the manager of the fish processing factory. As their boat reached the quayside the manager looked down and saw an unfamiliar craft, staring at Red Eric trying to see who it was. A German soldier passed behind and the manager sensed the danger. Instinctively, he knew the man looking up at him, but just couldn't put a name to what little he could see of his face. He noticed the young boy in the Faering and the penny dropped. He waved the Faering to a set of steps set into the quay.

The manager came to the water's edge, took hold of the Faering and, speaking in a low voice, he asked, 'Red is that you?

'Gustav, my good friend, I need your assistance and very badly. Is your covered slipway in the boatyard free?'

'Yes, it became clear last night, move along to the unloading winch, we'll take your catch and then row up to the slipway. The cradle will be in the water, just moor between the uprights.'

Red Eric did as he was bid, and by the time his catch of fish had been unloaded, the cradle was in the water. The Faering moved to the slipway, placed between the four uprights and made fast.

A steam winch pulled the cradle up the slipway, and the Faering disappeared into the boatshed. Gustav came quickly into the boatshed to see what his friend needed so urgently.

'Gustav, you will know the Germans are looking for me and my two companions. I need this Faering unloaded undercover. There are weapons that will be needed in the long occupation of our country. I also need to get this Danish Major out of the clutches of the Germans.'

Gustav replied his news had reached him, although he was certain the Germans on this side of Norway were not aware he'd made it this far. However, they were on high alert. After all, the British forces had only just retreated and the whole coastline remained in a state of flux.

'Gustav, what will be the best way to travel to Oslo. Are you still shipping your fish on the overnight train?' asked Red Eric.

'Yes, my truck departs at six this evening. It gets to the station at nine pm and the train arrives anytime between nine thirty to ten o'clock the next morning. I will take you and your friends the back way to my house next door. Get washed and changed. I would get a shave and a haircut if I were you, and your boy. That much red hair can be seen a long way away'

Red Eric grunted at the thought of washing and shaving. For the Major a shower and a change of clothes was the best news he'd heard in days.

They were quickly taken next door, where the housemaid took care of them. She found clean clothes for them all, including strong overcoats, strong leather boots and tweed hats. The Major was pressed into service as a barber. He even made a good job of giving Red Eric a shave, and both he and his son short back and sides. The transformation was amazing. Red Eric almost looked like a doctor or lecturer in a university, and his son an industrious student. Even his own mother wouldn't recognise him.

The Major thought about dying their hair a different colour, but cosmetic products had been an early casualty of World War II. With their ablutions finished the three weary travellers ate a hearty meal and retired to an upstairs bedroom to rest. Later, Red Eric packed a large leather bag with the belongings he wanted to take with him. He thought long and hard about what weapons he wanted to take on the final leg of his journey to Oslo.

The arsenal he had brought with him in the Faering had been taken to an underground store in the fish factory, covered over with rubber sheeting and covered in fish heads to deter close inspection by the Germans. Red Eric eventually decided on taking two British Sten guns, and two automatic pistols. Gustav had told him that anyone caught with German weapons would likely be shot out of hand. The German Army remained nervous after the recent battles, and continually on the lookout for foreign forces left behind by the retreating British Army.

These weapons were easy to hide and had little bulk. Only useful at short range, Red Eric recognised the need to change his style of fighting the Germans. He had to get his son to safety among his good friends in Oslo.

Evening came as Gustav returned to find the trio ready for their escape. The Major had done a good job in transforming Red Eric and his son into clean shaven and professional looking people. The Major found an old doctors bag that he'd cleaned up. Together the three of them looked very respectable.

The Major asked how to travel without identity documents. Gustav told him that the Germans had yet to register everybody and issue occupation identity papers. Many Norwegians were away from their homes with no documents at all. Local German commanders were issuing temporary papers to those Norwegians who could convince they were returning to their hometown. By chance, a local publican had come across a bag full of blank papers and helped himself without rousing any suspicions. More importantly, he'd stolen a spare stamp and inkpad to make the forgeries look authentic to all but the most rigorous examination.

The publican completed the documents needed for this dangerous journey with names of people from the Oslo region. Red Eric's documents described him as a court lawyer from Oslo collecting his young nephew after a road accident who needed specialist medical treatment in Oslo. The Major was described as a marketing and sales executive for one of Norway's largest manufacturer of wood pulping machinery. Other documents had been produced, including business cards, to add strength to the subterfuge.

Gustav brought his sister, the local nurse, to bandage the boy's head and right arm. The head bandage would hide his red hair, and the arm in a sling would complete the disguise.

At six o'clock a knock on the front door heralded the time had come to make tracks up the long winding road over the mountains to the railway station. The fish truck had no spare room, so Gustav found an employee to drive the spare vehicle belonging to the fish factory.

The journey over the mountains became slow and tiring, but at least the road had no military activity. When at last they reached the remote railway station they found it guarded by a German sergeant in charge of four bored German soldiers and the Norwegian stationmaster. There was little going on at this late hour. The freight train would be late, a normal occurrence even in peace time. The freight train made many stops at the remote communities needing their goods transported to Norway's capital city.

The rear of the freight train had a single passenger coach adjoining the guard's van. The coach an old corridor type, where each compartment could provide six bunk beds by rearranging the seat back rests to the horizontal position and lowering a bunk bed from high up in the ceiling.

The Sergeant checked everybody's papers with care but seemed to be satisfied. The freight train arrived in a cloud of steam. As its tender was refilled with water, the fishery workers made short work of loading the day's cargo into an empty wagon and emptying a container full of ice over the fish before covering them with a large tarpaulin.

Red Eric, his son, and the Major boarded the freight train quickly, organising a carriage compartment into a sleeping car. The Major was relieved; so far so good. The freight train would make directly for Oslo without any further stops. He wanted to ask Red Eric what would happen if and when they reached Oslo. Red Eric was not in the mood to answer questions, as he busied himself giving his son a quick snack, a small drink of milk, before putting him to bed on one of the middle bunks.

The steam engine made a juddering start as its wheels fought for grip to get the heavily loaded freight train on the move. The guardsman came to check their tickets and told them they could use the stove in the Guard's van if they wished to make a hot drink.

The freight train slowly made its way through the still night, as the railway track twisted its way around Norway's towering mountains, mostly following single-track roads that lined the many fjords.

During the night, Red Eric rose to make hot drinks to keep out the cold.

The carriage heating did not work, and his son had woken-up to complain. He found the guardsman dosing in his comfortable leather arm chair, but he had little to say. As the water heated for the drinks, Red Eric went out of the back of the guard's van to look around. Another clear night, the moon shone brightly and the countryside became bathed in an eerie silver glow. Nothing moved in the still landscape.

Red Eric took the hot drinks to the carriage compartment and woke his travelling companions. The Major took the hot drink without comment, and when he'd finished, he made his way to the far end of the carriage to find the toilet. He checked the other compartments; all were empty.

By early morning, the freight train had made up for lost time, and the landscape started to open up as the mountains gave way to rolling hillsides. The sun started to show in the eastern sky, and Red Eric was up and about looking out of the windows for signs of military life.

The train rumbled through a station, and Red Eric thought he glimpsed German soldiers ducking behind the station building. He asked the guardsman if the Germans were guarding all the stations as a matter of course. His reply was inconclusive, which Red Eric took to mean he hadn't really noticed.

Time to prepare for what had every chance of being a fraught day. Red Eric set about getting his companions ready, to prepare some food and hot drinks and be able to react to any eventuality. The Major rose from a deep sleep but quickly regained his focus. The freight train was taking them into danger; he had no idea where he was, or what Red Eric intended.

Breakfast consisted of hot coffee and the sandwiches packed the previous day. Red Eric took an automatic pistol from his bag and shoved it into a deep pocket in his overcoat. The Major followed suit. Red Eric's son tidied up where he could, but looked confused as to what would happen next.

With the carriage compartment returned to normal, now there was space to move about. Red Eric looked out the window and knew the train would soon pass another railway station. Red Eric ordered the Major to sit on the floor and keep lookout through the window. He positioned his son in the corridor, told him to keep a lookout and not be seen. Satisfied, he went into the guards van to keep lookout from the rear of the freight train.

The freight train rattled through the station. It looked deserted, but it wasn't. The signs were there. The back end of a hidden vehicle could just be glimpsed. A helmet, a German helmet, seen for a split second as it ducked down behind a windowsill. Red Eric looked up at the guardsman. He saw concern in the man's eyes, his posture stiff and unsure. Red Eric barked some questions at him; the guardsman knew something. What that was didn't matter, the Germans were up and about watching them and keeping a low profile; not a good start to the day.

Red Eric returned to the compartment to tell the Major his fears. The Major agreed with his observations, asking what plan he had in mind. Red Eric said in his opinion, the Germans would let the train proceed unhindered until it reached the outskirts of Oslo and entered into the main railway marshalling yard. The marshalling yard opened up into a wide-open area with good visibility for the watching Germans. He had a plan. About two kilometres from the entrance to the marshalling yard, the railway ran along the top of an embankment, passing over a bridge spanning a roadway.

Just before the bridge, a pedestrian tunnel made the connection from one side of the railway embankment to the other. The long tunnel went under the four railway tracks going into the heart of Oslo. In the area before the tunnel, railway points connected a branch line to the main line they were travelling on. The points were old, and the safety plates rattled as trains passed through the intersection. With the main track in poor condition, the trains slowed over this section of the track. The Major got the impression that today the train would slow down just that little bit more.

The plan, as the wheels of the freight wagons started to rumble over the points, the three of them would jump from the train, and slide down the battered side of the embankment, which had a rough pathway that dropped down to the adjacent roadway. The other side of the railway embankment was steep and faced with stone, which without ropes was an impossible escape route.

Red Eric said when they reached the roadway, they needed to rush through the pedestrian tunnel and turn left at the far end, then right into a second exit, left at the next junction and disappear into an old graveyard. At the end of the graveyard stood a small chapel, where someone would be waiting to guide them to a secret tunnel that led to a nun's convent on the other side of a small valley. With luck, they should be able to vanish before the Germans knew what happened.

The Major tensed with fear. He took the Sten gun from his bag, prepared it, put the safety on, and shoved it back in his bag on top of his few possessions. Red Eric checked the guardsman pretending to be half asleep. Red Eric returned to his companions, closing and locking the interconnecting carriage door behind him. He looked out of the window on the city side of the train. The point of departure was coming close, and daylight almost upon them with a slight mist covering the ground.

The freight train slowed to a walking pace, as the sound of the wheels rattling through the track points started up ahead. Red Eric opened the carriage door and flung it back. The Major and the boy took position at the door. Red Eric would jump first, the Major should hand the boy to him, throw out their bags onto the track, and then follow quickly.

'Now,' shouted Red Eric as he jumped from the train. The Major quickly handed down his son and threw their bags onto the track. The Major jumped down without effort. The three of them collected their bags and ran to the far side of the track, found the rough pathway and began their descent to the roadway below. Red Eric lifted his son on his shoulders, picked up one of the heavy bags and quickly made his way to the ground without problems. The Major followed close behind, a bag in each hand. Just as he reached ground he slipped, twisted an ankle and fell heavily.

'Shit,' he cried out in pain as he tried to get to his feet. Red Eric rushed over and lifted his friend onto his feet.

'Can you walk, can you run,' he demanded. The Major tried, but extreme pain shot up his leg.

'I'll take you on my back,' barked Red Eric. 'Boy give me one bag and you bring the other two.'

Red Eric strode through the tunnel heavily overloaded with the Major on his back. They reached the far end and the Major said, 'You can't carry me to safety. I hear the Germans running down the track. What's that on the other side of the road, looks like a road grit storage dump behind that half-height wall.'

Red Eric looked across, asking, 'What are you thinking?'

'Drop me behind the wall and give me a Sten gun and plenty of ammunition. I'll stop the Germans coming through the tunnel whilst you get your boy to safety.'

Red Eric knew the truth of the matter, thanked the Major and did as he was bid. The Major took position behind the wall, took a silencer out of his overcoat pocket and screwed it on to the automatic Sten gun.

Red Eric spoke quickly to his friend the Major. 'Don't let them take you alive. The Germans will torture you for the information you don't have. You have been a great soldier and thank you for my son's life.'

With that, he vanished. The Major settled behind the wall in a dark corner, resigned to his fate. He puzzled about what information he didn't have, but the sound of advancing Germans snapped him back into focus. Red Eric had left behind a small satchel, containing the ammunition he hoped to make good use off, plus five hand grenades.

He heard the Germans running through the pedestrian tunnel. His position looked almost directly into the tunnel. He lifted up the Sten gun and fired a long burst. Shouts and screams could be heard, and then retreating footsteps. It went quiet.

'The Germans will come to the top of the railway embankment,' thought the Major.

He slid further down behind the wall. The sun rose over the horizon, and the sunlight would be behind the Germans on the embankment. The Major put the ammunition clips into his overcoat pockets. He checked his gun and loaded a fresh clip. He waited some more, and thought he heard sounds in the tunnel. The Germans would be unable to hear his silenced gun, and the Major prayed this would give him a big advantage.

German soldiers appeared on the embankment, crouching low. He took careful aim and fired short bursts at each target. He hit two of them as the others dropped to the ground. The sound of a steel plate being dragged along the ground came from the tunnel. He fired another long burst into the tunnel, aiming low. Some shots hit the steel plate, others the feet of the German soldiers.

It went quiet again. The Major looked at his watch. Six minutes had passed. Red Eric should be clear by now. The Major moved his position to the other end of the compound, his ankle sending fires of pain up his leg. He made a strip of cloth from a piece of spare clothing and wrapped it around his ankle. It eased the pain a little bit, but his ankle was clearly in a bad condition.

German hand grenades started to drop down from the top of the embankment. The Major hid behind the wall, as they exploded harmlessly on the road. The Major expected the next volley to be thrown a greater distance. The Germans had not yet spotted his hiding place, but it wouldn't be long before they did. Three more hand grenades sailed down from the embankment. One landed beside him. He picked it up by its long handle and threw the grenade into the mouth of the tunnel. The explosion claimed more German lives.

The sun rose quickly, and the Major's position would rapidly become very visible. The wall he was hiding behind would not stop a directly aimed rifle shot. The end was near. The Major heard running footsteps coming along the road on this side of the embankment. The Germans dropped men down onto the roadway on either side of his position. They would rush from left and right at the same time.

The Major shrank back against the building on his left side. He could still see the tunnel entrance and the Germans attacking from his right. He took a grenade, pulled the pin and threw it into the mouth of the tunnel. Nothing, the Germans must have given up on that approach, which meant they'd a good idea of his position. The Major glimpsed German soldiers coming down the road from his right. They were ducking behind any available cover.

The Major lifted his Sten gun, took aim at the next fleeting target, and fired a brief burst. One soldier rose and fell heavily to the ground. Another

German soldier threw a hand grenade, which burst in the middle of the road. The Major ducked down behind his wall as it exploded, knowing full well the German soldiers would rush forward.

Three German soldiers broke cover running directly to the Major's position. He leant against his protective wall and opened fire. Two soldiers dropped to the ground, the third sprayed his position with a sub-machine gun. A bullet slammed into the Major's right shoulder, spinning him to the ground. He gasped with the pain and felt the blood flowing down his right arm. His Sten gun fell to the ground. The game was over. He dropped behind the wall, and grabbed a hand grenade with his good hand, and used his teeth he pulled the pin before placing is left hand inside his jacket holding the grenade.

A German officer leant over the wall and ordered the Major to keep very still. The Major laid his back against the building. His energy was draining fast. The German officer came up to him.

'Keep still Major', said the officer. 'I'll get a first-aid man to tend to your wounds.'

The German officer kicked the Major's Sten gun aside. The Major just sat there, waiting for the final moment. Another German officer arrived, a captain of the Gestapo. He started to ask questions, but the Major didn't hear them. He felt faint and light headed. He would have fallen over except the Gestapo officer took a hold of his good shoulder.

The Major came to, and muttered, 'Don't know' to a question about the gold. The Gestapo captain grabbed his injured shoulder and the Major screamed in pain.

'Where is the gold?' repeated the Gestapo captain.

'At the bottom of the Fjord,' gasped the Major, 'near the entrance to the sea, where it's very deep.'

The Gestapo captain shoved his face into the Major's, and shouted, 'And where is the artefact?'

The question was a mystery to the Major. It must be the big secret he never found out about. His strength had almost gone. He looked up at the Gestapo captain standing there and said, 'Come closer, I'll tell you.'

The Gestapo Captain knelt beside the Major. The Major smiled, as his jacket fell open and said, 'goodbye' as his left hand released its hold on the grenade.

*****

Chapter 23

The schooner powered across the North Sea, over rough seas to an uncertain rendezvous. It was another cold day; the North Sea was always cold, its temperature changed little during the year. Daylight arrived, reluctantly at first then, as a new weather front arrived, the darkness regained much of what it had lost.

The crew of *Samba Canção* reverted to three-hour watches and Calum and Mike slipped back into their normal routine of four-hour watches. Calum came on watch at six am, to find Mike hard at work re-wiring the schooner's many utility systems. Calum used some sharp words to get his good friend to get some rest; the coming day's programme would not be one of relaxing events.

He looked around the cockpit. The Port Watch were half way through the morning watch with the schooner sailing hard at her maximum speed. With copious amounts of power from the new rig, this required careful sail trimming and balancing. Calum remained pleased and thoroughly impressed with the way this young crew continued to work hard and mature in such a short time.

The strong wind settled down to a steady blow over the port quarter. At long last the seas started to align with the wind, enabling the schooner to surf down the face of the steadily increasing waves, and cover the ground fast. The visitors were fast asleep in any spare corner they could find, except for Mo. This member of the 'three blind mice plus one' was already up and about.

Mo lived at the stern of the cockpit with his radio station, which he rarely left. At last, some news came through as Mo shouted below for Buffty to show himself. Buffty came on deck in a flash to join his fellow hooligan. Calum joined with them to try and understand just what was going on? It seemed that the Albanian trawler had got back up to full speed after limping along on one engine. It transpired its crew repaired much of the damage inflicted by the crew of *Samba Canção*. Quite how this information had been gathered was not forthcoming, and Calum thought best not to ask too many questions.

The Albanian trawler was indeed heading for the previously rumoured destination of the Norwegian port of Mandal. A strange coincidence as, among other things, Mandal was the designated finish for the Youth Race they had long since forgotten about. Also, a local sea festival would be taking place there at the same time. It all sounded rather jolly except for the current matter in hand.

What worried Calum is why he had onboard some of the UK's finest purveyors of military violence when he could be sure the Norwegians wouldn't be shy of a few of their own. Buffty wouldn't come clean when asked a straight question. It also occurred to Calum this specialist member of the UK military didn't exactly have a firmed-up plan either for when they met up with the enemy. Landfall had been forecast to be mid-afternoon.

Calum asked what would happen if they caught up? Could the enemy still monitor the whereabouts of the schooner with whatever method of technical wizardry they'd used up to now?

Mo assured him the schooner was clean. During the night, an RAF Nimrod had over flown the schooner to conduct a careful in-depth spectrum scan of their electronic systems. Mo had collected all cell phones, and every other electronic equipment onboard had been shut down and isolated from the schooner's power supplies.

Mo told Calum the Albanian trawler had been as close as twenty miles in front, but now with full speed restored he expected it to arrive at Mandal by lunchtime. Clearly Commander 'H' had people on the ground at Mandal. The Albanian trawler would be directed to a corner of the main harbour, in an area reserved for ships waiting for immigration and customs clearance. Calum wondered what an Albanian passport looked like, and would they be dressed as nuns as briefly seen during the near collision with their counterpart at the 'Straights of Dover'.

Calum asked Buffty what plan he had hatched to rescue Marie. Calum hoped she had come to terms with her capture and thinking positively. Buffty stared down at the grating in the cockpit floor for a few moments and then looked Calum in the eye and said, 'Don't know, which means we have a problem.'

Calum riled and demanded more detail, what problem? Buffty commenced a long complicated story about a very secret organisation he'd been charged with exposing and stopping, by whatever means. The Albanian trawler had been stuffed full of electronic monitoring equipment which could only have come from the specialised defence industries in Silicon Valley who had been engaged on a long term and highly secret programme to provide the US Forces with new technology, years in front of everybody else, especially a resurgent Russia.

This development programme moved into the production phase, and the equipment onboard the Albanian trawler, the pre-production version, had been locked away in an out-of-town long-term storage facility. This classified, pre-production version was bulky but fully functional. It had been spirited away by whom nobody knew, and quite how it left the USA remained a total mystery. Parts of the system had been cloned and fitted to the Albanian trawler sunk in the collision off the Dover coast.

Clearly, whoever was behind the secret group had spent big bucks, though believed to be the Russians. The Russians denied all knowledge, which only proved a secret organisation existed. The possibility existed that the Russians had lost control of it, or there could be the likelihood that the Russians were not involved at all. The western intelligence communities were divided on the subject. If the Russians were not involved then they were definitely in trouble.

Where to start? Who knew what? There were no names. Where had they come from? Rumour had it this secret group had East German connections; connections who'd been 'sleepers' for a very long time. Their aims were unknown, but a few strange events, as yet to be solved, had been pencilled in as down to them.

The kidnapping of Marie was a complete mystery until it became known that her father, a famous professor of history, had mysteriously disappeared. Her father had been conducting field research, but his university had no idea of the subject. All they knew was that the Professor had a hobby researching ancient Viking history, which somehow seemed to be linked to a WWII massacre of an obscure Norwegian community near Holmestrand believed to be reviving Viking traditions.

The only other titbit of information came from the Norwegian authorities concerning a story about a cargo of Danish bullion and precious gems that had gone missing just after the invasion of Norway during WWII. The timescale matched the massacre at Holmestrand.

Sarra popped her head out of the aft master cabin skylight window. Buffty was not pleased she'd been listening in to his conversation.

'Want to know something Buffty?' Sarra asked.

'Anybody else down there with you?' asked Buffty sternly.

'No, quite alone,' said Sarra.

Sarra went on to tell them Marie's father had told his daughter a story about a company of Danish Rangers, of approximately forty men, a senior member of the Danish government and a cargo of bullion that had made a desperate dash from Århus to Norway just before the invasion of Norway in an old, but fast, train ferry. During the voyage, it wound-up up in the middle of the German invasion fleet on its way to Oslo but had managed to make its escape and headed for Larvik.

The Danish ferry discharged the troops and their cargo at Larvik, who rushed north only to meet with a force of raiders from the Viking community they were talking about. Further north, they'd run into and disposed of a reconnaissance force of German paratroopers south of Holmestrand but then ran into a bigger German force blocking the main junction on the south side of the town.

There had been a big battle, but the Danish force and their cargo escaped westwards into the mountains whilst the remainder of the Viking community plus many of the local population had set to and disposed of three companies of paratroopers and a column of regular German army troops in a particularly brutal manner. Revenge no doubt for the bloody massacre of the Viking community.

The Vikings caught up with the Danes as they rested at an old winter snow lodge at the top of a mountain pass. As far as could be discovered, the Danish officer in charge, the Viking leader and small gang of the Vikings escaped to the west with the bullion, whilst the remainder of the Danish and Viking forces made a fighting retreat north over some very rough mountain roads, mauling the advancing German force very badly. This force escaped and dispersed into the many towns and villages on the back road to Oslo, where they became one of the backbones of the Norwegian occupation resistance, which caused the German army so many problems before their eventual retreat to back to Germany.

The small group that escaped to the west crossed to the other side of the country, past and around the famous Hardangervidda plateau, and down into a system of deep fjords which eventually linked to the North Sea. Somewhere in this system of fjords, this small party of Vikings and the Danish officer had split up in two fishing boats.

One of the fishing boats had totally disappeared, along with the cargo of bullion. The other made its way to the sea, capturing a German patrol boat in the process. From there they conducted a suicide attack on a German naval base close to the exit to the sea, and after a brief bloody battle, they'd sunk a number of patrol boats before ramming a large German fleet destroyer, famously blowing it to kingdom come with about one and a half tons of high explosive packed in the bows.

According to Marie, her father, the Professor, had researched the ancient Viking holy sites, possibly the only place the bullion could have disappeared to. These holy sites were very secret, with almost magical, believed natural, qualities. What'd happened to the Danish officer and the Viking chief, no one knew.

One strange item concerned the Danish Minister, who had accompanied the original Danish expedition, and had wandered back from Sweden into Denmark after the war without any explanation whatsoever. Quite how he'd escaped from Norway had not been revealed.

So what was going on? To Sarra, it had become obvious. Buffty looked at Calum in amazement. This slip of a girl had the answer, and the best brains in the intelligence community had no idea what so ever.

'Go on,' said Buffty 'Let's hear your pet theory.'

Sarra smiled; since when was a mere girl supposed to have the brains to work something out.

'Well,' she said, 'not sure who the enemy is, but they just have to be ex-Nazis from way back when, and playing a very long waiting game. The Nazis must have had knowledge of the Danish shipment, and slept on this knowledge for a long time. Now the time is right for this bunch of lunatics to return into the confusion of world affairs and they're short of funds. The Danish bullion would come in handy, and the only man on the planet able to point the way is Marie's father, who knows a lot about ancient Vikings history, and a little about their secret holy sites.'

'You tell any of this to your father?' asked Calum.

'No, of course not. Marie only told me after the attempted ramming incident in the English Channel. She was really worried. She'd picked up a lot of little bits of information that suddenly clicked and left her a very worried person. She confided in me just to get it off her chest.'

'So why kidnap Marie?' asked Buffty, already knowing the answer.

Sarra gave him a withering look, 'There's a mystery man on the Albanian trawler. The one dressed in black with the funny hat, helmet, and headgear? He has Marie, therefore, he has her father. To make him talk. These Norwegians are a tough dour race when they want to be. My guess he won't talk, unless…'

Sarra left the rest of the sentence unfinished. She sat down on the cockpit bench seat looking glum and worried. Calum looked at Buffty and could also see his worried face.

'So,' said Sarra. 'What are you bloody war heroes going to do to get my friend back to safety?'

'Sorry,' muttered Buffty, 'not quite thought of a scheme.'

'Not thought of a scheme? Huh. You've no bloody idea, eh!' shouted Sarra, her voice rising in anger. 'All the best resources at your disposal, you've no bloody idea and that's not effin' acceptable.'

Sarra stood up and stomped below in a mounting rage.

Buffty looked up, 'Do you know Calum, she's right. Unacceptable! Do you have any ideas?'

Calum stood up shocked. He'd Britain's finest onboard, and they were asking him, Pah! Calum asked him to explain. Buffty told him the stolen electronic systems were so good, he had no idea how to approach the Albanian trawler undetected. Detection meant certain death for any captives. The forces they were dealing with were so evil as to defy belief.

'How about another parachute drop?' asked Calum?

'The parachute drop relies on some form of reference beacon, all detectable, not only from their frequencies but from their signatures,' sighed Buffty.

Calum had some distant idea of the concept he was talking about.

'How about an unaided drop?' asked Calum?

'Can't get the accuracy from the height we need,' said Buffty. 'We need something new. Anything known is already programmed into the electronics, absolutely bloody everything. It's a real shit and it's doing my head in.'

Calum looked out to sea. Something totally new? Now he understood the problem, and now he knew why Buffty remained at a total loss. He continued staring into space towards the west. Inspiration, he needed inspiration, not perspiration.

Mike came on deck for a look around.

'Eh Calum, seen this?' he asked.

'What?' said Calum, his train of thought distracted.

'Coming up very fast,' said Mike, 'Four yachts in close formation passing about a thousand yards to port.'

Calum groaned inwardly. It had taken weeks to get Mike's brain into nautical distances as a matter of course, and here was 'ye olde inches, feet and yards' maintaining his proud US traditions.

Calum looked out and focused on the four yachts. The light went on, Calum's brain rushed from obscure thought to the inspiration he desperately wanted.

'It's the 'Formula 59' Team,' he muttered out loud.

Buffty could see them now. How in God's name could these boys help?

'Mike,' Calum called out, 'get on VHF, Channel 16, and call 'Chalky Whyte' from 'New Masts and Sponsorship.'

Mike leapt to the task. Calum had an idea. It would be off the wall, but he didn't care. Two minutes later, no response. The Formula 59 team had reached the closest point of approach, and the CPA now started to open up. The four yachts were buried behind their huge bow waves, they would see little, but then they would only be on the lookout for vessels in front.

Calum turned on Buffty. 'You got a friend in the sky, looking down over us all?'

'Sure,' replied Buffty. 'What do you want?'

'Get them to check the electronic emissions from the four yachts. If they can raise them, can they patch them down here? Do it now or we'll lose them,' shouted Calum as he made his way down to the navigation station.

Mo quickly fiddled with his mini comms station at the stern of the schooner. He quickly reported the four yachts were running a high-speed LAN network, passing a lot of data between them, assumed to be sailing performance data. One yacht had VHF on standby, but there was no response.

Calum had a brilliant idea. 'Can your bird in the sky jam their LAN system? It would force them to talk to each other on the VHF to check out the problem.'

Mo passed rapid instructions to the circling Elint aircraft overhead, and soon the VHF burst into life, a lot of chatter from angry sailors totally engrossed in their task.

Calum started calling. 'Chalky Whyte, Chalky Whyte this is 'New Masts and Sponsorship' calling.' A familiar voice came on the air. Calum cut him dead, told him to listen and not talk.

'Go ahead,' said the familiar voice.

Calum replied, 'Stop, come south, and look for the 'new' masts, I need you real bad, over.'

'OK, over and out,' said the familiar voice.

To Calum's great relief the four 'Formula 59s slowed and changed course to the south.

'Soon be here,' thought Calum.

The four Formula 59 yachts arrived quickly, sporting their new hull colours, red, white, blue and purple. The purple yacht came hammering up from astern and parked off the schooner's windward quarter. Chalky Whyte appeared on the bow and looked over at *Samba Canção*. The sight of four Special Forces soldiers surprised him.

'What's with the pongos,' he shouted over.

'Big trouble,' shouted back Calum 'They're the cavalry, in fact, they're the best of the best, and in need of some serious assistance.'

'You need me to come over?' shouted Chalky Whyte.

'Save a lot of time if you did,' shouted back Calum.

Within sixty seconds, Chalky Whyte had made it over to the schooner. The two friends shook hands.

'What's up Doc,' he asked.

'It's a long story, but here's the quick version. We were laid up at the back of the Island of Terschelling hiding from the weather when this strange trawler turned up. At first light, we were all woken up by masked Albanian bandits, who forced everyone into the main aft cabin. They locked the door and boarded it up, and kidnapped Marie, our Norwegian princess. The Albanians opened the seacocks and left us all to our fate.'

Chalky Whyte's jaw dropped open.

'Anyway,' continued Calum 'We blasted the door off its hinges, shot the Albanians onboard, escaped, saved the schooner from sinking, just and no more, and persuaded the Albanian trawler to go away.'

'How did you do that?' asked Chalky Whyte.

Mo spoke up, 'They blasted the shit out of it with three AK-47 automatics, using tracer and armour piercing rounds at blank range. Nice job they did too.'

Chalky Whyte asked who the Special Forces guys were.

'Like I said,' said Calum, 'they're the calvary.'

'SAS, SBS? Asked Chalky Whyte.

'More special than that. Anyway, the problem is the Albanian trawler is headed to Mandal and will arrive in about an hour's time. They have our Marie, and here were guessing, we believe, her father. The baddies are looking for the secret location of a large haul of WWII bullion, the property of the Danish Government. We need a cunning plan to drop our guests on to the Albanian trawler, and your party trick of hanging a crew member from the end of a spinnaker pole when gybing is the one manoeuvre the Albanian trawler won't expect.'

Buffty looked confused. Calum explained when the Formula 59s were up to full speed the team had a party trick of hanging a crew member, in a harness, from the end of a spinnaker pole using a spare mast halyard. The manoeuvre, apart from when the spinnaker had to be tripped and gybed, was pure showmanship of doubtful value, but it was fun. Buffty winced at the word 'fun'.

Calum explained his idea that the Formula 59 team should continue to Mandal. The organisers of the Sea Festival could set up a course for a 'Fly-By' demonstration for the onshore spectators, and the sailing festival.

The course would pass close to the Albanian Trawler, and the racing team would brush past the Albanian Trawler, during a pretend race manoeuvre, the four hooligans would release themselves and drop lightly onto the Albanian trawler, kill all the Albanians, capture a mystery man in black, and rescue Marie and her father.

'Sounds simple,' said Chalky Whyte.

Calum looked at Buffty, 'You got a better plan or any plan at all?'

Buffty asked Calum to describe the intended sequence of events, slowly, in a language he could understand.

Mo spoke up, 'Monsieur Buffty, it is very simple. We drop from the sky 'idden' by the large bow wave of four very fast yachts.'

'And 'ow fast are travelling the fast yachts, Monsieur Mo, about thirty kilometres an hour. This is a little bit too fast, non?' replied Buffty.

Mo shrugged his shoulders and ignored the comment.

Chalky Whyte could see the problem, but he had a solution. The Formula 59s could disconnect their twin steering wheels, then by using two helmsmen, the steering wheels could be turned inwards, or outwards, giving a braking effect. They'd never tried it, of course.

Calum doubted the last remark. An unseen method of slowing a yacht down, especially on the start line, might be considered a useful tool.

Buffty got his men and their equipment together, with much to do, and prepare.

Chalky Whyte waved his yacht back to the schooner. Mike heaved a thick line over and the transfer of their equipment, the four 'hooligans and Chalky Whyte soon completed the transfer, and like that, they were on their way.

Carol appeared at Calum's side.

'And,' she asked, 'what happens next?'

'I guess we follow as quickly as possible,' replied Calum nervously. 'We will just have to wait to see what happens next.'

Mike organised the deck watch and got the schooner back on track. Calum went below to the navigation station, noted their position, marked it on the chart, and shouted the course up to Tom.

Calum asked for Sarra to come down to him.

'Sarra,' started Calum, 'let's keep most of this to ourselves. Do we have any method to monitor events when the Formula 59 team get in place?'

'Mo took most of his box of tricks with him,' replied Sarra. 'He did, however, leave behind a text monitor. As I understand it, he can send coded text messages to us here, and the machine decodes and displays the text in plain language. Hopefully, he sends better English than he speaks.'

Calum doubted that. Maybe his poor English was an act. His other languages sounded spot on, but how to know.

Calum had other things to worry about. God only knew what would happen next?

Chapter 24

Calum had little to worry about. Commander 'H' had pulled out all the stops, with his hooligans onboard the Formula 59 yachts, and two squadrons of Norwegian Special Forces in Mandal, he had all the skills needed to conduct every aspect of military endeavour.

The Mandal Sea Festival organisers played ball without hesitation. Rescuing a beautiful member of their Royal Family brooked no questions, and so everything was set for the Formula 59 team to make their dramatic entrance into the scenic beauty of the Harbour of Mandal.

The 'fly by' course started along the shoreline, where the public could see the Formula 59 team up close. The next leg took the speeding yachts on a dead run past the Albanian trawler, and finally, the last leg came hard across the wind so the Formula 59 team could reach their maximum speed and delight the onlookers with an unusual spectacle. They didn't know how unusual it would be.

The large fleet of spectator craft had been marshalled into the centre of the course. In truth, it was difficult to keep the spectators at a good distance from danger. Commander 'H' specified a four-lap demonstration, and the Sea Festival organisers broadcast the news to all and sundry.

The Formula 59 team arrived in a big hurry. In the brisk Force 4 northerly wind, the four yachts were up to full speed. Chalky Whyte had his team in very close formation, the yacht's impressive bow waves very pronounced to the average sailors eyes. The Formula 59 team were running their computer data link passing massive amounts of sailing data between each yacht. This allowed a small modification that Mo, the diminutive hooligan, had quickly put together. Buried deep inside the high-speed data link Mo had installed an internet voice link to enable the four 'hooligans' to converse in their favourite language, an obscure Arab dialect originating many centuries ago from the badlands of the Kingdom of Jordon.

The Formula 59 team screamed down the course past the cheering onshore spectators. They reached the turn mark together and headed downwind to brush past the enemy trawler. The Albanian crew pretended to enjoy the spectacle, trying to act as normal as possible.

On the next downwind pass, Commander 'H', watching from a Norwegian hospitality cruiser, could see the Albanian crew were bored and had retired below. He ordered his cruiser, to fly Flag 'S' at the dip. One more lap.

On the third pass, the deck of the Albanian trawler seemed practically empty. Sarra's father could see only one crew member in the wheelhouse dosing at his lookout post. Time to strike. He ordered Flag 'S' snapped to the top of the signal mast. The Formula 59 team swapped their crew members for the four hooligans who were about to put Calum's bright idea to the test, no practice runs, just do it. This is what they were trained for.

The four yachts engaged in furious place swapping manoeuvres the minute they left the top mark. With hectic gybes taking place along this leg of the course, the illusion of not 'seeing' the Albanian trawler was created.

The four yachts divided into two groups, careering past both sides of the trawler. At the last moment, their spinnakers were snapped behind the lee of their mainsails, the decoupled twin rudders brought the desired reduction in speed just as the spinnaker poles, each with a fully armed hooligan attached, brushed over the decks of the Albanian trawler. The arrival of the four hooligans on the enemy trawler heralded a brief but bloody battle.

Surprise was total, and a lot of Albanian blood was spilt in the pristine waters of Mandal Harbour. Buffty was the first to find the prisoners, a very scared Marie and her stoic father holding her tight to him. Meany kept right behind his leader.

'Where is the 'man in black', they shouted out. Marie's father pointed to a steel hatch in the bulkhead behind him. It had just slammed shut. Meany went to wrench the hatch open, but Buffty's large hand clamped round Meany's, bringing him up short.

'The hatch is spiked,' Buffty yelled. 'Look at those thin wires. You can hardly see them.'

Meany bundled Marie and her father up to the wheelhouse and into the fresh air, just as a Norwegian Special Forces RIB slammed alongside and bundled father and daughter into the waiting craft.

'The trawler's wired,' yelled Meanie. 'Get the fuck off this barge, it's going to blow.'

Mo and Miney appeared from nowhere and leapt over the side into the RIB, which blasted its way across to the support ship and Commander 'H' and his team.

Commander 'H' leant over the side and shouted at the RIB, 'Where the hell is your section leader.'

Mo shouted to the Norwegians to empty the RIB in double quick time.

His voice brooked no argument. Within seconds, the RIB blasted its way back to the Albanian Trawler. As the RIB got within twenty-five metres of the enemy trawler came a loud explosion. Mo instinctively ducked and killed the powerful outboard engine of the RIB. Mo looked over the water at the quickly sinking Albanian trawler. He edged in closer, looking through the hanging cloud of smoke for any signs of his leader.

A large hand appeared over the side of the RIB. 'Give me a bloody hand with this body', shouted Buffty, as he half pushed an unconscious prisoner over the side of the RIB.

Mo grabbed the prisoner by the hair, and the body quickly collapsed onto the floor of the RIB.

'This the man in black?' shouted Mo.

'Fuck it no,' cursed Buffty. 'He's gone down with his ship.'

They looked at the stricken trawler in her death throes as it rolled over before slipping underwater.

'You sure?' shouted back Mo. 'That trawler has an opening in the bottom of her hull, between the main cargo hold and the crews quarters. The trawler's fitted with a bloody moon pool. Your man's dead, maybe dead? I doubt it. This type of bastard, 'e don't die so easy.'

'He's dead,' shouted Buffty. 'He went the wrong way. He went aft, not forward.'

Mo could not be convinced. Edging the RIB slowly around the wreckage, he reached into a box of hand grenades. Grabbing one in each hand, using his teeth to pull the pins, he tossed them overboard to the far side of the floating wreckage. Ten seconds later two muffled bangs were heard. Dead fish started to float to the surface.

Mo remained wary and unconvinced. He circled once more and tossed more hand grenades overboard in the opposite direction. No result, only more dead fish. Mo cruised around the last remains of the Albanian trawler, slowly increasing the size of the circle. Mo killed the powerful outboard engine and let the silence regain the moment. The two comrades stared hard at the water all around them. No sign, nothing. The prisoner lying on the floor of the RIB started to move. Mo lifted him up, and with a vicious blow to the head, laid him out again.

Buffty smiled, pulled out a hand held communicator and spoke briefly in the strange Arab dialect to his Commander. In less than five minutes, a Norwegian Special Forces team arrived in a specially equipped RIB complete with hi-tech scuba gear at the site of the sunken Albanian trawler.

Four Norwegian scuba divers flopped backwards into the dark still waters of Mandal Harbour, with the helmsman holding station over the sunken Albanian trawler, muttering commands into a small boom mike attached to his helmet.

'Clever,' thought Buffty. 'They have underwater comms with the surface. He motioned Mo to drift their RIB over to the Norwegian craft. He looked across at the Norwegian pilot. All he received was a blank look, which said it all.

'Any video?' asked Buffty.

'Of course,' said the Norwegian RIB pilot. 'The cameras will be up in a few minutes.'

Ten minutes later the first of the four divers appeared. The Norwegian helmsman pulled him bodily backwards into the RIB. The diver took off his dive helmet and chucked it at the helmsman, who flipped a memory stick out of the dive helmet camera and popped it into a video reader. He stared at the screen intently.

He shouted over to Buffty, 'The 'moon pool' hatch had been found locked tight from the inside, but one of our divers is making an entry to what's left of the accommodation quarters. It's all horribly mangled down there. Doubt if we will find anything. There's a salvage boat on its way. We'll lift the trawler when it gets dark.'

Buffty motioned Mo to take him back so he could report to Commander 'H'. Commander 'H' listened carefully. Buffty had the opinion the mystery 'Man in Black' was dead and maybe in the remains of the trawler. Commander 'H' looked at Mo.

'Non mon ameis Commander 'H', le 'Man in Black' e' is gone, e' is alive, we will meet again, non?' said Mo, shrugging his shoulders.

Buffty looked away. Mo had been right before. All the signs were the man had been eliminated. Perhaps they were clever signs. Nothing seemed to be impossible.

Chapter 25

The schooner berthed in a quiet corner of the Port of Mandal, and a discreet force of Norwegian police politely, but firmly, kept away all intruders. No doubt a sound precaution, which did nothing but fuel the rumour mill spinning around the harbour. A press release had been issued, but it would not be long before the international press would arrive and make a complete nuisance of themselves.

The onshore spectators had seen, at a distance, the demise of the trawler. The sight of a bedraggled Norwegian princess, and her aging father, being hurried away under police escort did nothing to quell the rumours.

Within the hour, Commander 'H' arrived on the schooner for a briefing, wearing the disguise of a local Customs officer. Calum bid him welcome and took him below to the main cabin where Marie and her father were recovering from their ordeal. The three of them disappeared into the main aft cabin for a lengthy chat. Calum invited himself into the conversation by the simple means of bringing mugs of coffee for everyone.

Mike kept watch on deck as the four hooligans packed their equipment before disappearing in an unmarked van.

Commander 'H' and Calum returned to the main cabin of the schooner. Calum told everyone to pack a bag for two nights and get ready for a mini-bus to take them to a discrete hotel just outside the town.

Mike would go too as Calum prepared to stay onboard to oversee a gang of specialised workers conduct a rapid rebuild of the interior of the schooner.

Later that evening, Calum made his way to the hotel to find a big party in full swing. It became a fun evening with carefully selected local dignitaries making a big fuss over the young crew members. Calum badly needed a decent drink of draft beer. The hotel had done them proud and laid on a feast of local delicacies, hot and cold plates and plenty of carefully chosen wine.

The crew of *Samba Canção* were getting stuck in with gusto. Calum slid over to Mike to thank him for all his efforts. Mike felt very relaxed, assisted by the local beer.

'Mike,' Calum started mischievously, 'those parachute drop these guys did was very interesting. I know a good joke about parachute drops.'

'Go on then, I'm game,' said Mike hopefully.

'Well there was this champion parachutist, jumps from his aircraft, and is falling through the sky, pulls his primary ripcord and nothing happens. 'Bugger,' said the parachutist, and pulled the ripcord for his emergency parachute, again nothing happens.'

Mike started to smile, 'And?'

'OK,' continued Calum, 'The parachutist keeps calm, looks around, sees another guy falling to earth, and manoeuvres over to him. 'Good afternoon', the parachutist says to the other man as they plummet towards the ground. Can you help me? Do you know anything about parachutes?'

'No,' says the other faller. 'And I know even less about gas powered back boilers.'

Mike broke into a broad smile and then burst out laughing. He stopped after two minutes and said to Calum, 'Not bad, but if I'm laughing at your jokes it's time to turn in.'

Calum told him to behave himself and have another beer. He circulated among his young crew to tell them how proud he and Mike were of all they'd accomplished. He also whispered they should not talk 'shop' about anything to anybody. There were a lot of people more than interested in acquiring more details of the recent events.

Mike came up behind Calum and nudged him in his back, whispering the ginger haired Norwegian lady in the corner had been coming on kind of strong with the male members of the crew. Still the party proceeded apace but soon the fraught events of the last few days caught up with everybody, and with many thanks ringing in the ears of their host, the crew of *Samba Canção* struggled wearily upstairs to their waiting beds.

Calum and Mike made to join them but were interrupted by a bearded plain clothes policeman who asked them to join him for a nightcap. Calum looked at the man and broke into a huge smile; it was none other than Commander 'H'.

'Well done you two, I don't know how you managed it, but that was a mighty voyage you survived, in more ways than one,' he praised. 'It made a big difference to my Sarra. I guess the others have also grown up very quickly. Tell me, who did all the shooting when you persuaded the Albanian trawler to go away?'

Calum looked the Commander straight in the eye and told him it was just him and Mike.

The Commander smiled, 'You two can fire two assault rifles at the same time? Maybe not. The Irish laddy was one for sure, we know a lot about him. Nothing bad mind. The Londoner, Tom, used to be in the junior TAs, so he's another. Hum, four of you, putting up a very concentrated fire power, most impressive. The guns still onboard?'

Calum looked at the Commander. 'Yes, the armament of the US Naval Auxiliary, *Samba Canção,* has been stored in the regulation storage space.'

'Yes, yes, I know all about this US Navy connection. Not many people around here believe, but the US Ambassador to Norway has been well briefed by your chum in Grosvenor Square,' said the Commander smiling. 'By the way, Mike, his daughter has made it known you'd better get your sorry self home within the next few days, or else.'

Mike blushed, he hadn't exactly forgotten about the love of his life, but Jenny's pregnancy did not have long to go.

'Do I have couple of days?' asked Mike.

'I thought you would have had enough trouble, without pushing your luck,' replied the Commander

Mike took the hint and muttered something about checking the work of restoring the schooner; he just had time. Calum looked up at the ceiling. 'Just what was the most important thing in his life?' he thought.

The Commander rounded on Calum. 'I think I have the whole story, do you have anything else to tell me?'

'I had hoped you could fill in the blanks,' said Calum. 'First question. Are there any more of these bandits tracking us down? Who exactly are they, and what the heck do they want?'

Commander 'H' became more serious. He told them there were a few suspects under careful surveillance, but none in this part of Norway. As to the matter of the Danish bullion, very few people knew about it, either in Norwegian or Danish government circles. Those that did know were using Commander 'H' as some sort of go-between.

Marie's father, the Professor, evaded all questions on the subject, but Commander 'H' learnt more by looking at the man than anything else. Commander 'H' professed he didn't quite know what to do, but his superiors were bound to ask questions and demand answers.

Calum shrugged his shoulders. He'd nothing to offer unless anyone asked for assistance, and even then his priority had to be planning the return of his schooner to the Solent with his young crew.

The repairs to the schooner would be complete by first thing the day after next, and until then he thought it important to get his young crew back to normal and get the events of the last few days behind them.

It was time to turn in. All in all, the last few days had provided more than a sufficiency of action.

Calum grabbed a bottle of whisky and retired to his bedroom. After a hot bath and a stiff dram he was more than ready for a deep sleep and a long lie-in.

Chapter 26

The Search for the Gold

Two days later *Samba Canção* slipped quietly from the Port of Mandal on the morning tide at the unholy hour of six am. Calum couldn't believe it happened, but he'd been badgered by one and all to take the schooner on the hunt for the secret and sacred Viking King's funeral site. His crew could not resist one last adventure. Commander 'H', through various intermediaries formally requested his assistance, and Marie's father also became very persuasive until he gave in.

The schooner had a full crew, just raring to go, with Marie's father, and a Mr Holger Rudmose, a chum of his from the Danish government. He didn't look to Calum like any academic he'd ever seen. He was a fit strong man of average height, who looked like he had a military background. His luggage looked heavy, containing bulky objects not normally associated with yachting.

Before setting sail, Calum asked Commander 'H' for insurance, after all, he had the responsibility and safety for his young crew and the other passengers. For his troubles, he'd received a curious document from the Norwegian government promising, among other things, assistance as requested, compensation and reward for information leading to the recovery of any articles of interest. Talk about vague.

Samba Canção cleared Mandal harbour, as she prepared for a fast reach along the Norwegian coast in a strong southerly wind. Calum took the helm determined to get some practice helming his own yacht. He quickly found his course to the west full of hazards from crab pots and other fishing impedimenta. He threw the schooner into a smooth fast tack to head out to sea. It wasn't until all the sheets were wound in and the sails properly set on the new course that Calum realised he hadn't actually called the tack, and received a lot of dirty looks from the pit crew.

Calum smiled a well done at them, took the schooner into clear water, and then tacked back on to the original course, followed by murmurs of discontent from his crew. The schooner powered along, with just about one hundred and sixty miles to go to reach shelter for the overnight stop where the Professor would start his search.

The sailing turned out to be exceptional, and as the coastline slowly turned to the north, the schooner found a freeing wind and started to reach her maximum hull speed. Calum enjoyed his turn at the helm immensely and it didn't matter how many dirty looks he got from his crew, Calum was there to stay.

As lunchtime came and went, Mike wandered up on deck. He'd got a tad too close to the bottle the night before, and Calum didn't see the point of waking his good friend from a sound sleep with so many eager beavers onboard.

'Good afternoon Mike,' Calum whispered at him. 'How's the head.'

'Not too bad,' said Mike, as he grabbed a mug of strong coffee that Carol brought from the galley. 'We're away?'

'Oh, we're over six hours down range, running hot and hard. Want a spell on the helm to clear your head?' offered Calum. 'The pit crew are rebelling. I'm hogging the helm on such a splendid day for a sail.'

'Thanks,' said Mike as he slipped behind the wheel.

Calum disappeared below to talk to the Professor. Did he have a cunning plan? The Professor said they should get to the entrance of the Fjord by early evening, and anchor overnight at an abandoned navy base built by the Germans during the war. *Samba Canção* made short work of the voyage, and reached the abandoned naval base just as the sun went down. It was indeed a good anchorage, well sheltered from the wind and the sea outside.

Dinner was served quickly from the perennial pot of stew: first-day stew, not quite at its best. A box of beer appeared on deck as the crew settled down for a convivial evening in the fresh air. No one bothered to keep a lookout in such a deserted place. The next thing anyone knew a well-known voice came from a small rubber dinghy as it moored alongside.

'Bonsoir, mon amis,' said the dark shape. 'C'est Mo à votre service.'

Calum groaned inwardly. Now, what was Mo doing here? His heavy French accent with Belgian overtones still polite and gentle.

Mo spoke, 'You 'ave still the coffee ready?' he asked in a voice, this time more of an enquiry.

'Yep,' said Patrick. 'It's still below, and it's still 'ot and instant. It's all we 'ave.'

Mo ignored the mocking of his accent and proceeded to haul two large containers onboard.

'Look,' said Tom. 'He's brought Radio Caroline along. Anything else?'

Mo replied he 'ad brought a few bits and pieces for the adventure. Calum turned on him and asked what the dickens he was doing here.

'You 'ave a document from the Norwegian Government offering assistance, I 'am this assistance, mon amis,' he replied.

For some reason Calum became suspicious. A 'someone's walked over my grave' feeling came over him, but it faded just as quickly. Calum asked if his boss, Commander 'H' had an involvement in this escapade.

At this, Sarra brought the communicator up to Calum. 'It's for you,' she told him. 'It's Daddy.'

Calum listened to Commander 'H' ask the simple question if Mo had arrived with two containers. Calum told him 'Yes', and waited for more information. Commander 'H' paused and told Calum he wasn't far away and to keep this communicator with him, or Sarra, at all times.

The communicator went dead, as Calum stared at it a little confused. Time to turn-in. Calum set the night watches, two persons awake at all times, using the night vision binoculars to keep watch and keep the schooner safe. The crew thought this great fun, a part of the adventure, but Calum still felt concerned and had a quiet word with Mike, who agreed to keep an eye on things throughout the night.

Calum filled in the logbook for the day, instructed the duty watch to 'call all hands' at 05.30 hours and have breakfast ready for 05.40 hours. The schooner would sail at first light at 06.00 hours.

Calum took a quick shower, donned a clean pair of light coveralls and turned in for the night. He didn't let anyone see him place a loaded automatic .45 down the side of his mattress. Calum still worried about something he just couldn't put his finger on.

The crew arose on time, took breakfast, and the schooner slipped quietly from her mooring. The southerly wind dropped and progress slowed entering the fjord. The Professor told Calum that the prevailing wind would be contrary when they reached the fjord, so perhaps progress would be best achieved under power.

Calum gave the helm to Tom and went below to download any overnight emails. As he finished he set the chart plotter at its largest scale and switched on the radar. He found a chart on the navigation table with a large circle around the approximate position the Professor had in mind. It would take an hour to get there so Calum did a tour on deck, saw that everybody was resting where they could, and then returned to his bunk.

An hour later Carol brought Calum a coffee, and he arose much refreshed. He caught Patrick in the galley making a snack for the deck crew who had little to do but stare at the passing scenery. Knowing that the aft master cabin was unoccupied, he asked Patrick and Sarra to remove the fastenings of the seat backrests to get quick access to the guns stored there, and not to make this obvious to anyone else.

The schooner reached the fjord narrows. Despite the lack of any wind gradient in the weather forecast, a strong breeze blew down the fjord. Combined with the lack of sunlight on an otherwise clear day, it started to get chilly. Calum donned his waterproof jacket and went on deck.

The Professor explained he'd only a rough idea of where to search for the secret location, but thought he would recognise the area when he saw it. He'd brought a side-scan sonar set to pick-up the entrance underwater as he was certain it would not be visible from above. Calum stood impressed with his level of preparation.

The Professor stared hard at the vertical rock face rising out of the water's edge. The sun still needed to rise sufficiently to cast any light on the area of the search. The Professor signalled the schooner to slow down and get closer to the west wall of the fjord. Calum sat quietly in the cockpit watching the depth sounder, which could not even pick-up the deep bottom of the fjord.

The Professor commanded the schooner to heave to and maintain position.

Calum called out, 'Professor, are we near to where you think you need to be?'

'Not sure,' came the reply. 'My information is that we need the sun to rise above the mountain over on the east side of the fjord.'

'How much information do you have?' enquired Calum.

'Not enough in my opinion,' was the only reply the Professor offered.

Within the half hour the sun started to shine directly onto the sheer cliff face. Strange lichen plants covered the rock face, the sunlight changing their colour to an unusual hue. From far above, strange creepers fell down hanging some way from the rock face. Some of the creepers trailed into the water, and a slight mist rose among the trailing creepers.

The Professor motioned Tom to bring the schooner closer to the rock face. The Professor's companion, Holger Rudmose, unpacked a bag containing the side-scan sonar, attached it to a triangular frame and hung it from the schooner's guardrail next to the cockpit. A small handle allowed the sensor to be rotated in either direction. The apparatus contained a temperature sensor to detect the stream of warm water flowing from the secret entrance.

As *Samba Canção* slowly brushed along the rock face the sonar instrument indicated solid rock with an annoying beep. The temperature sensor merely confirmed the fjord was not an ideal place to go for a swim.

The schooner's progress along the rock face remained slow, and Calum began to wonder if this search had become a wild goose chase. The sound of the sonar with its pathetic beeping sound was getting on Calum's nerves. The Professor and Rudmose were starting to look a trifle nervous. They expected much, and little appeared to happening.

At long last the signal from the sonar changed, but only momentary. The Professor raised his hands and signalled Tom to let the schooner fall back before the wind. The signal changed once more as the Professor shouted out to hold position. Rudmose swept the sonar array to find the entrance they were looking for.

Tom asked the Professor if he wanted the schooner closer to the rock face. The Professor agreed but cautioned about getting under the overhang of the towering cliff above. The temperature sensor started to indicate a much warmer stream of water. The Professor rushed to the bow of the schooner and started to wave the schooner towards the rock face. The schooner approached very slowly. Tom had a difficult time holding position with the schooner beam on to the strong breeze blowing down the fjord.

A t last, the Professor could just about make out an entrance behind the overhanging creepers. With Sarra and Patrick holding the overhanging creepers to each side the schooner slowly entered a narrow channel. Calum looked nervously up at the masts, but there appeared to be plenty of space above them.

The Professor stared hard into the deep water of the narrow passageway, giving Tom a bewildering array of hand signals, to steer the schooner from one side of the channel to the other. As the schooner slowly inched its way along the passageway, strange underwater rock pillars were seen, ready to rip the bottom out of any craft that hit them.

The Professor suddenly recognised them from his many studies of Viking mythology, Drager Tenner, The Dragon's Teeth. Legend had it that the Drager Tenner were highly feared and revered. Strange and highly dangerous currents swirled around them, capable of dragging any unsuspecting craft on to them. Only by keeping exactly in the centre of the tortuous passageway could there be any chance of safe passage. Even then strange tidal currents flowed, greatly increasing the hazard.

Rudmose continued sweeping his sonar, watching for the underwater hazards and making copious notes in his notebook. Nobody noticed Mo, looking over the shoulder of Rudmose making notes of his own of the strange waterway.

The schooner entered a strange volcanic lagoon. Large clouds of warm dense mist rose eerily from its still surface. The far end of the lagoon looked completely fogged in. The schooner came to a stop in the middle of the lagoon as the Professor looked around anxiously trying to find the entrance of a cave that almost certainly existed. He asked Calum for the outboard powered inflatable to be lowered into the water.

The Professor returned to the cockpit and stood beside Tom, directing him to slowly bring the schooner around in a tight circle whilst he looked hard at the sheer cliff face that surrounded them. On one side a large number of creepers hung down, with the fine mist slowly rising between their entwined stalks. He motioned for the schooner to approach very slowly. Behind the hanging creepers the Professor suddenly made out two rock pillars standing high out of the water some ten metres apart.

Ordering Tom to hold position, he got into the inflatable tender gently bobbing at the stern of the schooner. Rudmose followed, and the pair of them set off, paddling over to the hanging creepers. As they passed through the creepers, Rudmose took a large machete from his backpack and hacked a wider path. They disappeared, as they entered, the first people in many decades, the sacred Viking Cave.

After a while, Rudmose returned alone, beckoning the other members of the landing party to help explore the cave. Calum told him to hang-on for a few moments whilst he organised the landing party, choosing Tom and Patrick for what was going to be an interesting day.

'Tom, Patrick, go down and bring two AK-47s, my automatic .45 and a satchel of ammunition,' he ordered, 'and bring two walkie-talkies from Mo's container. Mo you best come with us. Your communications set-up to talk to anyone outside this lagoon?'

Mo confirmed his equipment could communicate with the outside world.

'Mike,' said Calum, 'bring the other AK-47 on deck, plus the other guns too. Take the schooner to the far end and make yourselves invisible to anybody at this end of the lagoon. You can keep in contact by radio, so no worries.'

Mike wasn't quite sure Calum's precautions were necessary, who else would find their way into the lagoon? Seeing Calum looked serious, he said nothing. Calum grabbed an old haversack, filled it with a large bottle of fruit juice, snacks and biscuits.

It took two trips to get everyone, and their equipment, into the cave. For sure it was a dark and mysterious place, and the only light was the strange translucent sheen coming from what little daylight filtered through the overhanging creepers. With everyone landed, Tom took the tender back to the entrance and spiritedly hacked away at the creepers, making the light inside the cave a little more useful.

The crew of the schooner looked at the strange sight before them. Resting on the edge of a large flat slab of rock, at a slight angle toward the water, they saw an old Norwegian fishing trawler. The outer edge of the flat rock almost touched the water, with the fishing boat quite high and dry. Quite how it got there wasn't immediately obvious.

The Professor pointed to a large ordered pile of rocks at the far end of the great slab of rock. Hard to believe, but then he suddenly remembered the words 'Babyens Vogga', the 'Baby's Cradle'.

The Professor had at last discovered the many answers he sought. On the death of a Viking King, his funeral became a great state occasion. The Viking King's longboat would be burnt with his body, along with his worldly goods needed in the afterlife. During the funeral, one of the dead King's favourite wife's could follow her husband to the next world although this was rare. The inclusion of his favourite 'Thrall Woman' and a slave was common.

The ritual demanded sacrifice. Captured enemies, elders who'd plotted against the King, unfaithful wives, disloyal servants and many others could look forward to a gruesome end.

The funeral pyre would be constructed to form a great pillar of smoke and burn very hot. The strong updraft in the Viking King's Cave thought to aid in propelling the dead Viking King quickly to Valhalla and the afterlife. All that would remain would be some incinerated fragments of metal and few human and animal bones.

Odin established a law that all dead kings should be burned, along with their belongings in a great pile. The ashes were then cast into the sea or buried in the earth. Thus, said he, everyone will come to Valhalla with the riches he had with him upon the pile; and would also enjoy whatever he himself had buried in the earth. For men of consequence a mound could be raised to their memory, and for all other warriors who had been distinguished for manhood a standing stone; a custom that remained long after Odin's time.

The Professor now knew this to be a very important site for the Vikings and their rituals. No wonder this cave had remained secret for so long, and now the great mystery had nearly been solved, one he'd been racking his brains on for years.

The Professor jumped off the 'great rock' and with a powerful flashlight went to look under the far end of the rock. There he found human remains deep inside the overhang, chained to the floor of the cave.

Next he returned to look underneath the fishing trawler suspended above the water, and examined the surface of the 'great rock'. All around this area, close to the water's edge, were many markings in the rock's surface, all very old, all caused by great fires, a great many fires. There had been many funerals over the centuries.

Calum felt a small tremor under his feet. The great rock shuddered slightly, indicating the area was volcanic. Further examination under the great rock found a balance point along a raised ridge in the floor of the cave at its mid-point. Wisps of warm mist came from under the rock; perhaps a small fissure lubricated the point of balance?

Calum pondered about the large pile of large heavy stones.

'That's it,' he thought. 'They form a counterweight. With the rocks positioned inside the line of balance, the 'great rock' would tilt until its outer edge became immersed in the water. With the Viking King's longboat floated over the edge of the 'great rock', more or less where the fishing boat was positioned now, the funeral victims were dragged underneath the 'great rock' in chains.

With the pile of stones moved to the far end, the Viking King's longboat would slowly rise out of the water. The inboard end of the 'great rock' would drop down, but not all the way, bringing a strong sense of impending dread to the waiting victims.

When all became ready, a great pagan ceremony would be held before setting fire to the Viking King's longboat. As the flames consumed the longboat, its weight would reduce, the 'great rock' would pivot around its point of balance, and the inboard end would drop crushing the victims underneath.

Calum looked over at the Professor. 'You see what I see, the 'Babyens Vogga', the baby's cradle. It rocks to and fro, like a cradle, but without bringing much comfort to those underneath.'

The Professor came to the same conclusion as Calum. He nodded his agreement; all the years of hard work piecing together small fragments of mythology suddenly became clear.

Tom examined the hull of the fishing boat, its timbers were not fully dried out as expected with the decades out of the water. The wooden hull looked in reasonable condition, given the age of the vessel.

'Skipper,' he called out. 'This hull is actually quite tight, with very little cracking along the planks. Maybe it's been occasionally immersed to keep the wood in good condition. Perhaps the mist has preserved the timbers.'

Calum went around the hull with his seaman's knife. Some of the timbers were a bit soft with rot, but nothing too bad. The keel seemed to be sound with virtually no rot whatsoever. The hull had indeed survived the many years remarkable well.

Before Calum could say anything, Tom whispered that someone was watching them. He couldn't say where from, but the hairs were up on the back of his neck. He strained his eyes in the dark gloom of the caves recesses. The observer could be anywhere, but for sure they were being watched. Calum told the Professor, who was totally engrossed with his work.

'Someone is watching us you say?' asked the Professor. 'Legend tells us there should be a Guardian; who I have no idea.'

By now Patrick had climbed aboard the fishing trawler to look around in the cabin and engine room. He couldn't understand what he'd found. Clearly the fishing trawler had not been totally abandoned for all these many years since WWII, but someone had gone to a lot of trouble to make it look that way. In the cabins, he found old bedding, original bedding, dry and in good condition, if slightly musty.

In the engine room, the old fashioned diesel engine had not suffered from the neglect expected from many years of idleness. Deterioration, flaking paint and rust there was, but Patrick had the distinct impression it wouldn't take much to get this engine working once more. The oil dipstick had a reasonable level, but in the gloomy light, it was too difficult to see its condition and colour. The starting handle swung with little effort, and the cylinder lifters, although stiff from age, moved without too much trouble. The sight glass on a nearby diesel tank showed a low but useful level of fuel.

The galley was bare, but the ancient utensils were stored in an orderly manner, with no signs of any food, old tins or containers. The working surfaces were dusty and untouched, but how to tell how long they'd not been used?

Patrick thought some more, and then it came to him. The trawler had the look of a seaside caravan in January, one only used in the summer months. Very strange. He went on deck and shouted over the Calum.

'You coming aboard Skipper?' he asked. Calum answered by throwing his haversack up to him before climbing the rope ladder hanging down the side of the fishing boat. The others soon followed and began looking around.

Mo looked intently at the rotting canvas cover over the strong wooden beams of the cargo hatch, the access to the fishing hold, and Mo was looking for treasure. His eyes lit up, and Calum suddenly had a strange feeling about what exactly was going on. He looked at his two boys and nodded at Mo. Tom and Patrick said nothing, but they too saw the change. Mo had a great interest in what might be found in the hold of the fishing boat.

Calum looked around the cave, trying to show he was not looking for something in particular, but in the gloominess of the cave little could be seen.

The group stood around the hatch. To break the impasse, Calum asked the Professor who should enter the hold.

'Just Holger and I will be sufficient,' he replied crisply, without any details. Calum motioned his two boys to open the cargo hatch. Mo stepped forward, and then stepped back again. Calum pointed at the expanse of the cave and wanted Mo to face outboard, to stand guard. That's why he was here.

The hatch cover and the timber frames were quickly removed, as everyone gathered round to peer inside, eager to see if indeed the treasure had been found. Mo abandoned his guard and joined the others. In the centre of the hold stood a pile of ammunition cases, formed roughly in the shape of a pyramid.

The Professor and Rudmose were ready to descend into the hold when a high pitched young voice behind ordered them to stop. The command shouted in Norwegian, the meaning unmistakable. Everyone turned to see a tall strong looking youth about fourteen years old dressed in ancient Viking dress. The youth wore a large pouch strapped across his chest, carrying a German machine gun pistol with a short wire butt. Calum looked at the weapon; an original WWII weapon that looked to be in perfect working order.

The youth cradled the weapon, it seemed a part of him. The youth possessed a very strong face, broad shoulders, athletic build, very tall for his years and a mass of red hair flowing from under his Viking headgear.

The youth spoke to the Professor, again in Norwegian, asking who everyone was, and why had they violated the sanctuary of the Viking King's Holy Place. The Professor looked around, not scared, but very concerned. He translated the youth's question to English for the benefit of everyone, before giving his reply.

Rudmose explained he was a professor from the University of Oslo who'd researched the history of the Vikings. His friend, the Dane, represented the Government of Denmark, the rightful owners of the gold, if gold existed at all in the hold below them. The Professor went on to explain that the short Frenchman was a member of the UK Special Forces, to provide protection from evil forces encountered recently. The other members of the party were the crew from the schooner that had brought them to this place.

The red-haired youth stepped back, looking intently at everyone before him. His eyes penetrated their very souls. Calum found it a distinctly unpleasant experience and didn't know what to make of the situation. The youth, holding the grip of his machine gun pistol, motioned everyone to drop their weapons on the deck, to stand back and move away from them. Everyone did so, with Mo showing a marked reluctance to do so.

The youth stared hard at Mo. Even Mo felt unsure of himself. A muffled rifle shot rang out and a heavy bullet ripped into the planking between Mo's feet. Mo let his weapon slip through his fingers as it dropped to the deck.

The youth spoke for the first time in perfect English. He told them he was Ericsson, the 'Son of the Guardian', hidden high above, with a perfect view of everyone on the deck of the trawler. He ordered only the Professor and the Dane could enter the hold, the others should stand at the other side of the hatch, away from their weapons, and watch.

The Professor and the Dane lowered themselves into the dark hold using a knotted rope. Ericsson grabbed hold of the hatch side combing and dropped lightly down on his feet. Calum could see this young man looked very athletic and extremely fit.

The youth took out a torch and pointed at the ammunition case at the apex of the stacked pile. Taking a wicked looking knife from his pouch, he cut the metal bands securing the metal lid of the ammunition case.

The Professor released the rusty lid catches, raised the lid, peered inside the ammunition case and found half sized gold ingots wrapped in a heavy waterproof paper bearing the seal of the Danish Treasury. He removed one and opened the package. The youth moved to his side with his back to the others watching from above. The Dane stood on his other side to observe closely.

The Professor removed the wrapping paper from the half sized ingot revealing a rounded shape at each end, rather like a bar of soap. The Professor looked at it; something was wrong although his face gave nothing away. The ingot did not have the correct weight, the gold surface was not solid, and it wasn't gold at all. Ericsson held out his hand for the false gold ingot. As the Professor handed it over, the youth made it vanish, only to instantly replace it with another ingot that gleamed weakly in the half-light. The youth muttered something in Norwegian that only the Professor and the Dane could hear.

'Bad men coming, a trap is set, your gold is safe.'

The statement didn't seem to faze the Dane, but the Professor struggled to keep concern from showing on his face. The youth looked at the Professor, smiled and gave a knowing wink.

Ericsson spoke out in clear English, 'Mr Dane, please check the markings of the gold ingot from the list you will have in your pocket. You must make certain this gold bullion is correct.'

Ericsson handed over the real gold ingot. The Dane removed a crumpled piece of paper from his inside jacket pocket, took the ingot and examined its markings, consisting of a smelt number and date, a serial number and the royal seal of the Danish State Bank, the 'Nationalbanken'. The Dane looked surprised, he could see the gold had a slightly different hue about it and looked at Ericsson.

'It's very rare gold, not quite Russian pink gold, but very pure,' said Ericsson. 'It's part of an imperial consignment from former ancient kingdoms that formed northern Scandinavia many centuries ago. The jewellers will pay handsomely for it. The cargo consists of 2,025 kilos, four hundred and five ingots divided among the cases you see here in the hold. Is this the right quantity on your list'?

The Dane agreed that this was indeed correct. Above, Mo became agitated and wanted to come down into the hold. The youth stared up at him, daring him to make a move. Mo hesitated and stayed his ground.

The youth took the gold ingot and threw it up to Calum to look at. Mo looked on. The youth nodded for Mo to hold it and examine it also. Mo took the gold ingot and stared at it with strange staring eyes. He stopped, composed himself and reached over to his haversack and took out a small item of test equipment, a metal hardness tester. Mo used the instrument over the bottom face of the gold ingot. He became satisfied with the consistency and value of the readings.

The youth ordered the return of the gold ingot, which Mo did with great reluctance. The youth took the paper wrapping, and showed it to everyone, explaining the gold came from a special melt, and each ingot had been wrapped separately to prevent fretting during transport. The wrapper alone had an intrinsic value of about a hundred US dollars from collectors around the world.

The youth returned the gold ingot to the ammunition case. The Dane saw the youth conjured the rewrapping of the original ingot, as the real gold ingot vanished into thin air. Ericsson looked up at the Dane and smiled again. The Professor closed the ammunition case and locked the catches, before making his way back to the main deck of the fishing boat. The Dane and Ericsson followed.

Everyone started to talk among themselves, what to do next? What to do with the gold cargo? The Dane walked around the hatch, tripped and fell on top of Mo, stopping him from falling to the deck. Mo cursed him in French for his clumsiness. The Dane apologised and went to the stern of the fishing boat.

Calum quietly reached down and picked up his handgun, motioning for his two boys to retrieve their weapons and sling them on their backs. Calum was at a loss as what to do next and shooed his two boys out of the way of the others.

The Professor engaged with a heated discussion with Mo, who insisted on his idea of what to do next. The Professor insisted they should wait until the 'Guardian' of the cave made his presence known. Mo became more agitated, and Calum wondered why, becoming ever more suspicious.

The Dane wandered back, and tripped over a fitting on the wooden deck, falling to his knees. The Professor went to help the Dane to his feet, indicating that Mo should at least help. The Dane struggled to his feet, brushed himself off, apologising again for being so clumsy.

From the other side of the cave came a loud crashing noise, as a rock fall filled the air with dust and debris. Screams were heard. Everyone dropped behind whatever cover they could find. That side of the cave was dark, and Calum looked cautiously to see what had happened.

From high above, a pistol flare was discharged, and in the harsh glare, Calum saw a group of strange fully armed and sinister figures in military clothing coming down what remained of a dangerous winding path cut into the rock leading to a small opening in the roof of the cave.

Three bodies lay prone on the cave floor unmoving. Above the rock fall, a number of figures were frozen in fear. A loud rifle report rang out, echoing around the cave. One of the frozen figures dropped to the cave floor. The others turned to race back up into the open air. The rifle fired twice and two more bodies crashed to the cave floor.

Calum swore under his breath and shouted out for his boys to keep their heads down. The sinister figures on the cave floor searched upwards for the lone rifleman. Shouted orders rang out. Calum groaned inwardly, 'Not them again.'

'Who are they Guv?' asked Tom who'd moved alongside his skipper.

'Fuckin Albanians,' said Calum. 'I'd thought we'd seen the last of them. You OK? Pop your head up and check if they've seen us up here.'

Tom did as he was bid, and as he slithered back below the bulwark of the trawler he told his skipper he didn't think so. Tom appeared calm although his eyes shone brightly with heightened alertness

The Albanians returned fire to the unseen target above them. Their aim erratic and bullets sprayed in every direction. Pieces of rock flew everywhere, and a small rock fall crashed down behind them. It was starting to get even more dangerous.

Ericsson moved next to Calum and indicated they should drop down the blind side of the trawler whilst they had the chance. The Professor went first, dropping down onto the 'great rock' and then legged it over to hide behind the pile of stones. Calum signalled Patrick to get weaving and follow the Professor. On the other side of the trawler, Mo crawled on his stomach to recover his automatic weapon and backpack. Patrick made it to safety, as Calum told Tom to get a bloody move on.

Rudmose, with a heavy looking .45 automatic in his hand shouted to Mo to get off the trawler. Quite where that weapon had appeared from Calum couldn't tell. It begged the question why he even had it.

Mo collected his equipment, wriggled along the deck behind the bulwarks, entered the wheelhouse, came out the other side, crawled back along the deck and vanished over the side.

Rudmose smiled at Calum and invited him to follow the others. Calum shoved his .45 automatic deep into his jacket pocket and quickly made it to safety. Calum expected Rudmose to be right behind him, but the Dane did not appear at once. Above them, the lone rifleman continued choosing his shots, but the fire returned by the Albanians got stronger. Calum crouched beside Ericsson.

Ericsson dropped down from the 'Babyens Vogga' to the floor of the cave. Flares rained down at regular intervals, always from a different position. Calum knew there had to be a gallery above to give freedom of movement. The noise of the gunfire echoed harshly around the cave.

The top of a rough wooden ladder appeared behind the crouching party. Ericsson beckoned them to quickly follow. Rudmose was the last to descend as Ericsson led them up a small path and into a cave some fifteen metres above the floor of the cave.

In the harsh glare of the flares raining down behind the assailants, Calum could see two distinctive figures dressed in black, wearing strange protective headgear. The short one looked familiar, was he the one from the sunken trawler in Mandal? A rifle bullet hit this man-in-black in the chest. He fell backwards and picked himself up, his body armour saving his life.

Another rifle bullet hit the taller man-in-black, throwing him backwards and onto his back. The rifle fired twice in succession, hitting the soles of his boots. The man screamed in pain.

The short man-in-black ripped off his helmet to shout orders to the Albanians. Calum gasped, Garth Vidor, the ex-CIA man he'd met in the Marina in Lymington. The Albanians rushed towards the fishing boat; firing wildly in every direction.

Despite their good position to return fire, Rudmose held his hand out for everyone to remain still and unseen. The Albanians made it to the trawler.

Vidor and six of his men climbed onto the deck of the fishing boat and disappeared below.

Other Albanians crawled on their stomachs to the pile of stones at the far end of the Babyens Vogga, and started to roll them down the slope towards the fishing boat. The great rock began to tilt, as the trawler slowly re-entered the water. The engine of the fishing boat started.

A giant of a man in Viking dress, with a mass of red hair falling down around his face, appeared from nowhere. This was the Guardian. He handed his smoking rifle to Calum and shouted at the two boys to quickly follow him. Tom and Patrick looked at Calum who could only shrug an acceptance. Ericsson chased after them. The Guardian picked up two heavy wooden props and shouted at Tom and Patrick to bring the longest one they could find. Ericsson grabbed a shorter wooden prop and followed his father.

As the last of the stones rolled the down the sloping 'Babyens Vogga', the trawler became afloat, just as the remainder of the Albanians jumped aboard. The inboard end of the great rock rose to its maximum height, paused, and with a screech of tortured rock hung there before slowly starting its downward path. The two Vikings raced underneath to arrest the fall with their wooden props. The Guardian shouted for the long prop to be placed close to the edge of the great rock. Tom and Patrick struggled with the heavy and unwieldy wooden prop but managed to get it positioned in time to prevent the three shorter props from being overwhelmed by the vast weight of the Babyens Vogga.

The two Vikings emerged from under the great rock, and frantically grabbed more wooden props, placing them for added safety. Mo rushed forward, frantically shouting that the trawler was making its escape, with the gold. Calum wondered about the same thing, although there was little they could do about it.

The Guardian bid they should follow him. He strode quickly to the other side of the cave and ascended a short path into a hidden gallery. A hole in the rock face gave a narrow view of the entrance to the lagoon.

The Guardian leant forward to observe. The others crowded behind him, in time to see the trawler weaving in and out of the underwater obstacles until suddenly hitting, at almost full speed, one of the Drager Tenner.

The trawler impaled itself on a jagged underwater pillar of rock. It hung there for a few moments, before the base of the rock pillar collapsed, throwing the trawler forward. As the rock pillar collapsed, seawater rushed in, and the trawler quickly sank taking everyone with it, with little hope of escape. The water current entering the lagoon was strong, the water from the fjord at near freezing. Swirling whirlpools around the remaining Drager Tenner sucked any survivors down to their deaths. The Guardian stood up a grim smile on his face.

'The task is complete,' he said. 'and now we can complete our business. You, the skipper of the schooner? Best get your vessel to the entrance of the cave. And call also your Commander 'H'.

Calum made the call. The Guardian grabbed Mo by one of his wrists, twisted the arm with great force and placed him in an arm lock he would never going to escape from. Mo cried out with the pain.

'Monsieur Mo,' said the Guardian roughly. 'You have played your part well although you knew not your assignment. My friend the Dane is a member of, how you say, the European security services. You have the great hunger for the gold my friend. Where did this begin, Indo-China, or those dark places in South Africa? And now you know we know of your hunger. Your willingness to betray, and at what price you will pay for this hunger.'

Mo wriggled and squirmed, but the Guardian's arm lock was getting close to causing serious damage. He could handle the pain, but having his body broken apart was another matter.

Rudmose came to greet the Guardian. Mo looked up at him with a questioning look. Rudmose smiled down at him, 'The diagram you left for your friends on the fishing boat, it was wrong, No?'

Mo squirmed and breathlessly refuted the accusation. Rudmose smiled again, this time at the Guardian, and said, 'seems my copy had an error, naughty me for taking Mo's diagram and leaving mine behind.'

Rudmose took a piece of paper from his pocket and showed it to everyone. It was indeed Mo's diagram, his handwriting clear and unmistakable.

'Anybody else wish to see this proof,' he said. Calum suggested that perhaps Commander 'H' could have an interest.

Calum's prophetic remark had perfect timing, as a white parachute flare descended slowly from the roof of the cave revealing ten special force soldiers all in black and balaclava face masks. Three of them were perched above the break in the stairway. The rest were abseiling their way down to the floor of the cave. All were equipped with low-light vision headsets.

'Looks familiar,' thought Calum. 'The cavalry and about time too.'

A familiar voice called out. 'You gentlemen OK?' it demanded.

Calum shouted over, 'Yes thanks, Commander. Been up there long? Where's Buffty, on long weekend leave?'

'We've been watching for just a short time', Commander 'H' replied. 'Needed to get all the proceedings on video. I suppose the Danish gold is still in the trawler?'

Buffty appeared out of the back of the cave ripping off his headgear.

'Very funny, what's a long weekend and where do I apply?' he said, coming from the other side of the cave where he'd been photographing dead Albanians, finger printing them and making notes into a voice recorder.

Buffty went over to the wounded terrorist to check him out. His camera flashed again as the wounded man had his details recorded. He was lying in considerable pain, not helped by Buffty kicking his wounded feet. Calum considered luck was on the side of the good guys.

Rudmose joined the throng. 'I'm Holger Rudmose, Commander, we've met just the once I think. The gold is safe.'

The Guardian broke in with a bellowing urgent voice. He demanded quiet, which he immediately received. He told them the Drager Tenner had broken, and the Drager Munnen will close. Calum looked at him blankly.

'The Dragon's Mouth will close', shouted the Guardian, 'you have very little time to get your schooner from the lagoon and return to the fjord.'

Calum could feel strange vibrations coming through the soles of his sailing boots. Something seriously geological was afoot.

The Guardian issued a string of urgent instructions. He ordered his son to unearth four ammunition cases from under the 'Baby's Cradle' and bring them to the waters' edge. Calum, the level of urgency rising very quickly, took out his two-way radio and ordered the schooner to get the tender ready to transfer everyone.

Commander 'H' ordered two soldiers to prepare the wounded terrorist for evacuation. Commander asked if the man-in-black had been given any morphine. Tom told him there hadn't been time and the only morphine was onboard the schooner.

The Guardian decided to go with Commander 'H', and ordered his son to follow Calum. The tender hurried inside the cave with Sarra at the controls. Tom and Patrick tossed their AK-47s to her, and readied the ammunition cases for transfer to the schooner.

Tom asked the Guardian as to the contents of the ammunition cases. The Guardian told him they contained the diamonds and it would be useful not to drop them into the water. Patrick took a rope from the tender, made two handling straps and wrapped them around each case.

Tom jumped into the tender as Patrick passed the ammunition cases. 'Professor, there's room for you, look lively.' The Professor sat gingerly at the stern of a very overcrowded tender. Sarra pushed off and carefully gunned the outboard motor. In less than a minute, the tender came alongside the schooner where willing hands helped take the ammunition cases onboard and below to safety.

Then Sarra returned to the Viking King's cave, where Calum, Ericsson, and Rudmose were waiting. Calum looked back into the cave and saw the special force soldiers climbing back up with a forlorn Mo and Buffty right behind him.

The stretcher with the terrorist started to be winched out of the cave while the Guardian and Commander 'H' hooked on and took one last look around.

As the tender banged clumsily alongside the schooner, Calum jumped aboard issuing a string of orders. Calum gunned the main engine and swung the schooner towards the exit to the fjord, Ericsson raced to the bow to see if the way forward was clear. Ericsson worried that the Dragon's teeth had fallen, and now the Dragon's mouth would be about to close.

As *Samba Canção* reached the halfway point, rocks and boulders started crashing down from either side. Calum looked up at the masts. What he saw amazed him, bringing a deep fear. The tops of the cliffs were slowly leaning towards each other. The schooner slowed as the strong stream continued to rush into the lagoon.

'What's happening,' Calum cried out to Ericsson.

'The mouth is closing, keep going, full speed,' he shouted back.

The schooner's engine raced at full speed, close to bursting, as Calum watched the scene around him with increasing fear, with the schooner making very slow progress towards the fjord. The cliff tops were closing towards each other. Sarra and the other girls screamed and rushed below into the main cabin.

Calum ordered everyone below if only to save them from the falling debris. Rocks bounced off the schooner's deck; others were smashing onto the cabin roof. Suddenly, a tremendous noise of crashing rocks came from within the lagoon. Calum spun around to see the cliffs surrounding the lagoon caving in and crash into the water. The line of falling cliffs rushed towards the schooner as it struggled to reach safety, filling Calum with greater fear. The collapsing cliffs would soon reach them, surely the schooner was doomed.

Then, the collapsing cliffs caused a tidal wave to come from behind, lifting the schooner and hurling it forward with Calum steering furiously to prevent it being overwhelmed. Ericsson hung on grimly to the schooner's forestay. After a furious ride, the schooner was ejected into the fjord.

Calum reached down and slowly brought the main engine back to half speed. Bathed in sweat, his body shook from the shock of the great fear that had gripped him. Sarra jumped out of the main cabin to see what had happened, shouting with joy when she saw the schooner was safe. The others, hardly believing their luck, rushed on deck to congratulate Calum.

Thoughtfully, Mike arrived with a bottle of whisky. Calum grabbed it from his hand and took a large swig. He slumped down on the side bench as Patrick took the helm of the schooner. Calum sat with his head between his knees as he fought to control the panic that had racked his body.

The schooner circled around as her crew looked back at the entrance to the lagoon. It had gone, the cliffs had fallen inwards and all that remained was an indent in the skyline of the towering cliffs. It begged the question as to what had happened to Commander 'H' and his party, were they safe?

The question was soon answered as a military helicopter rose from behind the fjord skyline and made in the direction of the schooner.

The FM radio burst into life as the voice of Commander 'H' asked for a situation report. Sarra gave a brief, concise report, which Commander 'H' acknowledged, instructing the schooner to head for Stavanger, about ten hours sailing distance.

Chapter 27

The Adventure Ends

The schooner and her crew settled down to the overnight journey. Suddenly they were reminded of their hunger. The girls set to and prepared a substantial dinner. The other deck crew began to clear away the rock debris, checked the cabin roof for watertight integrity, and recovered the tender.

A much-recovered Calum went below to look around, pleased to find things as they should be. He had a quick word with the girls, telling them how relieved he was they had all come through the last two days with flying colours. He fished around in a locker and pulled out three six packs of beer, dropped one off them on the galley counter and retreated to the main cockpit.

He settled down at the stern of the schooner, next to Rudmose, handed him a beer and began some gentle questioning. It was time for Rudmose to fill in the gaps of the story. Eventually, Rudmose began to enlighten him, beginning with a brief overview of the Danish plan to move their treasury gold to safety. He knew most of the events that took place in 1940, including the events surrounding the Danish Treasury Minister, Eric Horskjaer, and his famous rifle.

Horskjaer had returned to Denmark shortly after the end of the war. He had mostly recovered from his ordeal in Norway, and over time, his dreadful nightmares faded. It became much later when the story of the artefact, the one the Nazis had been so anxious to get their hands on, became known.

It was eventually discovered to originate from a religious sect in Burma, but given the circumstances in that unhappy country, it was not possible to return the artefact. Eventually, the artefact was offered to the Temple of Gautama Buddha in Bodhgaya, India, traditionally considered the place of the Buddha's awakening. There it would be safe from the relatively few neo-Nazis whose presence continues. His rifle was donated to the National Armoury, where it is still stored to this day.

Rudmose continued, it was only by chance he'd met up with the son of the original Red Eric, the man he came to know as the Guardian of the Viking King's Cave. The Guardian, also called Eric, maintained a very low profile, but those in the know knew his special skills. He was a scholar and a tough professional negotiator who seemed to float between inter-government assignments. Other than that, the man remained a mystery, and seemed to go on extended vacations.

As a member of the Danish intelligence community, Rudmose knew something of his background, but not his deep knowledge of Viking history. The Danish government kept a very close eye open for any news regarding their lost gold, and their quest for knowledge remained a carefully guarded secret. All they really had to go on was the somewhat unfinished story from their former treasury minister.

Rudmose progressed through the ranks of his government's service until he was given the assignment to make yet another attempt to discover the whereabouts of the lost gold. Holger's investigation was nothing but thorough. Once he'd fixed on the Viking connection, it was only a matter of time before he knew Eric, the Guardian, was the man to approach on this subject.

It took a long time to gain the man's confidence, and luck would have it that Rudmose's work enabled him to do the odd favour for the former Viking. The Guardian had introduced Rudmose to the Professor who had single handily researched most of the Viking's history and recorded the history of the Vikings from their ancient and glorious heyday to their demise at the hands of a brutal German Army.

Rudmose's relationship with the Guardian progressed. During the same period, the European intelligence community at the highest levels, became increasingly concerned about a secret group of truly bad people who seemed to have no connections with the general run of things in the underworld.

This unknown group had carried out selective missions that didn't add up. That this group had been building its finances was a given, but why remained a total mystery? Intense investigations revealed very little. Their missions were being carried out by a ruthless band of ad hoc Albanians, known for their intense loyalty to their paymasters.

The group had no name and so it became known as the 'Gruppe Far-lige', Danish for 'dangerous group'. Eventually, it was decided that this secret group had former Nazi connections, and also discovered that the Gruppe Farlige had been underground for a very long time. The original sleepers could possibly be former German spies of various nationalities or Nazis who'd escaped from the Third Reich as the Allied Armies closed in. Clearly the generation gap had been bridged as the few names they had, were middle-aged, and not old age pensioners from Hitler's Germany.

Rudmose eventually discovered that the Guardian knew the secret of the Danish gold and where it had been hidden. Rudmose guessed correctly as it turned out, that the Danish gold would be secreted in a Viking King's sacred cave, but when he enquired, the Guardian always strongly denied any knowledge and quickly averted the question.

Deep examination of the subject concluded that the unknown group of terrorists also had some ideas about the Danish gold. They knew it existed and securely hidden, but where? That much gold would have become very visible if had it reached the world's markets.

It was guessed, more from rumours and scraps of information, that the Gruppe Farlige had some knowledge of the general area where the gold had disappeared, and investigations showed mysterious and unknown persons had been researching WWII German army records of war time operations in Norway.

It had also been discovered that a sweeping search of the general mountainous area had been quietly conducted by members of the Gruppe Farlige disguised as tourists, but try as they might, nothing even remotely useful came into the light of day. These tourists had been briefly seen by Norwegian Special Forces conducting training exercises in the same remote areas. A report had been filed as a matter of course, but it had taken some time before this information reached the right desk.

By chance, the Gruppe Farlige discovered from WWII German records, that Viking revivalists had been involved in the disappearance of the Danish gold. From this information came the idea of seeking out experts in the field of Viking history, which led them to discover that the Professor would be the key to a greater understanding of the subject matter at hand.

In the USA, members of the Gruppe Farlige were building their technical ability to monitor the US and NATO Security Forces methods of surveillance. Modern technology reached new heights, and it became known the computer industry in Silicon Valley had stored a working prototype of the latest surveillance system. As new systems went into production at the end of extensive field testing, the Gruppe Farlige decided to help themselves to the stored equipment and get ahead of the game for a major operation.

Then the USA and European security forces achieved a breakthrough, of sorts. The theft of the electronic equipment from the US authorities in California heralded the coming of the major event, the likes of which nobody in the intelligence world could make up their minds on.

Next, the events surrounding the schooner, the visit by Ex-CIA chief, Garth Vidor, and the knowledge that an unknown group of bad people were involved in surveillance of the schooner's preparation for the race destined to end in Norway, that two and two was put together, in a roundabout sort of way

With the kidnapping of Marie's father, the Professor, it became apparent that the event would take place in Europe and that the Gruppe Farlige were hunting for the considerable funds needed for whatever operation was being planned.

This led Rudmose to suggest the only source of considerable funds, without drawing too much attention, could well be the long lost Danish gold.

Rudmose fixed on the Viking connection, it was all he had. Eventually, he managed to persuade his friend Eric to confirm he was indeed the Guardian of the holy place of the Viking Kings, and that the Viking King's holy place had a great secret, namely the fishing trawler containing the Danish bullion. The Guardian too had become concerned there were indeed sinister people spending a great deal of time and effort trying to find the Viking King's cave, and not just for historical reasons.

How he knew this information was not revealed, as the Guardian would not reveal his sources. Strangely, it occurred to Rudmose the man needed help, although the Guardian would not say how, he suspected that his Danish friend had become involved with his government's intelligence services drive to discover the hiding place of the gold. Rudmose let the matter drop fearing to damage his friendship with the Viking.

Realising the importance of recovering the Danish gold, Holger conferred with his masters, and they quickly dispatched him to the UK to hold off-the-record talks with the British Secret Service. The Danish Government was, of course, more than keen to recover their gold, but they were prepared to wait just a little longer. Co-operation with the Norwegians would be vital, and a period of low-key negotiations became necessary to get the key players brought up to speed with the situation.

It didn't take Rudmose long to discover the British were not totally unaware of a threat to European security from this strange and unknown group, the Gruppe Farlige. The CIA had also become more than interested in the on-going events, and when the secret electronics were stolen from California, things picked up on their side of the Atlantic.

The British government put Commander 'H' to work to pull all the pieces together. The fact that he controlled a separate and secretive Special Forces squadron, whose main stock in trade was not getting caught at whatever they got up to, was considered a bonus. Commander 'H' had resources unavailable to many European government agencies, and discretion always his middle name.

Quite how Commander 'H' built on the faint idea that this secret group of terrorists had Nazi connections wasn't known, but he burrowed away and brought a most convincing scenario to the table.

The incident in the English Channel had been a very strange affair, and what clinched it for Commander 'H', was this attempted destruction of the schooner in the English Channel. The Albanians rescued from the attacking trawler clearly had no idea of their principal's master plan.

Eventually, the various secret services of the countries involved were persuaded to hand over whatever information could be remotely linked to the subject at hand and Commander 'H' slowly but surely started to close in. Progress increased rapidly when he received an urgent call from his daughter using a very out of date US military communicator.

The subsequent kidnapping of Marie, the Norwegian princess, daughter of the Professor, the attempted murder of the schooner's crew in the remote part of Holland, and the escape of the terrorist's trawler to Norway, all started to add up.

Clearly things were coming to a head, the Danish gold now confirmed as the target, but what exactly lay behind all this activity remained a mystery? There were a number of scenarios.

Perhaps an attempt to subvert the German government with all its troubles with Muslim immigrants was being planned. The problems with the Euro, currently being propped up by the German economy to the benefit of the Mediterranean countries in the Eurozone, were also considered. Added to this scenario came an increasingly fed-up German population who'd developed a nasty habit of not voting the way the German government, and its Chancellor, preferred. Did Russia have any involvement?

Anyway, why didn't matter. Why could take care of itself. How to head-off this unknown group off became increasingly more important.

The decision by Commander 'H' to parachute four of his hooligans onto the schooner was considered a stroke of genius. That the skipper of the schooner determined the means of dropping his men onboard the target trawler had also been lucky, and the result most satisfactory, up to a point. The sinking of the trawler had not been considered helpful, and the big question mark was who had escaped?

Rudmose revealed to Calum that he'd been mobilised at very short notice to Mandal to take charge of the onshore team comprising the Norwegian and Danish Special Forces. The whole episode could only mean one thing; the men-in-black and their Albanian thugs were determined to get the Danish gold no matter what. The Professor had earlier revealed the likely location of the Viking King's secret cave, and the rest of the story everyone knew.

Mike, Tom and Patrick dropped into the conversation. 'Hello Skipper,' said Tom. 'Thought we'd join the party. Is this a 'Come to Jesus' moment, when all is revealed?'

Calum smiled and went through some of Rudmose's conclusions. Patrick asked, did the day's events mean the end of the story. Before Rudmose could answer Tom butted in and asked a question.

'Holger, how many men-in-black were there, just the two, or are there any more?'

'Tom,' Rudmose answered, 'there will always be men-in-black, and we must always be vigilant against them. In this case, we have defeated our two men-in-black. The CIA man, the one known as Garth Vidor, we know about. He'd picked up the nickname Darth Vader long before he left the employ of the US Government. He was not a liked man, and the most difficult to track.'

'He'd been thoroughly schooled by his father, a ranking Nazi master spy. He used the old methods and hardly ever used electronic communications. He knew our capabilities on how to track him. He had mastered using drop boxes, microdots, even microfilm. His frequent use of letters and postcards had led to the conclusion he was using old school methods. He always thought ahead, so always had the time to use them.'

'By the time we'd cottoned on, we had to find some old timers to teach our guys the old ways. We found one in Prague, a Czech specialist in Nazi and KGB methods. Ninety-six years old and he did enjoy himself. Made the most of the comeback, brief as it was. Cost my treasury a small fortune.'

'Garth Vidor had the idea to kidnap Marie and her father. The attempt on the schooner in the English Channel did not come from him and frankly, it was a stupid idea by the Albanians. However, he did mastermind the events at the Island of Terschelling. He almost succeeded; you guys did well on that one.'

'Anyway, we know most of his contacts, and his passing will not be mourned.'

Rudmose continued, 'The taller man-in-black, the one we captured in the Viking's Cave, now he is a mystery. But Commander 'H' will take good care of him. The Commander will work on our mystery man in a variety of ways, some surprisingly simple. The Commander understands human nature almost totally. It may take some time, but these matters are no longer pressing, so time is not important. We are reasonably certain that this saga is over, but there will always be new ones to guard against.'

'And Mo?' said Mike. 'How did he fit in, and what will happen to him?'

'Ah,' said Rudmose, 'we did have some idea of his hunger for gold, and quite how he became involved with the bad guys we're not certain. Still, we were able to use him and Commander 'H' has him well under control. He emptied Mo's Swiss bank account to make him pay for his mistrust. More than three million dollars. Mo will be offered a chance to become solvent again. He has special talents, and his next mission will be doubly dangerous, and profitable, if he survives.'

Calum asked one last question, 'Holger, what ever happened to the survivors of the Danish Rangers.'

'Ah,' replied Rudmose, 'according to the Guardian, the retreat towards Oslo became a big success, and a lot of German soldiers died in the pursuit through some very difficult terrain. A few rangers died, most made it to Oslo. The wounded were treated and eventually smuggled into Sweden.'

Most of the remainder joined the Norwegian Resistance were they did sterling work. The sad story was regarding the Major. He'd stayed with the Red Eric until their supplies ran out. Stealing from the Germans would have drawn attention to the general area of the cave. The Germans searched long and hard for it. So Red Eric decided to make his way back to Oslo. They almost made it when they were caught in a German trap. The Major had died fighting, allowing Red Eric and his son to vanish.

The Guardian won't speak of his father, so that's all I know. What I do know is the story has finished. The Major can receive some long overdue recognition and a decent memorial. We all owe this man a great deal.'

'Well thanks for all that,' said Calum. 'I guess it's time to get organised for the night journey to Stavanger. By the way, what are the others doing below?'

'Oh yes,' said Patrick. 'The girls are raking through the diamonds. You may remember them?'

'Christ,' said Calum. 'Mike, you'd best go rescue the girls from any ambitions of becoming decorated in jewels. Tom, get your watch turned-in and rested. Patrick get your watch to carry out the checks for the night run, and get the log up to date.'

And so normality returned to the schooner, arriving in Stavanger early the next morning after a pleasant night's navigation through the Norwegian fjords. Fortunately, it was a quiet morning in Stavanger, and Commander 'H' organised a pilot boat to guide the schooner alongside a Norwegian Navy frigate. The crew of the schooner didn't have long to wait before the welcoming committee arrived.

With little fuss and no ceremony, Commander 'H' arrived with a Hans Worsoe, a senior member of the Danish Treasury, his counterpart from the Norwegian Government, the Secretary to the Norwegian Royal Family, and several special branch policemen. Included in the party came a pale individual, whose obvious characteristics marked him out for what he was, a member of the Amsterdam diamond trade.

The expected enquiry came regarding the diamonds, which had the girls giggling. Hans was definitely a dish in their eyes. Worsoe was slightly taken aback, he knew what they were thinking.

'Sorry ladies,' he said. 'I have come to see your precious cargo, perhaps you could lead the way, and you can have one last look.'

The crew followed Worsoe and his diamond expert below into the main cabin, where they pointed to the ammunition cases in the alcove that was Calum's favourite corner, the quarter berth behind the galley.

The ammunition cases were brought to the main cabin floor. The diamond expert looked in the two cases with the industrial diamonds and had little surprise they had been almost ignored. Hans beckoned two naval personal to remove them to the naval Frigate. The other two cases were opened.

'OK,' said Worsoe, 'let's see what we have here. Anything taken?'

'Not by us,' said Calum smiling, 'but it was a close run thing.'

Worsoe laughed. He could imagine the emotions of opening two cases worth several king's ransoms. The diamond expert was left alone to his work. Hans explained there were no details of whom the diamonds belonged to who.

The diamond expert quickly got to work on the first case. His long delicate fingers ruffled through the many packets, opening a few to take note of the contents. The crew of the schooner looked on in silence with great anticipation. The diamond expert lifted out the first tray to repeat the process on the deeper contents. Within another ten minutes, he lifted out the second tray to reveal the contents lining the bottom of the cases.

He looked up and smiled at everyone. 'Trying to guess the value are we?' he asked. Everybody nodded their heads in agreement.

'Hard to tell without more time,' the diamond expert replied, 'but very interesting. The top layer, in this case, were packed in Amsterdam, my home city. The packets all seem to contain about ten stones, roughly one to three carats per stone as an average I would say. Good quality, well worth the risk to try to get them to safety. The packets in the lower half of the case are from different dealers in different cities, mostly in the area containing

North Holland, West Belgium and parts of Germany.'

'You cannot see the difference in the packets, but I can tell roughly where they might have come from. This case has lost a few packets but I can't say how many. Holger reckons they were used by the original Red Eric to fund his escape, and to provide funds for his activities in the Norwegian Resistance. They would have been hard to use, the Nazis would have been on the lookout. There were odd rumours about stones turning up in Sweden, and this could be the proof.'

'Anyway,' he continued, 'count the packets at an average of 25 carats, say two thousand dollars a carat at wholesale prices, and you will get some idea.

You are looking at a lot of money, and it will take a long time to chase down the survivors of the former owners. Many will not be found, so the various governments will have to come to a conclusion what to do with them.'

Tom started to hand out some much-needed coffee, and everyone started to drift away into other activities whilst the diamond expert started to exam the second ammunition case. Forty minutes later he announced he was finished.

The contents of the second case, he announced, came mostly from the eastern European countries. The packets had the signs of being put together in Prague, Warsaw, Berlin and other cities with large Jewish communities. It was not only the Nazis that had everyone worried. Joe Stalin also became a big factor in the flight to safety.

'Anyway,' announced Worsoe. 'I am authorised to make a donation for all your valiant efforts, and to compensate for the dangers you experienced. Here is an official letter informing each of you of your ownership of the diamonds I am going to give you'.

Worsoe proceeded to give one packet to each of the young crew members who could hardly believe their luck. The crew were not to see that Calum and Mike received twice that amount, so happy were they shouting and talking among themselves.

Commander 'H' asked Mike to come on deck.

'Mike, this is an air ticket home, and a taxi is waiting to take you to the airport. The next flight is in forty minutes, I suggest you be very quick otherwise you'll miss being a daddy and a certain lady will not be pleased.'

Mike packed in record time and was gone. The other officials slowly left after copious congratulations and an invite to a grand dinner in a very upmarket local hotel.

The schooner and her crew enjoyed a few more days' relaxation with the hospitality of the Norwegians before preparing for the journey home. Adriana, not unaware of her husband's good fortune, arrived for what Calum cautiously labeled as a stock taking mission.

Three days later, the schooner arrived back in her berth in Lymington, with just a few friends more than curious as to the late return home.

'Let's see my husband talk his way out of this one,' mused Adriana.

THE END

41680482R00167

Printed in Poland
by Amazon Fulfillment
Poland Sp. z o.o., Wrocław